# Mariposa

## Book Three – Salvation

By

## Jeannie Hudson

ISBN:
ISBN-13:

## DEDICATION

TO MY REMARKABLE FRIEND,
TEDDY FUJAN, A WOMAN OF
WISDOM, INSIGHT AND ASTONISHING
LOVE AND RESPECT FOR HER FAMILY
AND FRIENDS.
THANK YOU FOR YOUR AVID
ENJOYMENT OF MY BOOKS AND
YOUR CONSTANT SUPPORT IN ALL
AREAS OF MY LIFE.
I LOVE YOU!!

# Cover Art

Dawn Newland grew up in the ranching country of the Cheyenne River of western South Dakota, where she spent endless childhood hours with pencil in hand sitting on a ridge drawing everything in sight. She studied with Art Instruction Schools of Minnesota after high school but is mostly a self-taught Western artist. Dawn paints horses and cowboys with the intense passion of one who knows her subject well. Her deep spirituality and intuitive style contribute to her ability to live with a foot in both worlds, taking her art on sashays out into the realm of 'magical realism.' She is represented at the 1875 Gallery of Sundance, Wyoming.

Prints of cover art are available

Dawn can be reached at

dawn.newland@yahoo.com

# Acknowledgements

Once again, I wish to thank my dear friend, Jill Schad, for her generous help with the technical processes in the publication of this book. I owe a huge thanks to my amazing friend, Dawn Newland for her stunning cover art. As always, she has captured the exact tone of my imagined *Mariposa.*

Great appreciation to my friend Marlene Hartzell for her proofreading and admiration for my work. Finally, I could not be more grateful to Peter Illidge for his insight and unending help with the complexities of editing and formatting and to Karen Perkins of LionheART Publishing House for recommending his services to me.

I once more acknowledge the use of Historical facts found in T.A. Larson's *History of Wyoming.*

# I AM

I am – yet what I am, none cares or knows;
My friends forsake me like a memory lost;
I am the self-consumer of my woes –
They rise and vanish in oblivions host,
Like shadows in love frenzied stifled throes
And yet I am, and live – like vapors lost

Into the nothingness of scorn and noise,
Into the living sea of waking dreams,
Where there is neither sense of life or joys,
But the vast shipwrecks of my lifes esteems;
Even the dearest that I love best
Are strange – nay, rather stranger than the rest.

I long for scenes where man hath never trod
A place where women never smiled or wept
There to abide with my Creator God,
And sleep as I in childhood sweetly slept,
Untroubling and untroubled where I lie
The grass below, above, the vaulted sky.

John Clare

## Anthem for Doomed Youth

What passing-bells for those who die as cattle?
Only the monstrous anger of the guns.
Only the stuttering rifles' rapid rattle
Can patter out their hasty orisons.
No mockeries now for them; no prayers nor bells;
Nor any voice of mourning save the choirs,
The shrill, demented choirs of wailing shells;
And bugles calling for them from sad shires.
What candles may be held to speed them all?
Not in the hands of boys, but in their eyes
Shall shine the holy glimmers of good-byes.
The pallor of girls' brows shall be their pall;
Their flowers the tenderness of patient minds,
And each slow dusk a drawing down of blinds.

Wilfred Owen

# CHAPTER ONE

**April 1892**

Harper Whittaker stood at the window of her *Mariposa* studio, looking out at daybreak unfolding beyond the spring garden where Kendrick, the caretaker, cultivated a bed of tulips and daffodils. She drew her shawl closer against the early chill. Overwhelming loneliness swamped her as tears cramped in her chest and her thoughts turned to her husband, Damien, who'd been away from *Rancha Mariposa* for over a month.

Damien and his partner John Carroll were imprisoned in Cheyenne for their part in a recent invasion into Johnson County where many known rustlers were hiding out. They had battled the thieves along with other damaging factors since they had come from Herefordshire, England in 1876 to join the men of vision, growing rich in cattle ranching on the Great Plains of Wyoming Territory.

In recent years, rustling had become a dire threat to the ranching industry, belatedly stirring members of the Wyoming Stock Growers Association to organize a foray against some of the most notorious thieves. Due to incompetence and lack of proper preparation, the raid quickly broke down in chaos with all the cattlemen involved arrested by the cavalry.

Harper literally ached for Damien. They'd rarely been apart since they were children, growing up in the pastoral idyll of Herefordshire. And they were destined to marry, long before their engagement was announced during a lavish ball at the Whittaker estate, Willow Rook.

Their wedding was postponed when Aunt Pris, Harper's guardian, decided her charge must see something of the world before she married, and abruptly sent her to Paris for a year of art instruction. Heartbroken, Harper complied, disastrously setting in motion the events that changed the course of their lives.

While she was away, Peggy Abbot, Harper's childhood nemesis, plotted to take Damien for herself. By the time Harper returned, she had learned that Peggy was not only marrying Damien but expecting his child.

As the Whittakers were about to embark on their journey to America, the sole means Harper could devise to go with them was to marry Damien's brother Brendon. And this rash decision prompted Aunt Pris to also accompany the Whittakers when they set sail for America.

In Wyoming Territory, they settled onto a vast ranch near Cheyenne where they began driving crossbred cattle north from Mexico to breed with their blueblood Herefords that soon arrived from England under the care of head stockman, Jamie Horncastle. Along with their fellow ranchers, they found monetary success greater than they could have ever imagined, even as the Whittakers' personal lives remained in chaos for the next ten years. Ten years that witnessed divorce, drought, disease and the deaths of Harper's first born son, Eddie and her ex-husband Brendon.

At last, Damien and Harper were married and claimed the happiness that had been stolen from them. John Carroll and Jamie Horncastle had gone into partnership with Damien and Brendon and despite drought and rustling, *Rancha Mariposa* flourished in the Golden Age of the Wyoming cattle barons.

Now Harper turned from the window and glanced at the half-finished oil on a nearby easel. She smiled at the scene of her daughter Delaney holding her brother Chandler on a garden bench, Riley, one of the resident beagles, sitting primly between them. During the past year, with the help of John's father, Granville Carrol, a barrister and old friend in England, Harper's art now hung in the top venues in Europe.

Thinking of Granville drew Harper from her reverie and she acknowledged a probing of hope. When she and Audra Carroll had visited Damien and John at Fort Russell after their arrest, she was so frightened by their predicament that she'd immediately sent a wire to Granville in Herefordshire. He was arriving by train shortly before noon today.

He was one of the top barristers in England, and she felt confident that he could unravel the complex legal maze in which the men found themselves. She acknowledged the first optimism that she'd felt in weeks.

Hearing footsteps in the hall, she watched Delaney, Rumor and Riley the most recent pair of beagles to live at *Mariposa,* scampering through the door. "Good morning, you three. What a nice surprise." She sat on a wide bench and drew them to her.

At five, Delaney was a perfect little replica of her mother with the same tangle of dark hair, and eyes the hue of violets. Harper's breath sometimes caught at the wonder of her.

"I couldn't find you in your bed." Her features betrayed her worry as she climbed into her mother's lap.

Her dejection sent pain through Harper. Their intrepid daughter had rarely shown any fear before her father left on the ill-fated raid. Delaney missed and grieved for him to a degree that frightened Harper, although it was the same with her. She prayed Damien would be home before Delaney lost any of her inquisitive delight in life.

"Why are you going to Cheyenne, Ma-ma? When will you come home?"

"Granville is coming to help Pa-pa. I'm meeting his train. I hope I can come back this evening. If not then, tomorrow I should think."

"I'll be so lonely while you're away."

"I know." Harper drew her close, resting her cheek against her hair. "And, I think, Chandler and our beagle girls may be quite lonely as well. So what you and Riley and Rumor must do is keep each other company while I'm away, and Ivy will need your help with Chandler."

Delaney smiled at the mention of her baby brother who was five months old and in her charge much of the time, especially lately because his nurse Ivy was in the last days of pregnancy. The father was Dom, Damien's son from his marriage to Peggy, Harper's girlhood archrival.

Having been abused and rejected by his mother as a very young child, Dom had become a rebellious lad, prone to reckless, delinquent behavior, including fathering a baby at fifteen. His parents did all they could to keep him on the straight and narrow. Toward that end, he now had his own tutor, Arthur, an engaging Harvard graduate with an abundance of common sense.

The means for educating the seven Carroll daughters, plus Dom, Delaney and Chandler had become an issue when John and Audra moved back to *Rancha Mariposa,* after living in Cheyenne the first years in Wyoming Territory. At that point, John had recruited young Arthur as well as Eliza Tilly, an Irish nanny in need of employment. Aunt Pris welcomed the two with a lavish dinner at the *Mariposa* and both had been hired.

"Eliza has invited you and Riley to join her and the girls during classes if you like," Harper told Delaney.

"I may be too busy with Chandler."

"Well, perhaps you may have time while Chandler is sleeping."

She brightened. "That'll be fun." She patted the beagles' heads, leaning down to peer at them. "Maybe you can learn to read."

Harper laughed and hugged her.

"Who's going to feed Chandler while you're away?"

She was a bit jolted by her perception. "Actually, he's begun drinking Greta's milk."

"Truly?"

"Yes, babies do well drinking goats' milk."

She sighed, relaxing against her mother. "Well, it's good Greta had a baby then."

"Why is that?"

"Because if she didn't have a baby, she wouldn't have enough milk for Chandler."

"Who told you that?"

"Luke. When I went to see all the baby goats. It's the same with the milk cows. That's why they have a calf most every year."

Harper nodded. "You're so smart. And now my darling daughter, we must go and have breakfast."

Delaney slid down and they made their way to the staircase leading downstairs. Halfway down, they met Roddy, Damien's valet. "I've packed a trunk with fresh clothes for Damien," he said. "I'll bring it down when you're ready."

"Thank you, Roddy."

When they reached the dining room, Dom and Arthur were already sat at the table drinking tea. For months after they came to work, Arthur and Eliza had resided in the apartments at either side of the villa where Harper and Brendon, and Damien and Peggy had lived during their marriages. Now since her marriage at Christmas to Jamie Horncastle in a festive holiday wedding at *Mariposa,* Eliza had settled into matrimony in Jamie's cottage.

Harper and Delaney sat at the table where Adare, the butler, served her tea, and milk for Delaney. Aunt Pris soon tottered in from her apartment, her newly-acquired cane tapping on the parquet floor. "Well, how is everyone this fine morning?" She leaned close to kiss Harper's cheek.

"If Damien and John were with us, it would be a perfect April day," Arthur said. "Are you ready to depart for town, Harper?"

"Yes, we're leaving at eight."

"I could drive you in and help you with Granville's baggage and the like," Dom interjected with the arrogant lift of his chin with which Harper was becoming less and less enchanted.

"Thank you but no. I need you and Arthur to help Jamie with the calving. You'll have to miss another day of classes."

"What a jolly good idea," Arthur said.

Dom gave him a peeved glance. "I hate that whole bloody business. It's really hard work and there's all the wet muck to deal with."

"You are a very annoying and ungrateful young man," Arthur told his charge. "If your father, John and Jamie hadn't been so diligent in tending the cows and making sure most of the calves were born healthy the past fifteen years, the gracious lifestyle you have enjoyed wouldn't be nearly so comfortable."

Dom scowled. "When I'm running things, I'll hire men to do all that sort of disgusting work."

Arthur sighed. "Well, I'm sure when and if that ever happens, that will be your prerogative. As for the here and now, *I* am in charge of what you do and you will do the work that's necessary, no matter how it may disgust you. As for me, I can think of nothing I'll enjoy more than being liberated from the classroom to do some physical labor outside on a lovely spring day. What could be nicer than having some enchanting baby calves at the end of it? Have you ever stopped to take a long look of all the charming babies frolicking about in the spring sunshine? If you enjoyed the largess of miracles all around us as much as everyone else, you might be happier."

"I love baby calves," Delaney remarked.

Dom glowered at her as though her giddy delight in all the young animals and life on the ranch in general was the standard to which his own lack of enthusiasm was being compared. He set upon his oatmeal, shoveling it into his mouth with total lack of finesse that brought a warning glance from Arthur. Soon enough, he asked to be excused and wandered from the table.

"Thank you for taking a firm hand with him," Harper said to Arthur. "His behavior has been worse since Damien's been away."

"Lately, I've tried putting my finger on the changes in him in recent months. When I first arrived, he was such a happy, engaging lad and I enjoyed spending time with him out of the classroom. But recently he's not been great company." He smiled and dropped his napkin on his plate. "Well, in any case, I'll keep him in tow and we'll hope he learns some manners eventually." He hurried to hold Harper's chair as she stood. "May I do anything to help before you go?"

"No, thank you. Luke should be coming for me any moment."

"Well, don't worry. We'll keep everything in order here. Greet Granville for me."

"I will." She turned to embrace Aunt Pris, then put her arm around Delaney as they headed to the front door. They sat together on a bench and Rachel soon hurried down the staircase with Harper's hat and reticule as well as a cloak in case the day turned colder later on.

Harper stepped up to a mirror to put on her hat, a smart teal affair with elegant dyed egret feathers picking up the matching tones in her traveling suit, which she hoped gave her an air of confidence she didn't altogether feel. Securing the hat pins, she gave herself a final inspection before she heard her son descending the stairs.

With a skip of delight, Delaney went to meet Ivy, reaching for Chandler who chortled with equal glee the second he saw her. She gathered him to her with practiced care, settling him on her shoulder as she bore him to Harper who opened her bodice to feed him.

"I wasn't sure if you wished to nurse at this late hour," Ivy said.

"I had aspirations of standing firm on that note but the pressure and pain this morning has changed my mind." Harper put the baby to her breast, covering him with the towel Ivy handed her. "I daresay, I'll be much more comfortable today, thanks to Chandler having breakfast."

Ivy looked doubtful. "Likely now but later on . . ."

"I shall just have to suffer," Harper said dismissively. "There's really no ideal time to wean a baby." She studied Ivy who looked like she might go into labor at any time. "How are you feeling?"

She reached for a dining room chair and sat. "I'm not sure at times. I just feel so fat and . . ."

"Well, Delaney is going to help you with the baby today so you get plenty of rest. I will alert Dr. Ritter as soon as we get to town so he can be ready to come when it's time. If that should happen today, send one of the men for him."

Ivy was looking at her aghast, her face quite white. "I don't require all that kind of fuss."

"You need a doctor and I won't hear any more about it. Don't forget you're having our grandchild."

"And my niece or nephew," Delaney said happily.

Ivy merely sat observing them in wonder. "Oh, I nearly forgot. I put extra cloths in your reticule in case you have leakage later on," she said, coming back to the moment.

"Thank you so much. You think of everything."

"Best to be prepared."

Harper looked down at Chandler who'd fallen asleep. He looked so content, she continued holding him for a time. Her heart clenched for a moment when she saw anew how much he resembled Eddie, the son she'd borne while married to Damien's twin Brendon. When that golden, perfect child had died, she'd thought she couldn't survive. Yet, she had with Damien's tender care. She'd healed in all the broken places and now, here was Chandler, Damien's son, their own beloved child.

Presently, she heard the carriage in the piazza and relinquished the baby into Delaney's competent arms, then hugged them both, bestowing kisses to their sweet faces. "Goodbye my darlings. I'll see you soon." She bent to pat Riley's head.

"Bye, Ma-ma. I love you. Tell, Pa-pa how much I miss him."

"I will darling." Collecting her things from Rachel, she turned out of the door into warm sunshine.

Luke leapt down and held the brougham door for her. "Good morning, Harper."

"Thank you, Luke." She settled inside and looked out at the maids, Delaney holding Chandler, and Aunt Pris all standing in a row.

She returned their fervent waves, Luke clucked to the pair of grays and they were off. The fragrance of April blooms from the front garden, wafted into the carriage, steadying her a bit. She said a prayer that Damien and John would be back at home very soon. She ached for her husband and feared for his safety.

Turning her thoughts firmly to the day ahead, she concentrated on the perfect morning unfolding beyond the open windows. The prairie was already green with new grass. The sight of it touched Harper deeply as she recalled the horrific conditions of the grasslands over the past years that'd led to the end of the glorious ranching industry that had beckoned men from all parts of the globe. It was perhaps the vast scope of success that had made the end so demoralizing.

If all the man pursuing the dream had approached the challenge with the foresight and humility of Damien, things might have had a much different outcome. As it was, the enormous resources of the American Great Plains—immeasurable tracts of nutritious grassland that had only a few years earlier fed millions of bison before the herds were decimated in the wholesale eradication of the Indians—were devastated by greed and over grazing.

Damien had been a steward of the land from the moment, the Whittakers arrived in Wyoming. He'd fenced the rich stream bottoms, erected irrigation systems and set hired men to the work of putting up tons of alfalfa hay and building barns and shelters. While other ranchers left their herds of longhorns out on the prairie to fend for themselves during harsh winter blizzards and plummeting temperatures, the Whittakers kept their Herefords sheltered and well-fed.

For some years, before the land was decimated by the huge herds of longhorn cattle being driven from Texas and Mexico, feed was sufficient to sustain the cattle and the weather remained ideal. The routine of driving free Mexican cattle from the far south and then fattening the herds on the lush grasslands in the public domain, enabled the ranchers to grow unfathomably wealthy. Most flaunted their lifestyle with lavish Cheyenne mansions and memberships in the Wyoming Stock Growers Association as well as the Cheyenne Club, a men's meeting place patterned after the exclusive men's clubs of Europe.

There seemed no end to the glorious lifestyle. Most of the cattlemen assumed the idyll would last. And it very well might have, had they all realized they couldn't continue using the land with no regard toward conservation. The Whittakers however, under Damien's guidance, began rotating grazing and spreading the rotting manure from the cattle pens and barns over the fields every spring, putting back what had been stripped away. Not many followed suit and after years of abuse, the prairie where once sheaves of curing grass had greeted the newly-arriving would-be ranchers, had become barren, the landscape scoured by hot winds. The plentiful rains of the early years had grown steadily sparse.

The general decline had culminated with the disastrous winter of 1886 when thousands of gaunt cattle were lost in the unending cold and blizzards. The Whittakers might have survived this calamity if they had remained united in their sensible and careful approach to whatever dilemmas they faced. But in this case, while Damien remained steady, Brendon engineered an insane plan to market starving stock in England and in the process, lost a large portion of *Rancha Mariposa's* livelihood as well as his life.

During the interim, the economy of the entire region had shifted. Most of the foreign investors from Europe and the American East had returned home, their hopes dashed. Thousands of small ranchers went broke and headed back from whence they came; still others merely changed their tactics and began nicking mavericks and the occasional cow or steer from the herds of the large ranches. This low practice had plagued Wyoming Territory since the first cattlemen had arrived and began accumulating their herds but as conditions worsened, it threatened the very future of the industry.

As soon as the Whittakers drove their first longhorns onto their ranges, they had been victims of rustling from two sources. Jose Martinez, one of their hired cowboys had proved to be a loathsome employee and was sacked after nearly killing Damien in a vicious attack. Fleeing the *Mariposa,* he'd joined forces with Jonathon Holt, another rancher with large holdings that abutted Whittaker land for miles. From that time on, the Whittakers suffered huge losses from the thievery of these two, and bad blood increased over ensuing years.

After the upheaval in the entire region following the reversal of fortunes in the wake of deteriorating weather and economic decline, the area reorganized into several massive ranches with sufficient backing to stay in business. Aside from these wealthy landowners that included the Whittakers were great numbers of small outfits comprised of a few acres of land and a huddle of shabby buildings. Much of the rustling now originated with these men teetering on the edge of ruin who weren't opposed to adding cattle to their herds by whatever means they could.

In recent years, the situation had reached the point of crisis. Members of the Stock Growers Association had been pushed to the limit of their patience as the thieves took up more and more disgraceful tactics in the pursuit of stolen beef.

Ultimately, with no other solution in sight, the ranchers, including Damien and John, had joined a vigilante invasion into Johnson County that had ended with the arrest of all the Invaders.

The men still remained in prison at Fort Russell. Harper hadn't seen Damien since she and Audra had briefly visited their husbands weeks ago. That fleeting interval had been so sad and disheartening she hadn't cared to return until now when Granville might be able to help.

As the carriage neared the edge of Cheyenne, Luke stopped the horses in the shade of a stand of cottonwoods. He alighted from the driver's seat and opened the brougham door.

"Shall we go to the depot?" He asked.

Harper consulted her pocket watch with the painted violets on the face. Shortly after nine. "The train is due at ten so we should wait there."

Luke considered her intently. "Are you all right?"

She smiled. "I am. Thank you."

He reached out to squeeze her hand. "I know you pick up *feelings* about things. What do you sense about this, what's happening with Damien and John?"

She thought about what he was asking and abruptly realized she was more optimistic today. The overwhelming fear was less, tempered by a probing of faith. "I'm more hopeful. Thank you for reminding me to stop and think about how I feel."

He studied her for some time. "Shall we get on then?"

She nodded and he closed the door, then climbed back up to gather the reins.

The train still hadn't arrived when they reached the depot and parked near the platform. Luke came to help Harper from the carriage and guided her to a bench. She clutched the cloak to her as there was still a chill in the air.

He settled next to her. "May I speak to you about Ivy," he said presently.

"Certainly."

Shifting his thin back against the bench, he said nothing for a few moments, evidently collecting his thoughts.

She gave him an encouraging smile.

"Ivy and I talk sometimes," he said at last. "It's nice in the back garden since it's warmed up. Sometimes we eat lunch together."

She waited for him to proceed.

"Our time together has become both habit and delight," he divulged with a grin.

"I see." She noticed not for the first time what a handsome young man he was. And he'd always been a favorite of everyone at the ranch because he was so sensitive and eager to help.

Since the very first summer at the ranch, when he'd driven a pregnant Harper in a buggy to sketch the rough and tumble crew of cowboys, she'd enjoyed his happy company and knew she could always depend on him. She especially loved the way he dealt with Delaney, teaching her to ride with the most gentle skill.

"Well, the truth is," he went on, looking at her directly. "I love her and I'm pretty sure she loves me too." He gripped his hands together, his mouth curving in a smile. Before Harper could comment, he seemed to gather himself with the sudden conviction he needed to get on with it if he was going to learn what he needed to know from Harper.

"The thing is," he continued forthrightly, "neither Ivy nor I can figure out just how it stands between her and Dom. He's the baby's father so doesn't he want to be part of her life after she's born?"

Harper saw the deep worry in his gaze and could have wept. How was it that this honorable young man had such yearning for what Dom had disregarded out of hand?

Since she and Damien had learned of Dom's illegitimate child, they'd made little progress in sorting the matter. Moral standards were perhaps a bit more lax in America than in England, yet there were very serious considerations to surmount. Now seeing the open love and longing in Luke comforted Harper as she struggled to answer his query. "Actually, Luke, I think the last thing on earth Dom wants to think about is his . . . d . . . daughter . . . . Why do you think it's a girl?"

He musingly shook his head. "Ivy's thought so from the start and I've come to like the idea of a wee lass."

"Am I to believe you're interested in marrying Ivy?"

"I'd do it in a heartbeat if I could. I've saved most all my wages so I have enough to build a cottage for us and I can support them." He grew pensive again. "Do you think Dom would allow it?"

"In showing no interest in his child, I'd say Dom has forfeited any rights."

"He might want her later on," Luke worried.

"Well, if you and Ivy should marry, it would be prudent for you to adopt the baby very soon. I should think Granville could be of help with that."

Luke's face came alight with hope. "Do you really think it could happen?"

"I do and the sooner the better as far as I'm concerned. Depending on what we learn from Granville about Damien and John, we may return to the *Mariposa* tomorrow or even tonight. We can arrange a wedding very quickly."

The passion in his pale blue eyes was beyond delight. "Do you think Damien will agree?"

"Yes, he'll be positively gleeful. He's very fond of Ivy and naturally, concerned that our grandchild be protected."

"I will cherish them both."

"I know you will." The distant whistle drew her attention. "Oh, good." She stood to straighten her skirt.

Any further talk was suspended in the noisy arrival of the train that rolled into the station amid squealing brakes and hissing steam. When quiet returned, Harper took Luke's arm and they moved to the nearest car where passengers alighted.

Granville appeared, carrying an umbrella, with his coat over his arm. When he spotted Harper, his handsome features broke into a wide smile and he clasped her to him. "Harper, my dear, how nice to see you. And Luke, how are you?"

"Good to see you, sir." Luke stepped forward to shake his hand, then turned to summon a porter to load Granville's luggage in the brougham.

"Shall we have breakfast so we can discuss matters?" Granville asked, guiding Harper to the carriage.

She felt much of her tension dissipate. "I'm so glad you're here."

"I'm just happy you let me know I'm needed."

Within minutes, Luke had driven them to the Plains Hotel a favorite of the Whittakers since the Inter-Ocean was destroyed by fire. When they were settled in the dining room, they ordered tea and breakfast.

"Now then, how do things stand with Damien and John at this time?"

"They're still under arrest at Fort Russell with the rest of the Invaders."

"I read with great interest the text of Governor Barber's telegram to President Harrison in *The New York Times*." He consulted her. "But that wire didn't get through, did it?"

"No, despite the lateness of the hour, Governor Barber sent wires to Senators Carey and Warren, instructing them to go to the White House and wake President Harrison. When they spoke directly to the President, he quickly agreed to send troopers from Fort McKinney to arrest the Invaders at the TA ranch."

Their food arrived and they all concentrated on it for an interval before they continued the discussion.

"From what I've managed to learn, Governor Barber has turned out to be an important ally for the Invaders," Granville said.

"Yes, once he assumed control over them, he's refused even to allow them to be questioned."

He smiled. "So what I've heard is correct then. The governor has completely frustrated the investigation of the Invasion into Johnson County. From my point of view, that is a very helpful development."

"Once Governor Barber assumed responsibility for the prisoners, they've enjoyed preferential treatment," Harper divulged. "According to a letter Damien sent to me with a stable boy last week, the prisoners have been allowed to roam the army base by day as long as they return to quarters at night. He said many of the men have spent their days at the Cheyenne Club or walked out of town to visit wives or girlfriends. Damien and John were too unnerved by their participation in the Invasion and the death of Nate Champion and Jose Martinez to break the rules such as they are."

"I'm pleased to hear that my son and Damien have kept their behavior above the fray. When hanging is the possible penalty for their actions, it's only prudent." He poured a final cup of tea and stirred it thoughtfully. "I'm getting the impression that there are a number of areas I can use to defend them or at least muddle the situation enough so some perspective can be gained." He laid aside his napkin and sat observing Harper. "What can I do for *you,* my dear? I mean as far as Damien is concerned. Are you worried about something I can explain . . . or . . ."

Harper laid her hand on his arm. "I want to see Damien alone. When Audra and I visited the fort, a trooper watched us like a guard dog. It was so disconcerting, I said we wouldn't go back under those circumstances. Audra did visit again a few days back and was able to speak privately to John because Governor Barber told the Cavalry that private visits between the prisoners and their families were to be allowed. I longed to see Damien but because you were arriving so soon, I decided to wait until I had spoken to you before I went."

Granville nodded. "I'd say that was wise. But it appears a precedence has been established so now I suggest we go to Fort Russell. While you spend some time with Damien, I'll speak to John. Later, I'll pay a visit to Governor. Barber and see if I can determine what the future bodes for the Invaders."

# CHAPTER TWO

## May 1892

When Harper alighted from the carriage at Fort Russell, she glanced at the men sitting and standing around the barracks. Most of the ranchers under arrest had attended dinners and balls at the *Mariposa* with their wives. Many had accompanied the Whittakers, John and Audra to the Cheyenne Opera House and the Gala at the Capitol when Wyoming attained statehood. Now the majority greeted her and Luke by name or raised hands in greeting. Their friendly demeanor went a long way towards quieting Harper's nerves as she followed Granville and Luke further along a cobbled walkway towards a grouping of wrought iron benches some distance across an open lawn dotted by shade trees. Several more cattlemen occupied the seats and they rose and doffed their hats when they drew near.

"Where would we find Damien Whittaker and John Carroll?" Granville inquired.

"Last I saw them, they were headed down to the stream there," a tall rancher wearing a black Stetson offered, indicating a thickening of cottonwoods perhaps a quarter mile down a slope abutting the running water. A breeze stirred the warm sunshine, fluttering the flag atop a pole to one side.

Harper took Granville's proffered arm and they proceeded toward the trees. When they topped the incline, they saw Damien and John sitting on a large slab of stone anchored at the edge of the stream.

Drawn by their progress along a converging walkway, Damien leapt to his feet, rushing toward them. In seconds, Harper was crushed to his chest, his heart pounding near her ear.

"Darling." He put her apart from him a little, looking into her face. "My, God, I've been out of my mind without you!"

"I'm here now," she said through her tears. "And I've brought Granville to get you out of this predicament."

"Ah, Granville." Damien leaned toward him to shake hands. "Am I ever so happy to see you."

"Good to be here, Damien. Now while you spend some time with Harper, I have a great deal to discuss with John. I have to determine how to get the charges dismissed against you two."

Damien stared at him. "Do you believe there's a chance of that?"

He gestured dismissively. "Much more than a chance. I just need time to sort everything. Now I want to speak with John." With a smile, he moved toward his son.

Luke came closer. "I'd like to find some things for Ivy," he told Harper. "Would you mind if I took the brougham downtown?"

"Not at all. Take your time." She gripped his arm and kissed his cheek.

With a wink, he strode toward the carriage.

"Come, let's walk a little." Damien looked searchingly into Harper's face as they proceeded along the path "Darling, how are you?"

"Right at this moment, I'm so happy to be walking with my husband on a lovely spring day."

He chuckled and pulled her into the shelter of some evergreens. His hands came up to cradle her face. "Ah, thank God, you're here." Leaning close, he kissed her tenderly, then led her to a flat rock large enough to sit.

She laid her head on his shoulder. "Delaney said to tell you how much she misses you."

"How is she?"

"Very sad."

"I miss her and Chandler. And you." He kissed her again as she twined her arms around his neck, savoring being so close.

"Have you heard anything about what's going to happen next?"

"Governor Barber comes every few days and is still manipulating the situation with an iron fist. He's been on our side from the start."

"Will there be a trial?"

"Eventually, I would imagine although Governor Barber seems intent on using the wait and delay defense. He's convinced the citizenry will gradually see that we were justified in invading Johnson County. I'm not sure he's correct in that assumption but time will tell."

"Granville plans to talk to him sometime today."

His gaze narrowed. "With Governor Barber?"

"That's what he told me."

"Well, I'm so glad you had the good sense to send for Granville. I can't imagine how you kept your wits about you long enough to see he's what we need. When you and Audra left the barracks after that last godawful visit, I could see no way out of this debacle. But once John and I learned his father was on his way, it made all the difference. We had hope again." He looked at her intently. "Thank you, darling."

"I was just so terrified. It was all I could think to do."

He drew her close until her head burrowed into the hollow of his throat. "I swear to you, I never for one moment thought that by trying to fight the threat to *Rancha Mariposa*, to our life in this glorious place, we would end up about to be tried for murder."

"Darling, I know that. When we spoke before you agreed to join the Invasion, I knew the risk. But I also wanted you to go ahead because the life we've built here is so precious. And we suffered so much because it was threatened. Because Jonathon Holt and Jose Martinez wanted to ruin us and they hated us so much." The length of her stiffened in his arms. "I wanted them destroyed and you did that. No matter what happens now, I'm glad you destroyed them. Glad!"

He studied her for a time. "Darling." He raised a hand to settle her head back against his shoulder. "Can we get through this to the other side and have the same life we had? Is it possible to become mired in such evil, to kill men in retaliation and then go back to the way it was?"

"Yes, it's possible. You are such a good man, an honorable man. Our life together will be just the same as before. Remember how much your children love you. How much I love you."

He managed a wan smile. "How could I forget?"

"I have news that will please you about Luke and Ivy."

"Does it have anything to do with Luke's high spirits today?"

"It does. He's told me how he wants to marry Ivy and she's agreed."

Damien pondered this a moment, then grinned. "I'll be damned. I daresay, this solves several problems in one fell swoop."

"My thoughts exactly."

"When?"

"Very soon, I hope, as Ivy will have her baby most any moment. I'm thinking I must alert both Dr. Ritter and a preacher while I'm still in town."

"How is Dom dealing with this turn of events?"

"We haven't discussed it but I'm quite sure he could care less."

"That might change now that Luke wants to marry the mother of Dom's child."

"I doubt it. He's made his feelings very clear and now, whether he likes it or not, he must deal with it."

"You're right, of course." A smile seeped into his eyes. "It is quite remarkable. I'm so fond of both Luke and Ivy, I wish them all the best. Where will they live?"

"Luke plans to build a cottage next to Jamie's. I thought in the meantime, they could live in the apartment Eliza used before her wedding."

"That's a good idea. Will you offer it with our compliments?"

"Yes. Living there will give them some privacy from the rest of the household."

"And Dom in particular," Damien said with a cocked brow.

"Yes. I do hope he'll behave himself. He's become even more inclined to act up lately. I daresay, you being away accounts for much of that."

Damien frowned. "Perhaps I'll have to make good on my threat to send him to boarding school."

"Oh, I hope it doesn't come to that. Despite his wayward streak, I can't help but think he'd be worse away from home. And he has met his match in Arthur. They're no longer pals like they were at first. Now Arthur's too caught up in plans for his coming marriage to be much amused by Dom's shenanigans so he's taken a sterner hand."

"That's good. Encourage him in that. Perhaps he can keep him in line until I get home."

"I've already told him I approve."

Footsteps coming along the walking path caught their attention and they watched Granville and John approach. "Well, John has filled me on all the details of the past two weeks," Granville said, taking a seat on a bench a short distance closer the stream.

John eased his long frame down beside his father.

"I believe I may have found a way to get you two released on bond until trial," Granville observed. "Perhaps all you prisoners."

Harper's heart leapt in her chest but she managed to remain silent, even as she gripped Damien's hand

"John tells me how put upon, the Johnson County authorities are feeling because they have to pay the expenses of keeping all these men here. The Texas Rangers have all escaped back to where they came." He lowered his voice and inclined closer. "And it seems the two trappers that were the sole witnesses to the killing of Nate Champion and Jose Martinez were in protective custody in the Converse County jail in Douglas. By some mysterious means, they've been broken out of jail and put on a train to St. Louis. I'm quite sure they will never be seen in Wyoming again." A slow grin lifted the end of his mustache. "Now, I see your man Luke has returned so I'm going to ask him to drive me to see Governor Barber so I can invite him to lunch." He rose gracefully and put on his hat. "Now all of you wait here and I will send Luke back with food for a picnic. I shall return as soon as I can." With that, he took his umbrella in hand and strode toward the brougham visible inside the gate.

As the sun climbed toward its zenith, those awaiting Luke's return moved into thicker shade under the cottonwoods. Harper removed her cloak in the warmth and soon settled back in Damien's embrace. "Do you think he can possibly do what he says?"

"There're many reasons my father is the paramount barrister in London," John said. "I've long since stopped underestimating him."

"Was it difficult studying law with such a high standard to emulate?" Damien asked.

"No, I always got on well with him and he recognized my talent for public speaking and the stage by the time I got to Oxford so it was his idea that I study law. And I loved the challenge of it. But after a few years, practicing law became too routine for my taste and that's when I began looking for a new opportunity and that's when Moreton Whittaker began writing to me about the prospects of cattle ranching here."

"And sixteen years later, here we are, prisoners," Damien said with a rueful grin, studying his friend and partner. "Has there ever been a vulnerable moment during our past weeks of imprisonment here when you wished you were back in Herefordshire practicing law?"

John tipped back his hat, not answering right away. "No," he said presently. "How could I even ponder that choice? If I hadn't heeded the call to come here along with you and all the other young men to this magnificent land, we wouldn't have had the friendship and adventure that's brought us to this point. I wouldn't have Audra and our seven amazing daughters." He looked intently at Damien and Harper. "Considering all, I'll stay the course. And what about you, my friend? Posing the same question."

Damien looked at him steadily. "Even with the risk that it could all end badly, I would not have missed one minute of the past sixteen years." He tightened his arms about Harper.

The cattlemen congregated about the barracks stirred and the sound of a triangle being rung announced the noon meal being served in the mess hall. Because Luke would bring them lunch, John and the Whittakers remained beside the stream and as promised, Luke soon arrived with food from The Plains—roast chicken, fried potatoes, early peas, and oatmeal cookies.

"Not quite up to Mrs. Goodeve's standards but tasty nonetheless," Harper said as she finished her meal with a glass of lemonade.

Her gaze settled on Luke who sat opposite. "Did Granville manage to have lunch with Governor Barber?"

"They were heading into The Plains dining room when I left. The Governor appeared to be listening closely to whatever Granville had to say."

They continued talking together until Luke left to fetch Granville. John wandered down to the edge of the water, leaving the Whittakers alone.

"Not knowing how long I'd be away, I decided to wean Chandler," Harper divulged. "Now would you please keep an eye out." She reached for her reticule and removed the linen strips Ivy had packed.

Damien shifted to shelter her from the men further along the stream. Once she'd replaced the soaked material with clean, he lowered his lips to kiss her collarbone, then tenderly nuzzled her swollen breasts. "My, God, I've missed you." His voice was thick with longing.

Soon enough, he replaced her fingers with his to do up the buttons of her bodice, smiling.

She lifted her hands to frame his head, her mouth settling on his to kiss him deeply, her body straining against him. "My darling husband, I love you so much."

"It's seems an eternity since I was home."

She studied him, seeing his exhaustion, the sharper planes of his features. He was much thinner and it hurt her to see him diminished by the recent weeks. Yet, as she settled back against him again, her arms atop his, she couldn't help concentrating on the tantalizing promise of a return to simple happiness like what awaited them at *Rancha Mariposa.*

"Do you know what I miss to the point of longing to weep?" Damien asked. "I mean aside from you and my children and our home?"

She shook her head, almost afraid to hear.

"Baby calves. This is the first spring when I haven't birthed dozens of baby Herefords and my heart aches to see them with their mothers, lolling about in the sunshine of green pastures."

"I don't blame you for that. Baby calves in the spring have always been one of my favorite parts of ranching. And you'll be happy to know there have been few difficulties this year. It's an omen for the future."

"I'm going to hold tight to that thought." He moved his head to kiss her cheek.

"Oh, good, they're back." She disengaged herself from him and he helped her up.

Harper attempted to read Granville's demeanor as he strode toward them with Luke and John. He laughed and clapped his son on the back which she interpreted as good news.

"Harper, my dear, I hope I didn't keep you waiting too long." He tucked her hand in his and embraced Damien to guide them back to where they'd been sitting under the shade trees. "We have a great deal to talk about," he said when they were settled again.

"Governor Barber agrees that the authorities in Johnson County are less and less eager to assume the costs of feeding and housing the lot of you. There would also be substantial charges for the preparation and presentation of the criminal cases." He placed both hands flat on his thighs, pausing for effect. "So," he finally went on, "he has agreed to release everyone involved in the Invasion on their recognizance until trial."

The gathering stared at him for some minutes without reaction. "When will the trial be?" Damien inquired.

"Sometime toward fall, I should think. I am not certain there will *be* a trial once this is all sorted. I've seen firsthand that the Governor wields considerable clout and he is very loyal to his friends in the Wyoming Stock Growers Association."

"When will we be released?" John asked.

"I tried my best to get that accomplished yet today but Governor Barber has decided for appearances sake, we wait until Monday. So I'll be staying on here in town to facilitate the arrangements and I will escort you and Damien home next week."

"Oh, darling." Harper turned to hug Damien. "Thank, God."

Although he'd begun shaking with reaction at the abrupt reversal of circumstances, he appeared determined to control any untoward response. He could only look into Harper's eyes, overflowing with tears and they were suddenly clinging to each other, weeping, struggling to accept what Granville had accomplished.

"You're coming home," Harper whispered. "Oh, I'm so happy." She looked up to see John standing nearby, his hand clasping Damien's shoulder.

He appeared on the verge of tears himself and Harper realized for the first time, just how deeply the two friends had been affected by the Invasion. She finally understood the gravity of their convictions that had propelled them into the midst of the conflict. She was humbled to think that what she had suffered at the hands of Jonathon Holt and Jose Martinez was the catalyst to force her husband to retaliate, to kill those responsible for so much pain and worry.

She longed to take Damien home where she could care for him and help erase the haunting images that must surely still move through his dreams. She glanced at Granville who'd come to sit next to her and now reached over to touch Damien's arm. "I'm sorry I couldn't get you out today but it will only be a few more days."

Damien wiped the dampness from his face with the back of his hand. "You've no need to apologize. You've accomplished what seemed impossible the morning when the Cavalry arrested us. I was never more certain of anything in my life than John and I were going to hang. From that total desolation, you've managed to get us released. How can I ever thank you for such a miracle."

"By always being the devoted friends to me and my family." He squeezed Harper's hand, giving her a smile. "Now, you should likely be on your way as Luke tells me a new baby may be born very soon at *Rancha Mariposa.* I wish it was possible for me to officiate at the wedding tonight but I must finish up here. I'll be honored to bless the union when I get there."

"Thank you for being here when we needed you so badly." Harper kissed his cheek.

"I'm just so pleased I could be of help. And Damien, John and I will be joining you on Monday. Now I'll wait for you at the gate." With that, he nodded at John and they strode toward the fort's entrance.

Laughing now with released tension, Damien grabbed Harper's hand, pulling her into the protection of the trees where they stood looking at each other with rapt delight.

"Darling, I'm once more indebted to you for asking Granville to come here. You always seem to know what will help the most."

"After a day or two of collecting your wits, you'd have done the same." She reached up to smooth the lines of strain from his forehead. "How lovely to think of you coming home, my love."

"We have so much to look forward to and . . ." his long fingers cupped her chin as he kissed her gently for the space of a heartbeat. "And now you must go," he murmured against her lips. "Perhaps our first grandchild will be born tonight."

She clung to him in the blind need to prolong their parting. As his mouth grew hard, demanding, she answered with overwhelming need of her own, accepting his probing tongue.

Molding the pliant length of her to him, he gloried in her intoxicating sensuality. They were lost in the enchantment until he abruptly wrenched his mouth from hers and, gathered her trembling body, merely holding her until they'd both regained control.

"Darling, I'll be with you soon." He traced a finger along her jawline, then stepped toward the boulder to pick up her cloak.

The sunshine had faded behind banks of rain clouds roiling in a massive bank to the west. The wind gusted along the stream as Damien wrapped the wool about her and they hurried toward the brougham waiting near the fort gate.

Luke and the others were staring at the swirling rain clouds to determine which way the storm was moving. It was soon clear that the wind was driving the maelstrom through downtown, then beyond toward the east. Only scattered drops of rain fell around them before shafts of renewed sunshine pierced the retreating clouds, banishing the chill.

"The gods grace us," Granville murmured as Damien handed Harper into the carriage. "May I bother you for a lift to The Plains?" He inquired of Luke. "I have a great deal of paperwork I must tend to before Monday so I should make a start this evening." He moved to embrace John and Damien, then climbed into the carriage next to Harper.

Once Damien had leaned through the open door to kiss her and John squeezed her hand in farewell, Luke guided the horses through the gate. Harper settled back on the seat, smiling at Granville. "What a wonderful day. When we got to town this morning, I was so afraid I thought I would be ill. Now Damien and John are coming home."

"During my many years of practicing law, I have learned that when a cause is just, and the souls involved are honorable, they are customarily vindicated." He grinned, squeezing her hand. "And I know of no two men with greater integrity than my son and your husband."

Harper couldn't recall a time when she'd felt so confident in the innate goodness of the life she and Damien along with John and Audra and Aunt Pris had forged here in the great, open American West. They and many others of the intrepid thousands who'd come seeking their fortune in cattle ranching had suffered at the hands of the mendacious factions that had come along with the rest.

Now, due to Damien and John's courage and Granville's willingness to bring to bear his vast knowledge of the law, they had been delivered from a disastrous state of affairs. When Luke stopped before The Plains, Granville gathered his coat, umbrella and valise and prepared to depart.

"Goodbye, my dear. I will look forward to seeing you on Monday." He stepped out and made his way toward the hotel's entrance.

Luke opened the door to consult Harper. "Shall I stop at Dr. Ritter's house?"

"Yes. And what are you wishes concerning a preacher coming to the country?"

"I've been pondering that question ever since we spoke before. I'd like to wait so Granville can marry us."

She gave him a smile. "All right then, let's see Dr. Ritter, then be on our way home."

He nodded with a grin, closed the carriage door and after a brief stop at the doctor's house, headed toward *Rancha Mariposa.* Halfway there, another thunderstorm overtook them and Luke stopped the horses to pull on his slicker before they continued.

The storm gradually settled into a steady rain that pattered pleasantly on the roof. Harper pulled her cloak closer, looking out over the intense green of the plains. While still living in Herefordshire, she'd taken for granted the verdant color of the rolling pastures and lush trees. In that idyllic setting, she'd never given a second thought to what might be the ramifications should a severe drought hit the British cattle breeders. None of the Whittakers or other ranchers from abroad had ever experienced what dry, hot weather and no rain could do to flourishing pastureland where the Herefords grew fat and prime for market.

It required the devastation of Wyoming summers when it didn't rain for months and the grass and water dried up and the cattle grew skeletal to show the ranchers who'd come in droves that they wouldn't always be blessed by ideal conditions on the American Plains. They'd erroneously believed the bountiful prairie that had sustained the vast herds of bison before the cattle came, would always be replenished by ample moisture and mild winters when the chinooks cleared the snow so the cattle could feed on the grass beneath.

Damien and John were among the minority of ranchers who became stewards of the land, putting in irrigation systems, planting and stockpiling hay, providing winter protection for their Herefords instead of leaving them on the range to fend for themselves. And they had prospered while others overgrazed their land which in turn led to a glut of thin cattle that forced prices down to ruinous levels.

The combination of drought, overgrazing, and low prices left the region vulnerable, something it hadn't been during the early years. The frigid temperatures and unending snow of the disastrous winter of 1886–87 was the death knell for the industry.

A shiver crept up Harper's spine as she recalled the terror and wreckage of those desolate months. When spring had revealed the range littered with dead cattle and scavengers feeding on what scarce rotting flesh remained on the starved carcasses, it had appeared as though a plague had crossed the region, leaving utter chaos in its wake.

Since that time, she'd found she loved rain whenever it came as she never had before. The healing moisture that replenished the streams at *Rancha Mariposa* invariably filled her with a sense of elation and confidence. Misty cool air touched her face now and she smiled, saying a silent prayer of thanks for the blessing of it.

Her heart still soared with relief and intense joy at the reality that Damien was coming home. She hugged her arms around herself, filled with such longing for him to be back in their life. She'd hardly been aware of the depth of the void after his arrest. She'd fought the agony of their separation by spending her days in headlong activity—caring for her children, riding Embarr, furiously burying herself in her art and painting, anything to exhaust herself so she could fall into deadened sleep late at night.

The strategy had been remarkably successful and she'd passed the days in a fog of dogged purpose without succumbing to utter despair. Leaning on the wise counsel of Jamie and Arthur, she'd managed to withstand the worry and dread that flooded her days.

Now the rain lessened as they crossed Lodgepole and she watched with delight as the clouds began dispersing into watery tatters that reflected the emerging sun in a kaleidoscope of orange and indigo. The new leaves of the aged cottonwoods shimmered with silvery droplets, the aspen quaked in gold scintillation. The world looked fresh and reborn, the damp, earthy smell exhilarating to Harper.

As the carriage approached the *Mariposa,* she saw Stephen, the new Mexican gardener in the front beds that were a glorious mixture of bright spring bulbs and flowering shrubs. The aroma of lilacs drifted through the window to Harper as Luke pulled up in the piazza before the front entrance.

The massive engraved door opened and Delaney burst forth, running to Harper when Luke came to help her out. She swung her daughter up into her arms, hugging and kissing her.

"Ma-ma, you came home! I'm so glad." She wrapped her arms tightly around her neck, then pulled back to inspect her. "Why isn't Pa-pa with you?"

"He had to stay in town a bit longer. But on Monday, he's coming home."

Delaney's face broke into merry fragments of glee. "Oh, boy, that is so wonderful!" She glanced back at her mother. "Did you tell him how much we miss him?"

"I did and he misses us just as much." When she put her down, Delaney began dancing in a circle.

Ivy had come from the house and stood holding Chandler wrapped in a small blanket in the cool fresh air. Luke stepped to her and kissed her cheek. "How are you, dear?"

"I missed you."

He smiled, catching her arm. "We have a lot to talk about. And Dr. Ritter is coming this evening."

She looked stricken at that. "Whatever for?"

"Harper thought it best." He watched her and Delaney enter the house, then returned his attention to the brougham, preparing to drive it to the carriage house.

Aunt Pris came to meet Harper when she reached the sofa before the fireplace where a modest fire burned. "Ah, my dear, you're back. Does that mean you have good news?"

"Wonderful news." She kissed her cheek. "Granville has been a tremendous help and managed to get Damien and John released until the trial."

"Oh, my, that is splendid!" She lowered her bulk onto the sofa, patting the pillow beside her.

Once Harper was seated, Ivy brought Chandler and deposited him on her lap. "So how did he behave today?" She asked Delaney as she snuggled against her.

"He was a very good boy," she said gravely. "But he didn't like drinking goat milk very much."

"Well, since I was able to come home so quickly, I've changed my mind. I'm going to continue feeding him myself."

Delaney grinned, clapping her hands. "Oh, that's good. That'll make him ever so happy."

Harper opened her dress and the baby was soon nursing eagerly. Delaney giggled happily.

"So how are Damien and John holding up?" Aunt Pris asked presently.

"Rather well, considering the grave situation they were in. But what Granville has been able to achieve has made all the difference, needless to say."

"Bless our Granville," she said with feeling.

"Indeed."

They continued there until Chandler was finally satisfied and ready to sleep. Ivy came to take him to the nursery. As she gathered him up with great care, Harper studied her. "You don't feel as though your baby is shifting or anything along that line?"

Ivy shook her head. "Nothing different today."

"Well, Dr. Ritter can probably tell you how close birth is. Now I'm going to walk out and speak to Jamie."

Delaney bounced excitedly beside her. "May I come? There's a new foal and I want to visit Matilda and her babies."

"I shall enjoy your company."

She ran toward the back hall for her cloak with Riley and Rumor dancing around her. They waited by the door until Harper joined them, then passed out into the rear courtyard where Riley tore after a cottontail that escaped under the fence along the driveway. As they walked towards the garden, the enticing fragrances of flowering fruit trees drifting around them in the misty remnants of rain, Delaney admonished Riley upon his happy return. "You mustn't catch that little bunny! You can chase him but don't you dare hurt him." She paused to squat down and grab his head, looking at him sternly. "I'll be very angry with you, if you do!"

Harper laughed at her stern words. "I think that bunny is too fast for our girls."

"That's good because they mustn't be mean." Past the garden, Delaney rushed ahead along the cobbled walkway passing through cattle pens. Some held cows that hadn't yet calved, others confined mothers with their pretty offspring waiting to be turned out onto spring pasture along Aspen Creek that bypassed the headquarters behind the *Mariposa.* Delaney was enchanted by the newborn calves and stopped often to peer between the rails.

"Aren't they beautiful?" She looked up when Harper paused beside her.

"I love them too," she agreed. "Do you know what your Pa-pa said he missed most about being away?"

"Me?"

"Of course you. But after you, baby calves."

Delaney clapped her hands, gazing at her in wonder. "I'm so happy we won't ever have to be without baby animals. Now let's go see the new foal." Grabbing Harper's hand, she pulled her toward the stables.

Luke stepped out into the breezeway as they went inside. "Did you come to see our new filly?"

"Yes. I just heard about her. Who's her mother?"

"Rose."

"Ah, yes. She came with us from Herefordshire when she was a baby herself."

Luke led them to a large foaling stall at the rear of the stable. When Delaney couldn't see over the door, he lifted her.

Rose's dappled hide was still dark gray despite her age, and the perfect filly was totally black. "What do you think of her?" Luke asked.

Delaney sighed happily. "She's ever so pretty but I hoped she'd be gray like Rose."

"You're in luck there because before she's a year old, she'll start turning dappled gray."

"Are you sure?" Delaney asked.

"Absolutely. Almost all gray horses are born black."

"Did you know that, Ma-ma?" She leaned closer to wrap an arm around her.

"Yes, I did actually. Pa-pa's gelding Beckett was born black."

"So why isn't Cadoc gray?"

"Sometimes it just happens that way," Luke said, lifting her down.

"Have you seen Jamie?" Harper asked.

"I think I had a glimpse of him driving some cows and calves out to pasture. He should be back soon enough."

"I want to fill him in on what we found out today. We'll just go visit Matilda and her kids until he shows up."

"Then I'm going to go have a word with Ivy."

"You do that and while you're at it, tell her Damien and I have decided that while your cottage is being built, you two should use the apartment where Eliza lived."

He snatched off his hat and stood holding it as he stared at her. "I can pay rent."

"We'll discuss the practical aspects of the arrangement when Damien gets home but feel free to move in whenever you like."

"You are so kind."

"As I've said before, we want only the best for our first grandchild. This is very exciting."

"What about Dr. Ritter? Ivy doesn't look like she's going to have the baby any time soon."

"Don't worry. We pay Dr. Ritter well so he won't mind checking Ivy over. If he thinks labor will begin soon, he'll stay here. If not, he'll come back when it's time."

"All right, then." He touched the brim of his hat and headed toward the *Mariposa.*

Delaney took Harper's hand and led her toward a pen at the back of the main barn. They stopped next to the enclosure where Matilda, a buff-colored goat, stood calmly chewing hay, gazing at them placidly. Her three spotted kids, only two days old, capered around her, bouncing onto a feed bunk to use as a springboard to leap atop the roof of their house before reversing and bounding back to the ground. After circling the equable Matilda in follow-the-leader formation, they hopped onto the roof again, dancing on the shingles, bucking and rearing until they descended once more.

"They have springs in their feet," Delaney declared, laughing at their antics. She raised the latch so she and her mother could go inside then bent to lift one of the tiny goats in her arms "Aren't they the sweetest things?"

"They are indeed." Harper took the comical little goat from her.

Delaney captured another and leaned against the feed bunk, cradling it in her arms much as she did her baby brother. They still lingered there when Jamie rode up and dismounted beside the barn.

"I see you've met our charming new babies." He got off his horse and wrapped the reins around a post before joining them, his scrappy terrier, Humbart, at his heels

"You may hold this one," Delaney offered, shoving her goat onto his lap when he sat on a manger beside her.

He laughed, fondling the floppy ears as Humbart poked his nose against the mottled hide.

Delaney chortled. "Humbart likes our baby goats!"

"But of course. He has excellent taste." He smiled at Harper. "It's wonderful seeing you back so soon."

"I have amazing news. Damien and John will be coming home Monday."

His warm blue eyes filled with delighted surprise. "Oh, Harper, I'm so pleased to hear that. How on earth did that happen?"

"Granville is quite a wizard with the law. He determined that Johnson County is running low on funds to pay the upkeep for the prisoners before trial so convinced Governor Barber they should be released until then."

"How fortunate you got him involved so soon. I know it must've been killing Damien and John being in jail."

"It was but Governor Barber was very helpful in that as well. The barracks at Fort Russell hadn't sufficient beds so the men were jailed at night. During the day, as long as they stayed on base, they were left to their own devices at Fort Russell."

"Ah, that's good then." Jamie deposited the baby goat on the ground and watched it scamper off to its mother and begin nursing lustily.

The other two upon seeing what it was about, ran to get their share.

"When does Granville say the trial will begin?" Jamie asked presently.

"When the investigation is finished. It's his understanding that lack of funds is hampering that as well."

"Perhaps that will work to the advantage of the Invaders in the end."

"Perhaps. Granville seems to be concentrating on the victory of getting them home. So I'm going to do that as well and enjoy the summer with them back where they belong."

"Yes, it is going to be a splendid summer for all of us. I feel strongly that most of our trials are behind us. We've never had a better calf crop and the weather bodes well for ample grass and hay." He fell silent a moment, considering Harper with a profound air of contentment. "Eliza is expecting our first child."

"Jamie, how lovely!"

"I've tried to put my thoughts into words to express how I feel about having a child. I thought finding Eliza after all the years of being alone was the ultimate gift but now, we're having a baby to bring us joy in the final years of our marriage. Could anything be finer?"

"I shouldn't think so. What is your secret wish? A boy or girl?"

He pushed his hat back. "Oh, it makes no difference at all. He or she will be cherished."

Harper thought of the impish lad her muse had placed in the painting of Eliza's school room. She was tempted to tell Jamie his coming child was a son but decided he would rather be surprised at the moment of the boy's birth.

Once he returned to his work, Harper and Delaney walked back along the path with the beagles frolicking around them.

They soon met Audra coming towards them on her daily walk. "I was so delighted when Luke came to tell me you were home." She hurried to throw her arms around Harper. "Is it really true that John and Damien are coming home?"

"Yes, thanks to Granville. They'll be here Monday."

"Thank God." Tears filled Audra's eyes and she moved to a wrought iron bench beside the garden and collapsed, hunting through her pockets until she found a hanky. "I can scarcely believe it's true after all these days when I've been worried sick."

Harper sat beside her. "It's true. I know exactly how you feel. It's hard to describe. Like being in a dark cave, then suddenly walking into sunshine." She gripped Audra's hand. "You and John and the girls must all come to the *Mariposa* on Monday evening for a celebratory dinner."

"How lovely. Luke also told me we'll be celebrating his and Ivy's marriage." Her face lit with pleasure. "How extraordinarily generous you and Damien are to bless them as you have. I've been concerned for months about Ivy and what would happen to her baby. I've agonized over the situation all the more because I care so much for her and because the baby is Dom's. I am so unhappy with that boy, I'd like to take him across my knee. Perhaps we should have done that more often when he was a boy."

"Damien and I never had the heart for it. I think it might have made him even more rebellious."

"I know you're right but he's so maddening. He is so brilliant and charming. He could accomplish the greatest things in his life but I just wonder if he will." She turned troubled eyes toward Harper.

"I'd like to shake him silly," she agreed, "but since he's too big for that these days, I'm putting my faith in God and Arthur who's very aware of his less complementary traits. He's agreed to exert whatever pressure is necessary to keep him in hand and have him ready for college in two more years. With Damien and I adamant on that subject, I believe our Dom will become an honorable young man all in due time."

Audra smiled. "I have complete faith in you." Her gaze settled on Delaney cavorting about the courtyard with the dogs. "And I thank God that his baby will be raised by two parents with as much good sense as Luke and Ivy."

"I too."

"How do you think Dom is going to react to the marriage?"

"Not well, I'm sure but I swear I'm going to slap him silly if he makes any trouble. He has little to complain about since he certainly had no desire to take responsibility for his behavior and his baby."

Delaney approached them and Audra reached out to hug her. "Your Pa-pa's coming home."

"I know. Isn't it wonderful? I've missed him so much."

Audra kissed her cheek. "If the rain stays away, perhaps you and Millie can ride tomorrow."

"Yes, we already decided while we were in school."

"All right then. Now I must go back. I'm sure dinner must be waiting."

"Goodbye." Delaney hugged her again.

"See you tomorrow, dear." Audra squeezed Harper's hand and they all proceeded to their respective dinners.

# CHAPTER THREE

**May 1892**

Dr. Ritter had arrived at the *Mariposa* while Harper was out. He'd already examined Ivy and speculated that she would not give birth for at least a week. Not having any pressing business elsewhere, he readily accepted Harper's invitation to dinner and agreed to spend the night. Aunt Pris was so pleased to have a guest that as soon as he finished eating, she ushered him into the parlor where she held court until he begged weariness and retired.

After feeding Chandler and putting Delaney to bed, Harper sought out Dom in the library where he sat reading by the fire. He watched her enter and settle in a chair opposite.

"Ripping news that Pa-pa and John are free," he said.

"Isn't it though. I'm just so happy."

"Me too."

"Dom, do you know that Luke has asked Ivy to marry him?"

He slammed his book shut and sat staring at her. "When did that happen?"

"He spoke to me about it this morning."

"He just wants her for fun and games."

"Don't be ridiculous, Dom. Luke has fallen in love with Ivy and is willing to assume responsibility for her and her baby in marriage. To put it bluntly, you should be grateful he's cleaning up your mess."

"I still say Ivy and her baggage should've been sent packing. That would've taken care of the problem."

"My dear Dom, with that kind of self-serving attitude, you are going to find your life much more difficult than it would be otherwise. I hope you never find yourself in dire need of help from someone you've treated as shabbily as you've treated Ivy and your child."

His look was sullen. "I don't want that bastard. She never should've tried trapping me."

"Did Ivy ever ask you to marry her, or even support her and the baby?"

"That didn't matter. Pa-pa makes me pay her every month."

"Because your father is a far more honorable man than you will ever be. It pains me to say so but it's a fact."

"Why are you so mean to me? You used to be so nice and took my side. Now you only find fault."

"Dom, I'm sorry to say that lately, you've done little to earn my goodwill. You've become arrogant and unkind. I simply will not stand by and watch you behave badly. I've always had such faith in you and seen your amazing potential. I refuse to watch you ruin your future."

"The only future I want is running *Rancha Mariposa.* I don't need to study Latin and English literature to do that, so I despise the notion I have to go to university."

"You miss the point of being a gentleman. You come from a lineage of English gentlemen and it is your destiny to take your place among them. As your father has explained to you, certain realities are expected in exchange for the successful and powerful heritage to which gentlemen aspire. A fine education is simply one of the requirements towards that end. So I would advise you to stop complaining before your father gets sufficiently weary of it and carts you off to boarding school."

Dom sat silently taking her measure. "With all the spring and summer work ahead, I doubt he'd do that."

"Autumn will be here soon enough, my dear. Now I'm off to bed. I do hope you will choose to give serious thought to what I've said and conduct yourself accordingly. Tomorrow, when your father gets home, I want you to be polite to a fault and watch yourself very carefully during the wedding. If you choose to be rude and obnoxious, it will not bode well for you. Do I make myself clear?"

With a grimace, he gave her a mock salute.

She hurried into the corridor before she was tempted to say more.

Monday, Mrs. Goodeve cooked all day in preparation for the meal to welcome Damien and John home from Fort Russell. By three o'clock, the delectable aroma of roast turkey filled the *Mariposa.* Luke had gone hunting at dawn and bagged a tender young hen for his wedding dinner.

When the Carroll daughters and Delaney were dismissed from Eliza's classroom, they traipsed upstairs to the ballroom where Harper and Audra waited with Aunt Pris and a number of Audra's ball gowns she'd worn during her various pregnancies.

Ivy stood amidst the finery, allowing the various dresses to be held up to determine which was most becoming. She'd brought Chandler up from the nursery and Harper sat on a bench feeding him.

When Audra lifted a sky blue silk and held it to Ivy's shoulders, Harper nodded her approval. "That one is perfect," she said, meeting the girl's excited gaze. "It compliments your rosy complexion and matches the lovely shade of your eyes. Do you like it?"

A slow smile curved her full mouth. "I adore it. It's so elegant, I'll feel like a princess."

"Well, let's see how it fits," Audra said briskly and set to the task of helping her remove her tent-like black uniform. When she stood in her undergarments, Audra draped the gown over her head and watched it fall in soft folds to the floor.

Ivy turned this way and that to view it in the long mirror. She quite glowed with happiness.

"You look very beautiful," Delaney declared, standing close to her best friend Millie Carroll.

"You do, indeed," agreed Aunt Pris.

Ivy clasped her hands together beneath her chin. "I don't know how to thank you."

"Just enjoy your wedding and live a happy life as Luke's wife." Harper gave her a smile.

"Oh, I will, I'm the luckiest girl in the world." Despite her ungainly shape, she twirled before the mirror as the others laughed at her high spirits. Catching her breath, she collapsed on the bench next to Harper, smiling at Chandler.

"Have you moved your things to your apartment?"

"Luke has put some of his clothes and such there but I think I should sleep in my usual bed for now so I can still care for Chandler."

"Oh, I should have told you sooner, Rachel will assume your duties in the nursery after your wedding. You'll need time to recover from giving birth and have your hands full caring for your own baby. You can take up your duties in the house in a couple months and your child can share the nursery with Chandler. So when I go downstairs, I'll send Sandy up to move everything to your apartment."

She still looked doubtful but soon agreed. "Thank you ever so much."

Eliza arrived and was soon dressed in a pale lavender gown cut to disguise her own growing midriff. "Will this frock do?" She asked with a little curtsy since she and Jamie were attending the bridal couple.

"It's just right," Ivy said.

"Shall Millie and I be your flower girls?" Delaney asked, coming to stand beside Ivy. "There are lots of lovely roses in the greenhouse for petals."

Ivy reached out to hug both girls. "I'd love it if you would strew loads of rose petals in my path. Thank you."

"Adare is fashioning spectacular bouquets for you and Eliza to carry," Aunt Pris observed when Ivy bent to kiss her cheek. "That man is quite the wizard with flower arranging."

"All of you make me feel very special."

"You *are* special, my dear." Aunt Pris caught her hand in her plump, bejeweled fingers. "Never forget it."

Chandler had finished nursing and Harper put him to her shoulder, gently rubbing his back until he burped with gusto, making Delaney and Millie giggle. Ivy reached for him but Harper shook her head. "No, I'll take him down. You're officially on temporary leave of nursery duty."

Ivy sighed blissfully. "A bit of rest sounds heavenly."

Harper patted her hand. "You've certainly earned it."

"May I put him to bed?" Delaney asked, reaching for her baby brother.

"What a good idea. Thank you."

Delaney cuddled him in her arms, heading downstairs with Millie and the other Carroll sisters trailing behind. Harper soon followed, intent on checking on the dinner preparations.

The Great Hall had taken on a festive air with the dining table laid with the best china, flatware and linen. Elaborate bouquets of pink and white roses graced the striking length of it. The butler still inspected his work with satisfaction.

"It all looks absolutely grand, Adare."

"Thank you, milady."

She continued to the kitchen where Mrs. Goodeve sat on a stool, putting the finishing touches on a small wedding cake elegantly iced with swirls of silvery frosting. "Oh, how extravagant!"

The cook looked up, her homely face wreathed in smiles. "Thank you, my dear. I wanted to give the happy couple something good-looking, them being such dearies."

"You've outdone yourself and they will be delighted." Glancing at the wall clock, she was filled with excitement. It was past five so Damien and the others were due any moment.

The front door bell rang and she hurried to answer it, Riley and Rumor capering at her side. After gesturing for them to sit, she admitted Jane Lamb, the musician who'd played at her wedding to Damien and at every ceremony since that'd been held at *Mariposa.* Today, instead of being accompanied by her brother and mother, her husband bore her cello and she was no longer the demure girl Jane Dooley. Adare strode from the back hall and ushered the couple to the spot with the best acoustics.

Too tense to be still, Harper let herself outside and briefly paced the courtyard before settling on a bench to wait. The evening was warm summer perfection. In only a matter of minutes, she spotted the brougham approaching along the curving drive that in due course ended in the piazza edging the courtyard before the front garden.

When the carriage came to a stop, she stood and smoothed her skirt, watching Damien step out, the picture of elegance. She ran to him and he curved the length of her against him. "Darling, how lovely to be home. Sorry we're so late but it took Granville some time to tie up all the loose ends." He looked intently into her face. "How beautiful you look."

She leaned close to brush his lips with hers before turning to Granville who'd alighted next to her. "Granville, so good to see you."

"Ah, my sweet Harper. It took much longer to get here than I'd have liked but at last, your husband is home." He took her hand, nodding at her.

Damien stepped toward the open door of the carriage and retrieved a small cage. The beagles came to investigate, peering up and whining. "I've brought a new friend for you and Delaney." Opening the door, he took out a tiny beagle puppy that he handed to Harper.

"Oh, Damien, how wonderful." She lifted the puppy to peer into his comical little face. "What's his name?"

"Huckleberry."

Delaney and the rest arrived in a clamor from inside and Harper gave the puppy to her, eliciting a cry of glee. "Huckleberry!" Holding him up, she rubbed her chin against his soft head. "Oh, Pa-pa, he's beautiful! Thank you so much!"

"You're welcome, darling. Tell me, how are you? I've missed you so." He lifted her into his arms.

"Not as much as I missed you!" Tears ran down her cheeks as she and the puppy were crushed to Damien's chest. "Pa-pa, are you really home?" She burrowed her head into his shoulder.

He held her close, rocking her tenderly. "I am, my sweet." At last, he put her down and they followed the others inside.

After giving John a hug, Harper led Granville to one side to ask if he was prepared to conduct the wedding ceremony before dinner.

"I'd like nothing more. Where are the nuptials to take place?"

She escorted him beyond the central fireplace where Adare had built an altar adorned with roses much like the one he'd constructed for her marriage to Damien six years ago.

"How charming. When shall we proceed?"

"I should think Luke and Jamie will be here shortly. Let me go up and see how the ladies are getting on. Why don't you sit and have some refreshment."

"Thank you. Don't be concerned about me. I'll be ready when you are."

Harper intercepted Roddy and asked him to serve Granville whatever he wished to drink, then escort Aunt Pris downstairs. Jane Lamb's soft cello music created a pleasant ambiance as Harper turned up the staircase. As she climbed, she heard footsteps behind and glanced over her shoulder to find Damien overtaking her.

With a grin, he pressed her against the bannister. Delight engulfed her in a blinding frenzy and she clung to him as overwhelming desire pouring over her.

"My God!" He said at last, chuckling. "It seems I've been away too long."

"But now you're home." Smiling, she laid her head on his chest, then shifted enough so she could look into his eyes, hunting for any change she might have missed when she saw him a few days ago.

He met her direct inspection straight on. "What is it, my love?"

"I just wanted to see if you're the same. If the horror you've been through has changed you."

With a sudden tortured intake of breath, he wrapped her close, holding her fiercely for perhaps a minute. "I'm the same," he said at last, looking at her again. "I will not allow myself to be altered by recent weeks. I won't let those two evil bastards steal any more from us. I'm back where I belong and you can count on me being here forever."

"You're not worried about the trial?"

"I'd be a fool if I said it doesn't give me pause. Yet, I've discovered a newfound faith in our future. I know with every fiber of my being, you and I and our family will endure here at *Rancha Mariposa* for a great many years to come."

"When you are old and gray and walk with a cane, I'll love you every bit as much as I do today."

"And the same is true of me. When your hair turns white and all the experiences of your life are etched in the lines of your face, you will be even more beautiful to me. And you will have all the greater hold on my heart." With a roguish grin, he pressed his forehead against hers as they lingered there a bit longer.

"When you accosted me here on the stairs, I was on my way to see if our bride is ready. Come congratulate the mother of your soon-to-be grandchild."

Just then, Roddy and Aunt Pris appeared above and Damien climbed toward them. "Damien, so nice to have you home," Aunt Pris said, lifting her hand for his kiss.

"So happy to see you back with us," Roddy said, giving his friend a one-armed hug before they continued down.

Guiding her with a hand on the small of her back, Damien followed Harper into the ballroom where the ladies waited in their finery. Adare arrived from the servants' quarters with a long flat basket holding the bouquets and boutonniere's he'd fashioned for the bridal party.

He set about pinning the rosebuds to lapels. Delaney and Millie careened into the room in time to claim the baskets of rosebuds and petals he'd prepared.

LuAnn, a new girl hired to fill in as ladies maid while Rachel returned to nursery duty had talent for styling hair. She'd put up Ivy's blonde curls in an elegant do. Now, she turned her attention to the girls' long hair, brushing it until it shone before tying it with grosgrain ribbons matched to their dresses.

"How beautiful you all look," said Damien before he embraced Ivy and Eliza. "And you two are positively enchanting," he told Delaney and Millie, dropping kisses on the tops of their heads.

Harper had stepped to the head of the staircase to look down into the hall where Jamie and Luke, in black frockcoats stood with Granville before the altar of roses. Audra had gone down the back stairs to join John when he arrived from town and now they sat to the side of the altar with the rest of their daughters except for the youngest Yvette who had joined Chandler in the nursery.

Harper was always amazed at what a handsome family they made—John dark and slender, Audra, blonde and willowy despite having borne seven babies—Ophelia, Bethany, Willa, twins, Olivia and Anne, Millie and Yvette, the baby, all blonde like their mother save for Willa who'd inherited her father's black hair and dark eyes. At fourteen, Ophelia closely resembled Audra, her eyes the shade of the best jade as John was fond of saying since he'd courted his wife after she first arrived in Wyoming Territory as Harper's governess.

The servants, as well as the cowboys and stable lads, all Luke's friends, had gathered near the spot where Jane Lamb played her cello. At the last moment, Mrs. Goodeve, who'd changed into a clean uniform and apron for the occasion, limped from the kitchen and sat in the chair Adare held for her.

Harper moved to the edge of the staircase and sat on a step to watch the wedding party descend to the hall below. When the flower girls came abreast of her, gleefully tossing rose petals on the Aubusson runner, Delaney darted across the stairs to quickly hug Harper. "I love you, Ma-ma."

Eliza came next with Ivy just behind, clinging to Damien's arm. She appeared to be bursting with happiness, the impression heightened somehow by her massive shape.

Harper's breathing quickened when her gaze shifted to her husband. When she'd seen him at Fort Russell, he'd looked quite thin and beleaguered. Now he appeared much as he had at any social event he and Harper attended together. Noting his lean and dapper mien in his frockcoat, she breathed a prayer of thanks that he'd come back to her unchanged.

When they'd all passed, Harper rose and fell in behind. Once he'd delivered Ivy into Luke's keeping, Damien led Harper to seats near the Carrolls.

He drew her close with one arm and she relaxed, finally able to enjoy the impromptu wedding she'd organized in such a short amount of time. She felt huge relief that now the baby would be born with legal parents.

As though reading her thoughts, Damien tightened his embrace. "This child will always be in your debt because you assured its legitimacy," he whispered.

"She's going to be a favorite of mine."

Damien started to speak, then merely smiled, pressing his lips against her cheek.

Harper looked around for Dom but couldn't find him. All the better, she decided.

Once Granville pronounced Ivy and Luke man and wife, the hall erupted in boisterous good wishes with the hired men crowding close to pound their friend on the back. Laughing, he pulled Ivy close and introduced her as his wife.

Mrs. Goodeve hurried back to her duties while Adare, Roddy and Sandy in his new role as footman broke out the champagne. To Harper's amazement, she saw Dom appear from the rear hall, impeccably groomed and dressed to the nines. After accepting a glass from Adare's tray, he walked through the group milling about the bridal couple. With head held high, exuding the confidence of someone much older, he stopped before Luke, extending his hand in congratulations.

Luke returned his smile. "Thanks so much."

Dom then turned to Ivy. "I'm very happy for you," he said, then leaned in to kiss her cheek.

She appeared rather stunned but recovered quickly. "We're so glad you could share our happiness. Thank you for being here."

With a little bow, he stepped back and soon accepted a glass of bourbon from Roddy.

"Our young Dom isn't quite as bold as he'd like people to believe," Damien said close to Harper's ear.

"Indeed, but I'm pleased he apparently took my lecture to heart."

Damien cocked an eyebrow. "Ah, and when did you feel obliged to lecture our son?"

"When I grew weary of his arrogance and general bad behavior."

He slanted a musing glance at her. "Well, if his show of manners and good grace this evening is any indication, you should perchance lecture him more often."

She slid an arm around his waist. "That may be my new policy."

"If he plans to hoodwink you, he has his work cut out for him."

"I'll be keeping an eye on him," she said with a toss of her head.

Luke escorted his bride to the head of the prepared table where they sat together. Harper and Damien followed and along with Aunt Pris took seats flanking the couple. The Carrolls took up a good part of one side of the table. When all the table space was filled, the overflow was escorted out into the courtyard where everyone settled at prepared tables and benches along the edge of the garden.

Constance, Adare, Roddy and Sandy began serving the food and a mood of merriment and goodwill settled over the celebration. As the meal proceeded, Harper watched Ivy who ate very sparingly which suggested she might be about to go into labor.

After Mrs. Goodeve's wedding cake was consumed with great appreciation, Damien and Harper circulated among the guests, saying good night and gently urging everyone out the door to continue celebrating in the courtyard if they wished. When the hall was nearly deserted aside from the staff clearing up, they approached Luke and Ivy sitting near the wilting altar of roses.

Settling on a bench, Harper studied Ivy. "How are you feeling?"

She managed a wan smile. "I'm purely fagged. . ." She lifted her eyes from her hands spread over her bulging stomach. ". . . and I had a couple of pains before . . ."

Luke stared at her in alarm. "We need send for Dr. Ritter . . ."

"I'll go send a boy to fetch him," Damien said, heading into the rear hall.

Ivy looked to Harper, her face creased with worry.

She gave her a reassuring smile. "It's likely to be a long night, dear. But little is going to happen right away. We need to get you settled in a room upstairs and then it's a matter of waiting for Dr. Ritter."

Holding to their hands, Ivy let Luke and Harper heave her to her feet. Then supporting her between them they proceeded up the staircase.

Upstairs, Gwen came to help settle Ivy in an empty bed chamber. After she lay propped with pillows, Harper heard the boom and reverberation of thunder beyond the windows. Lightning slashed the thickening twilight and wind gusted into the room, sending LuAnn scurrying to pull down the sashes.

Harper excused herself to check on Delaney in her bedroom, finding her staring out of a window, transfixed by the weather. "Oh, Ma-ma, isn't it wonderful?" She turned to watch her mother approach. "I love rain! And thunder and the lightning most of all."

Harper sat on the edge of a chair, taking Delaney's hand as they continued gazing out at the storm. "Here, let me help you with your dress so I can tuck you into bed." She began undoing her buttons. "You and Millie were so pretty tonight."

"I love weddings."

"Me too." She tugged her closer to lift the dress over her head. "Now, where is your nightgown?"

"Right here." She pulled it from beneath a pillow.

Once she was under the covers, Harper gathered her close. "Good night, darling. I'll send Gwen in to braid your hair so it doesn't get tangled."

"Where's Pa-pa? I want to tell him goodnight."

"He went to the stable to send a boy for Dr. Ritter."

She clapped her hands. "Is Ivy's baby going to be born tonight?"

"Perhaps."

"How lovely. Maybe I'll wake up tomorrow and the new baby will be here!"

"I'll send Pa-pa in to say goodnight a bit later."

"Thank you. I'm so happy he's home."

"Me too." With a final kiss on her forehead, she left the room and hurried to the nursery where Rachel rocked Chandler as she paced about in the intermittent flares of light. Seeing Harper, she came to put the baby in her arms.

Harper settled in a rocking chair to feed him while she watched the storm. She mused again that Delaney was truly her daughter. Since her intrepid little girl had begun sensing the sharp tension in the air before furious thunderstorms, she'd been as enraptured as Harper herself, feeling enlivened with excitement singing along every nerve as she begged to be held at a window to watch the riotous storms. Smiling, Harper looked down at Chandler's placid face, wondering if he too might pick up the exhilaration. Just now, she suspected his personality was far too easygoing to share the more unconventional tastes of his sister.

Half an hour later, Damien found her there and knelt next to the rocker. She reached out to touch his hair wet from the rain.

"Great timing." He reached for a diaper from a stack on a nearby table and used it to dry his head, then took Chandler from her.

Standing, he rubbed his tiny back, murmuring to him. "How I missed this." He considered Harper over his shoulder.

"I've missed watching you caring for our children."

He lowered himself on the edge of a stool. "Audra sent you a message when I got back in from the stable. She said she'll stay with Ivy." He bent to kiss the top of her head. "Which means we have time to become reacquainted after my absence."

"Reacquainted? What a delightful thought." She sat looking at him ruefully. "Bless Audra."

"Indeed." He moved his mouth to nuzzle her throat.

A tap on the door preceded Rachel who arrived to put Chandler to bed. Harper and Damien paused beside the crib, watching their son sigh blissfully as he settled into sleep.

Once they stepped into the hallway, Damien grabbed his wife, crushing her to him, his mouth hard as he forced hers open, tasting, probing, demanding. When a bolt of lightning sizzled into the garden, illuminating the entire front portion of the mansion, a tremendous crash of thunder followed.

Damien tugged Harper along the corridor and into their bedchamber. A window stood open and rain poured from the overhang of the balcony roof. He stopped a moment to strike a match and light a lamp.

Caught up in the charged atmosphere of the storm, they approached the open window, looking out at the front yard where the trees bent and gyrated in the driving wind, the flashes lit up the room around them. Damien stood behind, enfolding her. She pressed against him, feeling his arousal that kept pace with her own as his fingers began opening the buttons of her bodice. He tugged the silk off her shoulders and his hands covered her breasts.

The violence outside fueled their passion, their hunger for each other. A raw, familiar response coursed in Harper's blood. Damien's tortured breathing and the roughness of his hands stripping off the rest of her clothing, fueled her impatience and she pulled at his shirt and pants with equal fervor as they fed on the elemental force of nature drawing them along in its wake, into the maelstrom of light and booming sound.

Presently, they stood nude, tracing the planes of each other's bodies with intimate pleasure. Finally, they lay together on the waiting bed. Reckless abandon fused them in heedless surrender to their need to rekindle their carnal bond that had always nourished their love and commitment in the act that was both habit and joy.

At last they neared the necessary completion, and clung to each other like drowning comrades safe at last, straining toward the final ecstasy. Harper was first to move afterward, lifting her head to look at her husband in the glow from the hastily-lit lamp. "I'm so happy you're home."

"No more than I, my darling." He lifted a hand to trace the line of her jaw. "You are food for my soul. I shall never take our life here together for granted again."

"Did you ever?"

His eyes darkened in the lamplight. "I never thought so but I must have. Or I was overconfident about what we would accomplish with the Invasion. In any case, when everything went to Hell, and I found myself under arrest, I had never felt more bereft. It seemed I'd been wrenched from our life here at *Rancha Mariposa* and pitched into an abyss where nothing is certain."

He slowly stroked her arm lying across his chest. "Now that I'm back, even if it's not forever, it reminds me of just how precious our marriage is, how much we love and depend on each other. If I'm convicted along with the others, I'll do whatever I must to escape. I'll go on the lam if it comes to that until I find a place where I can send for you and the children."

"My dearest Damien, I have faith that all of you will be exonerated. The truth will be revealed. Outside of Johnson County, most know your cause was valid. Though it went awry in the end, they understand what you tried to accomplish was for the good of all ranchers."

He nodded glumly. "We were in the right certainly. We must never forget that. When a sheriff sides with known criminals, a situation has turned badly askew. The entire episode will go down in history as a defining part of history. Huge changes in the cattle industry will be implemented now. Such massive numbers of cattle will never again roam the plains at will."

"You knew that wasn't a workable arrangement from the beginning. Not on an ongoing basis."

"But it was the key to amassing a fortune at the start. We were guilty of engaging in the practice for longer than was prudent."

"Yet, you and Jamie and John knew a more stable way of life must replace what had worked early on. So many cattlemen apparently believed they could continue fattening cattle from Texas on the open range for decades into the future."

"Hard to believe anyone familiar with raising cattle would believe that, but it's a fact!"

Wind and hard rain continued battering the roof. A deafening crash of thunder impelled Damien out of bed. He grabbed his shirt, rushing to look out at the fury. "Dr. Ritter will have a hellish time of it getting out here in this."

"Perhaps it's better closer to town," Harper said, going to wrap her arms around him.

He shifted to pull her close with one arm. "We can only hope." Gathering his clothing, he began dressing. "I'll go say a belated goodnight to Delaney."

Harper moved to turn up the lamp and take a robe from a chair. "You'll likely find her with her nose pressed to the glass of a window, staring out at the violence. She told me again earlier how much she loves a thunderstorm."

He chuckled. "She's a bold one. Can you imagine the sort of pursuits she'll be up for in the future?"

"I can actually and I expect I will be her greatest cheerleader."

"I'm sure you and I will share that honor," Damien said with jovial resignation.

Soon enough, they parted in the corridor and headed in opposite directions. Harper entered the bed chamber where Ivy labored in earnest now with Audra and Luke gripping her hands from opposite sides.

Audra looked up as Harper approached. "This baby is a brave little soul to be venturing into the world when God is in such a temper."

Harper smiled, squeezing out a cloth from a basin and wiping Ivy's sweating face. "I'd guess she'll be a plucky one like her mother."

"She?" Audra inquired.

"Yes, it just occurred to me."

"Ivy wants a girl," Luke said, "so that'll be grand."

"Have you talked about names?"

"Ivy's set on Sawyer. After her father."

"Very nice," Harper said.

Dr. Ritter arrived at the *Mariposa* soon after midnight and Sawyer O'Dell was born eight hours later. She was fractious from the instant she drew her first breath, screaming at full volume for nearly an hour before she eventually quieted and assented to nurse.

Peering into the irascible red face the next morning, Delaney decided it was lucky the baby would be living in the apartment separated from the rest of the house by thick adobe walls. Clapping her hands over her ears, she shook her head. "How else would we sleep?"

"I should think she will become much quieter after a time," Harper ventured.

Delaney stroked her fiery red hair. "I hope so. But she is ever so pretty when she's not shrieking."

Harper's optimism proved unfounded. Sawyer suffered with colic that kept her parents up and pacing their bedchamber until the wee hours. Harper and Damien were immediately enraptured with their granddaughter and often went to the newlyweds' apartment to relieve her parents so that they could get a few hours sleep.

It was during one of these mercy missions in May that they came upon the solution to the sleepless nights. They had taken Sawyer down to the sitting room on the ground floor of the apartment that was remote enough to muffle most of the noise. Harper paced the chamber with the baby peering over her shoulder.

Damien perched on the arm of a brocade sofa, his mind moving back to the days when Delaney and Chandler were babies, both models of contentment. When his thoughts turned to Dom and he musingly recalled that no baby could be more cantankerous than he, the germ of an idea niggled at the back of his mind. His eldest son was born in New York some months after Peggy, Harper, Aunt Pris and the others had taken up residence in an apartment while Damien traveled on to their land in Wyoming Territory to begin establishing the *Rancha Mariposa*.

When he'd returned to New York to escort the women west, he learned that Dom had screamed night and day from the moment he was born. When Damien appeared, Peggy threw up her hands and refused to feed or otherwise care for the baby from that point on. Because his wife was so abusive, Damien readily accepted the challenge of tending Dom himself but was initially at a loss as to how he was to feed him. After conferring with Mrs. Goodeve, he'd decided to try giving the baby goat's milk and within hours of Constance buying some, quiet had reigned in the apartment. "Remember what happened when I got back to New York and began giving Dom goat's milk."

"I do," she said eagerly. "It was like magic. He'd been shrieking around the clock but when you fed him goat's milk, he became quiet and content very quickly. Mrs. Goodeve swore he couldn't tolerate Peggy's milk . . ."

"Because Sawyer is Dom's daughter, do you think it's possible breast milk could cause the same adverse response in both babies?"

"I wouldn't know for sure but I think it's worth giving this baby some of Greta's milk."

"As do I. Is there some in the scullery?" He asked because Aunt Pris had also become less tolerant of cow's milk as she grew older and Mrs. Goodeve always kept a small crock in the ice box?

"I'd say so. You take over pacing duty and I'll go see what I can find."

Damien stood to transfer Sawyer to his shoulder and Harper hurried through the door to the hall and ran to the rear hall where the ice box stood at the edge of the kitchen. She quickly inspected the contents, lifting out the container covered by a damp cloth.

Turning to the cook stove, she lifted a lid and poked the banked fire into flames. When she'd put some goat's milk in a small pan on the stove, she went further along the hall to ransack the cupboards in search of a bottle and nipple among those kept on hand.

Soon enough, she carried the prepared bottle back to the apartment and handed it to Damien who shifted the baby on his arm and pressed the nipple to her little bow of a mouth. She screwed up her face a moment but when a drop of milk escaped onto her lip, she gave a small gasp and took the rubber teat.

Damien grinned at Harper who went closer, leaning her head on his shoulder. They watched with wonder as Sawyer slowly drained the bottle, then drifted into sleep, a tiny smile leaving her mouth agape.

"Greta's triplets are going to have to share from now on," Harper said.

When they'd taken Sawyer back upstairs, Luke raised his head as they entered the bedroom. "You've managed to get her to sleep," he said in wonder, swinging his feet to the floor. Ivy snored softly, not rousing from her deadened sleep.

While Harper took Sawyer to the dressing room to change her diaper, Damien told Luke about the goat's milk and instructed him to not let Ivy nurse the baby from then on.

"Thank, God," Luke said. "Thank you for helping us."

"I'm just so happy we figured out what she needed," Damien said as Harper placed Sawyer in the waiting cradle where she continued sleeping peacefully.

The Invaders were formally charged with first degree murder and Granville and the other attorneys obtained a ruling that they should be tried in Cheyenne where sympathy was strongest. At a hearing back in friendlier territory, they pleaded not guilty before the District Judge and trial was set for August 22, then because of other pressing court cases, was immediately postponed until January 2, 1893.

By the end of the spring roundup in June, summer at *Rancha Mariposa* arrived amid intermittent rains, none as violent as what occurred the night Damien and John returned home, yet the continuous moisture and warm temperatures created ideal growing conditions for the pasture land. Grass was as abundant as the first cuttings of alfalfa.

Now that their wedding was scheduled for September, Arthur Wheeler and Laura Quinn would soon become permanent residents of *Rancha Mariposa.* After his previous summer of tedious work in a Cheyenne grocery store, then months confined to the classroom, he was eager to escape outdoors to join the men in the irrigation ditches and later, the hay fields.

Laura came to live at the *Mariposa* until the wedding and to her delight, was quickly pressed into service as back-up nursery maid. While she cared for Chandler and Sawyer, both of whom adored her, she looked forward to the time when she would have her own babies.

For her part, once Ivy could no longer breastfeed her daughter, she regained her strength with remarkable speed and returned to her duties as nursery maid where she spent long intervals every day and night feeding Greta's rich milk to Sawyer. Her change of diet had turned the wee fiery-haired harridan into the epitome of sunny goodwill.

Harper, Delaney and Millie found themselves in the nursery one afternoon in early June after the girls had returned from riding. Delaney rushed to inspect Ivy. "She's getting fat," she declared, taking in her pudgy cheeks.

Ivy placed her in Delaney's arms. "And she's so happy." She raised her gaze to smile at Harper. "Thank Heavens."

Delaney began humming and danced her toward the window. "When you're a bit older, you can come riding with Millie and me. I'll be getting a new horse before very long and then, you can ride Merry." She headed back toward the others and sat on a stool.

"I think Molly may be more Sawyer's size," Harper said.

"Maybe but Chandler will need Molly," she said with her usual pragmatism, then added wistfully. "I like nothing more than riding."

"Ah, yes," Ivy agreed. "But don't you think you'll have to give up riding horses one day when you have a husband and children?"

"Never! I'll ride until I'm a hundred years old. For my next horse, I want a tall Thoroughbred I can train to jump so I can ride in horse shows."

"I'll leave all that to you," Ivy said. "Horses frighten me no end." She rose and came to lift Sawyer and proceeded to change her before putting her down for a nap.

Delaney grabbed Harper's hand as they turned into the corridor. "I must talk to Pa-pa about my new horse."

"I'm sure he'll want to hear all about your plans."

"Maybe we should find a hunter in England. Do you think the Thoroughbreds are better jumpers there?"

"That may be true but I'm sure Pa-pa can advise you on the subject."

"Yes, he can. I'll talk to him tonight. Oh, look, here comes Dom."

They waited above the staircase until his dark head appeared and he climbed the remaining way upstairs. "Oh, hello there." He tousled Delaney's hair before turning to kiss Harper.

"How nice to have you home, Dom. I expect you're very tired after building hay stacks all day."

"Half dead is more like it. Roddy's running a bath for me."

"Then you can have a nap, if you like."

"I may do that."

"Do you want to see Sawyer?" Delaney inquired.

"Who's Sawyer?"

"Ivy and Luke's baby. I forgot you left for the roundup just before she was born."

He glanced peevishly from her to Harper. "So it's a girl, then?"

"Yes and very pretty."

He grunted and continued without comment along the hall toward his bedchamber.

Delaney shrugged, gazing after him. Harper wondered if his grudging goodwill following her dressing-down over his bad behavior was fading already.

Damien, John and Jamie rode along Lodgepole Creek later in June, inspecting the crossbreds as well as the fences. They'd reached some ramshackle buildings in the vicinity of Jonathon Holt's ranch headquarters that had been occupied by some of Jose Martinez's cowboys since the Mexican was killed in the Invasion. A dark-complexioned rider approached on a black horse. Something about the swarthy man sent a chill along Damien's spine as at first glance, he thought it was Jonathon Holt—but that was impossible.

Upon coming even with them, the rider pulled up and touched the brim of his black hat in a curt salute. "Afternoon, gentlemen."

Also stopping their horses, the trio observed him for a moment before Damien extended his hand in greeting. "Hello, my name is Damien Whittaker of *Rancha Mariposa*."

"I know who you are, sir. Your reputation precedes you. Indeed, I believe you were instrumental in the murder of my friend Jose Martinez." He studied each of them in turn.

"I beg your pardon, sir. Jose lost his life because he had been regularly stealing cattle from our ranch and others for years."

"Well, I wouldn't know about that," the horseman said. "In any case, that entire matter is in the past and I am only interested in the present. I am Randall Holt. Jonathon Holt was my grandfather and I have recently learned that after the death of Jose, I inherited his homestead. So we are going to be neighbors, Mr. Whittaker." Belatedly, he shook Damien's hand. "It is my understanding that relations between you and my grandfather as well as Jose have been rather tense over the years. As for myself, I hope we can forge a relationship based on mutual respect and goodwill."

"That would be our hope as well," Damien replied. Jamie and John both nodded in agreement. "It's our pleasure, meeting you. Now we'll get back to our work."

"Very well." Randall Holt wheeled his horse and galloped toward the cluster of shabby structures visible in a distant valley.

When he'd disappeared, Damien appraised the others. "Well, that was an unpleasant surprise." He lifted his hand to press his fingers to the bridge of his nose, staring at the ground. "I hoped we'd never have another Holt living near *Rancha Mariposa* in my lifetime." With a sigh, he looked up at the others and they continued.

"I'd never have foreseen this," Jamie said glumly, urging his horse forward. "But we must try to keep an open mind if we can."

"I agree," John interjected, "we must stay clear of any preconceived opinions where Mr. Randall Holt is concerned. Perhaps he is the antithesis of his grandfather and will be a welcome addition to Wyoming's cattle ranching industry."

"You're absolutely correct in that assessment," Damien agreed. "But I can't tell you how my heart dropped when I thought I saw Jonathon Holt approaching us back there."

"I daresay," John said with sincere perception because he'd lived through the same horrendous events at the hand of the man who'd brought such grief to their families.

A sense of time suspended filled the remainder of summer at *Rancha Mariposa.* It appeared more and more likely that the Invaders would be vindicated and freed in due time, yet with the murder trial still scheduled for Jan. 2, the matter lingered uneasily in everyone's mind. Granville often traveled to Cheyenne to work with Governor Barber and others preparing the defense of the Invaders. One matter they put into action was the disappearance of the two trappers, the sole material witnesses to the murders.

The two were mysteriously broken out of jail and taken to Nebraska where they were arrested and for the sum of one hundred, twenty dollars, a local judge granted a writ of *habias corpus.* They were then transferred to Omaha on a charge of selling liquor in Indiana. Much later, no accounting of the money was found, nor any record of the writ. The two potential witnesses were paid three thousand dollars each and put on a train for St. Louis where they disappeared forever.

Granville returned to the country after this particular chain of events had been completed. He assured everyone that the virtual evaporation of the only witnesses to the KC Ranch killings meant the Invaders were one giant step closer to freedom.

This news lifted much of the dread and at the end of September, the small, elegant wedding in the splendor of Stephen's autumn garden served as a happy diversion. Though Arthur and his student no longer enjoyed the close friendship that'd bound them in the early years of their relationship, Dom did agree to serve as best man. At sixteen, he was as tall as his father and extraordinarily handsome in his black frock coat. His outward maturity reminded everyone attending the wedding that in another year, he'd be ready to begin college so would be leaving *Rancha Mariposa* for an extended period.

Ivy and Laura had become such dear friends during the months they'd worked closely together in the nursery that Laura was adamant that Ivy be her attendant despite any awkwardness this might cause. The ceremony went off happily enough with Dom once more behaving with impeccable charm and good manners. After a lavish dinner in the Great Hall of *Mariposa,* the newlyweds departed for a honeymoon in Colorado before Arthur joined the fall roundup prior to he and Dom returning to the school room.

# CHAPTER FOUR

## November 1892

Some weeks later, Damien, John, Jamie and Arthur sat astride their horses near Carlin's chuck wagon at the dismantled campsite the final day of the fall roundup. A crew of cowboys circled the herd of steers bound for the shipping yards at Pine Bluff, waiting for Dom who would deliver the cattle.

Dom galloped up on Foxfire ready to deliver the steers for shipping. "Do you think Randall Holt stole the missing cattle?" He asked his father. "Don't you find it strange that he moves in and almost immediately, we're missing two hundred head of cattle?"

"Yes, I do," his father replied. "But right at the moment, there's nothing I can do about it."

Dom nodded without saying more. "I'll go now. Should I deposit the check in the bank?"

"Are you going to Cheyenne then?"

"I thought I would for a couple days before I start classes again."

"Very well, then, deposit the check."

With a jaunty wave, Dom rode toward the milling cattle. After the herd began the plodding trek to the railhead, he could think about the situation.

He had no doubt that this relative of Jonathon Holt was responsible for the most recent loss of *Rancha Mariposa* cattle. Who else could it be? Local thieves would be unlikely to steal cattle from anyone so soon after the Invasion.

During the hours before he and the cowboys made camp for the night, he continued to turn the matter over in his mind. He delivered the steers to the shipping yards the next day, dismissed the crew of riders, and was on his way to town soon after noon.

Tired after weeks in the saddle, he looked forward to his short stay at The Plains and kept Foxfire at a steady canter. He reached the hotel shortly after twilight and left his horse at the livery barn before booking a room for three days. After a bath, dinner and a quantity of bourbon, he considered going to Madam Charleen's Green Door, the brothel that had become his preference along The Row after he'd sampled the services at several others during the previous two years. Tonight, he was too fagged to seek immediate company but weeks of celibacy left him eager to see his favorite girl at The Green Door tomorrow. Eventually, he fell into bed, intent on being sufficiently rested when he sought her out in due time.

He sank into deep sleep and didn't come to until after three the next afternoon. His first order of the day was go to the brothel to book dinner in a private boudoir.

He arrived at seven, expecting to enjoy the usual routine with Clara Lou, hoping that she would be especially obliging after not seeing him all summer. She floated about his table clad only in a skimpy little wrap of a dress, her heady perfume tickling his senses.

After he had consumed an enormous T-bone steak, he lingered over a bottle of wine with Clara Lou draped across his lap, handy for kissing whenever the urge came. After a long time, he allowed her to lead him to the bed where she removed his clothes and her dress, then pushed him back against his pillows. He gave himself up to the delights of her experienced fingers and tongue; lamplight cast a friendly glow over them. Other than the occasional creak of the bedsprings, it was very quiet.

Dom gradually became aware of voices, faint but clear enough to decipher; he realized they came from the room next door, the boudoir of Madam Charleen herself. He had on occasion heard some remarkably arousing lewd talk from the chamber adjoining the one where he was being ministered to by Clara Lou; he hoped he'd be so lucky tonight.

Yet, straining to hear the separate words, he discovered it was not a passion-filled exchange. When he heard his father's name, he pushed Clara Lou away, rolled closer to the wall, pressing his ear to it.

". . . so it's safe now. Damien Whittaker's so scar't of hanging, he's not paying attention to much else. He's so damned wrapped up in his fancy wife and brats, I doubt he's keeping a close count of his crossbreds . . ."

". . . finished roundup . . ."

Dom struggled to hear a woman's voice and with Clara Lou's help, eventually identified Madam Charleen. "Years back, she was a very intimate friend of both Jonathon Holt and Jose Martinez . . . ." Clara Lou explained.

He stared at her a second before collapsing in a paroxysm of hilarity he had to muffle in a pillow. Raising his head at last, he gulped for breath. "Intimate friend. Oh, you are precious," he said before burying his face in the pillow again, his shoulders shaking. Presently, he looked at her again. "Who's that with her now?"

"New customer . . . some relation to Jonathon Holt. He's been coming here since the winter and only sees Madam." She ducked her tousled head, her eyes round, puzzled.

Dom laughed out loud, resuming his eavesdropping. He thought he heard the rustling of papers beyond the wall. Clara Lou began nuzzling his neck but he shoved her away, giving all his attention to what was being said in the next room. ". . . made an accounting of the work my men will do this winter as well as the proposed take for the next five years . . . ." A deep, nasty laugh interrupted the recitation. "Damien Whittaker may well wonder why engaging in vigilante justice had such little effect on the rustling of his cattle. In fact, he will find a year from now that the problem is worse than ever . . . ."

"Why do you hate Damien Whittaker? He's done nothing to you."

"Ah, my dear Charleen, you mustn't be naïve. My grandfather came to Wyoming Territory at the same time as the esteemed Whittakers. They all wanted to take advantage of the unparalleled opportunity for wealth and prestige. But what seemed unfair to my grandfather was just how wealthy his British neighbors were when they arrived, bringin' along their great, fat Herefords. They didn't wait even a proper amount of time before building their grand castles at their ranch as well as in Cheyenne. That hogish lifestyle galled him no end because he longed to live the same way but couldn't afford to. He did what the Whittakers and other ranchers did, hired cowboys to bring longhorns north but when he marketed his calves and steers, he always came up short of what he expected. There was never enough money to build a house, let alone the likes of that *Mariposa*.

"It didn't take long before Gramps Jon decided he'd just help himself to some of the excess the Whittakers had. What he done don't set well with some but it made sense to me. Before I was even involved with the ranchin', I applauded him. I'll like kickin' up my heels at the *Mariposa* just as much as Gramps would've if he hadn't got hisself kilt or whatever happened to him. He was a mean ole' bastard so it's easy to imagin' the things he must've done to end up gone from the face a' the earth.

"Same with Jose. He shouda been hung a long time back. I'll tell you sure, it galled me good when Gramps willed him his land and cattle so I was one happy bloke when I heard the Invaders knocked 'im off and the ranch was mine. He was a real reprobate but I loved Gramps so I plan to carry on the way that would please him most."

"You're a reprobate yourself," Charleen said.

"Just the way you like me. So I'm going to my ranch tomorrow, then I'm leavin' for New York on the evenin' train. So my men will come to you for their orders. I want you to put these papers in your safe. Later on, I'll be doing what I can to scare the Whittakers 'til they don't know which way to turn. I relish paying a visit on Mrs. Whittaker myself. I do believe she'll enjoy that."

A deep chill seeped along Dom's veins as the threat cut through his confusion. It was some time before he realized the talk had ceased beyond the partition. There came a short frenzy of heaving bedsprings as his brain struggled in a demented chase through the information that had been fed into it.

He slumped against the pillows, his gaze settling on Clara Lou. As her eyes slowly ignited with renewed interest, he realized she hadn't known why he was listening at the wall but thought he'd merely been feeding a lascivious streak she already knew existed in his nature. Rising, she came back and greedily renewed her exploration of his body.

His mind remained occupied with the pair next door; he was grateful when he lay spent with Clara Lou sprawled on top of him. She soon began snoring and he had the opportunity to think more clearly.

He'd longed for years to help his father with the rustling scourge but had always been gently rebuffed and told that he must concentrate on his lessons. Now was his chance to rid the area of the thievery once and for all. He'd been handed the ammunition needed to have his revenge against the longstanding ill-treatment that Holt and Jose Martinez had leveled directly at *Rancha Mariposa.*

He loathed the ill-treatment of Harper who'd always treated him as her own son. It was true enough that he often resented her when she required him to behave as well as she thought him capable. Still, he'd always known that she loved him and wanted only the best for him and it grieved him to know how shabbily she'd been treated. Jose had tormented her and killed Cooper, her favorite beagle. If he hadn't already been dispatched during the Invasion, Dom now felt empowered to the point when he would have gladly dealt with him.

He'd never been told or been able to determine what had happened that nearly caused Harper to miscarry Delaney, but he'd always sensed that Jonathon Holt was somehow involved. He hadn't appeared at the spring roundup the next day and indeed had never surfaced again, suggesting that he'd been killed as his grandson Randall had speculated to Madam Charleen. Dom doubted he'd ever know who was responsible and that didn't concern him. All that mattered was their nemesis was gone forever. But now, he *could* do something about Randall who in his loose talk with Madam Charleen had made it very clear that he planned to begin his own crusade of terror and larceny against Dom's family.

He had been handed the means to defeat him but he must get his hands on the papers Randall had mentioned to Madam Charleen. He briefly wondered if he might bribe Clara Lou to fetch the documents but discarded the notion. The fewer people involved, the better.

What he needed, he presently decided, was a diversion to draw attention from the madam's boudoir long enough for him to locate the evidence. He glanced at a clock beside the bed, pleased to see it was well past two. He was glad he'd come to the house late, planning to spend the night. From previous experience, he knew that every man still in the rooms wouldn't emerge until morning.

He grasped Clara Lou's shoulders, rolling her off him. Though more asleep than awake, she embraced him, murmuring her protest at his leaving. He whispered reassurance, tucking a blanket around her, then eased off the bed, snuffed the lamp and groped for his clothes. Eventually, he silently let himself into the hall, dimly lit by wall sconces turned low. All was still as he continued to the gaming parlor where a lamp burned on a low table among a cluster of gaudy velvet-upholstered furniture.

The room was empty. Dom hated to destroy the madam's property but it couldn't be helped. He reminded himself of the water closet's location before he knocked the lamp off the table onto the frayed Persian rug. The flames quickly spread into the circle of spilled kerosene as he fled.

He paused at the door to be certain the fire was large enough not to be smothered with a smaller rug, then dashed to the first closed door, pounding on it while screaming the alarm. He ran into the nearby water closet and turned the lock. He heard the corridor outside erupt with running people shouting their shock and fear.

After a minute or two, Dom stepped out into the turmoil of half-naked women and customers rushing toward the clogged staircase. He ran along the hall, finding the far rooms empty as he'd anticipated.

Crashing into Madam Charleen's boudoir, garish with gilt and blood red brocade, he was pleased to see what he assumed to be most of Randall Holt's clothing tossed carelessly on a chair. Scanning the room in the low illumination from a lamp still burning on a table, Dom eventually spotted the papers on a corner desk, evidently abandoned there before the two retired to bed.

He hastily gathered the documents covered with neat columns of numbers, and stuffed everything in his coat pocket, then blew out the lamp and hurried to a window. Yanking up the sash, he scrambled out over the ledge and dropped to the roof of the verandah circling the house.

Once he'd lowered himself over the edge, he dropped to the frosty ground and ran into the darkness, only stopping to look back when he was a block away. Most of the babbling, hysterical group that had spilled outside, creating a delightful spectacle for a front page story in tomorrow's newspapers. Yet, no fire company had been summoned; flames no longer licked out of the windows so Dom was confident as he continued to The Plains that Madam Charleen's gaming parlor wasn't beyond repair.

Upon reaching his room, he sank into a chair and collected his wits a moment before pulling the crumpled sheets from his coat. Staring at the neat accounting of information he'd risked his neck to steal, he trembled with shock.

Here was the explanation for years when Holt and Martinez had plundered Whittaker stock. Seven of Jonathon Holt's brands that were registered in 1876 were cleverly incorporating *Rancha Mariposa* designs. Dom assumed early officials of the Stock Growers Association had collected huge bribes in order to lay the groundwork for the wholesale rustling that had plagued the Whittakers and other nearby ranchers for at least a dozen years.

It had been a simple matter for thieves to add the lines needed to create what appeared to be Holt's duly recorded brands. Dom also found a list of four additional designs registered to Charleen Anderson and Jose Martinez that had been applied to mavericks.

Dom sorted through the data until he located the proposed plan for the immediate future. Incredibly, he saw that Randall Holt was plotting to steal ten thousand Whittaker crossbreds over the next fifteen years, killing cows whenever necessary to create mavericks. His hired men were to hack off chunks of hide large enough to remove the brands, then let the carcasses lie while calves were driven or hauled onto his range.

Randall assumed that lack of proof would save him from prosecution as it had his grandfather and Martinez. This was another reason he would spend much of his time in New York to deflect attention away from him personally. Everything was detailed and precise down to the lists of cowboys and the number of cattle they were to steal. Other names were specified as guards and lookouts.

Buried among the pages was a sheet unlike the rest, filled with more lists and figures. These appeared to be aimless scrawlings, notes no doubt jotted while Holt talked with Madam Charleen earlier. He'd likely planned to destroy it before the other papers were placed in the safe. Despite its untidiness, it was the most incriminating evidence that anyone had obtained against the Holts.

> *If rustling doesn't run the Whittakers out, they will be harassed in other ways. Other women there besides Harper W. Buildings will be burned one by one over time. Fires scare people like nothing else. Young children . . . kidnappings . . .*

Waving the sheet erratically, Dom leapt to his feet in trembling rage, pacing around the room. His head felt as though it might explode from the furious pressure within. How dare this diabolical man threaten to live one day in the *Mariposa*! Was it Jonathon Holt who'd devised the master plan to defeat the Whittakers? And had Jose Martinez and Randall Holt simply fallen into their prearranged roles when it was their turn?

The insanity of it was too much for him to fully grasp. Gradually his shaking temper eased and he poured a large brandy, and then returned to the chair where he remained the rest of the night, only falling into sporadic sleep sometime after dawn.

He came awake in mid-morning, stiff and groggy. After taking the wad of papers from his pocket, he went through them one by one, considering the appalling information once more.

Glancing toward the nearest window, he noted the gathering clouds in the distance. It looked like stormy weather was imminent. This reality impelled him to his feet. At some point during the past hours of mental turmoil, he'd made a decision.

He was not going to wait and see what Randall Holt did next. His father had spent much of the past sixteen years subjected to Jonathon Holt's abuse and later that of Jose Martinez without knowing what he was dealing with. Well, by some strike of extraordinary luck, Dom had become privy to evidence that he could use to fight the continuing threat. And he was going to act with all haste. He picked up the revolver and gun belt he'd discarded on a table and buckled them on.

After he donned his coat and stashed the papers back into an inside pocket, he wrapped a wool scarf around his neck and mashed his Stetson on his head. He went downstairs to settle his bill and reserve his room for two more nights before walking to the stable behind the hotel to collect Foxfire. Presently mounted, he checked his Winchester in its sheath. For years now, he'd been armed whenever he rode on the range.

As he headed out of Cheyenne, he dared wonder if Randall Holt would keep to what he'd said to Madam Charleen, that he was going to his ranch, then would catch the afternoon train to New York later today. Though it was spitting snow and the sky was low and threatening, there was little reason to think he'd changed his plans.

Some miles beyond the Lodgepole ford, Dom turned toward Holt's ranch, and eventually rode into the thick of the cottonwoods and aspen. He pulled up above the converging road that headed straight to the huddle of unkempt ranch buildings below the crest of a hill ahead. While he waited there, the temperature dropped and his coat and breeches as well as the gelding's hide became coated with the wet snow. At last, he spotted Randall Holt's buggy approaching from the ranch headquarters.

Dom pulled the rifle from its sheath and raised it to sight on the man who approached at a brisk trot. When he had come close enough to be recognized, Dom squeezed the trigger.

The bullet hit Holt in the chest. For a moment, there was no reaction, then the length of him jerked backward against the seat then pitched forward, the horse shying violently at the flopping thing just behind her. Shoving the rifle back in the sheath, Dom spurred Foxfire forward and caught the buggy horse by the bridle and led it further into the trees.

Time slowed to an eerie crawl. Dom dismounted and tied the horse to a branch, then approached the buggy. Holt was dying, his breath rattling in his chest. His blood soaked his coat and dripped down onto the floor of the buggy. When the corpse had ceased twitching, Dom was faced with the dilemma of what to do with it.

He acted quickly on the need to conceal it as well as the buggy. Considering the light in the west glowing through the clouds, he estimated he had at least two hours of daylight.

The weather was on his side as the wet snow had already partially covered the body and wiped out all the tracks. Dom approached the driving horse, pulled one rein free, then led the mare close to Foxfire, mounted and struck a haphazard course into the looming trees. The horses broke into a canter as they headed toward high country and Horse Creek. Holt soon slid off the buggy seat, crumpling on the floor.

As he rode, Dom decided that during his restless night, his mind must have been working out the details of his plan for vigilantism because now he knew the precise spot where he would dump Randall Holt. As he traveled into more rugged terrain, he had to stop once to open a gate in a barbed wire fence. It was difficult to keep a perspective on his location in the thick snow and he was grateful to finally near Horse Creek, its trees a black bank in the distance.

Once he'd found a shallow spot in the creek, he crossed with little difficulty. The land climbed sharply now and he ultimately had to abandon the buggy. The mare offered little protest when he dragged the body out and heaved it over her withers, tying it in place with rope from his saddle, looping it through the harness.

Twilight was nearing but Dom could still make out the hills and ridges in the silent snow. He eventually found the spot he sought by the landmark of the jagged bluff to one side. A deep gash of canyon slashed through thick pines for half a mile, the walls so sheer that he knew the body when pushed over the edge, would end up at near the bottom, at least half that distance down in the midst of boulders. With the present snow and the winter storms to come, it would never be found.

Dom stopped beside the precipice. He untied the corpse and dragged it to the rim, taking great care of his footing since the slushy snow was so treacherous, lest he could slip and fall over while the cadaver remained on top. Drawing a deep breath, he eased it past the edge and listened to the muffled descent.

When stillness returned, he turned to the horses and stripped the harness from the mare. After thinking a moment, he hurled the tangle of straps and metal into the canyon as he was overcome again with uncontrollable trembling. He stood shaking in the queer quiet a bit longer before he mounted, gripped the mare's reins and started for Cheyenne.

Only when he came onto the buggy was he pulled up sharply by the reality that he couldn't leave it there to stir up suspicion. He sat on Foxfire, trying to decide how he should proceed as the wet snow piled up. At last, he spotted a possible solution, a crevice opening up in the rimrock of the canyon wall a few yards to his right.

He urged the horses closer, eventually seeing that a craggy split in the rock angled down sharply until he couldn't see where it ended. It would do. Once he'd returned to the buggy, he dismounted and wrapped the reins around an aspen trunk, then placed himself between the shafts, gripping tightly, headed toward the cleft. Upon reaching the opening, he dropped the shafts and circled to the rear of the buggy, set his shoulder against the vehicle and shoved it down the incline.

He waited as the conveyance tumbled out of sight, the sound of splintering wood reassuring him before the stillness settled once more. He hurried to mount Foxfire, fetched the mare and continued toward lower country. When he'd crossed Horse creek, he stopped to draw out his jackknife and pry loose the mare's shoes that he hurled into the water, then slipped off her bridle, trusting her to find her way home or wander onto another home on the way. Once he reached the Lodgepole, high from recent rains, he threw the bridle into the water, watching the current take it out of sight.

As he rode toward Cheyenne, he pondered the chances of his afternoon's work going undetected. A lowkey optimism began to take shape at the back of his mind. He dared think perhaps he'd pulled it off. Exhilaration moved through him. Since he was twelve, he'd wanted nothing so much as to help his father fight the rustling that held *Rancha Mariposa* in a vice of worry and loss. He'd worked hard, patrolling the range and working on the roundups. He'd done his best but had never managed to do anything that really helped. Until now.

He rode in a daze, so exhausted, he could barely stay in the saddle. Nonetheless, upon reaching the outskirts of Cheyenne, he was so confident of his safety, he reached The Plains before he was hit again by the truth of what he'd done. In the glow from the streetlamps, he saw that he was covered with blood. His sheepskin coat was ruined.

Upon turning the gelding over to a stable boy behind The Plains, he stripped off the coat, rolling it so most of the blood was inside, then climbed the outside stairs to enter the upper hall where his room was located. Because he'd reserved his room for three nights, he was spared appearing at the front desk.

Once he'd reached the sanctuary of his room, he was relieved to see a blaze in the fireplace. He quickly added kindling to get it burning hotly, then placed the sheepskin coat in the flames that licked up around the wet leather as he added more dry wood. Though he was staggering with fatigue, he didn't go near the bed until he'd seen the coat and the rest of his clothes reduced to ashes.

Then he put on the change of clothing still in the bag he'd left in the room, crawled into bed and slept for fifteen hours. When he awoke the following evening, he was starving. After a bath, he dressed and ascended the staircase to the dining room where he ate steak and drank several bourbons before returning to bed and more sleep.

The next morning, he set his mind to his final task before he left town. He found hotel stationery, an inkwell and fountain pen, and settled at a table to compose a letter to Madam Charleen.

*Nov. 17, 1892*

*My dear Charleen. I have completed final tasks and now await the departure of my train for New York. After talking to my men and discerning the dicey atmosphere among the ranching community just now, I have decided to postpone the work we discussed last evening until greater stability returns. If the Invaders are acquitted, I should think that will calm the varied factions. So with that in mind, upon my return to Wyoming in 1893, I plan to proceed with strategies as we discussed. If it should appear fortuitous to continue at an earlier date, I will inform you. In the meantime, enjoy the coming months and know that I hold you in highest regard. I look forward to renewing our delightful association as soon as possible.*

*Faithfully yours, Randall Holt*

After sealing and addressing the envelope, Dom explained to the desk clerk that he'd forgotten his coat on the train a couple days earlier, and asked to borrow one to wear on a shopping trip downtown. The young man quickly accommodated him. Before he departed, he bought a stamp and rode to his favorite men's clothing emporium. He mailed the letter in a box outside the door.

His luck held as he found a sheepskin coat that was a close twin to the one he'd burned. Yet, it looked little like the one he'd worn on the range for at least two years. No help for that.

He selected a new scarf and gloves, put everything on the *Rancha Mariposa* account, then asked the clerk to return the borrowed coat to The Plains. Outside, he donned his battered hat, got on Foxfire and headed home.

His father's trial hadn't entered his mind since he'd last seen him at the roundup site. Now as he neared the ranch, he could think of nothing else. For perhaps the first time since his father and John were arrested, he was keenly aware of what might take place at the end of their trial.

He was suddenly gripped by a bleak sense of dread. He could not even imagine his life without his father and John. What was to become of *Rancha Mariposa* if they were executed? His thoughts dissolved into a morass of renewed shock as tears flooded his eyes. He let them come, pouring down the cold skin of his cheeks until snot ran in strings from his nose.

Shuddering, he scrubbed angrily at his face and finally fumbled a handkerchief from his pocket. He wiped halfheartedly at the mess but then gave up as great ragged sobs shook him anew. He abandoned any attempt at control and cried as he hadn't done since he was a small boy.

While Foxfire plodded stolidly towards home he continued weeping until he was empty of tears and all emotion save fear. He was abruptly terrified, feeling threatened in much the way the Invaders must. What if despite all his care, someone had seen him kill Randall Holt. What if the sheriff was waiting for him at the ranch?

Was he losing his mind? He straightened in the saddle and blew his nose, aware that he must pull himself together before he reached the *Mariposa.* Breathing deeply, he located another handkerchief and thoroughly wiped his face, then looked about him.

His brain had been in such turmoil ever since he'd mailed the letter to Madam Charleen, he'd taken no notice of the weather that he now saw that it remained gray and snow still fell in indolent flakes that floated aimlessly to earth. It must have snowed heavier at some point during the night because several inches covered the road. The sight calmed him as he realized again how well the horses' tracks up to the canyon beyond Horse Creek would be hidden.

He further regained his confidence as he neared the ranch headquarters. Once again, he was certain he'd done the right thing to thwart the threat of continued rustling. And he'd done it because he loved his family. And despite his irrational weeping jag, he'd been brave enough to risk his life just as his father had.

This reality bolstered his flagging spirits and he felt ready to face his family with the aplomb that would arouse no suspicion. He pushed Foxfire into a canter and by-passed the house to deliver him to the stables. Once he'd called for extra rations for his loyal steed, he headed toward the rear entrance of the *Mariposa*.

Mrs. Goodeve came from the kitchen when he stood in the back hall. "Ah, Mr. Dom, so good you're home." She came to embrace him, her gaze taking stock. "You're too, too skinny. Come, I 'ave soup on the stove."

"Thanks. I am starving but I'll wait for lunch."

"Go on with you, then. Miss. Harper's in the hall."

He hung up his wraps before heading to the fireplace where he found Harper and Delaney on the sofa with Chandler.

"Hello, darling." Harper rose and came to meet him, wrapping him in her arms. "It's so good to see you."

She smelled wonderful and he buried his face in her shoulder, suddenly battling new tears.

"I'm so happy to be home."

She leaned back to inspect him. "You look so weary."

"I didn't sleep well," he said vaguely, reaching down to tousle Delaney's hair. "How you doing?"

She laughed, hopping up and down. "Come see Chandler." Tugging his hand, she pulling him to the couch where his brother sat gurgling happily. "Pick him up. He's happy you're home too." She stood waiting until he reached down and gathered the baby, lifting him awkwardly, then jostling him on his hip.

"Come sit. We're waiting for lunch." Harper said.

Dom clutched the baby uneasily against him, both obviously uncomfortable with their proximity.

Watching them, Delaney finally lost patience. "Here, he likes to be up more," she explained, boosting him higher onto Dom's shoulder.

He scowled but drew the warm, little bundle closer, breathing in the clean, soapy smell of him. When she'd been born, he'd loved holding Delaney, so tiny and cute. What was the difference that made him so ill at ease with Chandler? No mystery really.

His jolly little brother was even more enchanting than Delaney had been at that age. Yet, Chandler was a threat to Dom's future

Abruptly, he wondered where his daughter was. He briefly wished he was holding her instead of Chandler. What was her name? Sawyer?

It seemed like his life was a strange and fragile dynamic where he was somehow disallowed. How was it that he felt as if he was looking in on his life from the outside? All the people at the *Mariposa* had someone to love except him. He felt a sudden jab of jealousy when he thought of Luke. If Dom hadn't been so hasty in discarding any loyalty toward Ivy, he might be married now and Sawyer would still be his daughter.

As he continued there, watching Delaney playing with the beagle Riley before the fire, he tried coaxing all the thoughts rattling in his brain back to reality, aware that even if he'd been willing, his father would never have allowed him to marry Ivy. Much as he hated the idea, he was still required to obtain a degree at Yale or Harvard before he'd be permitted to live his life as he saw fit.

Delaney left the rug and came to sit next to him. Her sharp, knowing gaze took his measure. "You look sad? Are you?"

"Why would I be sad when I'm home again?"

She shrugged. "I don't know but if you were happy, I think your eyes would shine more."

He continued scowling at her. "I'm happy enough."

"All righty, then," she said dismissively. "I'm going to take Chandler upstairs to see what Ma-ma is painting." She stood, lifted the baby and headed to the staircase. Before starting up, she turned back, taking the baby's arm to wave at Dom. When he chortled in delight, Dom couldn't help grinning.

When the afternoon continued with no one noting anything unusual in Dom's behavior, he relaxed, settling into the routine of being home. After lunch, he felt at ease enough to call on Arthur and Laura in their apartment. He and Arthur decided to take up Dom's lessons the following day. For the first time in his memory, he looked forward to losing himself in the customary schedule of academics in the comfortable warmth of the library.

As days followed one after the other, accumulating into weeks and still there was no sign of suspicion, he acknowledged relief and gave himself over to a new sense of purpose and responsibility.

# CHAPTER FIVE

### December 1892 – April 1893

As the trial of the Invaders drew near, nervous tension invaded the *Mariposa.* Eliza bore a son named Finnegan James in early December so Audra stepped into her classroom until such time as she was able to resume her teaching duties. If the students had thought they might have something of a vacation out from under Eliza's exacting standards, they were disappointed.

Audra seemed intent on counteracting the sense of troubled waiting that permeated the ranch headquarters by keeping her charges so busy with projects and lessons, they had no time to wonder and fret about the future. Her daughters and Delaney were so weary at night that they all fell into deep sleep.

Harper concentrated on her art, intent on having new work ready whenever Granville returned to England. Considering the gloomy atmosphere gripping *Rancha Mariposa,* no one could conjure up enthusiasm for the usual festivities of Christmas so the sole celebration was a subdued dinner in the evening. After the meal, the Whittakers and Carrolls retired to the drawing room where Adare served brandy. Ivy and Gwen soon departed to the nursery with Chandler, Yvette and Sawyer.

The remainder of the younger children congregated around Granville who read stories about Father Christmas and related tales of how he'd celebrated the holiday as a boy. Delaney and Millie came to sit on a loveseat between Harper and Damien. "We need to have fun tomorrow so we won't worry so much," Delaney declared.

Harper considered her troubled face. "What do you think we should do?"

She glanced at Jamie standing near the fireplace. "Maybe in the afternoon after all the cattle are fed, Jamie and Luke could put fresh hay on one of the really big sleds and come pick us up, and then we'll go for a long hay ride through the fields. We could sing Christmas songs if we feel like it."

Everyone in the room had fallen silent, listening to her. "Could we do that?" She prodded.

Damien lifted his arm to encircle her thin shoulders. "Of course, we can do that, darling. Shall we make it a special celebration just before John and I have to go away for the trial?"

"Oh, yes, Pa-pa, it will be ever so nice."

During the week preceding New Year's, all the young people from both houses filled the time with ice skating and sledding on the slopes above the stream. John and Damien were holed up in the *Mariposa* library with Granville most days, discussing final defense strategy for the trial. Unable to concentrate on work in her studio, Harper elected to go out with Dom, Delaney, Arthur and Laura, and the Carroll girls to join in the winter fun and was delighted when Audra joined them as well.

On New Year's Eve, the two friends left the skating pond as twilight fell and walked together toward the meal Aunt Pris was hosting to welcome in 1893. Audra caught Harper about the waist. "We're getting close to the end of it."

"The waiting, you mean?"

"Yes. Only one more day to get through. And with the hayride tomorrow evening, we'll have a lovely time before we have to face the trial."

"What do you think will happen?"

Audra scowled, then laughed softly. "I think it will soon be over and we can come home and take up our lives where they were before this whole nightmare started."

Harper hugged her arms around herself. "I shall never take one minute of my life for granted again."

"As though you ever did."

She glanced at her. "You're right about that but I did become a bit complacent on occasion."

"We all did, I think. Perhaps it's a good lesson to be brought up short."

"Perhaps."

Raucous laughter preceded Delaney and Millie, chasing each other through the clearing behind. "Ma-ma!" Delaney embraced her waist with both arms. “I didn’t know you were such a good skater.”

Harper kissed her cold cheek. “Your Pa-pa and I used to spend entire afternoons skating on the Layton in England. It was so romantic and he was so graceful.”

“I think you are very graceful as well,” Delaney said, a dreamy look in her eyes.

“She certainly is,” Audra agreed, draping her arms around Millie’s shoulders. “Like a swan.”

“Oh, please,” Harper laughed.

In happy camaraderie, they continued toward the beckoning warmth of the *Mariposa*

New Year’s afternoon, Jamie stopped the team of Shires outfitted with harness bells, in the piazza. Eliza shared the driver’s seat with him, holding Humbert the terrier in her lap. Finn had joined the other babies in the nursery with Ivy.

Harper and Damien, Delaney, Arthur, Laura, Roddy and some of the other servants clamored up onto the alfalfa. Rumor, Riley and Huckleberry got a boost from Damien, then capered about atop the hay, barking gleefully.

Everyone wore layers of sweaters, capes, caps, coats and scarves, extra pairs of woolen socks protecting their feet burrowed into the hay. At last, everyone was settled and Jamie drove toward Trail’s End to add Granville, John and Audra and their girls to his load. Though Harper had left Chandler behind in the care of Ivy, Yvette joined the party, snug in John’s arms.

Nestled close together in the fragrant alfalfa, the group was warm and comfortable under heavy blankets as Jamie guided the Shires along the driveway and then into pastureland along Aspen Creek angling past the rear of the houses. Hugging Huckleberry in her lap, Delaney began singing *Jingle Bells.* Grinning at her, Damien joined in, their voices in clear and true harmony in the still winter air.

Harper soon sang along with them, gesturing the rest to do the same. As the horses trotted on with their bells ringing merrily, she was filled with renewed hope and happiness.

Damien turned his head to look at her, a warm light in his eyes. She reached out to grip his gloved hand. How she adored this striking, honorable man, the father of their beautiful children.

Anger mixed in with the parade of emotions she'd been fighting since he and John were arrested. How could they be put in the same category as the evil men who'd kept up a constant reign of terror at *Rancha Mariposa* for so long before finally, matters had to been addressed with the Invasion. She leaned forward to hug Delaney as she remembered how this delightful child had been nearly destroyed by the criminal element that Damien and John had at last faced down.

She laid her head on Damien's shoulder. She longed for the waiting to be finished, for the trial to get underway. Now only one day remained before the legal proceedings commenced. During the course of the peaceful summer, she'd managed to keep her worry at bay most days while she and Damien delighted in the children and the pleasant warm days following one after another.

Harper had painted a great deal, pouring all her unease into her work. When Granville commented on the quantity of work she'd completed, he'd offered the opinion that her pain had added an edge of darkness to her art that hadn't been part of it since the years after Eddie's death. Though he'd never have wished her less than serene days, he believed the result of working so hard to banish her latest grief had the result of creating art with a new depth of genius.

Now as she sang along with *Silent Night*, she watched the winter gloaming settle around them as the anticipated full moon nudged up beyond the skeletal trees. A flock of ravens wheeled above, stark in the fading light.

"Look, Ma-ma, there go our raven friends," Delaney cried. "Do you think they're happy tonight?"

Harper laughed. She and Delaney had enjoyed a long appreciation of the black birds that inhabited the woods at the ranch headquarters. With her customary attitude of free thinking objectivity, Delaney had shared Harper's delight in the raucous interaction of the noisy birds that were sometimes joined by crows and rooks. They'd begun creating scenarios about the mixed flock whenever they spotted them, discussing their mood and what they were up to.

They often speculated that they were on their way to a funeral because a flock of crows is called a murder and they thought they were decent enough to attend a funeral after a murder. Other times if the birds appeared particularly shiny and orderly, they reflected they were going to Parliament since a gathering of rooks was called a parliament.

As the deepening darkness was overcome by moonlight, Jamie guided the team deeper into the woods along the Aspen. The immense horses easily negotiated the snowdrifts among the tree trunks.

Delaney and Millie began singing again and soon enough, their high spirits infected the rest and everyone sang at the top of their lungs, the sound soaring through the night quiet. Luke had lit several lanterns and now he came back along the sled, hanging them on the uprights on one side.

In the new illumination, Harper glanced around and suddenly realized Dom was missing. She bent to speak in Damien's ear but he was also at a loss.

Delaney and Millie, craving more excitement, crawled over to Granville to convince him to tell some ghost stories. Always eager to oblige when asked for entertainment, he grinned and settled the girls on either side of him. "How about *The Legend of Sleepy Hollow?"*

They both clapped enthusiastically. "Oh, yes," Delaney cried. "That's a good one!"

The group was soon listening intently to Granville's dramatic baritone.

Unbeknownst to the rest, Dom had chosen to stay behind and have a word with Ivy. He'd waited until the revelers had been gone from the house for an hour, then climbed up to the nursery.

Ivy answered his tap on the door, a bit startled to see him. "I thought everyone was off on the hay ride?"

He shrugged with a grin. "I decided to stay here. Could I see Sawyer?"

"I don't see why not." She turned toward the row of cribs and lifted the fiery-haired lass who gazed happily at Dom. "Isn't she a pretty one?"

Dom reached a finger toward her and she grasped it between both chubby hands. "She's beautiful."

"You may hold her if you like." She came closer and Dom carefully lifted the tot who snuggled against him.

He carried her to a bench and sat with her on his lap. "How old is she now?"

"Eight months. Hard to believe, it is."

He grinned down at her as she brought up her hands to pat his face. "Maybe I should've taken more time to think about things," he said after a while.

Ivy frowned at him, sitting in a rocking chair. "What do you mean?"

"I didn't want any part of being a father," he said gloomily. "But now that I see her, I find I wish I could go back and claim her as mine."

Anger shot through Ivy. "Well, you can just forget that idea! She belongs to Luke and me now with everything legal. Granville drew up the papers himself so put the notion of changing your mind right out of your head. You've always been spoiled and gotten everything you want. But not this time, Mister!" She got up and marched to the bench, reaching for her daughter. "And don't you start bothering us! You made your decision and it's final. I don't want you confusing Sawyer by butting in at this point."

She held her close, staring defiantly at him. "You hear me?"

He sighed. "I hear you."

"Could you tell me one thing?"

He stared at her. "What would that be?"

"Where did her red hair come from?"

"Ah, that. My mother had hair that exact color. It was lovely as I recall."

"I'm sure."

He reluctantly got to his feet. "Thanks for letting me see her." With that, he strode out the door.

After hours in the cold, the throng eagerly sat down to Mrs. Goodeve's supper of chicken and dumplings, apple and walnut salad with New England cranberry pie for dessert. "Why is it called New England pie?" Delaney wondered when she found it very much to her liking.

"Because cranberries grow in New England," Aunt Pris explained.

"Well, I think we should grow them here."

"That wouldn't be possible," Arthur interjected, "because they grow in bogs."

Delaney studied him as though she thought perhaps he was feeding her a line.

He raised his hands for emphasis. "It's true, I swear. Cranberries are actually very strange fruit. They grow on short vines. During winter, the bogs are flooded to protect the fruit and keep it from freezing. The following autumn, the bogs are flooded again and the fruit floats so the berries in the water are raked up in the harvest. The Indians used the fruit for medicine, even putting it on their arrow wounds."

Delaney pondered what he said, slowly chewing her final bite of pie. "Thank you, Arthur."

Everyone was weary and Granville, Damien, Harper, John and Audra would depart for Cheyenne early the next morning so the group soon headed to bed or to Trail's End. Damien and Harper climbed the staircase and settled Delaney in bed.

Once she was tucked in, she hugged them both.

"Wasn't it a wonderful evening?"

"It was lovely," Harper agreed. "You were so clever to think of it."

She giggled as Damien's mustache tickled her neck when he kissed her. "Good luck tomorrow, Pa-pa! I'll say lots of prayers for you all the time you're away."

"Thank you, darling. And don't you worry. Your Ma-ma and I will be home very soon. You tend to your studies and take care of Chandler and Sawyer."

"I will, Pa-pa. I love you so."

"And I, you, my dearest Delaney."

Delaney turned to look at Harper. "Ma-ma?" Tears sparkled in her dark eyes and she lifted her arms.

"Our sweet girl," she said, bending to pick her up. "You are so precious to us. Now you must be strong and brave. We'll say goodbye at breakfast. Now have nice dreams." Wiping the tears from beneath her eyes, she kissed her forehead. "Good night."

Damien turned down the bedside lamp and drew her with him into the corridor and on to their bedchamber. They entered the dressing room and Harper bent over Chandler sleeping peacefully. She kissed his cheek.

Damien went to the hearth to stir the fire to new life and warm. At last, they approached the window, standing together to look out into the moonlight for a time before he gathered her into his arms. With his usual sensitivity, he sensed her dread and sought to console her. His mouth floated to her throat, then edged up to kiss her with a tenderness that made her want to cry.

Yet, as they found the bed and he began undressing her, her fear grew remote for a time. He was restrained and gentle in his lovemaking; his mouth and body worshipped hers with growing demand but even as she presently lay nude beneath him, she was unable to reach the final plane of satiation and rest.

"My dearest, Harper," he pleaded at last as her teeth nipped the skin of his naked shoulder. He held her tighter against him a moment, then studied her in the lamplight. "I'm not going away forever."

"How can you be certain?" Her violet eyes glittered with fear and love.

"Granville is very confident this will be finished quickly now. And, I believe him."

"The people of Johnson County would like to see every one of you hang."

"Only because they never understood our intent, never knew we were going to Buffalo to protect them, not attack them." He took her face between his hands and kissed her with infinite compassion, then appraised her once more with sharp, knowing eyes. "Believe me, Harper, when I say we will all be home very soon."

"I shall not be able to bear it if we aren't."

His hands and mouth gradually offered new comfort, kneading the stiffness from her limbs, finally concentrating on her breasts, stomach and thighs until she lifted her body in silent longing. When he took her once more, the desperation was gone; she was carried quickly to completion.

They lay together in the firelight, the warmth like a blessing around them. Soon enough, they were claimed by dreamless sleep.

Dawn lay cold and desolate over the plains as they set out to Cheyenne the next morning. Luke drove the landau that comfortably accommodated Damien and Harper, John and Audra, and Granville who was in fine fettle and gave every indication that he enjoyed the drive immensely.

Harper clung to Damien's hand, trying desperately to calm her breathing and find the pool of serenity within herself that had sustained her for the past eight months. She had often found herself floundering in dread and doubt but had always managed to gradually bring herself to a core of tranquility by concentrating hard on hope and all the reasons she believed Damien would ultimately be vindicated. And she was able to do the same now.

When Damien looked into her face, she gave him a confident smile, kissed his cheek and mouthed the words, "I love you."

With a sigh, he rested his head against her hair.

The long-awaited trial of the Invaders could not have been more anti-climactic. The plaintiffs filed into the court room and the attorneys took their places before the judge who appeared quite bewildered by the whole affair.

When he learned that Johnson County had still not paid for the accumulated room and board of the prisoners as well as their guards while they were under arrest, he asked when the outstanding balance would be settled? As soon as he was told Johnson County had no money left in its treasury, he stared at the gathering in total disbelief, then slammed his gavel down with a resounding bang. "All charges are dismissed!" He shouted.

The room erupted in an uproar as plaintiffs, as well as spectators, struggled to absorb what had just occurred. Granville threw back his head and laughed in great, roaring guffaws. That his behavior was unseemly in the solemnity of the court room didn't concern him at all and he continued enjoying his victory for some minutes; he pounded John and Damien on the back and pumped the hands of onlookers in congratulatory excess. "Did I not tell you, not to worry?" He finally asked, drawing out his handkerchief to wipe his florid complexion.

They could only gape at him for the space of several minutes. Harper was first to recover. "You are positively extraordinary," she ventured. "Thank you!"

"It was a stirring adventure," he declared.

"It's truly over?" Audra asked, wiping tears.

"It is, my dear. Thanks to Governor. Barber and our friendly judicial system. Now, please allow me a few moments to speak to Governor. Barber and some others I've grown fond of during these proceedings. Then let us retire to The Plains where I shall buy us an extravagant breakfast to mark the end of our collective anguish of the past many months." He strode toward a group of men conversing with the judge.

The rest made their way to the carriage parked outside. Damien caught Harper in a joyful embrace, whirling her about. She clung to him, dizzy with relief.

As 1893 continued, *Rancha Mariposa* settled into a period of calm and prosperity as the Whittakers and Carrolls recovered from the rustling and the resultant misfortune of the previous years. Dom appeared content to concentrate on his studies in preparation for going east to Harvard.

Delaney grew taller and continued to delight everyone at the ranch. Chandler and Sawyer matured from babies to toddlers who first walked, then ran, keeping Ivy constantly in motion as she sought to keep them from calamity.

Delaney and Damien had long discussions about the new Thoroughbred she desired. Granville agreed to look for just the right horse for her when he got back to England. He remained in

Wyoming until June when he departed for Herefordshire with a dozen of Harper's new paintings to be placed at the *Louvre* and other outlets. He left with the promise to visit again much sooner than he had in the past.

Shortly after Granville's departure, Dom joined Damien, John, and Jamie on the usual roundup. There had been no word concerning Randall Holt during the winter, leading Dom to believe that his part in their nemesis' disappearance would remain safely hidden. Evidently Madam Charleen concluded that silence was the best policy where the vanishing of her new partner in crime was concerned.

It was only when no decline in the head count of *Rancha Mariposa* crossbreds was found that Damien and the others took notice and dared wonder what accounted for the welcome change. Dom could scarcely school himself to present an indifferent demeanor when he longed to shout with delight at the success of his plan and be praised for his ingenuity.

Only when Luke traveled to Cheyenne for supplies that he delivered to Carlin, the roundup cook, did the news of Randall Holt's disappearance become public. Luke reported that a Pinkerton detective had already started an investigation but had so far, uncovered very few clues. One fact did surface, Dom surmised from an interview with Madam Charleen. "He was to take the train east but had to ride to his ranch first. He never returned from the country. With the new snow that afternoon, there were no tracks, nothing to suggest what happened to him."

"Perhaps he did get back to town and took the train after all," Jamie suggested.

"I believe that is the conclusion, the Pinkerton man came to," Luke agreed.

Damien seemed a bit dazed by the development. "Apparently, there's no mystery why our count's where it should be."

"That and the new climate since the Invasion," John pointed out.

Following the Invasion, the political atmosphere in Wyoming shifted dramatically. The friendly judicial system that protected the cattle barons could not protect them from Wyoming voters. The Republican Party was closely associated with the cattlemen and the Wyoming Stock Growers Association. Republican U.S. Senator Joseph Carey had recently served as president of the organization.

The 1892 election had been a landslide in favor of the Democrats. Republican U.S. Senator Francis E. Warren lost his seat. Then in 1894, following the nationwide Panic of 1893, Wyoming voters threw out the Democrats, the party in power during the economic crisis. Francis E. Warren wouldn't be returned to the U.S. Senate until 1895.

Despite mixed electoral results, there were permanent and positive changes in response to the Johnson County War. The most important was the Wyoming Stock Growers Association was altered for the duration when it was opened in 1893 to all the stock growers in Wyoming.

The small cattlemen were invited to join and this abruptly halted the overwhelming hostility of the cattle barons toward the lesser stockmen. It also stopped the confiscation of suspected rustlers' cattle at point of sale by the Wyoming Livestock Commission.

# CHAPTER SIX

## June 1893 – August 1894

The discussion of what had become of Randall Holt became less and less energized as 1893 gave way to 1894. The *Rancha Mariposa* head counts remained steady as peace descended over the Wyoming range. Still Damien, John and Jamie had known for some years that the time of the open range in Wyoming cattle ranching was coming to an end.

A month or so following the 1894 spring roundup, the Whittakers, Carrolls, Jamie and Eliza, Luke and Ivy, and Dom met in the *Mariposa* drawing room to discuss a new policy to be implemented on the ranch. The first order of business was a report from John that Randall Holt's attorney had written to him, authorizing him to end the employment of all the cowboys and other hired men on the Holt ranch and sell the land.

The next matter to be discussed was the phasing out of the crossbred stock at *Rancha Mariposa.* Everyone was in agreement that it was time for the Herefords to come to the forefront of their company. Damien, John and Jamie had already discussed this transition with many other ranchers and discovered a large demand for any Hereford breeding stock and weanling heifers they might put on the market. This development assured a profitable future apart from the traditional marketing outlets.

Holt's range was to be divided into dozens of plots suitable for small cattle ranches and several of his men expressed interest in buying starter herds of his crossbreds. These men who'd been nicking *Rancha Mariposa* stock for years would likely steal scattered Herefords but without the leadership of the Holts and Jose Martinez the devious work would be of little consequence.

The summer was taken up by the liquidation of the Holt property as well as the regular work at *Rancha Mariposa.* After the spring roundup, the crossbreds were confined in fenced pastures along the Lodgepole.

Another advantageous development for the ranch was the arrival of many new settlers eager for claimed-up homesteads which the divided Holt ranch provided. This congregation of small-time farmers and ranchers served as a buffer along one edge of *Rancha Mariposa* land against squatters that might otherwise have been an unwanted presence.

Dom completed his education in the library school room in the spring soon after he turned eighteen. The time he'd dreaded for so long was upon him and he would be enrolling at Harvard in September.

Though the onslaught of new enterprises at the ranch intrigued him and he hated to be leaving during these important transformations, he had gained enough maturity by this time to accept his fate with some semblance of equanimity. And he took huge personal pride in the changes, to some extent, the result of his bold action two years before.

At noon on the final Saturday in August, Aunt Pris hosted a farewell luncheon for him at the *Mariposa.* He sat in the Great Hall with her before the other guests arrived.

"Are you excited about this new adventure?" She asked from her chair opposite where he reclined at the end of a sofa.

"I am," he said, giving her a smile as he leaned forward to rest his elbows on his knees. "Arthur tells me it's quite a rousing place to be so I'm looking forward to it."

"Well, it is my fervent hope that you will enjoy yourself tremendously while you obtain an excellent education."

"I'll do my very best. Thank you, Aunt Pris for hosting this luncheon for me."

"It is my pleasure, dear. We will celebrate again when you come home for Christmas."

"I doubt I'll be here then as I wish to finish my studies as quickly as possible. Arthur says if I skip holidays and continue with my classes during the summer, I'll be able to obtain my degree in June of '97. So that's what I plan to do."

"My goodness, that is an admirable goal but we'll miss you horribly if we don't see you for three years."

"I'm sure it will be worth it. I'm very eager to take my place with Pa-pa, John and Jamie in running *Rancha Mariposa.* We'll be entering a new century soon so it's going to be ever so exciting."

"Indeed." Her gaze drifted to the entrance beyond the staircase where Sawyer ran ahead of Luke from their apartment entrance. "Ah, here's our Sawyer."

The pretty two-year-old careened around the corner and rushed to her. With one hand, Sawyer clutched Aunt Pris's lavender skirt, and twirled to shyly inspect Dom. "Hello, Dom, Dom."

"Hello, Sawyer. You look very pretty today."

Smiling, she cocked her head, melting his heart. She wore a dress the color of forget-me-nots that perfectly set off her carroty curls. "Thank you."

He longed to draw her into his lap but Ivy and Luke had made it abundantly clear that he must treat his daughter with friendly respect and keep his distance. This attitude enraged him but because he knew he'd be given no leeway, he chose to make no unwanted overtures. He hoped by the time he returned, the bond with the comely little girl that he felt so keenly now, would have faded to something more manageable.

Luke strode into the sitting area, greeting Aunt Pris with a kiss on the cheek, then sat on the sofa beside Dom. "Are you ready for your new adventure?"

"Yes. After hating the idea for so long, I'm finally eager to be on my way."

"Since I only have a fifth grade education, I must say I'm quite envious of you." He shrugged. "That hasn't held me back so far but only because my aspirations aren't particularly lofty."

Dom nodded. "Lately, the thought has occurred to me that I might wish to get into politics one day so I imagine my education will be an asset if I ever actually pursue that path."

"What path is that?" Damien inquired, briskly descending the staircase to join them.

"Running for Governor one day."

Damien sat elegantly in a chair next to Aunt Pris, reaching out to lift Sawyer onto his lap as he appraised his son. "Are you serious?"

"Perhaps. I was just saying that if I should decide to go after something like that, my education will likely be of help."

"You have no idea of all the ways it will be of benefit throughout your life."

"I'm in complete agreement with you, Pa-pa," he said with a bit of a sheepish grin. "Sorry it took me so long to see it your way."

Damien granted him a tolerant smile. "I'm only happy that eventually, you came around, belated though your capitulation was."

Harper, leading three-year-old Chandler with Delaney trailing behind, came down the stairs. Still holding Sawyer, Damien rose to meet them. "Darling," he said softly, catching her hand to draw her to the chair next to him, then bent to drop a kiss on Delaney's hair.

When he sat again, Delaney approached, catching both of Sawyer's hands and laughing into her jolly face. "You're so beautiful."

"Thank you," Sawyer piped before she spotted Rumor coming downstairs and ran to sit on a step and pull the beagle close, chattering into her ear.

Delaney squeezed into the chair beside Damien, gazing up at him. "Did Granville say what day my horse can leave New York?" She asked, referring to the letter from England he'd received, telling them when her new Thoroughbred hunter could be picked up after arriving from Surrey.

"Yes, he did. By the time Arthur and I get Dom settled in at school, your horse will be ready to come home with us."

She clapped her hands at the news. "I can hardly wait. What's his name again? I forget."

"Destino."

"Oh, yes, I remember now. Ma-ma says it's just right because maybe it'll be our destiny to be champions at horse shows."

"I'm sure Ma-ma's onto something." He leaned his head against hers. "Can you keep a secret?"

She studied him quizzically. "Of course, I can."

"I'm bringing home a horse for your mother as well,"

Her violet eyes widened. "Truly?"

"Yes. Her name is Avalon. That's where King Arthur lived, you know."

"I know. It's a very pretty name." She looked up when the front door opened and the Carrolls trouped in. She soon hurried off to see Millie. Soon after, Arthur and Laura arrived from their apartment, accompanied by Laura's parents, Theodore and Jessica Quinn.

When everyone was settled about the fireplace, Adare and Roddy arrived with champagne while Constance served hot canapes fresh from Mrs. Goodeve's oven. Dom smiled graciously when Damien and Arthur both offered toasts to his success. But his attention was glued on three-year-old Yvette Carroll who'd enchanted him from the first time he'd seen her as a baby. With white-gold curls falling over her shoulders, she was spectacularly lovely. The delicate planes of her face might have been formed of the finest porcelain and her pale blue eyes always seemed to be dancing with amusement.

All of the Carroll girls were uncommonly pretty but Yvette, the youngest was in a league all her own. Dom had been half in love with her since she was born. And because no one had imposed restrictions on his attention as they had with Sawyer, they were already friends.

Spotting him now, she came running and climbed into his lap, giving him a delighted smile. "Dom. . .y."

He shared some of the pastry he was eating and she consumed it daintily, then accepted half a stuffed egg from the tray Constance passed. While she chewed tiny bites, Dom marveled at her perfect features, her long blonde eyelashes that she'd already learned to bat in female coquetry.

Dom could well imagine what a tease she would be at sixteen. The image even now stirred his blood. Though he'd be well over thirty, he dared hope he might have the good fortune to court her.

All too soon, luncheon was served and he had to surrender her to Ophelia, the eldest Carroll daughter who was very attractive in her own right. Because Dom had lived with the Carrolls for much of his boyhood, he knew her well and bestowed a playful kiss to her cheek as she picked up her sister.

Jessica Quinn who was known to be quite an imbiber, had already downed considerable champagne and veered a bit as her husband escorted her to the table. Harper beckoned Roddy to mention he should serve her in moderation at lunch.

Once Harper had sat with Aunt Pris and Damien at the head of the table, she gripped his hand beneath the linen. Because he, Arthur and Laura were accompanying Dom to Cambridge to get him settled into his living quarters, she already felt a pang of distress at the prospect of staying behind. But because she'd received three commissions for art within a month, all due before Christmas, she felt obliged to stay at home.

Reading her mood, Damien leaned in to kiss her cheek. "I'll be back before you know I'm gone."

"I wouldn't go that far," she demurred, "but I'm sure I'll manage to keep busy."

The meal passed with everyone in high spirits and soon it was time for the travelers to depart. Luke had already loaded Dom's trunks and the rest of the baggage in the wagon Stephen would drive to Cheyenne while the rest traveled in the Victoria since it was such a perfect warm afternoon.

After hugs and goodbye kisses, Damien and Dom got into the carriage. Harper stood with her hands draped over Delaney's shoulders as they watched the Victoria circle about in the courtyard and turn along the driveway heading toward the road to Cheyenne.

Delaney wiped at tears, glancing helplessly at her mother. "I wish Dom wasn't going to be away so long."

"I know, darling, but just think what fun we'll have when he comes back."

Millie came to stand beside her friend and put her arm around her. "Don't be sad. We'll be so busy, he'll be back before you'll miss him much."

Delaney managed a smile and caught Millie's hand as they followed Harper back inside where the luncheon guests had gathered in the drawing room. Audra looked up as they entered, then stood to embrace Harper. "I'll soon face this day myself. Come tell me how it feels when the first leaves home?" She led her to a bench near an open window that admitted the sound of chirping finches in a lilac bush.

When they were settled, Harper collected her thoughts. "I'm immensely proud that I had a part in raising an honorable young man whom I hope will be a huge asset in our world. I hate that he's going to be so far away for so long but I'm delighted that our Dom has in the past few years matured into someone sensible and caring."

Audra smiled. "At least, John and I shall be spared from seeing Ophelia traveling so far afield to pursue a higher education. To my knowledge, none of our daughters harbor aspirations along that line."

"What do they want to do with their lives?"

Audra laughed. "I doubt any of them have much of an idea at this point. Except for Millie who, like Delaney, wants to ride horses every day of her life. If they can find a means to make a living at that, they will be set."

Harper's gaze fell on the two young friends sitting together on a sofa across the room reading, as was another of their shared delights. Yvette and Chandler played with Huckleberry and Riley on the rug while elderly Rumor peered out from her napping spot beneath a hutch.

Harper was gradually possessed by a mix of joy, pride and contentment. Time marched forward. She and Damien had begun life in this place with no conception of what hardship and wonder awaited them.

When trouble came, they suffered to the depth of their souls. Yet, because of their commitment to each other and this way of life, they'd persevered, stronger than before with restored dedication.

"Well, my dears, all this food and good company has quite worn me out," Aunt Pris declared from her nearby chair. "I must excuse myself and have a nap." She firmly positioned her cane and leaned forward, waiting as she now required help to rise out of whatever seat she settled in.

Jamie and John quickly went to her aid and with one on either side, gently hauled her to her feet. "Thank you so very much for a lovely time," Jamie said, offering his arm to escort her to her apartment.

John came to sit next to his wife, draping an arm about her shoulders. "Perhaps we should gather our brood and depart as well," he said presently.

Audra leaned her head back, smiling. "I was just thinking of those lovely years when Dom lived with us in Cheyenne while he was in school. He was just like one of our own."

"I always enjoyed having him in our lives," John said. "He was such a bright young man."

"Damien and I have always been so grateful to you for letting him be part of your family. I've always thought your lovely girls had a gentling influence on him, smoothing out his rough edges."

"They've always loved him like their brother."

"And I had a bit of the experience of having a son," John said, "for which I'm grateful."

Jamie strode back into the room and knelt on one knee beside tow-headed Finn who'd fallen asleep on a loveseat. Eliza dozed in a rocking chair nearby. Gathering the boy in his arms, Jamie stood, then reached down to take his wife's hand, drawing her up before they approached the others.

"Thank you," Eliza said with a smile before they departed with the rest of the gathering trailing them outside.

"I'm so happy for them." Harper sat on a bench in the piazza to watch them disappear toward their cottage behind the *Mariposa.*

"We're blessed to have them in our lives," John said, bending to lift Yvette as his family prepared to head back to Trail's End.

Because the warm afternoon was so perfect, they had walked. Now all save for Millie who was staying overnight headed back through the front garden. Harper and the girls soon entered the quiet house and climbed up to her studio where she immersed herself in the first commission, an extravagant, brilliant-hued treatment of the summer garden.

Delaney and Millie busied themselves with water-colors. But after half an hour, they were intent on escape and decided to go ride their horses.

Damien was due home on Saturday, near the end of September but as a surprise for Harper and Delaney arrived a day early. Harper had gone riding with her daughter and Millie astride Merry and Molly. As had been her habit all summer, she held Chandler in the saddle before her on Embarr. The old stallion had mellowed from his spirited youth so made a perfectly dependable mount to carry a small child.

Thinking back to the days when she was a girl and the chestnut was in his prime, Harper was saddened by his advanced years. She often wondered why God hadn't created lifespans more compatible between man and his treasured animal friends.

She and the girls guided their mounts along the drive leading to the stable. Luke appeared and took Chandler when Harper handed him down, setting him on his feet.

Sawyer darted out of a stall, laughing when she saw the boy. She threw her arms around him, nearly toppling him over.

"Do you want to ride Merry?" Delaney asked her little brother.

"Yes, I do! Lift me up, please." Once he was in the saddle, she led the little horse back along the cobbled driveway.

Harper smiled when Millie made the same offer to Sawyer who accepted with equal enthusiasm. "The stable is becoming a favorite spot of Sawyer's," she observed.

"She loves staying out here with me," Luke agreed. "And it keeps her occupied while Ivy is working."

"It appears she's becoming a very good rider."

"Took to it like a baby duck to water," he said with a grin. "I believe I shall have to begin giving riding instruction to all the youngsters residing here now."

"That's an excellent idea. You did such an amazing job starting Delaney and Millie and it would be wonderful for the other three to have the same opportunity."

"Four actually. Don't forget Finn."

"Ah, yes, Finn . . ." she turned her head when Delaney shouted at her as she returned with Chandler.

"Ma-ma! Look!" She pointed behind her at two horses trotting along the walkway.

Harper stared, then was running to meet Damien astride a handsome dappled gray, ponying another grey, the second almost dainty in bone structure.

He pulled up beside her, then swung down and pulled her into his arms, kissing her soundly. "Hello, my darling wife. How do you like these fine Thoroughbreds I've escorted from New York?" He bent to sweep Delaney into his arms.

"Is this Destino?" She asked, reaching out to stroke his neck.

"Yes. Do you approve?"

"Oh, Pa-pa! He's so grand! And is that Avalon?"

"It is." He put his intrepid daughter down and again reached for Harper, drawing her around so she could see the mare. "This is my surprise for you, darling."

Harper's fingers drifted to her mouth as she took in the exquisite horse that was a strange shade of gray without dapples or other markings. "I've never seen such a color. How lovely."

"It's called rose gray and I thought it perfect for you."

"I love her already. And I love you for bringing her to me. Now my old and dear friend Embarr can retire and spend his days lolling about in green pastures and sunshine when he's not teaching our children to ride."

Delaney and Millie had turned their mounts over to a hovering stable boy and came to inspect Destino closer. Chandler and Sawyer tagged behind.

"May I ride him?" Delaney asked, looking longingly up at the huge hunter.

"Yes, you may." Damien began adjusting the stirrup leathers to fit her, then lifted her into the saddle.

Delaney's face broke into fragments of pleasure. "Oh, Pa-pa, thank you so much. He's so gorgeous." Gathering the reins, she urged him down the cobbled path. Upon reaching the rear garden, she turned him about and trotted back past the Herefords lazing in the pens.

Her parents watched, amazed at the ease with which she handled the massive beast, at least twice as tall as Merry. Harper slid her arms around Damien's waist, laying her head against his chest. "For our daughter, bliss is a great, tall hunter from England."

Grinning, he lifted his hand to cradle her face a moment before they started walking along the driveway to the garden where they sat together on a bench at the edge. "Dom said to tell you he misses you and Delaney already."

"I daresay no more than we miss him. He didn't mention Chandler?"

Damien frowned. "He's likely still deluding himself that his brother is some threat to him."

Harper glanced at the boy sitting on the cobbles with Huckleberry sprawled across his lap. Her heart contracted as it always did when she considered him closely. How much he resembled Eddie with his golden curls and cherubic features. "Does that beautiful child look like a threat to you?"

Damien chuckled. "I'm hoping that his charming personality will win Dom over by the time he's old enough for it to matter?"

"Did Dom like what he saw of Harvard?"

"Considering how much he disliked the notion of going to college, he appeared rather delighted. His roommate seems a jolly sort so I believe they'll be mates before the week is out. The venerable old campus drew me back to my days at Oxford when I was Dom's age. I hope he feels even a small portion of the joyous anticipation I felt when I arrived there. Arthur was positively giddy to be back and had a wonderful time showing Laura about and visiting his favorite professors. If nothing else, his enthusiasm for the place must have made Dom curious to discover for himself what Arthur liked so much about it."

Harper reached a hand toward Sawyer who'd come into the garden and picked a handful of daisies she now presented with a coy smile. "Oh, thank you, sweetheart." She sniffed the blooms. "Are these for me?"

She nodded, then turned her smile on Damien and took half the flowers in her fist and held them out to him.

"Thank you, Sawyer. I love daisies."

"Me too."

He placed her on his lap and she beamed at him. Leaning closer, he kissed her forehead, eliciting a giggle. "I sometimes want to weep because Dom can't claim this little one," he said, glancing at Harper.

"I feel the same but otherwise, she's in a very good place with two parents who adore her."

"Not to mention, grandparents who feel the same. Still, my son's a fool."

Just then, they heard the clopping of hooves and watched a buckboard turn toward them with Arthur driving. Harper saw the vehicle carried the baggage from the journey east.

Arthur pulled up the team and got out to help Laura down. "Hello," he said with his usual grin, stepping forward to kiss Harper's hand with a bow. "We had a splendid time in Cambridge but it's a delight to be home!"

Laura gave Harper a smile and touched Sawyer's hair. "So nice to see you. Is Delaney pleased with her new horse?"

"She's positively over the moon," Harper said, "and here she is now."

They all watched her appear on Destino from the trees, cantering along the creek. "Oh, he's lovely," she declared, stopping before the little group. "Merry has a wonderful smooth way of going but Destino is even better. I truly love him." She slid down from the saddle and raised the stirrups. "Now I'm going to get him in his stall for the night. He must be very tired."

"No doubt. We'll see you at dinner then," Damien said, putting Sawyer down for the walk to the *Mariposa.*

Delaney hugged her father once more. "Thank you again. Pa-pa. So much."

"My pleasure, love."

# CHAPTER SEVEN

## September 1894 – June 1897

Dom was caught in a storm of anticipation and dread as the train approached Cheyenne. He was nearly home and it felt as though he'd been away for far longer than the three years it had required him to graduate from Harvard.

He'd fought the idea of leaving the ranch for college ever since his father had broached it when he was still a boy. Yet, now that he was returning instead of departing on the venture, he had to admit that his college career was the adventure Damien had predicted. Being rather obsessed with getting his degree in the shortest time possible, he'd buckled down from the start, studying hard. He even limited the enticing pull of rowdy pals, accommodating girls and alcohol to weekends and holiday.

When it was time to head home, he was actually quite sad to leave his friends and Maylene, a favorite girl at a brothel. Still, those sacrifices were a small price to pay for returning to Wyoming to assume his promised position at *Rancha Mariposa.*

His eyes settled on Caldwell Bartholomew snoring in the corner of the seat opposite. This lanky young man who always reminded Dom of Washington Irving's portrayal of Ichabod Crane had become his dearest friend.

The two of them had lived together and been virtually inseparable since Dom had arrived. Caldwell hailed from Virginia where his family owned a Thoroughbred horse farm that had supplied cavalry mounts during the Civil War and now provided top hunters and racing stock for the aristocracy of the east. The two friends had spent most every holiday there and Dom had come to love the venerable place.

Now Caldwell was accompanying him to Wyoming for a visit and had voiced some interest in moving there permanently. Dom would like nothing better as he'd come to depend on him and couldn't imagine living any distance from him.

As Cheyenne appeared ahead, Dom kicked the foot sprawling into his space. "We're almost here, Cal."

He slowly unfolded himself from the curled arrangement of his limbs on the seat and straightened his back, squinting as he peered out the window. Yawning, he scratched his chin and mashed a wide black hat on his tousled head.

The Union Pacific whistle sounded as the engines hissed into the depot and came to a stop. Dom leaned down to look out the window at the siding outside. "Oh, they're here. My family's here. Come on."

The porter opened the door and Dom ducked out into the corridor with Caldwell close behind. Damien, Harper, Delaney and Chandler waited at the bottom of the steps. Harper stepped forward to embrace Dom, then pulled back to look at him closely. "Oh, darling, you look so grown-up."

Grinning, he kissed her cheek. "It's so very nice to be home." He reached out to shake Damien's hand. "Hello, Pa-pa,"

"Dom, it appears you've survived college in good form." He squeezed his shoulder. "We've missed you, son."

Delaney stepped closer, barely controlling her excitement. Dom hugged her close, swinging her in a circle while she laughed with delight. "Wow, you've grown a foot," he marveled once she stood still before him.

"Not quite." She scowled at him, then leaned in to peck him on the cheek.

Chandler, thin and coltish at six years old, hung back, observing. Dom made no move to speak to him but rather turned to introduce his friend.

Damien offered his hand. "We're honored to have you with us, Caldwell."

"Thank you Mr. Whittaker. Dominique has regaled me with so many stories about Wyoming and *Rancha Mariposa,* I had to come see it for myself."

"We're so happy you did." Harper pressed his hand, meeting his gaze in her disarmingly forthright manner.

"Now," Damien said, "we shall be off to The Plains for lunch to welcome you. We've brought the Victoria since it's such a splendid day." He led the way toward the carriage.

A porter loaded the trunks and baggage into a cart driven by a lad Dom didn't recognize. "This is Tim Beecham, our new stable boy," Delaney said, seeing his confusion.

Dom saluted him by touching the brim of his hat. When they were all seated in the Victoria, Chandler had managed to sit between Dom and Caldwell. Once they were underway, he glanced shyly at his brother. "Hello, Dom."

He was abruptly made uneasy by the very sight of the boy, a small version of his father with his lean body, tawny blonde hair and gray eyes that had the same warm, discerning depth that often made Dom nervous. In the past, it always seemed when Damien looked at him, he could read everything he was thinking and the same was true now of Chandler.

Similar emotions had rolled over him when Harper was pregnant with Chandler and later, when he was a baby. He'd loathed him with every fiber of his being. But gradually, because his brother had turned out to be a funny little lad who didn't seem like much of a threat after all, he'd basically forgotten about him. Still, while Dom was away, Chandler had grown until he looked shockingly like their father.

Dom had always been unnerved by his own dark coloring, a throwback to his mother's unsavory family. As a child, he'd longed to look like Eddie, Harper's golden boy from her marriage to Dom's Uncle Brendon.

And now, meeting Chandler's frank gaze, he wished he looked like him. Caldwell watched him with a peculiar expression as though he was trying to figure out what was wrong with him.

Dom smiled at him, then jostled Chandler's knee. "So what have you been up to since I've been gone."

"Riding Molly, mostly. And Arthur's been teaching me things so I can start my lessons in the fall."

"Well, good for you. Do you know that Caldwell's family raises amazing Thoroughbreds? A lot like Destino, if the descriptions in Delaney's letters are to be believed."

"Really?" Chandler glanced up at him. "That good?"

Caldwell smiled. "I'm proud of them but from what I've heard about Destino, he must be very special."

"He is!" Chandler said, his eyes alight. "And Delaney rides so great! You should see them."

"I will," Caldwell said. "I'm very much looking forward to it." He winked at Delaney who considered him ruefully from the front seat.

Once they'd continued to the hotel and settled at a table in the dining room, Damien considered Caldwell. "Do you have plans for the summer?"

"Well, sir, though my degree is in banking so my prospects are rather broad, I must say I'm a bit at loose ends at the moment. Dom has told me so much about working in the beautiful outdoors here, I'm quite intrigued with the idea of hiring on at your ranch for a time, if you are in need of another man."

"We always need good help. Much of what we do here is done on horseback and I understand you are an excellent horseman."

"Indeed. Hardly anything gives me more pleasure than a fine piece of horseflesh."

"Well, we can discuss your employment at *Rancha Mariposa* whenever you like," Damien said. "Now let's see if we can order some food." He motioned to a waiter.

When they were presently served roast beef, everyone save Chandler concentrated on the food for a time. Much to Dom's aggravation, Chandler began plying him with unending questions about his time in the east.

At first, he answered curtly but finally, tired of the game, he ignored him. When the boy persisted, Harper spoke quietly to him and he subsided, giving full attention to his dinner.

Dom watched warmth seep into his father's eyes as he winked at Chandler. He felt foolish and overwhelmed by a new aversion toward the child who was clearly first in his father's priorities.

Now in wake of the uncomfortable scene between his sons, Damien's voice had become guarded, his eyes shadowed. Dom had the bewildering feeling he found him frightening somehow.

Despite the present uncertainties, Dom was determined to make himself indispensable to his father in the years ahead. When Chandler was old enough to threaten his position at *Rancha Mariposa*, he would deal with him. As the eldest son, Dom felt he should garner a majority of company stock on principle alone but he doubted his father would agree.

His thoughts flickered into a dangerous, black region in the past. He gave his head an impatient shake to clear the images. He must bide his time and fight Chandler only when he became a real menace. At six, he was no problem. There were plenty of years to battle him for precedence.

Dom had wanted to rid himself of the nuisance as soon as he learned Harper was expecting. He recalled now, how agitated he'd been at the news and how on the drive home to the ranch after a winter stay with the Carrolls, he'd struggled to form a plan.

He'd thought he would catch a rattlesnake and throw it in front of Harper's buggy horse as she returned from sketching one day. But, before he could act on the perverse idea, fate intervened and something else nearly caused her to miscarry. And, it hadn't mattered in any case because in the end, she didn't bear the son Dom dreaded but Delaney. Now looking at his fetching sister across the table, a chill went through him at the thought that his rage might have caused her death.

"It is indeed splendid having you home, Dom," Damien remarked, stirring his tea as the meal wound down.

"You can't imagine how much we missed you," Harper agreed. "We were all so eager to go to Cambridge to see you receive your diploma. Why did you ask us not to come?"

"All that foofaraw is just for show. After working so hard for my degree, all I wanted was to get home and begin my life here in earnest." He forced a smile. "No more time spent dealing with this dubious business called education."

"Don't let him fool you," Caldwell interjected. "He positively relished all the amusements that intersperse the dubious business called education."

Dom shot him a lethal glance and Delaney giggled. "Incidentally," he went on, "I want everyone to call me Dominique from now on."

"Why?" Damien asked.

"Dom is rather childish, don't you think? I feel Dominique is more appropriate for a man beginning his life's work."

"I've always thought Dom was a perfect name. I loved it the moment Pa-pa, who'd already come west, wired us in New York to say that's what you would be called." Harper stated.

Damien soberly studied his son. "Well, if you're certain that's what you want, I'll do my best to remember to address you as Dominique. But I must say, it makes me a little sad."

"Me too," Delaney said with an accusing look.

Dom hadn't expected this reaction and felt a bit defeated.

"I say, Mr. Whittaker," Caldwell said in an effort to lift the mood, "are you about to invest in an automobile?"

He smiled musingly. "I've been traveling about atop a horse or behind one for so many years, I believe I'll require quite some time yet before I can adjust to being transported by a machine."

"Having grown up among some of the best horseflesh in the world, I wholeheartedly agree with you. Still, I've seen some magnificent autos."

"All in good time perhaps." Harper lifted Damien's hand and stroked it between hers.

"Now we should get home," Damien said. "Aunt Pris is absolutely aquiver at the prospect of having you back, Dom. And meeting Caldwell."

"We're just going to have such a nice time while you're with us," Harper said, threading her arm through Caldwell's as they trouped out to the waiting Victoria.

"Thank you, Mrs. Whittaker."

"Oh, you must call me Harper." She inclined closer and kissed his cheek.

While the carriage moved out, Dom glared into the distance, irrationally peeved that his homecoming had become so upsetting.

By the following day, he'd grown steadily more disgruntled when no one remembered to call him Dominique. After correcting everyone several dozen times, he teetered on the edge of an explosive temper tantrum.

Fortunately Caldwell intervened and confronted him in his bedchamber where Dom sat staring out a window. "Do you know how stupidly you're behaving?"

Dom refused to look at him.

He stepped closer, suddenly clipping him on the shoulder. "Do you?"

Dom leapt up and paced to the door and only spun back when Caldwell rushed after him. "Don't touch me!" He snarled, staring at him, wild-eyed while his face grew flushed and he began to shake.

Caldwell had become rather adept at dealing with Dom's erratic behavior while at Harvard. Now he threw his arms around him, holding him so tight his frantic bucking and twisting finally quieted. "Stop this nonsense!" He ordered, shoving him into a chair before pulling a stool close so he could sit in front of him.

Dom slowly lifted his chin. "I just wanted to use my full name because it's more distinguished and makes me seem older."

"Why the devil do you want to seem older?"

"So my family will have some respect for me."

Caldwell shook his head, incredulous. "They already respect you, you ridiculous ingrate! They likely don't like you much when you're surly and throwing your weight around. But, if you smarten up and start acting like a college graduate instead of a two-year-old, I'd say your future looks rosy enough."

He continued musing over Dom's mournful demeanor. "Your family clearly holds you in the highest esteem so I recommend you stop feeling sorry for yourself and give you and everyone else a chance to grow accustomed to you being home. I see how happy your family is that you're back and how much they respect you as you begin your work here." He poked his face close to Dom's. "I daresay *you* will be able to see that soon enough." He gave him a playful punch on the shoulder. "If not, old chap, I'm going to be obliged to knock you silly. And you know I can and will do that."

Dom mulled over what he'd said, presently recalling a few occasions when Caldwell had been unsuccessful in jollying him out of a snit and had indeed physically took him to task. Gradually good sense began to return. He had little doubt if Caldwell was pushed much further, he'd bash him and that wouldn't bode well for his desire to impress his father with his maturity and fine judgement.

In a sudden, quicksilver shift of mood that was his wont, he sprang up and clapped his friend on the back. "Thanks, mate. I have been acting like an ass."

Caldwell rolled his eyes heavenward. "I'm glad you concur. Now let's go find your brilliant young sister and admire her new Thoroughbred. Perhaps she'll agree to ride out with us so I can see your magnificent *Rancha Mariposa.* Incidentally," he added as they headed outside, "you'd best watch your step around Delaney, or you'll wake up one day and discover *she* is the new ranch manager."

"She's ten."

"Nevertheless, she's the smartest person around here, and that's saying something when we see what her parents have accomplished. Good Lord, Dom, your mother has paintings at the *Louvre.*"

"She's amazing," he agreed. "And actually Delaney's a pretty brilliant artist in her own right," he added with surprising grace. "If she ever gets tired of riding horses, she'll probably have art in the *Louvre* herself."

"No kidding." He digested the information as they headed along the cobbled drive to the stables. "So you see yourself how smart she is."

Dom nodded glumly, feeling some of his newfound goodwill fading. He loved his sister so much he'd never thought of *her* as a threat but now Caldwell had planted a seed of doubt.

Caldwell stopped to inspect some massive Hereford bulls in one of the enclosures beside the walkway. "Bloody big guys," he marveled when they moved on.

After being dressed-down so soundly, Dom wasn't especially eager to go along on the ride around the ranch headquarters. But he was resolved to behave better than he had since arriving home. Once they reached the paddock where Delaney performed intricate dressage maneuvers, he managed to conjure up enough interest in her quest for success on the horse show circuit that he could see what a phenomenal mount she had in Destino.

As they watched, Caldwell praised the huge gray lavishly. "What a grand one you have there," he called when she soon rode toward them.

Her lovely face lit with pleasure. "Isn't he though?" She glanced at Dom. "And what do you think?"

"He's the best horse I've ever seen this far west." He glanced at a golden-headed boy sitting on an overturned pail next to the fence. "Who's that?"

"Finn Horncastle."

"Wow, he's gotten big. What's he doing out here?"

"He's my trainer."

"Oh, of course," he said facetiously. "Do you think you can show us around the ranch? Caldwell's rabid to see what we do here."

"Is that true?" She asked, glancing at the loose-jointed young man who towered over Dom.

"I'd love to take a ride with you," he said with a wink.

"Well, let's be off then." She guided Destino toward the stable, pulling up beside Finn who jumped up.

"Go get Merry. We're going riding?"

"Oh, boy!" His gave her a gap-toothed grin, tugging his flat cap lower. "Shall I take Destino in for you?"

"Please. Thank you." She slid off, raised the stirrups and handed him the reins. "And what are you going to tell Tim?"

He stopped. "To cool him out carefully and rub him down with liniment before he feeds him."

"Excellent! And ask some of the other lads to saddle Foxfire, Belle and Swan and bring them out."

"Yes!" He said with enthusiasm and led the big gelding towards a gate in the rail fence.

Delaney turned to join Caldwell and Dom lounging on a long bench outside the nearest stone horse barn. Sitting between them, she removed her helmet that she turned in the circle of her fingers.

"Is Finn your own little slave now?" Dom asked.

Turning her head, she considered him. "Don't you dare give him a bad time! He wants to be a stable lad and one day, ride horses like I do. Jamie likes his work ethic. I just like him. He's very engaging and I love having him help me whenever he wants." She pointed a warning finger at her brother.

He threw up his hands in mock fear. "Well, excuse me. I didn't mean to offend."

"You'd better find a better attitude, big brother," she replied soberly. "I know what you're up to when no one is watching. I missed you while you were gone but I didn't miss your meanness and bad manners. You look grownup now and I hope you are because no one likes a man who acts like a brat."

"Well, aren't you the authority all of a sudden. How old are you now? Ten? Ten doesn't make you an expert on anything."

She looked daggers at him. "I just say, you better watch yourself."

Caldwell was astonished when Dom actually stuck out his tongue at her. He reached out to squeeze Dom's arm. "On this high note, I'd like to begin our ride." With that, the testy exchange ended and Finn soon appeared on Merry with three lads leading the other mounts behind him.

Mounted on her chestnut filly she'd named Belle, Delaney led the others past the stables toward the Aspen where she urged her horse down the bank and into the ford to cross to the opposite bank. Spring runoff had swollen the stream to a depth that required the horses to swim. Once across, she pulled up to look back at Finn who gamely urged Merry into the water. The little mare struggled a bit when she reached the deeper flow but continued boldly and soon came scrambling up the incline.

"Good job," Delaney said as Finn guided Merry to ride beside her.

"She's a goer," he said proudly.

"Indeed, she is."

They spent most of the afternoon riding in the spring splendor of greening trees and lush pastures where herds of Herefords grazed. Caldwell admired the cows and calves, recognizing the quality of the beasts. By the time they returned to *Mariposa* for dinner, Dom's spirits had risen enough so he managed to be cordial to Delaney and everyone else during the course of the evening.

The following afternoon, his father asked to see him in his study. Suspecting what was afoot, Dom felt more confidence than he had since coming home.

Roddy soon arrived with a bottle of bourbon. When they'd been served and his son sat before his grand ornately-carved desk, Damien raised his glass. "It is truly wonderful to have you home. I'm very pleased with the way you comported yourself at college and now I'm anxious to discuss your future at *Rancha Mariposa*."

"Thank you, sir." He was elated by the praise and hoped it boded well for the specifics of his role in the management of the ranch.

"I've spoken to John and Jamie, and Granville when he was here last year. They are all in agreement with my proposal to transfer ranch stock into your name and set up a monthly stipend. Does that sound reasonable to you?"

"I should think so."

"You sound uncertain."

He swallowed some bourbon. "I'm merely curious about the numbers."

Damien slanted a dubious glance at him. "Well, yes, the numbers are quite an important part of our agreement. You already have a generous bequest of stock you were given when you were born and we're prepared to offer you an additional block worth twenty thousand dollars along with a salary of one hundred dollars per month to start." He studied him for reaction.

Dom drained his glass in an effort to remain calm but didn't reply.

"Well?" Damien prompted.

"I was expecting a more generous arrangement."

"Were you indeed? Well, for the time being, you'll have to be satisfied with this. I don't believe you'll be reduced to a pauper. Your accumulated stock has grown to a substantial amount and Aunt Pris has made rather large deposits over the years to an account that you can draw on at any time."

"She has?" This bit of news was a considerable surprise.

"She has. She likes to think her bequests will allow you to live as a well-heeled gentleman with good prospects while your livelihood is assured by your hard work here."

"Are you saying I can use her money however I want?"

"That is her wish. I'm quite certain she expects you to use the money wisely."

"Has she opened accounts for Delaney and Chandler?"

"Of course. As in your case, they will only have access when they turn twenty-one."

"How much is in my account?"

He lifted a small leather bound passbook from a desk drawer and held it out to him. "You can see for yourself and I'd advise you to keep careful records of your withdrawals and deposits."

Dom half rose to take it, then sat again and dared glance at the balance. His heartbeat accelerated when he saw that over seventeen thousand was available to him.

"Is that more to your liking?" Damien asked.

He grinned. "I'm pretty amazed actually. Why would Aunt Pris do this?"

"Because she is very proud of you and our other children and rather feels as though all of you are her grandchildren. She's always been very generous as you may recall."

"I must thank her." He appeared as if he might leap up and go find her that moment.

"Actually, she is hosting a dinner this evening to welcome you home. You can speak to her when we have drinks in the drawing room. Now I'd like to finish up our own business here. Are you satisfied with what I and the others are offering? Now that you know you won't be poor as a second string cowboy?" He added with a lifted eyebrow.

Dom had the grace to appear a bit chagrined. "I'm sorry I sounded ungrateful. It's just that I've worked so hard."

"Yes, you have. From now on, you'll be working with me, John, Jamie, Luke and Caldwell if he decides he wishes to be a cowboy for a time."

"Have you spoken to him?"

"Yes, and he's going to let me know his plans in a day or two."

"I hope he stays. He's ever so much fun to be around." He gaze narrowed. "A lot like Arthur when he first came here. Back then, he was a real pal but then after he met Laura, he got pretty stuffy."

"As I recall, you were behaving badly about that time. I believe he realized he had to stop being your friend and become your teacher with new resolve in order to have you ready for Harvard in time."

Dom gloomily considered this, finally nodding. "I think you're right. I guess I was something of a popinjay."

Damien grinned. "To say the least. In any case, as I was about to say, you will answer to me until I tell you otherwise. You know the work as you've been doing it most of your life. I must tell you that Chandler seems to be a born stockman and he's already fond of joining us when we deal with the cattle. And when he's not helping Delaney, Finn comes along as well."

Dom sighed. "Are you telling me I must deal with boys riding out on Molly and Merry when we're working with the Herefords?"

"I'm telling you they'll help from time to time because they love it and are very good at it. We're proud of them both and as for them getting in the way on ancient children's ponies, you may be interested to know they've both mastered riding big stock horses."

He pondered this silently, still frowning.

"Dom, I do hope you aren't going to begin a senseless discussion of your ill feeling towards your brother. I love all of my children equally. If we are all to work effectively together one day, you are going to have to make an effort to come to terms with that reality."

He was briefly warmed by the naked entreaty, the love in his father's direct gaze. As in the past, he yearned to please him above all else. "I will do my best for you, Pa-pa."

"That's all I ask. You will be paid a monthly allowance as we discussed, against yearly dividends."

"Is rustling still a big problem?"

"Not so much now, thank God. I still look back on the Invasion with distaste and embarrassment but I must say, it helped us immeasurably. Except for scattered incidents, our ranges are free of thievery. I daresay we've also been helped because a number of ranchers who got no satisfaction during the Invasion, have since had their revenge by hiring assassins to eliminate their enemies."

Dom pondered this, knowing his killing of Randall Holt wouldn't be excused under any circumstances. He wished he could tell his father what he'd done, thinking how pleased and grateful he would be but he also knew the luxury of such confession was never to be.

"Jamie, John and I have made a decision about the future of *Rancha Mariposa*," Damien observed. "Others may prefer to continue breeding crossbreds. But we believe the time has come to bring our Herefords to the forefront of American ranching. We've been careful to maintain the purity of our Herefords even while we outcrossed them with longhorns and crossbreds. We've been very fortunate in pursuing this practice, managing to accumulate a fortune since arriving from Herefordshire. Yet, now that we've been delivered from rustling and bad weather that plagued us along the way, we can afford to concentrate on breeding the finest Herefords, much as we did in England. Once we've sold off the remaining mixed herds, we will continue raising sizable herds of Herefords for beef. And just as your grandfather and his ancestors did, we will also give much attention to raising the finest Hereford breeding stock that will be in great demand as other ranchers endeavor to improve the quality of the beef they produce.

"For many decades, our Herefords have been among the finest beef cattle in the world, a source of immense pride for generations of Whittakers. That very reality is what prompted John, Brendon and me to embark on our foray into American ranching. And now more than ever, I look to the future with pride and hope that we Whittakers will take our place in history as a family who brought our prime cattle to this country and dared to make our mark." He paused to consider Dom. "I have been blessed with a family in which I take utmost satisfaction. I expect you, my eldest son, to move into the future at my side as we continue to strive for success based on integrity and ceaseless effort."

"You have such a way with words. I think you should have delivered the graduation speech at Harvard."

"Why, thank you, my boy." He rose and came around the desk, shaking his hand before embracing him. "We must dress for dinner now. We mustn't keep Aunt Pris waiting."

They both headed upstairs and Damien found Harper already dressed, sitting before the mirror in their dressing room. He deposited a kiss on her neck. "Ah, you smell delectable, my dear."

She smiled at his image in the glass. "Have you and Dominique finished talking?"

He frowned. "Are you going to keep calling him Dominique? I've already given up on that."

"I believe he'll soon realize it's quite an impossible request of us who've always loved calling him Dom." She waved a slim hand dismissively. "He'll soon give it up."

Damien nodded at her grateful. "Thank heavens. And, yes, we have finished and you'll be happy to know it is my opinion that he has become quite an honorable young man ready to take his place as an integral part of *Rancha Mariposa*."

Harper turned about to meet his gaze. "Oh, darling, I'm so glad. I've been so worried about him over the years."

He lowered his lean frame onto a stool. "As have I." Taking her face between his hands, he pressed his lips to her forehead, stirring a small fissure of pleasure in her soul. "There have been times when I hadn't a clue what was to be done about him."

"Do you think it was his time at Harvard that made the difference?"

"I daresay. And I think Caldwell was very helpful in changing his outlook."

"Then we shall always be grateful to Caldwell."

He stood and drew her up into his arms. "Parenthood can be quite the conundrum, can it not?"

She searched his eyes. "Do you think he has a better attitude concerning Chandler?"

Frowning, he pulled her closer. "I'm not so sure about that but I made it clear he needs to get over his ill will toward his brother. Otherwise he's going to find himself at a great disadvantage because already, Chandler is making himself very useful to me and the others. And he's doing it with the greatest good humor."

"I have faith, Dom will rise to the challenge," Harper said, slowly disengaging herself from his embrace to inspect herself in the mirror, leaning back to rest her head on his shoulder.

"You look divine, my dear." He nuzzled the soft curve of her throat.

Smiling gaily, her gaze floated down over the sumptuous summer gown Aunt Pris had ordered from Paris and presented to her last week. As the end of the 1800s neared, ladies fashion had evolved and the bustle had disappeared. Waists had become narrow above the new circular skirts that fell gracefully over the foundation garment below. Harper took in the elegant lines of her cactus green *peau de soie*, with lace edging the short frilled sleeves. The gown exposed a provoking décolletage and her arms were left bare save for bracelets of fine jade.

Harper lifted her hands to encircle the slender waist, thinking she still looked quite presentable after bearing three children. Damien covered her fingers with his. "You're barely bigger than when you were sixteen. I still sometimes find myself wondering what I ever did to deserve such an exquisite wife."

"You exaggerate, my love."

He gently turned her about so he could look into at her face. "Exaggeration is not one of my vices." He tapped the end of her nose. "I adore you, Mrs. Whittaker."

They presently descended to the hall where Aunt Pris held court while drinks and appetizers were served. Dom and Caldwell sat on either side of her on a brocade bench. She caught both their hands in her bejeweled fingers, smiling coyly as though she were a debutante entertaining beaus. "It's such a treat having you home, Dom."

"I want to thank you for your generous gift."

She simpered, releasing his hand to take up her fan and gave him a flirtatious look around the edge. Grinning, Dom thought she must have been a force to be reckoned with among her friends when she was his age. "I am just so proud of you, having received your degree from such a prestigious college as Harvard. Because you accomplished so much in such a short time, I wanted to reward you by providing funds for you to use as you wish."

"Thank you so much." His lips brushed her crepey cheek.

"You're very welcome, my sweet." She lifted her bourbon from a table drawn close and swallowed a large mouthful before turning to Caldwell. "I understand that you are going to stay with us for a time. How lucky we are."

"I'm looking forward to it, Miss Begbie," he said with a wink. "Perhaps Dom will make a cowboy of me."

She patted his knee. "Well, you couldn't have a better teacher as he's been working side by side with the men since he was a mere lad."

"I grew up on my family's horse farm so I hope I won't be labeled a hopeless blackhorn. Is that the proper word?"

Dom snickered good-naturedly.

"I believe the word is greenhorn," Aunt Pris said.

Dom soon lost track of the conversation between the two, his attention settling on Delaney sitting across the room with Millie, Chandler and Sawyer.

He noted anew his sister had grown several inches. Her thin frame and graceful carriage was much like Harper's and he could see she would be beautiful once her coltish appearance mellowed with age. He hoped she would stop being such a little bluenose.

It was extremely vexing to note again what a handsome lad Chandler was at six. He wore a light blue suit that complimented his pale coloring. When he met Dom's inspection, his steel gray gaze was more than a little unnerving.

His attention was abruptly arrested when Sawyer preceded her parents into the hall, coming to sit near Aunt Pris. He was momentarily convulsed with excitement at the sight of his daughter, a droll little mite, now five. Freckles sprinkled her impish face and her flaming red hair cascaded over her shoulders. She abruptly stopped to inspect him with sharp periwinkle eyes.

He winked and after a few seconds, she smiled, nearly causing his heart to stop. "Hello, Sawyer?"

She considered him a moment more, then turned to her father who lifted her onto his lap where she sat soberly regarding him and Caldwell.

"How are you, Dom?" Luke asked.

"Very pleased to be home."

"I'm sure. We've missed you."

Ivy merely granted him a smile. She was as buxom and pretty as ever; the past three years had seemingly given her a new serenity.

The Carrolls arrived and gathered around him for hugs, kisses and the bestowing of good wishes. Once they were settled in a group before the fireplace, he had a chance to study them. "Where has Ophelia gotten herself off to?" He inquired at the eldest daughter's absence.

"Oh, didn't I write you when she married?" Audra asked. "Remember Jane Lamb, the cellist? Ophelia married her brother Isaac. They live in Cheyenne. They were sorry they couldn't be here this evening but promise to come visit you soon."

"It's so great to see all of you again. I've missed you something awful." With a jolt, his eyes came to rest on Yvette. For a moment, he couldn't think.

He'd been charmed by her from the moment she was born. She'd been an exquisite baby with white-gold curls framing her delicate features and eyes the color of forget-me-knots. He felt his heart swell with love. He realized once again, he could never be happy until he claimed her as his own. But, as usual, when he considered how he would make his most fervent wish come true, he was stymied.

Fifteen impossibly long years lay between them. When she was eighteen, he would be thirty-three. It wasn't likely her parents would be in favor of her marrying a man so many years her senior. Nonetheless, he was as certain he would have her one day as he'd been when he first saw her as a baby. This inevitability lay snug in his heart, warm as a blessing.

Within a week of Dom and Caldwell arriving from Cambridge, they had both settled into their work at *Rancha Mariposa*. Caldwell proved to be a willing pupil in learning the rudiments of a cowboy's duties although he had little natural talent for the job.

At first, Dom was a patient instructor. Their friendship and mutual sense of humor paved the way along the rocky road of learning new skills that had little in common with Caldwell's years at his family's Thoroughbred farm.

When the cattle were gathered on the various *Rancha Mariposa* ranges for the usual spring work of branding and castration of the bull calves, Caldwell had little stomach for the brutal practices of slicing off genitalia and burning designs into hide without benefit of any kind of pain killer. Upon witnessing the procedures for the first time on a calf he was helping secure near the branding fire, the blood suddenly drained from his face and he keeled over in a dead faint in the dirt. The calf leapt up and raced back among the bunch of other waiting victims.

Dom had been wielding the branding iron that he flung back into the fire before stomping to where Caldwell lay and shouted down into his face. "What the blazes is wrong with you!?"

He groggily pushed himself up on his elbows, staring at him. "I don't know what came over me. I saw that poor animal's hide cooking and . . ."

Dom's sudden rage slowly cooled and he reached down for his hand, hauling him to his feet. "Well, I daresay this business is pretty grotesque if you're not used to it." He glanced at Chandler on his horse, roping a calf. A new stab of anger went through him when he remembered he had been several years older before he'd learned to rope.

Before he could scream at Caldwell again, he noted his father observing him from astride Beckett, his features creased with an emotion he couldn't name but did not wish to have unleashed on him. He hastily reached out to lay his hand on his friend's arm. "I apologize for yelling. Do you think you can buck up so we can carry on now?"

Caldwell grinned in relief. "We employ anesthetic when we geld our horses," he said in explanation. "I'll do my best to stiffen my spine as my father has often requested me to do".

Dom noted with irritation that Chandler had deftly settled his lariat around a calf's hind legs and waited to haul it to the fire. Caldwell stepped forward with another cowboy, gamely helping him immobilize the beast on the ground.

When the branding iron was applied amid a sizzling cloud of smoke, Caldwell threw his head back to stare into the sky but he held his ground and didn't waver again the remainder of the morning. Indeed he was soon quite adept at the routine and was eager to take on other ranch work such as haying, repairing irrigation ditches, and mending fences. By the end of August, he was as tan and as fit as any of the other cowboys.

Dom had acquitted himself well during his first summer back from the east so felt that he and Caldwell deserved a break before the fall work commenced. Damien agreed to them spending a week in Cheyenne and they rode to town the first Saturday in September.

# CHAPTER EIGHT

## September 1887 – January 1900

Upon reaching Cheyenne, Dom and Caldwell rode to The Plains where they booked rooms for the week. After dinner, they discussed plans for the night. After plying Caldwell with a quantity of brandy, Dominique persuaded him to join him at The Green Door.

As they entered the front hall of the brothel, Clara Lou spotted them from an upstairs hall and came racing down to launch herself at Dom, throwing her legs around his waist as she clung to his neck, kissing him as if she wished to devour him.

"Good, Lord!" He protested, grasping her arms to place her away from him.

"So sorry but I'm just ever so happy to see you!" She clasped him to her again with a little squeal. "It's been soooo . . . long. I was wondering if you'd decided you didn't like me anymore."

"You know that would never happen." He put her firmly back from him again and held her there with a hand spanning her side. "Tell me, is the madam hosting a game tonight?"

"Indeed."

"Can I get in?"

"I 'spect so. Wait here and I'll ask." She dashed out of sight along a hall and was just as quickly back to escort them to the gaming parlor.

Madam Charleen, resplendent in royal blue silk displaying an amazing expanse of cleavage, swept up from the table to greet them and they were soon seated on either side of her. She called for the waiter to bring bourbon and made introductions to the other players who took in their youth with barely-concealed glee.

Though Caldwell had some experience playing poker with his father's business associates, this was Dom's initial foray into gambling. He soon proved he was possessed of astonishing beginner's luck. By two o'clock in the morning, he'd managed to relieve the others of five hundred dollars.

Ecstatic, he was eager to take Clara Lou upstairs but had the presence of mind to wait long enough to find out what Caldwell wished to do. "Would you like to meet one of Clara Lou's friends?"

Caldwell threw up his hands in good-natured refusal. "Oh, no, thank you. I've had quite enough fun for one night so I'm off to my lonely bed." He gave Dom's arm a fond squeeze. "You've had ripping good fortune tonight. I'll look forward to seeing you in the morning." With a jaunty grin, he turned to the rear door.

Dom watched his departure with some misgiving. He'd wanted to show him the kind of good time like they'd often enjoyed at Harvard. It'd not gone as he'd planned but ended with Caldwell short a month's wages that were now in his own pocket. He felt badly about that even as he was still delighted that he'd done so well at the gaming table. He thought he should follow Caldwell and try to make amends but Clara Lou was waiting and he soon headed up the stairs.

Later, Dom tried his best to rekindle goodwill with his friend and convince him to return to the game the next evening, but he'd had his fill of revelry in Cheyenne and decided to save his money and return to the serenity of the country.

Dom was sad to see him go, yet happy enough to continue his carousing alone. The luck that had graced his first attempts at gambling continued and when he finally returned to *Rancha Mariposa,* he brought with him a full purse and a growing appetite to return to the gaming table at every opportunity.

He soon fell into the habit of riding to Cheyenne once or twice a week, playing poker long into the night, then returning to take up his duties at the ranch, usually not in prime condition after consuming too much alcohol. The money Aunt Pris had gifted him declined at an alarming rate, yet he refused to curtail his gaming. Though he slumped into a fearful existence where the newfound joy and confidence he had brought home with him from college had faded, he managed somehow to keep up with his ranch work. Much of the time, he was physically impaired by lack of sleep and debilitating hangovers, yet he struggled on, holding grimly to the hope his luck would soon return.

His friendship with Caldwell suffered the same fate as had his relationship with Arthur years earlier. Caldwell was much more serious and sensible than Dom and quickly tired of his chase after raucous entertainment. He preferred to concentrate on his work at *Rancha Mariposa* and making friends there. Ironically, he and Arthur became friends and when Laura bore a son, Ashley, in the fall of 1899, he was asked to be his godfather since the Wheelers were of the Episcopalian faith.

Dom's debacle was the only thing marring the peace at *Rancha Mariposa* as Wyoming neared the end of the 1800s. He guarded his secret so rabidly no one suspected how much he was suffering.

By winter, he was in a devil of a financial fix, having depleted all of Aunt Pris' gift and run up a sizable debt as a result of Madam Charleen's liberal credit policy. She'd been generous in paying his gambling losses and by November, he found he personally owed her more than ten thousand dollars.

He could well imagine the mortification he would experience if he went to his father, yet time was running out. He was unable to try recouping because Madam Charleen had curtailed his access to her tables until he paid his debt in full. It wasn't likely that he'd ever be able to win back the total amount in any case as his monthly wages wouldn't cover his initial stake.

Aunt Pris and Harper wished to celebrate the enduring prosperity and happiness that had so blessed the Carrolls and Whittakers since their arrival from England. Harper and Damien would soon reach their Chrystal wedding anniversary and Damien's fifty-third birthday also neared so they resolved to celebrate the two events with a huge ball at the *Mariposa* on New Year's Eve, 1900. Weeks before, Mrs. Goodeve began planning the extravagant menu while Adare shepherded his staff in a massive cleaning of the mansion from top to bottom.

Granville Carroll would be arriving for the ball and planned to stay on for a year or two. As usual, he'd be taking Harper's latest art with him when he returned to Europe. Both Harper and Delaney were possessed of greater anticipation of his coming visit because Delaney had completed some watercolors her mother thought of sufficient quality to be included in the collection they'd be showing to Granville. They'd both worked hard in Harper's studio as well as out of doors during the years since Granville's last visit.

During good weather, they'd loved riding Destino and Avalon out along the stream beds where they sketched the cattle, the horses turned out to pasture, wildlife and the three beagles that now lived at the ranch. After Cooper died at Jose Martinez's hand, Riley was still in residence. A year or two later, another female puppy named Rumor came to live and to everyone's delight, had litters of beagle babies that had been given to a dozen new owners, most at the ranch. Finally, Huckleberry had arrived.

Delaney delighted in capturing the merry little dogs in a variety of watercolors that beguiled everyone who saw them. She'd sold a dozen of them before Harper intervened and insisted she save the rest to show to Granville.

While Harper concentrated on grand, abstract canvases, Delaney explored the gardens in various seasons. She visited the barns and stables to render comical likenesses of goats, chicken, geese, foals, calves, milk cows and pigs.

Caldwell was quite fascinated by the art produced by both of them and tended to tag along on their excursions outside and came to the studio to watch as Harper's sketches became amazing paintings. As Delaney added final touches to her carefree watercolors, she told him he should try drawing and painting himself. For some time, he begged off with the excuse that he couldn't spare the time, but eventually, he joined them on an odd Sunday and discovered he harbored some artistic talent.

Delaney was overjoyed at his success and appointed herself as his instructor. Harper watched their interaction with amusement but didn't interfere unless she noticed Delaney, in her enthusiasm, imparting incorrect information at which point, she offered mild correction so Caldwell didn't pick up any bad habits.

Aside from his attention to art, he also became infatuated with Anne Carroll who presently became as attentive as he. At nineteen she was the image of her mother, tall and lissome, with a great, curly mane of pale blonde hair that fell to her waist in shiny waves. She'd been indistinguishable from her twin Olivia when they were girls but now they looked quite different. Olivia, though, beautiful in her own right, lacked the sparkle of fun that lay in the depths of Anne's jade eyes.

Observing her and Caldwell together, no one could quite fathom the attraction from her point of view. While she was altogether fetching, Caldwell was far from handsome with his exceedingly tall, somewhat ungainly build, a long Roman nose and dark hair that always appeared unkempt. Yet, his generous and caring nature and droll good humor were quite irresistible to Anne who found him to be the most interesting person she'd ever encountered.

As for him, he adored the ground she walked on. Despite Dom's loyalty to both, he watched their flourishing relationship with jealous ill-will. He'd long since tired of his rough and tumble liaison with Clara Lou and buried his emotions in his imprudent longing for Yvette.

As was her customary habit, Aunt Pris organized a shopping expedition to Cheyenne to outfit the *Rancha Mariposa* ladies with the very latest ball gowns for the New Year's ball. During the decade preceding the end of the century, the focus in ladies fashions had switched slowly from the skirt to the bodice. Skirts grew plainer while bodices exploded with layers and frills, becoming either short at the hip, or long as jackets.

By 1899, sleeves had slimmed considerably and the corset had changed to the S curve. Skirts had grown narrow in front.

Social gaieties were at their height and the question of ball gowns was one of serious import for women of all ages. Thin fabrics were the most fashionable and the embroidery and trims were marvelous.

Harper chose a dress featuring the popular S shape with a very tiny waist that accentuated her svelte figure. The designer had employed a novel fancy pairing of chiffon and *mousseline de soie* with the sleekest satin. The delightful gown in primrose featured a plunging décolletage and long, snug sleeves that set off Harper's slender arms.

Now on New Year's Eve, 1899, she and Damien sat at the head of the extended dining table at *Mariposa,* as guests of honor. After weeks of concentrated effort, Aunt Pris hosted the event to celebrate Damien and Harper's anniversary and the beginning of the new century.

At the conclusion of the prime rib of beef dinner, Harper looked out over the gathering of their family and friends. Aunt Pris reigned over the proceedings from her seat next to Granville Carroll halfway down the table.

Damien smiled at Harper, then whispered in her ear. "You look so lovely tonight, my darling. I can scarcely wait to dance with you. Remember, all the balls of our youth?"

Smiling, she kissed him. "How could I forget? You were my knight."

"And you, my lady, as you are this evening."

She touched the pearl and cameo necklace he'd given her earlier, a fine compliment for the enticingly low neckline of her gown. Watching her, he lifted one hand, tracing a finger about the delicately-carved image. "Did I tell you, this lady is Athena the Huntress?"

"Yes, you did. I love her. And I cherish you."

"The feeling is mutual, my dear." He held her face in his hands, his mouth settling on hers. After perhaps a minute, he considered her musingly.

She was abruptly aware of everyone watching them and laughed softly. Their guests applauded and Damien, unfazed, raised his glass to them.

Adare and Roddy presently served champagne and toasts were soon underway. Lifting her glass, Aunt Pris spoke first. "Since we arrived here in Wyoming a bit less than twenty-five years ago, we've been blessed with unending opportunity. We have succeeded in grand fashion, not only monetarily but in our loving interactions with family and friends. During our quest, we've had the most honorable leadership from Damien and Harper, John and Audra, and our treasured friend Jamie. More than a dozen children have been born since we arrived here, and will now enjoy the vast opportunities of living as citizens of the United

States of America." Glasses were raised around the table amid a clamor of approval.

John lifted his glass next. "To our dear friends Damien and Harper who are celebrating fifteen years of marriage."

"Thank all of you so very much," Damien said. "We are blessed and honored to be here with you this evening. And we are deeply grateful for all the years we've worked side by side with all of you as we made our dream here a reality. America and Wyoming have been very good to us and we look with great anticipation to the coming years as we watch our families carve out their own futures as vital parts of *Rancha Mariposa* and the Hereford beef industry that we had such a large role in creating here. I believe as my cherished father Moreton Whittaker observes us this evening from the afterlife, he is filled with huge pride and shares the joy of our huge accomplishment. After all, it was he who first had the vision that we have all lived over the past twenty-five years."

Granville and a few others offered their own toasts. When silence settled over the gathering, Harper reached out to slide her arms around Chandler and Delaney who stood between their parents. "And now, let's all continue to celebrate upstairs in the ballroom," she said in gay invitation, smiling at the children who both hugged her.

Damien reached for her hand and they headed toward the staircase with Delaney and Chandler marching behind. In the ballroom, a military band from Fort Russell already played. Damien swept Harper onto the dance floor and other couples quickly followed, creating a grand tapestry of sumptuous ball gowns in rich winter hues of claret, sapphire, turquoise, emerald, jade, viridian, rose, topaz, aquamarine, peacock, garnet and heliotrope.

Harper felt as young and carefree as she had years ago when she danced with Damien in the ballroom at Willow Rook in Herefordshire the night he'd asked her to be his wife. How young and naïve she'd been that night despite having been wooed by him and his twin brother Brendon since she was a little girl.

Both Whittaker twins had treated her with the greatest care and respect. It was only when she'd chosen Damien and he asked her to marry him, that she discovered what it was like to be loved by a man who desired her body as well as her heart. She'd been caught off guard by the urgent physical need he stirred in her. Aunt Pris had told her it was improper for women to have such feelings so she'd tried to deny them but Damien hadn't allowed that.

He'd told her she must never listen to Aunt Pris about such things and he wanted her to enjoy their physical love as much as he did. Soon enough, he had stirred such passion in her, she'd desired him just as much as he lusted after her.

It was then, in the midst of their greatest happiness that Peggy Abbot had betrayed them and stolen Damien from her, forcing her to marry Brendon in order to follow Damien to America. Ten years had passed before they could finally marry and now that was fifteen years ago.

And at last, after such suffering and loss, that part of their life was over, and they were together again. They had lost those ten dreadful years but they still had the future. They still had Dom and were to become the parents of two more beautiful children, their Delaney and Chandler. They were so very blessed.

Damien studied Harper. She was no longer the girl he'd been destined to marry. Now she was nearly forty years older, yet she was still so beautiful it sometimes made his heart hurt. A few silver strands threaded through the black tumble of her hair that had enchanted him from the time she was a tiny little girl.

He tightened his embrace, pressing her close to his body, fitting her head into the hollow beneath his chin. "Ah, my darling, I could stay here forever, floating within your orbit."

She sighed contentedly. "What an enticing notion." Lifting her face to his, she looked into his dynamic face, glorying in the reciprocal tug of arousal in her lower stomach.

He shifted a little, sliding his arm around to curve her to him, his mouth growing hard, urgent. Groaning, he insinuated his tongue past her lips, amazed at her eager response, the yielding hunger of her mouth, her total surrender that even now, after so many years as her lover, occasionally caught him off guard.

"Good Lord," he breathed when he pulled back a little. Lamplight shot scintillating lights through the fathomless amethyst depths of her eyes. "I remain convinced that you bewitched me with your lavender eyes when I first saw you having tea in Aunt Pris's parlor all those years ago."

"You are absolutely correct about that, my dear," she said with a toss of her head.

"You conducted yourself like you were sixteen that day. No wonder Delaney has always comported herself like someone much older."

"We Whittaker women have been eternally ahead of our time."

Grinning, he guided her to the edge of the ballroom as the music ended. "Would you like something to drink?"

"Lovely. I'll just sit here a little." She stepped to a bench where Delaney and Millie sat side by side in their party dresses of claret and emerald velvet, their long hair dressed with small sprays of white silk forget-me-nots. Harper settled between them. "Are you two having fun?"

"Tonight is so beautiful," Delaney said. "It's fun watching everyone dance. Especially you and Pa-pa. Your dress is gorgeous and Pa-pa looks so dashing."

"Caldwell and Anne look nice tonight," Millie remarked as the pair twirled past. "I love the shade of Anne's gown."

Harper took in the sky blue satin that fit her shapely young figure like a glove, a garland of ivory silk roses caught about her tiny waist. Slim cream evening gloves accented her slender arms. "Ah, she is so very pretty." She examined the information that had gradually seeped into her mind. It seemed like there would be another wedding in the spring.

As she glanced across the room in search of Damien, she spotted Olivia, Anne's twin, lovely in orchid satin, on the arm of an attractive young man she didn't recognize. If their animated interaction was any indication, they appeared to be quite taken with one another. "Does Olivia have a new boyfriend?"

"Oh, no, that's just Jackson. He's Laura's brother who's been at Yale, becoming a lawyer. When he graduates in the spring, he's going to work for his father, Mr. Quinn."

"Who's going to work for Mr. Quinn?" Damien asked, arriving with champagne for himself and Harper, punch for the girls. He sat beside Delaney, serving the drinks from a tray.

"Jackson." Delaney answered.

"Ah, yes, I spoke with him earlier. Seems a fine chap."

Harper laughed at the sight of Chandler dancing Sawyer across the floor. Even at nine, dressed in a small tuxedo, he already had the lean, finely-cut features of his father. He guided Sawyer masterfully through the waltz, having learned his dancing lessons well from Arthur who decided he and Finn should be instructed in the basics of social etiquette as part of their education.

A year younger, Sawyer was a rather odd-looking child, her hair still the brilliant orange she was born with. She'd lost none of the freckles that abundantly dusted her face, and since she was in the process of losing her baby teeth, she possessed an engaging gap-toothed smile. Just as Chandler had inherited his father's charm and ease of movement, Sawyer, too, had much of Dom's grace.

Smiling at the miniature dancers' antics, Damien glanced at Harper. "What joy it is to watch our granddaughter take her first steps into the big wide world. I never asked, was it a blow to your feminine allure to have a grandchild when you were only thirty-five?" He nuzzled the bare expanse of her elegant neck.

She arched an eyebrow. "My dear Mr. Whittaker, I don't recall suffering a decline. Who could resent the arrival of such a delightful little cabbage as our Sawyer?"

"You are a remarkably sensible lady."

Sawyer's five-year-old sister, Doreen, suddenly appeared next to Chandler and began persistently tapping him on the shoulder. After this continued for a short time, he stepped back, bowing to Sawyer before taking Doreen's hand and drawing her with him as he continued the waltz.

Sawyer, looking slightly bewildered, spotted Damien and came to stand by him. "Doreen took my Chandler."

Harper clasped her hand. "Sometimes that happens during a ball."

Sawyer leaned her head against Damien, staring up at him before turning her gaze back to the dancers. "I was having fun."

He hugged her as she clambered onto his lap where he cradled her tenderly. "I think he'll want to dance with you again before long."

She pondered him gravely. "All right then, I'll rest here."

True to his word, Chandler soon led Doreen toward them, reaching out to claim Sawyer before abandoning Doreen to Harper who cuddled her for a time while they watched as the two joined the dancing once more.

Damien chuckled. "Ah, the romantic intrigue that's in store for us in the future."

Harper's heart filled with the wonder of the coming years within their amazing family. Still holding Doreen, she slid her arms around Delaney and Millie.

Presently, the older girls joined the dancing and Luke arrived to collect his younger daughter who'd dozed off. "Time for bed, little one," he said, lifting her into his arms. "Wonderful party," he added before heading out.

"Thank you, dear. I hope you're not leaving so early."

"No, as soon as I get our girls to bed, I'll be back so Ivy and I can enjoy the rest of the evening." While Doreen slept on his shoulder, he veered to gather Sawyer from where she dozed next to Chandler, who'd put his arm around her.

Damien and Harper soon returned to the dance floor where they remained until the servants laid out a lavish late supper on long tables. The platters and tureens offered the seafood Mrs. Goodeve had ordered from New York along with a vast assortment of savory canapes, desserts, thick soups and hot chocolate with the option of adding brandy or bourbon.

Aunt Pris was ensconced with Belle Henning in chairs close to the fireplace. Harper went to speak to them, thanking Belle for the book on herbal cures she'd presented to her and Damien as an anniversary present.

"It is my great pleasure to be here with you and your family on such an auspicious occasion."

"We adore having you with us. You must know that you're responsible for Damien and I having reached fifteen years of marriage."

The old woman peered at her with the snapping gentian eyes that had once intimidated Harper before she learned what an ancient, wise soul she possessed. "How's that?"

"Your medicine brought down Damien's fever after he was beaten by Jose Martinez and was near death."

Belle absorbed this, eventually nodding in remembrance. "I do recall that now. I'm happy I could help."

"It was life changing."

Once the food had been consumed, everyone gathered before the tall windows, looking down into the front garden, lying in its winter sleep. Three stable lads moved about in the glow from the lamps and suddenly a huge spray of fireworks erupted, spreading over the house as the revelers gasped and clapped.

The explosive spectacle, a gift from Granville, continued for half an hour, a glorious mix of brilliant sparkling colors shooting into the winter night. When the finale came at last, it was a seemingly endless intermingling of pinwheels in every bright color spinning in overlapping spirals until the last upsurge that spread out and hung in the air for an extended heartbeat of time before it gradually dissipated into darkness.

The older children who remained up jumped about in a delighted reaction, approaching the windows to peer out in case there was something out there still. The band struck up *The Star Spangled Banner* and everyone began singing the lyrics as they stood with hands pressed to their hearts.

Once the brief tribute was over, a grandfather clock in the hall struck midnight and the gathering broke out in applause followed by a general round of hugs and kisses. As his mouth broke from hers, Damien looked intently into Harper's face. "To 1900, darling, our best year ever."

The band merged into *Auld Lang Syne* and couples began dancing once more. Caught in introspection, they softly sang the melancholy song as they held each other. Harper laid her head on Damien's shoulder, tears filling her eyes. Not tears of sadness but of gratitude and joy as she reflected on her good luck at being at this place in time with the man that she'd loved forever.

They'd weathered much difficulty during their years together. And now, they stood on the edge of great accomplishment and hope.

John and Audra approached after a while and they switched partners, then did the same with Jamie and Eliza, Luke and Ivy, Arthur and Laura. Finally Granville came to claim Harper for a dance.

"What a splendid evening, my dear," he said as he masterfully swept her into a waltz. "I am so honored to be here to share in your happiness."

"You are a vital part of our family and our life here so we certainly couldn't celebrate without you."

"I'm honored."

"Have you given more thought to moving here permanently? I know that has been on your mind for a long time."

"As a matter of fact, I have been considering it more seriously of late. I'm thinking I may wish to return to Herefordshire once more to put my affairs in order and, of course, ensure that you have a continuing market for your art in Europe. After that, I would take up residence here at *Rancha Mariposa* and only travel to England when business dictates."

Harper smiled with happiness at his words. "Oh, that is so magnificent, Granville! Have you told John and Audra?"

"I told them that it was a distinct possibility. As a matter of fact, I made up my mind as I enjoyed the festivities this evening. Why would I ever want to live in England when there is so much joy waiting for me here?"

"Precisely my thought," she declared, leaning up to kiss his weathered cheek. "We so love having you here and to have it a permanent situation will be a titanic blessing."

"You flatter me."

"It's absolutely true." As the music came to an end, she curtsied. "Thank you so much."

"My great pleasure, Harper." With a bow, he released her hand.

She rejoined Damien, scanning the crowd for Dom. She hadn't seen him since dinner but soon spotted him lounging on a bench where Yvette sat on Bethany's lap at the other end.

He attempted talking to Yvette but she was so tired she lay against her sister, hardly acknowledging him. Harper made her way toward them.

Dom glanced up when she approached. "Harper, what an ace party! Are you having a wonderful time?"

"Indeed, I am but my evening wouldn't be complete without dancing with you."

She thought she saw the hint of a scowl but he quickly rose and offered his arm. As they made their way onto the dance floor, she was nearly staggered by the smell of bourbon emanating from him.

He drew her into his arms and propelled her into the rhythm of the music. "Hard to believe you and Pa-pa have been married for fifteen years," he observed in an attempt at conversation.

"It is, though it doesn't seem nearly that long to me. I adored your father from the moment I saw him when I was four. I think I knew even then what a lovely life we would have together. And I was absolutely right."

"My mother must've caused you a lot of grief."

"Yes, but we always knew we would end up together so that made it a bit easier to get through that awful time."

"Are you even sad that my mother ended up insane while you have this brill life?"

She studied him, trying to read the direction of his thoughts. "Your mother was always jealous of me and coveted what was mine, and that included your father. So what happened after she tried to steal him from me was merely the consequence of her stepping into territory where she didn't belong. The only good thing that came out of her treachery is you."

"But wouldn't you have rather had Eddie live instead of me?"

"Dom, you are as dear to me as my own sons."

"I've never believed that." His voice was slurred by alcohol, his gaze unsteady.

"It doesn't matter to me what you believe. I'm telling you the truth. I don't know what is happening in your life just now but it seems to me you're very unhappy!"

The music ended and they returned to the bench. "As I was saying, you haven't been yourself for some time. When you returned from Harvard, you were so happy and confident, we were all delighted and thought you were on your way to the life you deserved at last. But soon enough, you appeared to sink back into the misery and discontent that seems to have plagued so much of your life."

His mouth twisted into the same frown that she'd seen so often when she confronted him about some unappealing subject over the years.

She touched his arm. "Maybe I can help if you tell me what is wrong."

Shaking his head, he averted his gaze to the windows. "There's nothing wrong."

She wrapped her arms around him, trying to ignore his atrocious breath. "Darling, I love you so. If you won't let me help, please be careful. Now it's time you got some sleep. Come, I'll walk you to the stairs."

He groaned but let her escort him. "Just one more glass of bourbon," he said when they passed the serving table.

"No more bourbon. You need to go to sleep." When they stood at the top of the staircase, she paused and he put his arms around her.

"Thank you, Harper. I love you."

"Goodnight, darling." She watched his unsteady progress down the steps.

"What did our number one son have to say for himself?"

She glanced at Damien beside her. "He said nothing is wrong."

"That is what he told me also. I did my best to find out what's troubling him but he stonewalled me. What do you make of our challenging young son?"

She collected her thoughts for a moment. "Something's causing him pain. I feel so badly for him. When he first came home, I thought that all of his private suffering was behind him."

"As did I."

"Oh, dear," Harper said as they turned back to their guests. Dom wasn't the only one who'd had too much to drink. Jessica Quinn appeared to have passed out in a chair near a fireplace.

They hurried to her. Arthur and Laura tried without much success to revive her.

Harper approached Aunt Pris and asked for her smelling salts, then returned to Mrs. Quinn. She held the vial beneath her nose but got no response.

"It's no use," Arthur decided. "I'll just carry her down." With efficiency born of long practice in dealing with his mother-in-law's excessive drinking, he drew her up into his arms and proceeded downstairs with Theodore and Laura, thin and pale in late pregnancy, close behind.

As she saw them disappear, Harper thought again what a tragedy it was their family was afflicted with such a heart-rending condition. She hadn't seen Jessica at a social event for several months as she was kept isolated most of the time lately so she wouldn't embarrass her family. "What a lonely, hopeless life she must lead," she said when Damien took her hand.

"It's hard to imagine," he agreed, leading her back towards the band.

All of the children, even Delaney and Millie, were in bed; Aunt Pris and Granville had retired. Harper and Damien and the remaining guests continued dancing until after three, when those staying the night at *Mariposa* descended to their rooms in the gallery readied with fires kindled much earlier. The servants had also warmed the beds and provided hot water for the washstands.

Stable lads arrived in the piazza with carriages to transport the Carrolls and their guests to Trail's End. When Damien had closed the front door after the final visitor, he turned to Harper waiting nearby and held out his arms to her. "Happy Anniversary, darling."

She stepped eagerly to him, kissing him with all the pent-up desire of the night. "Take me to bed," she finally begged.

He obliged by picking her up and carried her up the staircase, his heart pounding more from arousal than exertion. Outside their bedchamber, she reached to turn the doorknob and he crossed to the bed in two strides, laying her tenderly on the linen that had been turned down and nicely heated.

With her arms still wound about his neck, she pulled him down with her, her mouth meeting his in ravenous need. She lost all sense of time, aware of nothing but his love pouring over her in an enchantment of sensation and sound. As he slid off her gown and then, her gauzy under things, one piece at a time in a slow erotic unveiling, he spoke to her, spinning the web of her desire as he'd done a thousand times.

As he removed the pins, her hair tumbled about her shoulders and his fingers combed through it before he held her head steady, his mouth teasing, devouring. She arched her body, desperate for his intimate touch as his hands spanned her waist, then roved lower, moving over each rib before reaching the center of her pleasure. He finally kissed her where his fingers probed.

She moaned with ever greater need. Damien's loving had grown familiar over all the years they'd been together. Always pleasurable and renewing but sometimes routine.

This night was new. She felt every nuance of his kiss and touch with acute sensitivity that flowed along each nerve, leaving her trembling on the edge of completion. The act of taking, his body merging with hers was so unbearably sweet, she cried out as her nails raked his back. When at last, they both reached the glorious end of it, she lay utterly spent in his arms.

He lifted himself onto one arm, using the other to gently brush the hair from her face. "My darling, I cherish you with every fiber of my being. I can think of nothing more splendid than spending the next fifteen years at your side."

"Only fifteen? You may be interested to know I plan to live to a hundred. Perhaps longer."

He grinned at her in the lamplight. "Do you really? Well, then, I daresay I'll have to adjust my expectations."

She burrowed close to him as the fire died down to a rosy glow.

# CHAPTER NINE

## January 1900 – May 1907

During the first days of the new century, heavy snows swept over the ranch headquarters. The weather made travel to Cheyenne impossible so Dom had no choice about staying at home. With his debt preventing any gaming, he concluded perhaps it was fortuitous that he was stuck in the country, working hard every day with the other men to keep the Herefords fed and watered.

Harper used the isolation to concentrate on her art in preparation for Granville's last journey back to Herefordshire. He'd been enthusiastic about her sizable inventory of rather dark, somber works completed during the grim months following the Invasion. His opinion had proved to be a valid reading of buyers' fancies and all the work had sold since he delivered them to the galleries after his most recent stay in Wyoming.

Now he recommended that she produce more of the same for him to take back with him when he departed for Herefordshire once again in March. However, with the return of good fortune to *Rancha Mariposa* and the sparing of Damien and John from severe punishment for their part in the Invasion, Harper's heart sang and she was incapable of getting in touch with the dismal emotions that had inspired the bleak images that sold so readily.

"Well, then, you must listen to your heart as always," he conceded when he sat in her studio in mid-January.

Tossing her head, she came to join him on a sofa. "Oh, thank you. I don't want to disappoint you but I simply cannot find that joyless place where my mind resided for so long."

"No worries," he said, considering her wryly. "It was gratifying to sell your last paintings so readily but I much prefer seeing you so blissful once again." He gave her hand a reassuring squeeze.

"What of Delaney's work?" She asked, pointing to a watercolor of the beagles on a nearby easel.

He studied the picture. "It's absolutely charming and I foresee nothing but success for her should she choose to continue painting. As for her present work, I fear it lacks the sophistication to compete in the European art market. That is not to say it won't be viable in time, but for now, I feel we should let her gift develop while she pursues her other interests. Once I've returned from Herefordshire, I would cherish the chance to give her lessons, and at which time I feel her work is competitive, I will be delighted to put it on the market." He lifted his kind gaze to Harper. "Does that sound reasonable?"

"Yes, it does. You're very wise. While Damien and I want her to have every opportunity for success, we also want her to work at her own pace. And as you know, she has other aspirations. She wants to ride in competition."

He smiled drolly. "I must say, I'm eager to see her pursue that goal. Can you imagine what a grand sight the two of them will make. Her so tiny and striking astride her huge beast of a hunter. I predict they will be formidable in competition."

"I agree. I never realized when she was born that she would wish to pursue such adventures."

"She's such a gutsy little maid," he agreed. "Much like her mother."

A gratifying period of calm and prosperity held *Rancha Mariposa* as the new century progressed. When word reached the ranch that Queen Victoria had died at eighty-one, Aunt Pris insisted on having everyone in both houses gather for a mourning tea in her honor. The group convened in the *Mariposa* parlor and Granville read stories about the queen's life and her funeral from *The Illustrated London News* that he'd subscribed to since moving to Wyoming.

Harper was saddened by the death of the portly queen whom she'd seen in parades and appearances on the Buckingham Palace terrace several times as a girl. She had always adored the pomp and ceremony of public outings by the royal family. She particularly loved seeing the gorgeous black and white horses with their plumed bridles that pulled the various royal conveyances.

Edward the Seventh, the eldest son of Victoria, succeeded his mother as king. According to Granville, he was already famous for his mistresses, said in many circles to number more than a dozen.

Aunt Pris simpered at hearing this news and allowed that she doubted any child of Victoria would stoop to marital infidelity. Granville dared propose that King Edward the Seventh would likely be best remembered for his philandering.

Vast changes swept across Wyoming with the turn of the century. The hired men at *Rancha Mariposa* concentrated on the usual ranch work as well as new projects to keep pace with these transformations. Because the days of the open range were long past, the entire ranch was enclosed by fences.

This work took several years to complete and was carried on in all seasons save winter. The materials were hauled to the far corners of the land in wagons pulled by Shires. Because of the large distances that had to be dealt with, the men once again began using the many line shacks built during the years of open grazing.

Now the crude buildings contained beds, rough though they were, so the men weren't required to return to the ranch headquarters each night. Indeed, most returned only when more wire and posts were required.

As ranch manager, Dom chose a number of crew bosses from among the men to supervise the fencing as well as expansion of the irrigation ditches and the construction of additional hay corrals. All of the improvements were directed at increasing the efficiency of feeding the Herefords.

Caldwell asked for a fencing position and was sent to a remote location beyond Horse Creek where he labored in relative solitude with a few other men. He enjoyed the hard work and the casual camaraderie. The physical toil was a welcome balance to his quest to become a serious artist. When he wasn't occupied with the ranch work, he spent hours painting under the tutelage of Harper and Delaney.

Once the fences traced the outer contours of *Rancha Mariposa,* the work was concentrated closer to the headquarters where the land was divided into small paddocks and pastures. It was during this final phase of work that Anne Carroll began driving a buggy out to bring Caldwell lunch or baked treats that she had made herself.

When he'd first come to *Rancha Mariposa,* he'd met the Carrolls and had enjoyed conversations with most all the daughters at various social events. He thought them a fetching lot but it was Anne who made the greatest impression. Tall with a delicate build and lovely features, she was perhaps similar in looks to her twin Olivia, yet in personality, the two were very different.

Olivia had struck Caldwell as being insipid and even a little vacuous, prone as she was to fits of giggles whenever she was flustered. On the other hand, Anne was a serious and elegant girl who wore her shiny mane of blonde hair loose over her slight shoulders.

When the fencing was completed and he was back at the headquarters, she sometimes stopped to admire Caldwell's sketches when he worked outside in the evening or early morning. They often spent some time talking about art in general and he'd realized to his delight that she knew a great deal about the subject. She adored Mary Cassatt's work and one day, brought out a book of her paintings to show him.

"I'd love to paint like her," she'd said wistfully as they paged through the book together. "Look at all these lovely faces of women and girls, mothers and daughters and sisters."

"They're very nice indeed," he agreed and from that day forward, they enjoyed a bond begun by their mutual love of art that gradually became their united quest

Within a few months, he'd coaxed her to try painting herself and in the ensuing years, whenever the weather grew colder and winter took over the ranch, they spent all their idle hours in Harper's studio. As they worked together, their art improved dramatically and they fell in love.

Their new status happened so slowly and easily, it was 1907 before they decided it was time they shared their good fortune and joy with all their friends and family. Naturally, they confided in Harper first, and of course, she wasn't the slightest bit surprised.

Caldwell traveled to Denver to buy Anne a delicate diamond ring that caused her to cry with happiness when he gave it to her upon his return. They set the date for their wedding for the autumn.

Dom was given a reprieve and eventual deliverance from his financial fix when his father sent him on his first official business outside of Wyoming as spokesman for *Rancha Mariposa.* A week after the Hereford calving was finished in May, 1907, the men turned their attention to the crossbreds, organizing their private roundups within the vast fenced ranges of their property.

On the final day, Damien asked Dom to ride home with him. "I must say after losing stock for over twenty years, it still strikes me as curious when our count comes up to expectations. I daresay I'm experiencing the uneasy sense of security his victims must feel when the school bully is expelled."

"I doubt the Holts and Martinez would've ever gotten the best of you, sir. You and John had slowed up the rustling considerably."

He nodded glum agreement. "I know it's irrational but I'm occasionally plagued by the notion that there may be yet another Holt lurking about, ready to begin stealing from us again."

Dom observed him, incredulous. "Since the land has been sold, I'm certain that won't happen."

Damien grinned. "I daresay, you're correct about that. In any case, I asked you to ride with me tonight because I have a job for you. We've reached the juncture where we're ready to begin selling off our crossbreds. I've consigned three thousand head of cows and calves to a man near Boulder, Colorado. I want you to make the delivery."

Dom's mind raced ahead. At last, here was his chance to redeem himself.

"You should be on the trail by June and you'll collect a nice bonus in Boulder. Is that agreeable with you?"

"More than agreeable, sir." He could scarcely keep his voice steady. Such a bonus would doubtless be sufficient to get him in a game in Colorado; he might well win enough to pay off his debt.

They discussed further details during the remainder of the ride. Upon reaching the *Mariposa,* they went to the parlor for a drink before dinner. Harper and the children waited there.

Harper stepped into Damien's arms, kissing him without reservation even as Delaney and Chandler waited for his attention. When he finally turned to them, Harper greeted Dom. "How were the roundups? Was our count still up?"

"No loss except for a few wolf kills. We found the partial carcasses."

"It's so nice to have this ranch enjoying the unfettered success like we had at the beginning of our venture here."

"It's been a long siege," Dom said, his gaze resting on his half-brother.

Almost sixteen, Chandler was fast becoming tall and elegant as he'd never possessed the awkwardness of adolescence Dom recalled from his own youth. For some reason, his brother's graceful bearing filled him with rage.

He shook his head in an attempt to clear it of the unworthy emotion. At present, he had no reason to feel badly about Chandler who still had to go to college before he could assume the kind of responsibility with which Damien entrusted Dom. Nonetheless, he couldn't dismiss his ill will as he watched his father interacting with his brother.

"Pa-pa is sending me to Colorado with the herd of crossbreds," he divulged to Harper.

"I know. He's very proud of the work you've done all winter."

"One can but try." He forced a smile, recalling how restive and filled with discontent he'd been during all the months he'd toiled with the rest in the calving sheds. Thank goodness for the deep snow that'd kept him from straying from his work because now he was being rewarded. There was no reason to be jealous of Chandler, he reminded himself once more.

"Chandler, have you said hello to your brother?" Harper prompted when he wandered over.

"Hello, Dom." With a wide smile, he politely extended his hand. "Did you have a good time on the roundups?"

"It was swell." He pulled him close in a one-armed hug.

"Pa-pa says I can help next year."

"You'll like that," he said even as it seemed an invasion of his personal territory that Chandler would soon be working with the men much as he'd done as he matured. His adult objectivity knew his attitude was unfair and of no particular importance but he was unable to push it aside.

As though she read the drift of his thoughts, Harper slipped her arm about his waist to pull him close as they followed Damien and Delaney to the dining table.

Final arrangements were made for the trail drive the second week in July and Dom was on his way to Boulder with the herd. Twenty cowboys rode out with him. Carlin, the elderly trail cook, had become too crippled with arthritis in recent years to continue working so had retired to a cottage along the Aspen.

Wally, another rather aged cook from Montana had been hired to take Carlin's place in the chuck wagon that rattled along beside the herd. The days on the trail were broiling hot, dusty and acutely disagreeable. Dom and his crew were overjoyed to reach their destination the first week in August.

They neared a ranch headquarters two miles south of Boulder in early afternoon. Dom was wondering if someone was home to take delivery of the herd when a horseman galloped out from the gathering of buildings among spreading cottonwoods along a winding creek. The rider stopped to speak to two or three of the lead cowboys before Dom was pointed out, then came the remaining distance. He reined in with a flourish, raising his hat, his rank mustang rearing and chomping the bit.

He was a dapper fellow no older than Dom. "Welcome, Mr. Whittaker. I've been looking for you for the past three days. I'm Sidney Wallace."

"Is your father home?"

"I'm afraid not. He had urgent business in Denver. When you didn't show up earlier, he had to go on. But he'll be back day after tomorrow to pay you. In the meantime, you can go into Boulder with me. We have a house there and I'll show you a whale of a time. For now, we've a fenced pasture back behind the barn so we'll just push these Ma-ma's in there and I'll have my men keep a close eye until we come out with my father on Thursday."

"I'll have my own men stay with them," Dom interjected. "Where can they make camp?"

"Down there in the meadow." He pointed vaguely, then with a whoop, wheeled his horse and tore back past the buildings, presumably to open a gate.

When he returned, he helped drive the cattle. Getting the beasts through the narrow opening in the fence was no small task but after a frustrating half hour, some of the lead cows deigned to pass through the gate and the rest soon followed.

After Dom gave the okay for ten of his men to ride to town, on the condition they should be back before midnight, the rest followed Wally and his chuck wagon to the camp site. Sidney was so eager to be off, he refused to let his guest even wash up in the dilapidated ranch house before the two departed.

The Wallaces' town residence was by no stretch of the imagination similar to the *Mariposa,* yet it was a large brick home, majestic when compared to their country quarters. "You'll want a bath," Sidney ventured when they stood in the front parlor. "The tub's at the end of the hall. You have suitable clothes in there?" He nodded to the warbag in which Dom carried what few personal items he'd brought with him.

"Suitable for what?"

He slanted a sardonic eyebrow at him. "Whatever you like. Dinner . . . girls . . . ?"

"Well, I've not brought a frock coat."

"Frock coat indeed." He chuckled, draping an arm over Dom's shoulders. "We seem to be similar in height and weight so let me lend you some things. Some pressed trousers and a jacket have got to be preferable to whatever's been wadded up in that bag since you left Wyoming."

"Thank you very much." Dom followed him to the bathroom. He enjoyed a long soak in the tub before dressing in the clothes

Sidney produced. By the time he was outfitted to his satisfaction, Sidney had also changed and led the way to the drawing room.

"You go to school somewhere, Whittaker?" He asked, pouring bourbon.

"I graduated from Harvard a couple years ago."

"Good show, old boy. The furthest east I've gotten is St. Louis."

"You were born here then?"

"Not *here* but at that ghastly house at the ranch. My mother died during the blessed event and I'm afraid my father hasn't been quite right since." He lifted a hand to forestall any sympathy Dom might have offered. "He's not a mental case or anything, just drinks himself senseless three or four times a week. Much too often, I admit. I've taken over more and more of the responsibility for the ranch and the situation works nicely to my advantage, if you get my meaning." He drained his glass, then refilled it and Dom's before stepping to a window to survey the street. "What shall we do tonight, my friend?"

Before Dom could answer, he rattled off a list of possible diversions, then declared in his agreeably presumptuous manner that they would have dinner and proceed from there. Within the hour, they were seated in a lavish dining room at the Boulderado Hotel. Sidney ordered bourbon and a variety of appetizers and they settled in to getting acquainted.

"So where did you father hail from?" Dom inquired.

"Upstate New York. Albany actually, where my grandfather owned a shipping company. My father had an older brother who inherited the family business. My father was required to seek a living elsewhere so he lived in New York City for a time and that's where he met my mother who'd come from England to work as a nanny. They married and came west to claim up a homestead and that was the beginning of our ranch here."

"I wondered where your English accent came from."

Sidney waved his hand dismissively. "Oh, that. By the time I was born, my father had picked up my mother's accent that rubbed off on me over the years. And where did your own accent originate?" He asked, prompting Dom to tell the story of his family.

"Well, I'm afraid we're nowhere near your upper crust status," Sidney concluded after he'd finished. "Still, luck's been with us. My father brought five herds of longhorns from Texas back in the day and that paid well. I'd like to buy some Herefords as I feel that's where the future lies in cattle ranching but so far, my father is adamant about sticking with the longhorns. So that's why we bought your stock," he said in conclusion, emptying his glass as he looked around for a waiter. "Well, now we need some food so we can get on with the evening."

He ordered steak for both of them but hurried Dom through the meal, eager to get on to a brothel at the edge of town. Once there, he threw himself at the entertainment with the same flighty approach as he'd eaten dinner. Much sooner than Dom would've preferred, they were outside and mounted on their horses, heading out again.

Accustomed to the leisurely service at The Green Door, Dom was put off at being rushed, particularly since he hadn't visited Charleen for months. And it appeared he was hurried back outside for nothing more pressing than sitting across from the perplexing Sidney in a dim tavern half a mile down the street. If this is what Sidney called a sporting evening, he might've given him some lessons.

Yet, he soon learned there was a reason for the mad dash from home to dinner, to bed, to the bar. Sidney held him in a long, contemplative gaze. "You ever enjoy a little friendly poker, my boy?"

"On occasion." He struggled to keep the excitement out of his voice.

"I know where there's a game on at eleven. You want in?"

"What's a stake?"

"Five thousand."

Dom sucked in his breath. "I won't have that kind of money until your father pays for the herd."

He fingered his mustache. "I'll stake you. If you do well, you can pay me later. If the night doesn't pan out, Thursday will be soon enough. I'll cover IOUs for as much as you like."

Dom considered the offer that seemed too enticing to pass up, yet his good sense warned him that it could turn out badly, putting him further in debt without any money to try recouping his losses in Cheyenne. He slugged down more bourbon while Sidney waited.

Finally, he was overcome by the hunger to play. It might well be foolhardy but if he didn't try, how was he ever to get his finances back on an even keel? "I'm in."

Sidney gave him a thumb's up and a dazzling smile. "Good man!"

The game in a dark little room was cast by a curious group—a paunchy, mutton-chopped man of indeterminate vocation; a tall, cadaverous speculator vaguely reminiscent in coloring and bearing to Jonathon Holt; the latter fellow's mistress who appeared deceptively brainless; Sidney and Dom. Bourbon flowed freely but wishing to keep his wits about him, Dom drank only enough to keep up appearances. He enjoyed modest success during the early hours, parlaying Sidney's stake into a bit over eight thousand dollars, yet with the passing of midnight, luck took flight. At two in the morning, he wrote his first IOU, promising himself that if his fortune didn't change, he would bail out after the very next hand.

He was forthwith dealt a straight flush but the rest were also graced by the gods. Betting proceeded briskly for two rounds of the table, then a slow battle of wits ensued. Dom had hoped his sobriety would give him a slight advantage but the others' mental acuity appeared not to have been hampered in the slightest by their impairment.

He was caught in a laborious test, no longer in control of himself and his reactions as he scribbled IOUs with no orders from his brain. Whenever the others' cards bested his, he rushed on, not heeding the clanging alarm in the distant reaches of his mind, nor Sidney's questioning looks across the table. He was helpless, hunting for the surge of exhilaration that always attended victory. When the rest stood up at four o'clock, he begged them to stay.

It was only when Sidney wrote out checks for all three of their fellow players, that reality crashed over Dom. He remained at the table, much too sober, the beginning of fear growing in him as the fat man, the skinny man and the loose woman filed out.

Sidney returned his check record back to his pocket and shoved back his chair. "Time to hit the hay, old boy. Tomorrow night, we'll have another go at these rounders."

Dom knew he already owed him a great deal of money but his offer of another chance to win back his losses stilled his panic, filling him with a giddy feeling of well-being. Still resembling a coiled spring even at the late hour, Sidney led the way to the horses outside

Having retired at five in the morning, they slept until dinner time the next day. At six o'clock, they once again set out in pursuit of entertainment; the evening proving to be a near repeat of last night.

After a quick supper and a fleeting stop at the same brothel, they again convened in the tiny room for another game. The players were the same. After an hour or two, Dom had the feeling of being trapped in a shadowy stage drama. He reacted, spoke, scrawled his name, all as if directed from something outside himself. Yet, tonight, he won two large pots. When the rest had left them, he was confident Sidney had been repaid with some to spare.

Sidney worked over a sheet. "Lady Luck smiled on you toward the end there," he said presently. "Quite a remarkable comeback, my man. You only owe me a bit over four thousand."

"Four thousand!?" Shock shoved into his brain like so many shards of ice. "How is that possible? I won over twenty thousand tonight."

"Indeed you did, old boy, but you were into me for twenty-five when we stopped yesterday. You should be well pleased to have chiseled that down to such a manageable sum. Come along now. We can't sleep the day away like yesterday because Father will be coming in on the train at ten. Now we can catch a few winks, then I'll buy you breakfast at a place near the depot."

Dom's thoughts stampeded toward the inevitable confrontation once he got home. When his father learned he'd not only spent every cent of his bonus but two thousand dollars of *Rancho Mariposa* funds besides, he would be outraged. And when Dom went on to ask him for ten thousand to pay Madam Charleen, he might well boot him right off the ranch. Dom's worry was apparently evident to Sidney as they dismounted and walked toward the town house in the dim light of dawn.

"You concerned about the money, old chap?"

"I simply won't have enough," he blurted, aware his circumstances couldn't deteriorate further.

"You told me you can take your bonus when Father pays up."

"I know but it's not that much."

They continued inside. "I trust you for my part," Sidney said, punching him on the arm. "You can send me a wire when you get home."

"You're very generous."

He stopped to scan Dom's haggard features. "There is another option. One that would benefit us both. Come, let's have a little hair of the dog." Ushering him to the drawing room, he poured bourbon. "We can perhaps reach a mutual arrangement that will benefit both of us." When Dom had named a figure, his eyes took on a calculating gleam. "Very fair, I must say."

"My father is a very fair man."

"And so is mine. He would pay a good deal more without feeling in any way cheated." He walked to a desk, sat and drew out a pen and paper.

Dom tried to decide what he had on his devious mind as he jotted figures.

"Do you think this would be an outlandish price?" He inquired shortly, holding out a piece of paper.

"Certainly not," he said when he'd digested the figure. "The stock carries over sixty percent Hereford blood."

"My point exactly. At the higher price, we could garner a nice sum."

"My father would never hear of that."

"Come now, my man, don't be dense. Damien Whittaker will have his originally-determined price and you and I will split the difference. Once I've taken what you owe me, you'll still have a nice chunk." He smiled. "There's virtually no chance of us being tripped up. Your father will never know what was actually paid here and by tomorrow night, mine won't be able to remember. You with me?"

Dom was momentarily jolted by the proposal that would save him from the consequences of his actions. He didn't hesitate long. "Yes."

"Good show, my man. Now when we take Father out to look over the cattle, take your cues from me. We won't have much trouble with him as he'll go along with whatever I say. Once we've gotten the check, I'll bring you back to town and we'll make the split. Now we must make up a new bill of sale." He rummaged in the desk until he found a blank document, then began copying the information from the one Dom produced.

Able to imagine all too clearly his father's rage if he ever learned he'd gone back on his word as a gentleman, Dom slept only restively before it was time to leave for Boulder. Sidney drove them to town in a buckboard and after breakfast, they met the train. Leonard Wallace was a spare, diffident man and Dom understood instantly how his son could manipulate him so readily.

"Father, let me introduce Dom Whittaker. He arrived with the cattle day before yesterday."

Leonard extended a trembling hand, peering at him through spectacles. "Nice to meet you, young fellow. How is your father?"

"Very well, sir."

"Glad to hear it. Fine man, your father from all I've been able to learn about him and his cattle."

"Yes, he is."

Sidney herded them to the carriage and they were underway to the country. Seated beside his son while Dominique occupied the rear seat, Leonard lapsed into silence.

Dom was astonished to see him draw a flask from his pocket twice before they reached the ranch. They immediately drove out to view the herd. As the carriage bumped across the pasture toward the beasts, Leonard made an effort to rise to the occasion, taking off his glasses to polish them. He gave full attention to appraising the cattle while Sidney drove through the thick of the herd. "Fine, fine," he murmured from time to time.

"What are you paying per head, Father?" Sidney inquired.

Leonard jerked his head around. "It's been some time since I spoke to Damien Whittaker. I believe it was . . ."

Sidney glanced at Dom. "Do you have the figures with you?"

"Of course." He drew the bill-of-sale from a pocket inside his coat and passed it forward.

"Yes, that is correct," Leonard declared when he'd glanced at the paper.

Sidney eventually turned back to the ranch house. "I expect you'll want to rest now after your trip, Father."

"Yes, the train ride always tires me."

"If you'll make out the check, we'll drive back to town so Dom can send a wire to his father. Here's the bill of sale."

Leonard took the forged paper, then handed it back to Sidney. "Just make out the check and bring it to me to sign." As they entered the front door, he veered toward the drawing room where his son poured him and Dom bourbon before disappearing.

When he sat opposite the cattleman, Dom became aware of how impaired Leonard was. If he hadn't been in so much trouble, he'd have been sorry for taking advantage of such a pitiful person. As it was, he was fervently thankful for the chance to save his skin. He knocked back his bourbon, hoping Sidney would come back quickly.

When he did return, carrying the check on a tray that he presented to his father for his signature, Dom stood, watching the old man scrawl his name, then stepped forward to shake his hand. "Thank you so much, Mr. Wallace."

He tipped his head back to inspect him over his spectacles. "Goodbye, Dom. My best regards to your father."

With a nod, he strode toward the front door and made his way to the carriage. He climbed in to wait for Sidney and was possessed by an unnerving mix of elation and shame. Leonard Wallace's acceptance of his son's treachery was acutely unsettling.

Yet, Sidney had evidently pulled off a similar scheme many times before as he was in high spirits when he came out. He leapt up beside Dom, handing him the check. "Didn't I tell you this would be as simple as taking toffee from my Great Aunt Penelope?" He jerked his head toward the house. "He's going downhill like a runaway goat these days."

"Do you do this sort of thing often?"

"Let's simply say, I'm doing very well for someone my age," he replied as they sped toward Boulder.

"Won't you defeat yourself in the end? Wouldn't it be wiser to bide your time until you inherit?"

"I'm not that patient, old boy. Besides, Father did so very well in his early years here, his holdings are extensive. If my mother hadn't died, he would likely be one of the wealthiest men in Colorado today. Unfortunately, I've no aspirations toward ranching myself. Once Father's gone, I'll sell everything off. It seems a much more practical approach to take what money I can as I go along rather than waiting for it to hit me like a runaway train one day."

Dom was anxious to be on his way home. Once they entered town, they went directly to the Wallaces' bank. When the check was processed, he wired *Rancha Mariposa's* proceeds to their Cheyenne bank, and not wanting a record of the extra money, he folded the cash into the corner of his saddle bag.

"Can't tell you how much I've enjoyed your visit my man," Sidney said when Dom prepared to mount Foxfire. "My father may find he needs a consignment of *Rancha Mariposa* Herefords in a year or so."

"If he does, I'll be happy to make the delivery," Dom declared, swinging into the saddle. "Goodbye, Sidney." He pushed the gelding into a canter, heading toward the meadow where Wally and the cowboys waited.

# CHAPTER TEN

## July 1907 – October 1909

Dom arrived in Cheyenne three days later. He sent the men on to the ranch while he stopped at The Green Door overnight. He welcomed the chance for a leisurely bath and dinner, then went upstairs with Clara Lou. Much later, he extricated himself from her and began to dress.

"You goin' so soon?"

"Yes. I want to see Charleen."

"She ain't playin' tonight."

"I don't want to play tonight but I must see her nonetheless. Go tell her. Go!" He swatted her bare behind.

Grumbling, she pulled on a shift and passed into the hall. She was soon back. "Charleen will see you in her boudoir." He gave her an absent-minded kiss before heading next door.

Charleen reclined on a red velvet chaise, a bright pink wrapper barely corralling her voluminous bosom. Her face was well rouged, her auburn hair swept grandly up in corkscrew curls, her green eyes were mesmerizing; she exuded sex like a powerful perfume.

Dom stood before her. Despite his recent session with Clara Lou, he felt himself responding to blatant invitation in her spellbinding regard. Compared to the slapdash service in Boulder, Clara Lou's unhurried attention had been delightful, yet drowning in the verdant depths of Charleen's eyes, he was as eager to partake of her as if he hadn't had a woman in months.

"Well, Dom Whittaker, what a nice surprise to see you after all this time. I've been concerned about you."

"I've come to pay you what I owe."

She pressed the tips of plump jewel-laden fingers together, gazing steadily at him. "Well, you can't imagine how happy that makes me."

He reached out to place a stack of bills on the table before her. "It's all there."

Languidly, she picked up the money and counted it before laying it aside. "I'm so pleased to say you're welcome to join my games whenever you like. We've missed you."

"Thank you."

She smiled. She had to be nearly the age of Harper and like her, her face was firm, saved from the ravages of time by the classic beauty of fine bones. With slow, languid movements, she spread her arms, causing her wrapper to fall open, exposing a glimpse of her alluring body beneath. "Come to me, Dom."

He eagerly complied, amazed that she could see how much he desired her. They soon moved to her huge ornate brass bed draped with red gauge curtains from each corner and piled high with silk covered pillows in all sizes.

With sensuous dispatch, she divested him of his clothes in erotic ritual that further provoked his carnal appetite. Finally, she gathered him close, every part of her soft flesh inviting, with none of the sharp jutting angles of a younger body.

He was awash on a glorious river of sensation—voluptuous moist flesh touching, teasing, engulfing, heating his blood until the deep need expanded, exploded. As he lay shaking within her plenteous embrace, he raised his head from her perspiring cleavage.

Pressing her lips to his forehead, she stroked his hair as she might have small child. "You must come see me again soon," she said presently. "Come, prepared to play."

When Dom arrived at the *Mariposa* the next day, no one was about when Roddy ushered him into the hall. "Ah, Dom, you're home then. Your father's out riding with Jamie and John. Chandler went with them as well but they shall return shortly. I'll tell Harper you're home. Would you like a glass of bourbon?"

"Thank you, I would." He seated himself in the parlor to wait, accepting the glass.

Sitting in the quiet, enjoying his drink, he heard a soft sound out in the hall that pulled his attention to the door. A blonde head suddenly appeared around the jamb.

Yvette had grown since New Year's. At sixteen, she remained the most stunning child. He found himself quite at-sea in her enormous Wedgwood blue eyes. She shyly edged inside, her hands clasped behind her back. Clad in a stylish little dress the exact color of her eyes, she leaned forward, the corners of her mouth curving up in a faint smile. "Hello, Dom. It's very nice to have you home. Did you have a lovely time in Colorado?"

"I did. Colorado is very pretty."

She nodded, perching on the edge of a sofa. "There's going to be a wedding soon."

He narrowed his eyes. "Who's getting married?"

"Anne and Caldwell."

Digesting this, he tried to tamp down the stab of envy shooting through him. It wasn't fair. He'd brought his good friend home with him from Harvard, expecting they'd spend most of their time together as they had at college. But, Caldwell had never cared for the pursuits Dom enjoyed. Instead, he'd decided to take up painting for God's sake. And apparently courting Anne Carroll, though Dom hadn't been aware of the serious nature of their liaison.

"So when is the wedding going to happen?"

Yvette shrugged. "Before long, I'd say." She left the sofa and strolled to a chair closer Dom, moving with the assurance of a woman who knows she is beguiling and has the undivided attention of a man. Once seated, her back straight, ankles crossed and hands folded in her lap, she smiled serenely at him.

Her feminine aplomb, as always, both intrigued and disturbed him. Still, he was helpless not to fall under her spell. Years later, he would recall that precise moment when he totally lost his heart to her. They remained there, still chatting when the others arrived.

Aunt Pris appeared first. She'd gained such poundage in the past few years, she was now a great round sausage of a woman stuffed into her purple watered silk. Dominique rose and she hobbled close to enfold him in a smothery embrace, then held him at arm's length as she had when he was ten. "Dom, I'm quite unhappy with you," she said, leaning heavily on her cane, her lips pursed. "Why is it that you never find time to visit me?"

"It's not that I haven't wanted to," he lied, uncharacteristically annoyed. In truth he'd always been fond of her and appreciated her generous gift when he'd returned from Harvard. Still, he'd often hated her tendency to meddle. Besides, nothing made him less likely to do something than being hounded about it. He was grateful when she waddled to a chair as Audra and Harper hurried in.

"There you are!" Audra said, descending on Yvette. "I couldn't imagine where you'd gone."

"I came to say hello to Dom." She beamed at her mother.

"So you did. How are you, Dom? How was your trip to Boulder?"

"It went well, thank you."

"Have you heard the news? Anne and Caldwell are going to be married."

"Yvette told me. That's wonderful."

"We're so pleased. Did she also tell you that Ophelia is expecting a baby?"

"No. You're first grandchild."

"Indeed, though I'm not sure I'm quite up to that. Oh, here is our mother-to-be now."

The eldest Carroll daughter entered, greeting Dom warmly and accepting his gallant kiss to her cheek. She wore the same vigorous mien of good health that had attended Audra and Harper when expecting.

As she settled beside Audra, he thought about the hushed reminiscences he'd heard as a boy about his own mother's hatred of everything to do with motherhood. The talk had invariably put him in touch with a lost, aching void somewhere deep inside him.

Now, he forced his mind back to the moment. He wanted to speak to his father before dinner so turned out into the hall to wait for him on a sofa before the fireplace. Presently Damien came through the front door with John, Jamie and Chandler. Observing the three of them unaware gave Dom the opportunity to see what he'd not noticed before. John had aged to the point where his hair was totally gray and the flesh of his face had begun to sag. Curiously, Damien, though nearly as old as John, appeared at least ten years younger, the elusive deterioration of age still at bay in his face and graceful carriage. They had nearly reached the parlor, when Dom rose, calling to his father.

"Dom!" Joy charged his voice as he strode back to him and caught him in a hug. "When did you get back?"

"Not long ago. May I have a word?"

"Of course. I must change before dinner. Come upstairs with me." He led the way up the staircase. "How was the drive?"

"Beastly hot and dusty but we got the herd there in good shape. We didn't lose a single calf."

"Excellent." They entered the suite Damien shared with Harper, everything in perfect order. "I'll be back shortly." He turned into the dressing room to wash up. "What did you want to tell me?" He asked when he emerged, pulling on a clean shirt.

"I sent the money to the bank."

"Yes, Jim Becker spoke to John. You did a fine job, Dom. I'm very proud of you."

"Thank you, sir. I did my best." Warmed by his approval, he refused to consider what his father would've said had he known all that had taken place in Colorado.

Dom's fortunes turned appreciably after his business transaction with Sidney Wallace. With the cushion of funds, he was able to steadily increase his capital at Charleen's tables. After he first experienced her vast inventory of delights, he wasn't content to return to Clara Lou. He became one of Charleen's few private customers.

He knew he'd had a close call in escaping his father's wrath. Feeling so fortunate to be back in his family's good graces with a handsome balance in his bank account, he vowed to make himself even more valuable to his father at the ranch. As summer progressed, he limited his gaming and only partook of Charleen's charms on occasional weekends. When he did ride to Cheyenne, he went on Saturday night and always returned Sunday evening so he was back at work as usual the next morning.

During the remainder of summer, Dom's responsible approach only broke down once when his luck during a Sunday night game at The Green Door seemed unending and he played on until three in the morning, winning one huge pot after another. Yet, after a few hours sleep, he headed home for the final days' work during the fall roundup.

Without stopping at the *Mariposa,* he rode toward the amassed herd where his father, Chandler, Jamie, Luke, Caldwell and John and the cowboys were branding and castrating calves. All looked in his direction when he pulled up Foxfire and tied him with the other mounts before walking to the branding fire.

"Hard night in Cheyenne?" Damien asked but there was no animosity in the inquiry.

Dom grinned. "I was on such a roll I couldn't afford to leave earlier."

"Well, good for you. Now you can join us poor working men. If we keep up the pace, you should be able to drive the consignment of steers at least partway to Pine Bluffs yet tonight."

"Wonderful," he agreed, pulling on his gloves as he moved to the branding fire where Caldwell handed him a heated iron.

While he worked, he noted with pleasure how the influence of Hereford blood had become more and more evident in recent years. Thousands of *Rancha Mariposa* crossbred calves and those of their neighbors had taken on some variation of the characteristic red and white coloring. He could hardly imagine how happy this proof of their attainment made his father, John and the others.

A portion of *Rancha Mariposa's* purebred Herefords had always been isolated to keep the bloodlines undiluted. With more and more Herefords being imported in recent years, several unrelated bulls had been purchased to prevent a reduction in quality through inbreeding.

Pride filled Dom when he considered how profoundly Whittaker Herefords had improved the quality of the beef cattle produced by Wyoming ranchers. For perhaps the first time, he fully understood what his father and John had set out to do when they brought the hardy stock from Herefordshire when he'd been but a baby.

Markets had remained depressed into the 1890s and all the ranchers had seen the harsh consequences of overgrazing. All *Rancha Mariposa* cattle had been fed in winter for years and because it was impossible to harvest enough hay for the vast numbers the ranch had once had on its books, the total now rarely exceeded ten thousand head. The care of this many cattle involved an incredible amount of effort nonetheless so fifteen additional men had been hired and a second bunkhouse built since Dom had returned from college.

As Damien had predicted, the work at the roundup wound down by mid-afternoon and Dom departed with a crew of cowboys for the shipping point at Pine Bluffs. On the trail, he was in high spirits, relishing the success of his trip of Colorado. He couldn't imagine all the other opportunities that might present themselves in the future.

He didn't get back to the *Mariposa* until the morning of Anne and Caldwell's wedding. An hour before the marriage was to take place in the Trail's End parlor, Luke and Joe, a stable lad, arrived at the front entrance of the *Mariposa* with two flower-bedecked carriages to transport everyone to the other mansion. As he and the rest filed into the festively-decorated parlor, Dom was momentarily overcome by the sense of coming home.

Prior to the Carrolls moving to *Rancha Mariposa* to stay, he'd spent most of each school year living with them in Cheyenne. Aside from the pain of being temporarily wrested from the security of life with his father each year, he'd always been content with the Carrolls, finding them an engaging, extraordinarily caring family.

His easy enjoyment was rudely shoved aside when he glanced across the room and spotted Caldwell pinning a rosebud to Arthur's lapel. While his friend hadn't formally asked him to be his best man, he'd thought that once he arrived for the wedding, that would be the first order of business. Now he was swamped with incredulity, shocked by betrayal and possessed by an overwhelming compulsion to bolt from the house.

Only Harper noted his agitation and quickly came to his side, gripping his arm. "Darling, what on earth is wrong?"

He could only shake his head, swiping frantically at sudden tears while he tried to wrench free.

Harper held tight to him, walking with him as he headed toward the front door. "Dom, stop it! Tell me what's wrong!" When they reached a bench in the foyer, she pulled him down beside her.

"He picked Arthur instead of me."

Insight dawned. "Darling, Caldwell and Arthur have become very close friends. You've been busy with other responsibilities and . . ."

"I still believed we were friends and I'd be his witness!"

She grasped his hands, looking up into his miserable face. "Sometimes when we're young, we don't think things through carefully enough. I'm sure Caldwell meant no harm but merely thought you and he had moved on to other priorities . . ."

He tried twisting free of her again but she withstood the effort. "Dom, listen to me!" She was deadly calm by this time. "You're making a scene now. There's no time for this as they're waiting for us to begin the ceremony. We'll talk about this later, but right now, I want you to wipe your face and usher me back to the parlor."

By some miracle, he managed to stand up and Harper finished wiping up the wetness of his tears. She turned him toward the hall, fixed a radiant smile in place, and holding to his arm as though she'd been planning on being his escort all along, guided him to seats next to Delaney.

Now as he sat among the rest, he quickly regained his composure and some objectivity while he observed the bridal couple. He'd seen little of Caldwell during the summer and hardly recognized him.

When he'd arrived from the east, he'd been rather unsettled, unsure if he wished to stay on as an employee of *Rancha Mariposa* or return to his family in Virginia. Now, standing with Anne before the altar, he appeared as calm and confident as any man positive of his place in the world. Anne, her adoring sea green eyes locked on his, was clearly tail over teakettle. At twenty-two, she was slim and vivacious. If the drowning torrent of passion so obviously passing between them was any indication, they were embarking on a union as ardent and enduring as that merging the Carrolls, or Dom's father and Harper.

For a brief span, Dom found himself yearning for just such a total immersion of himself into the orbit of another. This longing was fleeting as he had too much yet to accomplish to saddle himself with a wife who'd doubtless become a bloody bore within a year.

He continued his contemplation, finding Yvette seated in the second row of chairs. His heart surged as he took in her dainty demeanor, her palest yellow hair. He recalled that she was his ultimate goal and nothing else mattered very much.

He resolved to work hard in the coming years, striving for success and the finest reputation so when she was of age, he could claim her as his own. He could imagine nothing more lovely than having her at his side as his enchanting wife.

His attention passed to others in the gathering. He saw his father, strikingly handsome as ever, stood beside Chandler. The two resembled each other to an uncanny degree. Save for his brother having no mustache, Dom decided Chandler was a right doppelganger of his father. The thought made him smile.

Despite his good intentions, he battled a sudden surge of panic, forcing his eyes from the pair as he acknowledged his old envy of his brother's place in his father's heart. Yet, after a time, he realized for perhaps the first time that the emotion might be unfounded. Since his return from Harvard, he'd enjoyed the closest working relationship with Damien. Though Chandler was almost an adult at sixteen, he still represented no peril toward Dom at the moment. Nonetheless, the feeling that he was less than his brother had plagued him for so long, since Chandler was a baby and as hard as he tried, he could not banish it. Right then, he doubted he ever would.

His glanced at Harper beside him and was so grateful she'd saved him from a really embarrassing situation where he'd have been left looking like an utter fool. As though reading his heart, she squeezed his hand and gave him a small smile.

She still possessed the knowing, refined bearing that always set her well apart in any group of women. He could understand his father's utter delight in her. He was often warmed by memories of the secure circle of her arms when his mother had been so cold and cruel. If not for her love and concern for him over the years, he'd no doubt be floundering even further out on the river of self-doubt that so often swept him toward despair.

Pulling himself back from his gloomy introspection, he decided to put on a good front and enjoy the wedding supper. When the guests fell into a line to congratulate the newlyweds, he stood behind his parents, Delaney, and Chandler.

Delaney turned around to smile at him. He'd long since decided her behavior toward him was a constant barometer to show him how everyone else regarded him. When he first came home from Harvard, she had often unnerved him with her overtly suspicious attitude. But soon enough, despite his nefarious deeds, she appeared to regain her faith and they salvaged their mutual goodwill. "Hello, Dom. I didn't have the chance to see you before."

He winked and kissed her cheek. "How're you and your riding coming along? Are you ready for the show ring yet?"

She laughed. "Not quite, but I will be when it's time."

"Glad to hear it." He watched his parents' interaction with the bride and groom. When they moved on, he grinned at Anne who gave a little giggle of pleasure as she wrapped her arms around his neck. "You look so pretty. I hope you and Caldwell are very happy."

"Oh, thank you, Dom . . ."

He kissed her cheek, held her close a moment more.

She beamed at Caldwell. "Did I ever tell you, darling, that Dom lived with us when we were children?"

"No, but he did," her husband replied. "From his glowing report, those years were among his favorites. He talked endlessly about you and your sisters while we were back east."

Anne considered him. "I can't imagine how boring our life would've been if you hadn't been with us."

"I always loved living with you." He shook Caldwell's hand before moving on, having decided he'd rather die than ever have him know he'd been so presumptuous as to think he'd be his best man.

A bit later, he encountered Ophelia, and was rather taken aback at her very pregnant state. She, too, seemed overjoyed to see him.

As he continued mingling with the guests, he was able to talk with all the Carroll sisters and by the time the bridal couple prepared to depart for their honeymoon in Denver, he felt much better, no longer out of place. The friendly rapport he'd enjoyed with nearly everyone present bolstered his ego and he was once again on firm ground, confident in what he was accomplishing at *Rancha Mariposa.*

And indeed the ranch prospered during the next months; all who worked actively with the cattle grew more secure as the region's economy stabilized. Rustling on all ranges became less and less a matter of concern as hired gunmen continued dispatching scattered thieves. One of the most notorious assassins, Tom Horn, had been hung in Cheyenne in November, 1903, amid general emotional furor. After this spectacle, the stealing declined still further. The years merged one into the next in uneventful succession.

During the earlier time of endless open range, cooperation among the cattlemen was essential for survival and individual success. With the erection of miles upon miles of barbed wire fences, an era of ever greater self-sufficiency evolved. The final organized roundup for the general region was held in 1909.

All of *Rancha Mariposa's* range had been under fence for several years, a move made necessary with more and more settlers moving into Wyoming along with numerous sheepmen, all competing with the cattle ranchers for space. Consequently, *Rancha Mariposa* hadn't participated in the public roundups for the same amount of time.

Numerous cross fences were built to make more efficient use of the pastureland. The unending gates that now had to be opened and closed to travel to and from Cheyenne caused all to look back fondly on the time of the vast open grasslands. Still, the changing scene brought any number of exciting developments, not the least of which was the arrival of the first scattered automobiles in Wyoming. These contraptions chugged along the rutted roads, coughing and sputtering and causing innumerable runaways among the horses still employed by most people. Dom, at first, found the new-fangled autos particularly annoying.

One May evening when he and Chandler rode home from checking on cattle far from the ranch headquarters, they came onto a picnic spot between Aspen and Lodgepole. A young couple shared the supper laid out on a blanket.

Dom had completely lost patience in recent years with squatters and trespassers who were not above cutting fences to reach a spot they found to their liking. Hardly a month went by when he didn't evict some unscrupulous party from *Rancha Mariposa* land. Weary and short-tempered after a long day, he was in no mood to look kindly on picnickers.

"What the devil are you two doing on this land?" He shouted when they were within earshot.

Startled, the man, a gangly youth of no more than twenty, scrambled to his feet. "I beg your pardon, sir. This was just such a fine place for a picnic."

"How'd you get in here?"

He shrugged sheepishly. "Through about a dozen gates. I closed every one . . ."

"Well, get the hell out and if I ever catch you in here again, I'll press charges for trespassing."

"Right away, sir." The lad rushed to throw the food back into an empty basket while his companion wadded up the blanket.

When he and Chandler continued over a rise, spotting the couple's Ford parked close to the Lodgepole, he couldn't resist teaching the pair a lesson they wouldn't soon forget. Ignoring Chandler's indignant protest, he shook out his lariat, draped a loop around the car's bumper and dragged it toward the water. Once it was sitting out in the middle of the stream, he recoiled the rope, pushing Foxfire into a canter.

Chandler followed close behind. "Why in hell did you do that? They were leaving."

"Chandler, if you know what's good for you, shut your bloody mouth. Right now, I'd as soon knock you off that horse as look at you."

"You can be despicable."

"You have no idea how true that is, little brother, and you're getting harder to stomach every blessed year. You're getting to be way too much of a smart aleck and I'm liable to give you a good thrashing if you don't change your ways."

"I'd love to see that. Pa-pa would kick you right off this ranch," he declared before falling silent.

Dom welcomed his sullen reaction. He was delighted that he'd struck a nerve. Chandler was usually so even tempered he could rarely goad him to react. And he was right. All too aware of their father's loyalty to his younger son, Dom knew better than to harass him with more than verbal abuse.

If he wouldn't be a real threat to him in the future, Dom would probably have liked him a great deal because at sixteen, he was an extraordinarily engaging young man, talented, well-mannered. When Chandler was twelve Harper had shown him a tintype taken of their father at that age. Dom had been swamped by insane jealousy. If he hadn't known different, he'd have sworn the thin, fair youth with light hair neatly combed, ascot tied rakishly, was Chandler, not his father.

Looking into the laughing, already sensuous eyes, Dom could well understand his popularity with girls from a young age. Studying that old picture, he'd realized for the hundredth time how much he resented his own swarthiness, the reality that even in physical appearance, Chandler was more pleasing.

Although, he handled himself well in any social gathering, Chandler wasn't nearly as attracted to girls as Damien had been at his age. Instead he applied himself diligently to his studies with Arthur and to his work with the cattle.

Still, he and Yvette Carroll had become fast friends; indeed, their rapport appeared to go much deeper than that. Of course, this enraged Dom, who'd long since decided she was his. It seemed Chandler had similar intentions. Dom ultimately saw the reason his brother wasn't much interested in other girls was because he'd already settled on Yvette.

Because she was barely sixteen, Dom still had some years to wait before he could pursue her. It was clear, nonetheless, if he was to guarantee his future at the ranch and win the girl he wanted for his wife, the time was approaching for him to declare warfare on Chandler.

# CHAPTER ELEVEN

## November 1909 – June 1913

The difference between him and Chandler in their father's eyes had never been clearer to Dom than when his brother was allowed to attend the University of Wyoming at Laramie while he had been exiled to Harvard for three years. Chandler divided his time between Laramie and the ranch, giving his attention to the three most important things in his life—his education, Yvette and *Rancha Mariposa.*

Much to Dom's vexation, his brother and Yvette grew closer. He often felt totally impotent in his inability to spend time with her himself but he was all too aware of how her parents as well as his own would view him fraternizing with her when she was sixteen years his junior. Indeed, his advanced age when compared to hers filled him with unrelenting hopelessness. If he wasn't allowed to court her openly, how could he ever compete for her?

Still, at her eighteenth birthday party at Trail's End in November, he saw for the first time she was within his grasp. The Carrolls had hired a string band for the occasion so there was dancing after dinner.

Unimpressed with the few unescorted women in attendance, Dom was disinclined to join the couples on the dance floor. Instead, he sipped champagne, watching the various pairs, finally settling his attention on Yvette and Chandler.

Yvette had negotiated the brief awkwardness of adolescence, emerging as a tall, graceful young woman with a striking bearing. Dom noted the hem of her embroidered muslin dress showed an inch or two more ankle than current fashion deemed seemly. He didn't realize it just then, but that slight daring was an indication of her nature that he would use to his advantage one day.

Her wavy mane was still much lighter than blonde hair usually is, a strange ashen-gold shade. The silvery mass of it fell rippling down her thin back, nearly reaching her waist.

Dom was newly worried by the depth of love in her face tipped up to Chandler's. Jealousy raced along every nerve and he left his chair in disgust, presently wandering out on to a balcony. He leaned on a railing, staring out over the Aspen bathed in white moonlight. Turmoil whirled through his brain as he searched vainly for the means to undermine Chandler's hold on what was most dear to him in all the world.

The night was unseasonably mild for November. He'd moved restlessly to the far end of the balcony when a soft footfall caused him to turn about. Yvette stood beside him, framed in the lamplight from an open doorway.

Startled, he struggled to find his voice. "Happy Birthday, Yvette. What a nice party."

"Thank you."

"You and Chandler seem to be getting on splendidly."

"Of course. Mother thinks it will be grand when we marry one day."

"What do you think?"

"Oh, I know it'll be splendid. I think we've always known we'll be together. Harper told me that's the way it was with her and your father. She said their love was preordained and it's the same for Chandler and me. And he's divinely handsome, don't you think?" She leaned her elbows back against the railing, her breasts thrust forward. As she slid her eyes toward Dom, he caught a flicker of heat, the smoldering suggestion of an eager sexuality he doubted she yet knew she possessed.

The fleeting glimpse of this hidden part of her was quickly banished as she brought down her arms, straightened her back and cast him a demure look as if to see if he'd noticed her slip in decorum. He had indeed.

For over a dozen years, he'd acknowledged her shy, childish interest in him, betrayed in an occasional unknowingly coy glance, a slow smile. The attention had been intriguing but infantile. Her inspection a moment before had been something else altogether.

Dom embraced the certainty that she'd inherited the potential for the same lusty enjoyment of sex that had blessed her parents.

In this, he could best the genteel Chandler but realized he must approach the matter cautiously.

Over twice her age, he likely appeared ancient to her. The mere thought of him kissing her would doubtless be so shocking she would run from him in horror. It was essential that the sensuous nature he detected in her be awakened slowly.

She lingered there, the fine bones of her face brushed with lamplight. "I haven't had the chance to thank you for my wonderful birthday present. I shall put it to good use."

"I don't know how appropriate the gift of a bridle is for such a lady as yourself." He'd wanted to give her something personal such as jewelry or a bolt of fine blue silk, the color of her eyes, but knew such offerings would have appeared scandalous. He had settled on a bridle for the blooded Thoroughbred gelding her father had bought her in Philadelphia.

"It's splendid and will set off Centaur nicely. Have you seen him yet, Dom?"

"No but I've heard he's a grand one."

"Oh, he is! Such a shiny black. I think he's even more beautiful than Delaney's Destino."

"Ah. Do you plan to follow her into the show ring?"

She shook her head, causing her pale curls to bounce alluringly. "I daresay not. I'm not half as good a rider as she is. I just love riding for itself. I feel so brave and free when I let Centaur run."

"I still have difficulty sometimes remembering you're one of the Carroll sisters. Not only are you much prettier than the rest but I can't really recall any of them riding a horse."

"Then your memory is bad because Millie used to ride Molly all the time with Delaney. And Bethany liked to ride Harper's stallion Embarr." She lifted a saucy brow.

He laughed. "I stand corrected."

Chandler strode through the nearest door. "There you are! You'll catch your death out here."

"Oh, fiddlesticks!"

"Yvette, for heaven's sake. If your mother sees you out here in the cold without a wrap, she'll be convinced you'll catch pneumonia. And I'll be to blame." He wrapped an arm around her and she leaned into his warmth. "Shall we go in?"

Her mouth turned up in a pouty smile. "All right, if you promise we can dance until dawn."

"Your father may have something to say about that but we'll give it our best effort. Dom." With a nod at him, he led her away.

Dom might have been further disheartened by their obviously enjoyment of each other save for the smile Yvette threw him over her shoulder. The future would no doubt see a deepening of their attachment but he was newly encouraged about his own chances with her.

When Chandler left to begin his study at the University, he and Yvette visited each other every two weeks when one or the other caught the train in either Laramie or Cheyenne. In the meantime, she was courted by Dom at the ranch. Now that she was of age, neither her parents nor Damien and Harper expressed any reservations about their long horseback or buggy rides or the evenings they spent talking in the *Mariposa* gardens while they watched the sunset.

She loved both of her chivalrous men and no longer assumed she would marry Chandler although she couldn't imagine life without him. Yet, when she was alone in some secluded spot near the Aspen or Lodgepole and Dom kissed her with a commanding, fierce adoration she'd never experienced in Chandler's arms, she grew unsure. These solitary trysts invariably left her feeling astonished by her own physical responses. She felt wild and out of control and more often than not, was left longing for more.

And when she took the train to visit Chandler which she did so often, she was thrilled to see him. They spent every bit of the weekend together, walking on the tranquil campus, picnicking close to a brook, visiting the library where they borrowed novels and poetry to share by reading to each other, and occasionally stealing away to a hidden spot to hold each other. She adored every minute of their time. When Chandler took her tenderly in his arms and lowered his mouth to hers, her heart raced and the blood pounded in her ears.

His kisses weren't the carnal assaults to her senses that Dom's were but rather, gentle rituals that stirred her to the bottom of her soul. When she lay in his arms, trembling with the force of their love, she often wanted to run away with him, marry, and have the decision made, the matter finished. But instead, she soon kissed him goodbye and got back on the train, taking away her longing and her confusion.

Once she was back home, she clung to the memory of each moment with Chandler, his touch, the pressure of his mouth on hers, his tender declarations of love. She wanted to do nothing, until she was with him again, except reimagine over and over the time they'd just spent together.

Sometimes when Dom asked her to go out in a carriage with him, or walk in the garden, she wanted to shout at him to leave her alone, that she belonged to Chandler and didn't want to go anywhere with him anymore. But always when she thought back to the last time she'd succumbed and the frenzy of desire he'd stirred in her, she wasn't strong enough to resist.

The three of them continued in this mad, delightful, disturbing merry-go-round of emotions as Chandler followed Dom's example and doubled his efforts in the classroom so he could finish his studies in three years. A constant sense of bewilderment and perplexity followed Yvette as she vacillated between them.

Chandler graduated from the University of Wyoming in May 1912, and received the same amount of *Rancha Mariposa* stock Dom had received twelve years before. And though Dom officially remained manager of the ranch, Chandler was made a partner immediately, on equal ground with his father, John, Jamie and Granville, while Dom had waited ten years before he reached that status. The immediate inclusion of Chandler into the hierarchy of ownership while he'd been required to serve an implied probationary period enraged him.

His outlook wasn't improved when Chandler came home and took up his ranch duties. Expecting he would soon propose to Yvette because there was no longer any obstacle to prevent it, he increased his efforts to have her for himself.

The first Sunday after Chandler's return, Dom was riding back to *Mariposa* after checking on an ailing cow. He was nearly home when he saw Yvette race past Trail's End on Centaur. Desperate to speak to her, he wheeled his horse and raced after her.

As he nearly caught up with her, she leaned over the black's neck, urging him forward until he had to spur his horse to keep her from pulling away. He chased her for over a mile before she pulled up in a copse of aspen.

She sat staring at him as he rode closer. Her face tense, her eyes filled with anger.

"Are you trying to escape from me?"

Tossing her head, she averted her stormy gaze to the water of the nearby stream. "Actually, I rode out here so I could think, thus I wasn't expecting to be run down by a mad man."

He lounged in his saddle. "So I'm a mad man now am I?"

Scowling, she sighed. "I just want everyone to leave me alone."

Studying her, he tried to decide how to deal with her peculiar mood. There was a new cold clarity in her eyes that terrified him. "Why are you behaving like this?" He inquired presently.

"I didn't plan on you." She stared straight at him. "Since I was two years old, I've loved Chandler. After my eighteenth birthday, I was sure I would be married to him and that made me very happy. I had such a lovely life with my family and friends. And knowing the man I loved with all my heart would be my husband made my life so settled. I had nothing to worry about."

While she continued glowering at him, a tear wandered down her cheek and she wiped distractedly at it. ". . . and then, you came crashing into my life. Up until then, I never really thought about you. Whenever I saw you, you fascinated me to no end but I had no idea I would fall in love with you. But you hit me like a wagonload of rocks."

Now he stared at her in alarm. "Are you telling me you're finished with me?" He dared inquire.

She shook her head. "No! Certainly not but I can't stand being torn between you and Chandler. I love you both so much and I can't bear giving up either of you. So I'm running away."

"You're joking?"

"No, I'm very serious. Lately, I've realized I don't want to marry either of you. Not right now. And then, Eliza told me she's expecting twins and she wants to stop teaching when the babies are born. I've always thought I'd enjoy teaching and I'd be rather good at it. So that settled it."

Dom frowned at her. "I can be dense at times. I confess I can't make heads or tails of what you're saying."

"Well, I decided I want to get my teaching certificate and take up Eliza's job when she retires. I spoke to my father and he told me it only takes a matter of months to get a certificate to teach school. Nine I think he said."

She'd relaxed now, warming to her topic as she continued. "So I'm going to live in Cheyenne for as long as it requires to get my certificate, then I'll be ready to take Eliza's place next year."

"What about me?"

"You will be living here and working. As will Chandler. I need an extended time away from both of you or I'll go mad."

"But I don't want to be away from you." Dom felt ill at the thought.

"Chandler isn't too keen about the idea either but I've made up my mind. I'm going to take whatever time I need to decide which one of you I want to marry. Or I might meet someone else I want to marry."

"My heart will break." His voice trembled.

"No, my dear, it won't. You can perhaps call on me in town occasionally. But it will be on my terms. I can't stand any more pressure. You can't imagine how awful it's been lately, traveling to see Chandler and losing my heart to him all over again. Then coming home to have you beg and plead for me to be with you and having the same thing happen. If I subscribed to the teachings of Brigham Young, I could marry both of you. As it is, I want time to sort things out."

"When do you believe you can make up your mind?"

Leveling him in an impatient frown, she picked up her reins and turned her horse toward home. When she'd taken Centaur to the stable and walked along the cobbled drive toward the

*Mariposa,* Chandler stood up from where he'd been sitting on a bench beneath a crab apple tree at the edge of the garden.

"Darling." He came toward her.

She stopped, watching him approach, her breath catching as she took in his familiar, graceful stance. "What a lovely day." The fragrance of apple blossoms hung in the air, nearly intoxicating in its sweetness.

Stepping closer, he folded her close, merely holding her for a time as though he sensed the agitation in her. Finally, he leaned back, searching her face, his gaze troubled. "What's wrong? You're trembling."

She didn't answer but slid her arms around him, laying her head on his chest, listening to the steady beating of his heart beneath her ear. Willing the cadence to calm her, she dared wonder how she'd come to her present state of tension and distress. She'd been so happy and contented for so long with this tall, beautiful man whose sensitive pewter eyes had always looked at her with such sweet longing that her heart ached with the delight of it.

How could such a deep, all-encompassing love have been turned into the debilitating confusion and uncertainty that pursued her now? After a long time, she slowly lifted her head, tears flooding down her face. "Oh, Chandler, I'm so sorry."

Alarm darkened the shadows in his eyes. "Darling, whatever is the matter?" He brought up one hand, wiping his slender fingers along her cheek. "Come, sit with me and tell me what's wrong." Leading her to the bench, he settled her next to him, still holding her, peering at her as he searched for the reason she was in such a state until she looked away and let her head settle against his shoulder.

He frantically searched for the reason for her state. At breakfast, she'd been her customary sunny self, eager to be off on her morning ride. He planned to take her to dinner in Cheyenne later that afternoon and ask her to marry him. Now, he was at a compete loss, unease plummeting through him. Whatever could have caused this appalling transformation? "Please, Yvette, tell me."

She haltingly lifted her face and allowed him to mop up her tears with his handkerchief. "I don't know how to tell you."

"Sweetheart," he said softly, "we've always trusted each other and been able to talk about anything."

"But now, I feel I've betrayed you. I haven't been honest . . . ." She gripped his hand, trying to put it all in words. "I've been seeing Dom in between visiting you in Laramie."

With a little smile of relief, he drew her close again, rocking her. "I've known that ever since I left for school. We talked about it. That you were free to see him if you wished . . . ." He trailed off, staring at her with new fear. "Has he done something improper? Has he hurt you?"

"No! No, he's been a perfect gentleman."

"Then I don't see what the problem is. You and I aren't betrothed. Indeed, we talked a great deal about that and I told you, I didn't think it was fair to you to talk about marriage until I graduated . . ."

"I know that," she broke in. "But you don't understand all that's happened. Dom has also fallen in love with me. I'm quite sure *he* would like to marry me."

He stared at her with real alarm now. "Are you telling me things have gone that far between you!?"

"We've done nothing improper!" She hastily added. "We've done nothing but kiss . . . but I've grown fond of him and . . ."

"Are you in love with him!?" He suddenly demanded, gripping her arms to set her away from him before he leapt up and paced some distance from the bench. He finally stopped and stood still, the entire length of him rigid.

"Please, Chandler, don't shut me out. I need you to understand that . . ."

"What is to understand!?" He shouted, whirling to face her before stalking back to sit on the other end of the bench. "I trusted you. I knew you and Dom were friends. That was clear enough but I thought you *loved* me!"

"I did! I do! Oh, my sweet Chandler, I do love you so!"

"Yet you also love Dom?" He held her in his contemptuous regard.

"I never meant for that to happen." Pressing her hands together, she struggled for control but she couldn't stop crying.

"Oh, really? Well, where does that leave me? Or my brother for that matter?"

Frantically, she wiped her face with his damp handkerchief. "I don't know. I'm so sorry. I never thought I could ever love anyone but you."

"Well, I can certainly understand that as it's precisely the way I've felt about you since we were children. Of course, I didn't feel the need to cultivate friendships with other women!"

The harshness of his words caused new tears and her thin shoulders convulsed in sobs.

He wanted to go to her and offer what comfort he could but he was too angry so he stayed where he was, watching her weep. "It might interest you to know," he said at last, "that I planned to drive you to dinner at The Plains this afternoon and ask you to marry me."

She could only stare at him helplessly, feeling as though her heart would break. She watched in disbelief when he slid closer and dropped a ring in her lap.

"That was my grandmother's," he said dully. "For some reason, my father chose to give it to me instead of Dom. I daresay because he and the rest of the family and all our friends were under the impression that I would be the first to marry."

Numbly, she picked up the ring, an exquisite gold filigree design enclosing a large, perfect sapphire. Looking at it made her feel physically ill. It would've been such an honor to wear it as Chandler's wife and she could see how it wounded him when she finally handed it back to him.

Studying it for a long while, he finally put it in his shirt pocket and returned his attention to her. "So what do we do now?"

She drew a quavery breath, abruptly determined to make him understand what she had decided with Granville's advice and counsel. Choosing her words carefully and having finally gotten her weeping under control, she told him what she'd told Dom earlier.

Silently, he absorbed all she said, then sat in silence for so long, she finally asked what he thought. "You truly believe you'll enjoy teaching?"

"I do. Growing up with all my sisters, I adore children and I believe I'll be rather good at being a mother. But what I want most right now is time to sort out my thoughts and feelings. I truly could not make a responsible decision about marriage at this time. I've become too bewildered. I adore both you and Dom but I don't know which of you I want for my husband. Time is the only thing that can help me. I don't want to hurt either of you and I beg you to let me find my own way for a time."

"Have you any idea what you're asking of me? Until a short while ago, I thought we would be married soon. For the past three years, I've held to the certainty that once I graduated, we would be free to marry. I love you with every fiber of my heart and soul and I can scarcely imagine how lonely I'm going to be with you living in Cheyenne while you study for your teaching certificate."

"You can come visit me."

He shook his head. "And I daresay the same invitation will be offered to my brother?"

"I daresay, as seeing both of you on occasion, is the only way I can foresee to determine with which I want to spend the rest of my life. And I may be terribly presumptuous because perhaps one or both of you will decide you want to marry someone else entirely."

"Speaking for myself, I can't see that happening," he said with some of his usual objectivity. "I will fight for you to my last breath."

She smiled. "I do love you so and I always will."

"I can say the same." He leaned closer and let his arm fall around her shoulders. "Since I have no choice, I will give you all the time you need but I will never cease wanting to be your husband."

After Yvette took charge and radically changed the direction of her life, an uneasy calm settled over *Rancha Mariposa.* She'd rocked both her suitors, leaving them groping for their equilibrium but she held true to her course, refusing to bend to the pleas from either. They reconciled themselves to her terms with the awareness that they must allow her the room she needed if one or the other wasn't to be eliminated from the game altogether.

That is not to say they suffered their fate gladly. They both entered a patch of gloom that manifested itself in different ways.

Dom grew more angry and rebellious than he had been for all the years Chandler had been away in Laramie. He was soon planning his revenge on his brother, intent on making him look like a total fool. Yvette would surely throw him over as hopeless and not deserving of her continued interest.

Chandler grew philosophical, deciding that ranting and raving and making life miserable for himself and everyone around him was a huge waste of time. Instead, he threw all his attention into performing his duties at the ranch with as much responsibility and dispatch as his new position warranted.

When he wasn't occupied with his other work, he became interested in Delaney's quest for success in the show ring and began advising her in the advanced training of Destino in dressage, cross country and show jumping. Granville had long been a part of the country gentry in Herefordshire and had a keen eye for fine horseflesh and knowledge of training Thoroughbreds in the three disciplines of English horsemanship. Both Delaney and Chandler were soon asking him for pointers and he gladly became part of their team. Soon enough, he took over as head instructor.

The three of them began spending hours every day, either in the cool of early morning or evening in training exercises in a wide flat meadow behind the stables. Delaney and her great, tall Thoroughbred became fit and proficient as the weeks passed.

Granville made inquiries and found that various towns in Colorado hosted horse shows at various times during the year. Delaney and her coaches decided tentatively that she might make her debut the following year.

After the spring work was finished, Dom reacquainted himself with Madam Charleen and her gaming tables and fell into his old habit of spending half his nights in Cheyenne. His father and Harper watched his return to debauchery with great concern, although they understood what Yvette's about face was costing both of their sons.

Their worry over the situation deepened as they watched the animosity build once again between Dom and his brother. While Chandler appeared to be coping with his customary good grace, Dom buried his emotions in the dark pursuits of which he was so fond.

While Yvette prepared to leave the ranch in the fall to take up her teachers' normal training course in Cheyenne, she treated both brothers with courtesy and concern. Rather soon after the upheaval in his life, Chandler was happy enough to go on rides and walks with her. They'd soon schooled their passion to a new dimension. There was no lessening of their love and deep caring but they found they could be near each other without becoming embroiled in the hot turmoil of their emotions. When they weren't so sure of what the future held, they were able to see clearer and listen as each spoke with thoughtful appreciation.

For his part, Dom couldn't muster the same equanimity. He stayed away from the *Mariposa* as much as possible and during the rare times when he deigned to spend an hour or two there, he was barely civil to anyone and studiously ignored his brother.

When Damien grew weary of his behavior and called him on it, he began taking his meals with the cowboys in the bunkhouse and often slept there when he wasn't in Cheyenne. This brought back bad memories for the Whittakers as Dom's mother had been fond of commiserating with the cowboys which led to all sorts of unacceptable behavior.

Yet, because Dom was of age and free to make his own decisions, they chose not to make an issue of his rebellion. "Why do I feel like Dom is reverting back to behavior we'd expect from a child rather than our adult son?" Damien asked Harper one summer evening when they'd returned from a ride and seen him drinking with the cowboys outside the second bunkhouse.

Threading her arm through his, she laughed as they walked. "I've ceased to be surprised by anything he does. I do wonder if we shouldn't have been so tolerant of his wooing Yvette when Chandler was away. Looking back, I'm afraid that was quite improper and it led to the sticky situation we find ourselves in now."

"I daresay we've reached a time in our lives when we must allow our children to deal with their own problems, particularly when they're of their own making."

"Perhaps things will grow calmer once Yvette has taken up her studies in Cheyenne."

"We can but hope," he agreed ruefully. "I must send one or the other to take possession of the bulls we've purchased near Denver. I'm tempted to dispatch Dom but I believe it's the perfect mission for Chandler to prove himself as a valuable part of the ranch management."

"When must the bulls be brought home?"

"Next week." They came abreast the benches at the edge of the garden that were a favorite stopping-off spot for most everyone living at the *Mariposa* and the cottages above the stream.

This evening, they found Granville, Chandler, Delaney and Finn pausing there after their customary training session with Destino. "Good evening," Granville said as they sat opposite.

"How did our future champions perform this evening?" Damien asked with a wink at his daughter.

"They were splendid as usual."

"Excellent! Can you find time from your training duties to travel for a few days on ranch business?"

"But of course. It's not as though Delaney is going to a horse show in the near future. What do you need me to do?"

"Bring home the bulls we bought this spring in Colorado?"

"I can leave whenever you like." He glanced at Granville with a grin. "I will leave our pupil in the capable hands of my partners."

"Oh, good," Delaney interjected, "it will be like a holiday for me because Granville isn't as much the task master as my little brother." She laid her head on Granville's shoulder while she smiled at Chandler.

Granville in his eighties remained as debonair and delightful as ever and was beloved by everyone. "There is such a thing as overtraining," he said mildly.

"My thought exactly." Delaney kissed his cheek.

Finn approached to sit beside her. He had matured to be slightly taller than his father and much more handsome. His personality was every bit as engaging as Jamie's and his crystal blue eyes held the same depth of caring and good humor.

During the last several years, he'd appointed himself as Delaney's helpmate in her preparation for the horse show circuit. In that interval, her regard for him had evolved from happy gratitude for his constant presence and eager help to something she couldn't yet quite comprehend. All she knew for sure is she never wanted to be far from him and most everything he did fascinated her to no end.

For a long while, their age difference had cast them into the roles of grownup and child which hadn't diminished their great admiration for one another. Now older, they'd leveled into more equal status.

Watching the interplay of emotions passing between them, Harper wondered if either realized what was happening. It seemed quite clear to her that they cared deeply and were well on their way to falling in love.

The thought pleased her and she could envision nothing more lovely than having her beloved daughter courted by Finn. As the son of Jamie Horncastle, Finn was fun and caring, and possessed the finest moral integrity.

As she pictured the future once Delaney and Finn realized what a profound course they were embarked upon, she was inspired to throw her arms around Damien's waist, giving him a dazzling smile. He looked down at her, puzzled.

She stood on tiptoe to whisper in his ear. "I have something lovely to tell you later."

Clearly he remained clueless and absently granted her a smile and kissed her hair before returning his attention to the others.

"So, we're all set then?" He asked Chandler. "Let's plan on you departing for Colorado next Friday. The seller insists on you making the transaction for the bulls on Saturday."

"I'll be ready," Chandler agreed.

In bed that night, Harper molded herself to the contours of Damien's body, resting her head on his shoulder as she idly traced the contours of his lean face with her fingertips. "Have you noticed that Delaney is completely smitten by Finn and vice versa?"

On the verge of sleep, he only belatedly grunted good naturedly, then eventually lifted his head to study her in the dim lamplight. "Are you certain?"

"Completely. I'd say an engagement is imminent."

"Do they know that?"

"I believe it's not yet dawned on either of them. But that's not to say, it won't, very shortly."

"Ah. I wonder if Jamie and Eliza know."

"Likely not, as along with the rest of us, I think they've gotten so accustomed to the Delaney and Finn's close friendship, they haven't noted how it's evolved lately."

"But you, my wife of the spiritual realm, would never miss such developments." He chuckled.

"So true." She snuggled closer and threw her arm over him as they both thought about the delightful development before they fell asleep.

# CHAPTER TWELVE

## June 1913

Upon hearing that Chandler was going to Colorado instead of him, Dom set aside his immediate rage and concluded this was the perfect opportunity to sabotage his brother's mission and assure his first major job for *Rancha Mariposa* was badly bungled. He was called to a meeting with his father and brother the same night that Chandler had been told of his task.

Seated with his sons in his office, Damien appraised them while Adare served bourbon. "This transaction is a bit trickier than normal," he presently divulged, "because the seller Thomas Kelley, certainly the most eccentric man I've ever known, has informed me that he will only accept payment in cash and he must have you take possession of the bulls on Saturday. He cannot do the deal on any other day." He shrugged with an exasperated frown.

Dom struggled not to betray his excitement when he realized this was precisely the situation he needed to make Chandler look like an incompetent boob. Sipping bourbon, he forced himself to listen carefully as his father outlined the timetable for the plan. Once the specifics were settled, Dom returned to the bunkhouse, then saddled Acer and rode for Cheyenne to enlist the help of Clara Lou.

When he reached The Green Door and had climbed the stairs with Clara Lou, she studied him peevishly from a low stool in her boudoir, absently jerking her foot. He hadn't personally partaken of her services since he became one of Madam Charleen's select clients

"You sure you'd not prefer Madam?" She inquired sarcastically when he hadn't explained himself after several minutes.

"I need your help and I'll pay you well."

"I wonder. I ain't had the chance to please you in years."

"You will please me very much by helping me."

Her amber eyes took on a sheen of interest and she ceased bobbing her foot, waiting.

He explained what he needed her to do.

She spread her hands. "Your brother's goin' to Denver. What's that got to do with me?"

"Quite a lot as a matter of fact. I want you to do something for me in Colorado."

"Why?"

"This is the first chance I've had to settle things between my brother and me."

"I don't know how I'll do it."

"My dear, Clara Lou, with all the astonishing tricks in your bag, you can accomplish what needs to be done where anyone else would fail."

"I 'spect your fine brother thinks himself too much the gentleman to lie with me."

"True enough but as long as he doesn't know who you are, he can be convinced to have a roll in the hay."

"For all you know, he's still a virgin."

"Then he'll be all the more eager. I doubt it's true in any case. He's too much like our father. Damien Whittaker was bedding girls all over Oxford when he was in college so it's unlikely he's managed to preserve his virtue 'til now."

Clara Lou observed him with amusement. "Am I to be Sarah Bernhardt or maybe Mary Pickford for the fine Mr. Chandler?"

"Nothing so extravagant. Posing as a chamber maid will do nicely. You'll earn a nice bit of cash if you pull this off."

An enigmatic smile tugged the perplexed tautness from her mouth. "If the money is nice enough, I can do my best work."

"I'm sure you can." He reached down to catch her hands, drawing her from the stool to kiss her before lowering her to the bed.

"When will I go?" She asked some time later, her mind having clearly not been entirely on the details discussed earlier.

"I'll arrange a room in Denver. You'll go there Thursday and wait."

"With you?" She asked with a leering grin.

"No, I'll join you later on Friday, then come back so I'm on hand when Chandler's frantic wires arrive. It's going to be marvelous and I don't want to miss any of it."

"You're a very wicked man, Dom Whittaker."

"Only enterprising."

Clara Lou traveled to Denver Friday morning and took a room at a boarding house within a short distance of the Brown Plaza Hotel where Chandler was staying. When Dom arrived at her room that afternoon, he dispatched her to the Brown Plaza to learn her way around. Dressed in an up-to-date dress of blue georgette, her hat large and elaborate, she looked the part of a lady and didn't appear out of place in the elegant hotel. Later she would don the shabby dress she'd brought along as her chambermaid costume.

Dom had instructed her to hang about outside Chandler's room and somehow make him notice her when he arrived. Then it wouldn't seem strange when she took it upon herself to knock on his door later on.

Eager to be on his way back to Wyoming, Dom waited none too patiently for her to return from her scouting mission. He presently heard her key in the lock and watched her enter. She stopped, staring at him, then wrung her hands distractedly. ". . . I beg your pardon, sir . . . I . . . I know I'm behavin' unseemly but . . . I couldn't get you off my mind. And I got this here bottle from a frien' . . . ." She snatched a nearly full bottle of brandy out of her bag and stepped closer, her eyes imploring, wide with lust.

Standing before him, still clutching the bottle, she ran the tip of her tongue along her gaping lips. "Please, sir," she sighed, "you'd find me a real pleasure . . . ." She set the bottle on a table, then consulted him musingly. "Will that line work on your fine brother?"

He grinned, then laughed outright. "I should think that will do nicely but don't get so caught up in your fun that you forget to give him plenty to drink. He also takes after his father in that regard and holds his liquor well."

"I'll see he's restin' real comfortable when I make off with the money."

"I've no doubt." He raised an eyebrow. "You should be on the stage." With a shake of his head, he strode to the door. "I'm off then."

"Couldn't you wait a little?" She asked, following and reaching to touch him, her hands reinforcing the notion.

"No!" He shoved her away. "Save your lust for my brother. It should be safe for you to come home in a week. If not, I'll send a wire."

Clara Lou paced about her room, nervously wondering if she was up to pulling off the scheme. Earlier, when she'd seen Chandler leave the elevator and stride along the corridor to his room, she approached from the opposite direction, trying to decide if the tall, fair gentleman was him as all she had to go on was a tintype Dom had given her.

When he'd nearly reached her, she abruptly lurched and lost her balance, her arms waving erratically before she crumpled to the carpet. Alarmed, he leaned over her. "My, dear, are you hurt?" His engaging gray eyes met hers.

Grasping his hand to climb to her feet, she retrieved her hat that had come unpinned and secured it back atop her curls. Straightening her skirt, she gave him a smile. "Goodness, I don't know what happened. Perhaps my new shoes don't fit as well as I thought. In any case, have a pleasant afternoon." With that, she'd left him, looking after her, puzzled.

With a little smile, she decided he most assuredly would remember her later. She paced to the window and looked out over the grounds at the rear of the boarding house.

Though she probably shouldn't since she was working, she uncapped the brandy and poured a healthy amount into a glass. After swallowing most of it, she sat in an upholstered chair to wait. Drowsy, she closed her eyes, savoring the quiet and the soothing spirits.

She had no idea how much time had passed when she suddenly woke, the room dark around her. Sitting bolt upright, she didn't know where she was and panic jolted through her.

By degrees, her mind slid back and she remembered why she was there. *What time was it? Had she missed her chance to seduce Chandler?*

Rattled, she leapt up and flipped on the electric lights, staring at the brandy bottle that was now empty save for an inch or two at the bottom. How was it possible that she'd drunk nearly the entire bottle?

She wasn't accustomed to drinking alcohol in excess, let alone when she was working, as she had been since she arrived in Denver. Totally at a loss at her behavior, she struggled through her virtual intoxication, pulling on the shabby wrinkled dress that'd been stuffed in her reticule. Unable to recall why she needed to dress like a chambermaid, she inspected herself in a mirror, seeing a wild woman with hair sticking out in every direction. Smoothing it as best she could, she groaned but quickly pulled herself together and headed out.

As she walked towards the Brown Plaza, she realized that she had slept much too long. There were hardly any people on the street that actually seemed quite deserted. She noted a few saloons were still open, raucous music drifting into the night but otherwise it appeared Denver had gone to bed.

When she reached the Brown Plaza and walked through the deserted lobby, her heart hammered. Within minutes, she stood in the corridor outside Chandler's room. She almost hated to disturb the quiet but knocked on the door nevertheless.

There was no response even as she rapped again. The alcohol in her brain caused her to sway, resting her shoulder against the wood. Perhaps she dozed; in the next moment, she fought to remain standing as the door opened.

Chandler caught her as she fell forward. "What's the meaning of this?" Hauling her upright, he peered at her. "What are you doing back here?"

She could only stare at his rumbled countenance. It appeared she'd awakened him from sound sleep and he was having as much trouble as she comprehending why the two of them were confronting each other in the doorway of his bedchamber in the middle of the night.

If there had been some plan for her to say something to him, she had no clue what it was. All she could do with sag on the door jamb.

As he studied her, Chandler seemed intent on figuring out who she was and why she was there. Abruptly, understanding dawned. "Ah, now I remember you." He wagged a finger at her. "My brother's friend Caldwell went with him to The Green Door one night. They didn't know it but I followed them and hid in the front parlor when we first got to the house. That's where I saw you and watched you go upstairs with Dom."

His words served to bring her out of her stupor. Now she could only stare at him.

"I'd like to get back to sleep now. So you should take yourself off and abandon whatever it is you thought you were going to do here tonight. You know who I am so if my brother gives you any trouble because you failed here, let me know and I'll take care of it. I won't let him hurt you. Now off you go. Goodnight."

Stunned, she turned away as he closed the door.

Dom spent Friday night gaming at The Green Door before he rode to *Rancha Mariposa* the next morning. Some three miles from the ranch headquarters, he heard a horse somewhere beyond a stand of aspen. He pulled up just as Yvette charged into view astride Centaur. He hadn't seen her since she'd told him she was going to school to become a teacher and delight coursed through him at the sight of her tiny frame controlling the great force of the gelding.

"Dom!" She cried breathlessly, reining in beside him. She flung her head back, catching the sun on her face beneath her wide hat.

"Are you certain you can manage that beast?" He teased with a grin as the gelding tossed his head, batting the air with his front feet.

"We understand each other." Her hands gently communicated with his mouth through the reins and he ceased his dancing and stood still.

"When are you moving to Cheyenne?"

"Very soon. Race you to the Lodgepole!" Before he could reply, she was off, leaning low against the gelding's straining neck.

He urged his horse after her but Acer was no match for Centaur when he was rested and now he was weary after the trip from Cheyenne. Yvette reached the Lodgepole ford well ahead of him and sat there laughing, exhilaration pinking her cheeks.

"You've a real charger there," he said when they turned to ride side by side along the road at a more sedate pace.

"What happened to Foxfire?"

"He was twenty-seven so I finally made him retire. He's earned it. He's a wonderful horse and half Arabian so that's why he's living so long but I didn't want him working so hard anymore."

"What's this one's name?" Yvette asked.

"Acer."

Laughing and twisting this way and that in the saddle so as not to miss any of the delights along the route—twin fawns, the wild flowers in the meadow, the never-ending expanses of golden clover that covered the plains in vast folds as far as the eye could see in all directions. The warbling song of meadowlarks quavered in the quiet as the birds flashed yellow in the grass

Yvette's unbridled pleasure was catching and Dom found himself seeing the familiar sights with new enjoyment. When they parted on the cobbled driveway, he rode toward the *Mariposa* while she turned in the direction of Trail's End. He'd only ridden a short way when he pulled up and sat watching her until she disappeared. He couldn't decide what to make of her friendly behavior toward him. She'd behaved as if there was no rift between them. Shrugging, he presently rode on towards the stables. Perhaps she sensed that matters were now radically altered between them.

Within a matter of hours, Chandler would have passed from glory to humiliation. Dom smiled as he visualized Yvette's reaction once she learned what dastardly exploits Chandler had been up to.

When he entered the *Mariposa,* he found the household having lunch at the dining table. After washing up in the rear hall, he approached his parents, a probing of unease touching him at the serenity of the scene.

His father nodded as he took a seat next to him. "Nice of you to join us."

For some reason he couldn't pinpoint, Damien's smile put him off guard. "You seem surprised to see me," he ventured at last.

Damien lifted an eyebrow. "Not at all, but we were under the impression you preferred taking your meals with the men these days."

As the rest around the table waited for his answer, Dom felt heat suffuse his face. He was suddenly off balance. *Why had he come here for lunch today?* He hastily picked up the glass of wine by his plate and drank most of it. He realized with the arrival of real worry that he'd wanted to be with his father when word arrived of Chandler's folly.

Now, as he took in Damien's placid demeanor, he saw he still awaited his explanation. "I've missed spending time with my family," he lamely offered.

Damien clapped him on the back. "Well, we're delighted to hear that. We've missed you."

He concentrated on the plate of food Constance had placed before him.

"We saw Yvette ride up with you," said Harper from across the table. "Did you have the chance to speak with her?"

He nodded. "She's going to be moving to town next week."

"How do you feel about that?" Delaney inquired.

He leveled a peevish frown at her. "I daresay, my brother and I have no choice but to wait for the silly girl to make up her mind."

"She's going to teach school for quite a while, I think," Delaney observed.

"I doubt that. Once she's living in Cheyenne, I'm sure she'll find she's quite lonely and will come to her senses."

"I don't think so," Delaney rejoined.

Dom tiredly turned his gaze to his father. "No word from Chandler, then?"

"Oh, yes, apparently everything is on schedule. Your mother and I are riding out after lunch to meet him. He made the transaction and put our bulls on the train this morning." He glanced at the grandfather clock next to the kitchen entrance. "He should be well on his way here by now."

Dominique pushed his plate away, feeling suddenly ill. *What the devil had happened to thwart his careful plan?* He motioned to Adare and asked him to bring a glass of bourbon that he drank down while lingering at the table.

Harper already wore a riding skirt so she and Damien immediately departed for the stables. "What do think Dom's up to?" She asked as they walked past the magnificence of the summer garden.

He reached for her hand. "I couldn't say but I agree he did have a dubious look about him."

"Why is it that we can always depend on our eldest son to be on the verge of veering off course?"

"I can feel some empathy for him just now because I recall how devastated I was when my own wedding plans were blasted all to hell."

She managed a little laugh. "That was an awful time but in the present situation, Chandler is in the same boat as Dom and he appears to be dealing with the setback with his usual good grace."

"True enough but that's the way Chandler handles things in general. He's not easily knocked from his even-handed approach to life."

"Thank God," said Harper as they entered the stable yard.

Two lads hurried out, then dove back toward the stalls to fetch Avalon and Jasper, the black Thoroughbred stallion that had replaced Cadoc and Beckett who'd both been retired along with Harper's old friend Embarr. The stable boys assisted them in mounting and they turned the horses along the cobbled drive, soon heading along the rutted track that still served as the route to Cheyenne.

The afternoon was perfect with pleasantly warm temperatures and the blue sky filled with puffy white thunderheads that was so typical of Wyoming summer days. Damien and Harper rode close together, occasionally catching hands as they'd always done when they rode horseback together. Glancing at her rugged, tanned husband, her heart still quickened.

He was leaner, his handsome face more lined and weathered than when they'd first come to this vast, wild land so many years ago. Yet, to her, he was every bit as physically appealing now as he'd been as the dapper young Englishman who had first stolen her heart.

They presently pushed their mounts into a canter and continued at that pace until they topped a rise and saw the parade of Hereford bulls plodding toward them with Chandler riding at the head of the line. His gelding neighed in greeting to the other horses. To their considerable amazement, Damien and Harper saw that the lead bull wore a halter and was being led by Chandler who held the attached rope in his gloved hand.

Behind the leader, the other bulls followed, as docile as milk cows heading to the milking barn. Chandler grinned, raising his hand. Not wanting to disturb the serene progress, Damien and Harper stayed some distance back, presently turning to proceed to the ranch.

Damien inspected the prime stock with appreciation. As expected, these mature bulls were the finest Herefords he'd seen, aside from his own herd. Their blood would be a valuable addition to the *Rancha Mariposa* purebred breeding program.

Harper took in his pleasure. "Aren't they wondrous?"

He guided Jasper closer to her mare and leaned to kiss her. "My father would have loved Chandler's little parade."

When they neared the ranch headquarters, Jamie and John rode to meet them in case their help was needed. Dom, Granville, Finn and Delaney sat at the edge of the garden to watch the arrival.

As they observed, Chandler turned down the driveway with the bulls still doggedly following. Delaney clapped with glee while Dom could scarcely believe what he was seeing. This triumphant return of his brother leading the enormous beasts with the same ease as one would handle a family of goats filled him with such outrage, he could hardly see. He still couldn't imagine what had transpired last night at the Brown Plaza to have allowed this to happen. But, he was going to find out.

When the riders and Herefords had passed by him and continued on to the pasture where the bulls would be held until they were turned out with various herds of cows in July to ensure calves arriving in March, Dom headed to the stables. Within minutes, Delaney, Granville and the others saw him riding out like the Devil, himself, was after him.

With Clara Lou still in Denver, he had no choice but to take the evening train there if he was to learn what had happened to derail his careful plot. Now, assuming his brother would have a tale to tell their father, he had every desire to stay away from the ranch long enough for the matter to blow over.

Everyone watched the new Herefords file into their pasture, still as docile as dogs. Chandler dismounted and approached the admiring group.

Damien swung down and strode to embrace his son. "Good show, my man. I've never witnessed quite that kind of bull whacking."

Chandler laughed. "Well, sir, Thomas Kelley likes his Herefords tame. He claims that most of them are his pets and delights in feeding them by hand when they're calves so they stay bonded with him even when they're full grown. It's quite the most remarkable thing I ever saw. When he's out in the pasture with them, they all tend to follow him around and that does stir up a certain amount of jealousy but he manages to make them behave."

"I'll be damned," Damien finally replied. "Well, they are certainly a handsome lot." He touched Chandler's arm. "You did a fine job, son."

"Thank you, sir. I do need to have a word when it's convenient."

"Certainly. I'll meet you in my office."

Half an hour later, Damien sat behind his desk, savoring the bourbon Adare had brought him. A few minutes later, Chandler joined him, accepting his own glass.

"So what's on your mind?" Damien asked.

Tension tinged his voice when he finally spoke. "This is very difficult but I believe Dom was up to some chicanery while I was gone."

Damien's gaze narrowed. "Go on."

"It was just so strange and then it seemed to come together in the back of my mind and I knew it was Dom." He sighed and swallowed some bourbon as he tried to sort out his words. "I'm not making much sense, I know, but when I arrived at the hotel on Friday, I'd nearly gotten to my room when I noticed this woman approaching. When she came level with me, she suddenly stumbled and ended up falling at my feet. I helped her up, determined she wasn't hurt and she went on her way. After dinner that night, I was tired and knew I had a big day getting the bulls to the depot yesterday so I retired early.

"This is where it gets very peculiar indeed. Sometime in the middle of the night, I was awakened from a sound sleep by a knock on my door. I finally managed to answer it and found the same woman staring at me. Earlier, she'd been wearing a rather elegant blue dress and a huge hat. Now she had on a very wrinkled brown dress and looked altogether unkempt and reeked of alcohol. She carried a nearly empty bottle of brandy and seemed to be offering me some. It took me awhile to get a hazy grip on the situation and immediately I thought my brother was responsible. It abruptly occurred to me that I'd seen the woman at The Green Door in Cheyenne when I was a boy."

"How the devil did you come to that conclusion?" Damien asked in his own confusion.

"I remembered seeing her there a long time ago. When Dom came home from Harvard with Caldwell, the two of them went to town one night and I followed them. They ended up at a brothel and I slipped inside without anyone seeing me. That's when I saw that woman take Dom upstairs. About the same time, I saw Caldwell leave and when I went back outside and got on my horse, I saw him ride back to The Plains. After that, I headed home and I don't think anyone realized I'd been gone as everyone thought I'd gone to bed."

"You little scamp," Damien said drily.

He shrugged with a wry grin. "I just thought everything my brother and Caldwell did was so exciting. I couldn't help myself."

"I remember some of that."

"So getting back to being woken up in the middle of the night, as soon as I recognized the disheveled drunk at my door as the same lady I saw with Dom at The Green Door, I realized I was the target of some sort of scheme the two of them had cooked up."

Damien digested this as he drained his glass, then rose to circle the desk. He retrieved the bottle and refilled both glasses before collapsing into the chair next to Chandler's. "One thing is sure," he said at last, "your brother is going to be the death of me with all his cloak and dagger exploits. I dared think he'd given up most of his underhandedness, but now I see that was too optimistic a conclusion." He lifted his glass in a little toast. "I promise you, I'll get to the bottom of this. And I want you to know I could not be prouder of you."

"I do know that, Pa-pa."

"Good."

When Dom went to the boarding house, he found Clara Lou still in a drunken stupor. The sight of her in such an impaired and helpless condition enraged him as he stepped toward the bed where she lay in a crumpled heap, tears flooding her eyes the second she saw him.

"What the hell is the meaning of this!?" He yelled, stripping the rumbled blanket off her.

She whimpered, crawling toward the edge of the mattress to escape but he caught her hair, yanking her back, a scream smothering her sniveling.

He leapt astride her, one hand grasping her face so he could stare down at her. "What happened here . . . ?" He broke off, then continued with mocking sarcasm. "Oh, but of course, *nothing* happened. My brother just breezed on home with those bulls like a conquering hero. My father is absolutely delighted with him! Do you recall what *you* were supposed to do to prevent that happening?" His hand jostled her face. "Do you!?"

"Yes . . . but I drank the brandy . . . I drank too much and slept . . . too long . . . when I went to the hotel, it was way too late. He just looked at me like I was crazy . . . ."

"He looked at you like you were *drunk*!" He raised his hand, striking her face. "I daresay he laughed at you, you stupid bitch!"

Her weeping had become a high keening as he stood up, staring down at her with utter revulsion. "Well, you're going to have to get yourself home from this fiasco. I'm done with you. As far as I'm concerned, you're trouble and I'll be surprised if Madam Charleen even takes you back. You'd be better off to hire on at some house down here and crawl yourself up from the stinking pit you've dove into. Damn you to hell!" With that, he spun on his heel and left the room.

He caught the next train back to Cheyenne and fell into Charleen's welcoming arms to lick his wounds. After three days, he decided he must go home and deal with his father. He deplored the idea, thinking he'd be found out forthwith. His father was no fool and Chandler had likely spilled it all. That was all beside the point because he must maintain his standing at *Rancha Mariposa* by whatever means necessary.

He reached the *Mariposa* early in the morning and greeted his father and Harper in the Great Hall where they lingered at the breakfast table. "Good morning."

They both studied him for a long moment before Damien nodded toward an empty chair beside him. "I'm glad to see you decided to grace us with a visit this morning. I assume this is a visit, or are you back to resume your duties?"

He stared at his hands twisted together in his lap, frantically hunting for some means to explain his dereliction. "I am most certainly back." By painful degrees, he lifted his eyes to meet his father's, not forthrightly but in feeble flickers before he stared away again. "I don't know why I ran away . . ."

"Oh, come now, we all know why. It was because your greed and ill will toward your brother caused you to attempt sabotaging him and making him look like a fool in my eyes. Well, my man, you've managed to do nothing but make yourself into an utter laughingstock. And now I want a word." With a nod at Harper, he shoved back his chair and strode toward his office with Dom reluctantly following.

When they were seated, Damien observed his son from behind his desk. "Do you have any sort of explanation for your behavior?"

A scowl twisted Dom's mouth. "Since Chandler's been back from the university, it seems everything he does, is perfect in your eyes." He shrugged. "That scared me, I suppose. I wanted to do something to prove to you I can do as well."

Damien continued studying him while he tapped his finger on the blotter, appearing as if he could barely control himself from bolting the room. "Well, what you've managed to do with your flimflam is make me completely enraged and disgusted with you." He abruptly stood, slamming his fist into his hand as he paced to peer out the window. "I'm at a loss to know what to do with you. Harper and I have given you more second chances than anyone should be allowed. And there have been many stretches when your behavior has pleased us no end. We've been so very proud of you. Yet, invariably, you soon fall back into your old behavior."

"I'm very sorry, sir."

He swung back to level him in a cold stare. "Oh, are you really? I wouldn't know about that as I can no longer trust you."

"Please, Pa-pa. I will do better. I give you my word." His eyes implored him with the same wounded expression that had always tugged at his emotions when he was a boy.

Damien had rarely been able to resist this demeanor of hurt and self-doubt. But now his revulsion was sufficient that he was unmoved.

"What are you going to do?" Dom inquired uneasily.

Damien paced back to his chair and sat apprising him for some minutes. "Well, patting you on the head and accepting your assurances to do better and be better hasn't been helpful in the past. Apparently you cannot cultivate a more kindly attitude toward your brother and that seems to be the reason for most of your deception and trickery. So this time, I'm going to take a hard line with you. I, no doubt, should have done that years ago and perhaps we wouldn't find ourselves in this ridiculous fix now."

Dom started to speak but was cut short with a vicious slash of Damien's hand.

"The first thing I'm going to do is demote you to the status of a newly-hired cowhand . . ."

"You can't do that!"

"I can and I just did. As of this minute, you have no more authority than that lad Joseph we hired last month. The way I feel right now, I'd like to say this status will continue until you appear to have regained some of your good sense. But I'm going to make it a probationary state for the next six months, then we'll go back to business as usual except for one significant difference. I'm making Chandler foreman in your stead. That status change will be permanent."

Dom had gone pale. "How can I ever continue on here with my brother lording it over me?"

"Please, spare me your whining. You say you're sorry for behaving so badly. Well, I could sack you and no one would blame me for an instant. But I choose to give you the opportunity to prove to me that you're the young man I've always assumed you to be. I'm no longer certain of just what you are but I'm prepared to let you see what you can do to redeem yourself. If you don't wish to accept my terms, you can leave the ranch immediately."

"You must be joking?"

"Hardly. I just want to be very certain you understand how serious I am about this."

When he'd come home, Dom had expected his father's wrath but had no clue of the extent he was to punish him. Now he floundered in the import of his new circumstances. "Am I allowed to go to town?"

"Short of locking you up somewhere, I can't keep you here all the time. However, if I were you, I'd bear in mind that you will no doubt make more progress getting back in my good graces if you concentrate on your work here than if you continue seeing your nefarious friends in Cheyenne. But the decision is entirely yours."

He mulled this over for a time, then decided, he didn't have much choice in the matter. He'd tried something that had failed miserably. If he was honest with himself, he had to admit that he needed to take a new tack in dealing with Chandler so he might as well get on with it. "I'll do my best," he declared at last.

"I'm very glad to hear that." Damien busied himself with papers on his desk for a while, then lifted his gaze again. "Have you left any loose ends that need to be dealt with? Chandler seemed to think you'd lured a prostitute to Denver to help you with your scheme. Did you deal with her properly?"

Irritation touched him. "Actually, I left her there drunk out of her mind. Her doing, not mine. I advised her to try for employment at a house in Denver."

"What right did you have to do that?"

"She didn't do what I told her, what she was hired for."

"You mean she didn't hoodwink your brother so you could take advantage of the situation?"

"That's one way of putting it."

"Well, since you are the one who knows where she is and how to contact her, I want you to send her enough money so she can go back to Cheyenne if she wishes. It's the least you can do since we both know she did you a huge favor when she drank too much and was unable to follow through."

"Very well," Dom agreed presently. "Now, if you will excuse me." With great relief, he left the office and soon wandered outside through the back hall and ended up sitting on a bench in the rear garden. In his depression, his thoughts turned to Yvette. He longed to talk to her.

He continued there, seeking to sort out the turmoil in his mind, trying to locate some means to face his new status. Soon enough, he gave up. There was no tolerable way to work with Chandler and the others. He would suffer the greatest embarrassment in the days ahead and wished he could get far away from *Rancha Mariposa* before anyone else discovered his disgrace. But he'd resolved to stay and face whatever the future held. Did he really have the strength to do that?

A flash of blue from somewhere near the Aspen caught his eye and he watched Sawyer approach. Seeing him, she stopped. "Hello."

He nodded, a bit undone by the sight of his daughter whom he hadn't seen all summer. How was it possible that he had fathered this striking flame-haired woman who must be twenty-one now. The incredulity of it struck him every time their paths had occasion to cross. "What have you been up to these days?"

She shrugged, then lowered herself on the bench next to him. "Oh, I've decided to move to town and find a position. I'm going to live with Yvette while she's at the teacher's school."

This information startled him. "When are you going?"

"My parents and the Carrolls are taking us in tomorrow. We already have a room reserved at Myra Foxe's Boarding House. I think it will be great fun."

Wincing at her failure to acknowledge their blood tie, he studied her a moment. "What kind of position do you want?"

"I'm going to learn how to type so I can work in an office, I think."

"Ah, that's good then." On impulse, he looked at her closely. "Do you know who I am?"

"Of course, you're Delaney's brother." She laughed softly. "Oh, I see what you mean. Yes, I know you're my father. My mother told me that a long time ago and recently gave me all the money you've given her since before I was born. She says it's good to have a nest egg to help until I'm drawing a good wage. When I was about twelve, I always thought you were terribly handsome and it was a surprise when Mum told me who you are to me. Of course, I always loved my real parents and wouldn't have guessed who you were. But, it makes me feel special that my grandparents are Harper and Damien. They've been so special to me since I was a wee baby." She fell silent and sat gazing out into the garden where hummingbirds flitted about a patch of bee balm.

"Funny isn't it, how things turn out?" She said after a time, sliding a glance at him. "Even though my parents are the best in the world and I'm so lucky to have them, I also have a connection to you. Do you remember when my grandparents discovered that I'm allergic to any milk but goat's?" She shrugged when he didn't reply. "It was the same with you when you were a new baby in New York after your parents arrived from England. You screamed all the time and finally your father found you some goat's milk and you were fine after that. Isn't that interesting? You and I are the only two in all our families who could not drink cow's milk when we were little. Isn't that the most amazing thing?"

"Amazing. It may interest you to know you very much resemble your grandmother, my mother. She had the same brilliant hair."

She digested this as voices reached them from the direction she'd come earlier. They watched Chandler and Yvette coming toward them, holding hands and chatting animatedly.

Catching Yvette's delighted smile, Dom groaned under his breath. Was it possible this day could get any worse?

"Hello, Dom," Yvette said, stopping before him. "Has Sawyer told you, we're leaving tomorrow?"

He nodded as Chandler said something to Yvette only she could hear, kissed her cheek, then with a curt nod, continued to the *Mariposa,* disappearing inside.

Yvette sat beside Sawyer, linking arms with her. "Are you all packed?"

"Nearly. Mum's hemming my new shirtwaists. I love them and they'll be just the thing for my position. So smart."

"I like them, too," Yvette agreed. "They were a bit too staid for my taste at first but now they're lovely with all the lace and embroidery trims."

"I'll see you first thing in the morning." Sawyer stood, and heading past the *Mariposa* to the cottage next to the Aspen where she still lived with Ivy and Luke.

Following her with his eyes, Dom finally looked at Yvette. "So you're really leaving?"

"Of course. It's going to be wonderful. I can't wait to get settled. I'm so happy Sawyer's coming with me. We'll have a fabulous time together."

"I'll miss you."

Inclining closer, she draped one arm around his neck. "I, too, but you can come visit me if you like."

"Somehow sitting with you in a boarding house parlor doesn't have the same appeal."

She lifted an eyebrow. "Well, under those circumstances, perhaps I can think. I never could when you were nibbling my ear, trying to kiss me every minute we were together."

"I found you intoxicating. I still do."

"Yes, I know, and of course, I feel the same but we'll be all the better for some time apart."

He frowned. "I can't imagine anything much worse."

"You're sure to see the wisdom of it," she said firmly, brushing his black hair back with her fingers. "Besides, Chandler tells me you've been a very bad boy and tried to get him in deep trouble. Instead, you've ended up there yourself."

Looking at her dismally, he caught her hand and pressed it to his lips. "It's true. After you told me . . . we couldn't be together, I daresay, I went a bit crazy. I wasn't thinking clearly."

"How in the name of heaven could you plan to do something so awful, stealing the ranch's money and blaming it on Chandler?"

Miserable, he shook his head. "I can't explain it. I tried to tell my father why but I couldn't. I just become so frightened sometimes."

"Darling, you have nothing to be afraid of. Just stop and think how lucky you are. You have such a lovely family. Your father and Harper adore you as does Delaney . . ."

"Chandler doesn't."

She scowled at him. "Only because you're so obnoxious to him. He would like nothing better than to love you as only a younger brother can. But you've pushed him away and done your best to make his life miserable since he was only a boy."

"My father will always favor him. He's already demoted me and made him foreman."

"Well it doesn't require a lot of intelligence to comprehend why he did that. You're likely lucky, he didn't dismiss you outright."

"He threatened that." He raised his eyes to meet hers, so filled with love and concern that his heart hurt. "What am I to do? How can I do my work with everyone looking at me, knowing what I did?"

"Dom, you are an honorable man with such a capacity for love. I know life has been hard. I know how awful you were treated by your mother. I'm so, so sorry about that but your father and Harper have always tried to love you enough to make up for that. And, of course, my own parents have always loved you like you were one of their own children. You have been blessed as few men are. You must accept that and begin living up to what everyone expects of you."

Tears had crept from his eyes and now wandered down his striking face. She tenderly wiped away the wetness with her fingertips. Smiling, she hugged his head to her. "We both have much to do now. If we work hard, we can accomplish what we must and perhaps one day, we'll end up together. Perhaps not. But regardless, fate will lead us to where we belong."

He lifted his arms to embrace her. "If I could be with you, I know I could be better. Please, Yvette, marry me and help me be strong."

"I can't. Not now. You must be strong on your own." She snuggled against him, giving herself up to the joy of being held so close to his heart. How tempting it was to give in to his need for her.

She had little doubt that she could prop him up, bolster his confidence. If she was at his side, he would become strong enough to succeed as Damien wished. Yet, she would be sacrificing her own wish to triumph and accomplish something worthy apart from her future as a wife and mother. And that she could not do.

# CHAPTER THIRTEEN

## June 1914 – October 1915

After the fiasco in Denver, Dom was sufficiently chastened that he had resolved to police his behavior with extreme care. He swallowed his chagrin at losing his title of foreman and settled into his position as a mere cowboy with good grace. Although the men took their lead from Damien and Chandler and treated him with the respect he'd become accustomed to, he chafed at the reality that he no longer commanded any real authority. Nevertheless, he made every effort to stay the course and refrained from traveling to Cheyenne until he was half out of his mind with his hunger for some sort of entertainment and mental stimulation.

He'd remained hard at work at the ranch for a total of five weeks before he finally rode to town, using the excuse of visiting Yvette. No one offered the slightest protest and he left early on Saturday morning the first week in August.

Once he reached town, he made inquiries and soon found himself on the street in front of Myra Foxe's Boarding House. Leaving Acer tied to the hitching rail, he bounded up the steps and rang the bell.

Soon enough, a plump little woman wearing an enormous apron opened the door. "Hello, may I help you?"

"I'm here to see Yvette Carroll. Is she in?"

The lady peered at him over spectacles for a brief span. "And who might you be?"

"A friend. Dom Whittaker."

"Well, wait here, young man and I'll see if Miss Carroll wishes to see you." She gestured toward a cluster of wicker furniture circling the wrap-around porch.

"Thank you," Dom said with a courtly bow, watching her recede back into the Victorian mansion painted a startling lavender shade. He settled into a rocker to wait.

Mrs. Foxe was absent for some time before she arrived back on the verandah with Yvette in her wake.

Dom stood, his heart surging at the sight of her wearing one of the stylish shirtwaists in a lovely deep burgundy color over a handsome gray skirt. He was astonished to note that the hem was a few inches shorter than had been the fashion forever, exposing an intriguing expanse of low, elegant boots laced over her shapely ankles.

As he stepped forward, she moved eagerly into his embrace, accepting a kiss on her cheek. "How are you darling?"

She laughed softly. "I'm well. I've been in school for over a month now and I'll have my certificate before Christmas."

"So you'll be back home for all the yuletide fun?" He speculated.

"Yes." She twirled away and sat on a nearby bench upholstered in calico, still observing him expectantly. "My mother will only have to fill in for Eliza for a matter of months. The twins are due in September and I'll be ready to begin my teaching duties in January." To his annoyance she looked altogether thrilled with herself.

Leaning back in his chair, Dom watched her with wavering enthusiasm. He'd missed her so desperately in the past weeks and he'd hoped she might have suffered the same so she would be as delighted to see him as he was to be with her again. He'd hardly expected her detached reception though he likely should have.

It was suddenly and belatedly clear to him that she was doing precisely what she'd told him she'd decided was the best course for her life in the foreseeable future. He realized that he hadn't believed what she told him until this moment. He'd thought she couldn't be serious when she said she no longer wanted to marry him. That she needed time and space to decide if she ever wished to be his wife.

Now looking into her laughing Wedgwood eyes, he finally did believe her. Though, she still captivated him every bit as much as she ever had, he knew that if he had any chance of having her for his own forever, he must play by her rules and give her what she wanted. "Is Sawyer finding town life as agreeable as you have?" He inquired presently.

"Oh, indeed, she's already found a position in an attorney's office. A woman who's been employed there for some years is giving her personal lessons in using a typewriter. Sawyer's well on her way toward full-time employment."

"Well, that's good then."

"Yes, it is. Sawyer is a very enterprising young lady." She slanted him a musing glance. "Like her father. I must say I still find it difficult to believe she is your daughter. You apparently came close to setting a record for being the youngest man to father a child."

"Not hardly," he scoffed, turning his hat in a circle as he considered her. "Come downtown and have lunch with me?"

"No, thank you. I have to study all of today and tomorrow to be ready for an examination on Monday."

He groaned under his breath. "You're positively dreary company."

She narrowed her gaze. "I'm sure you can find someone livelier among some of your old friends." With that, she rose and turned to grasp the handle of the screen door leading indoors. "Goodbye, Dom." She had the audacity of blowing him a kiss over her shoulder.

He watched her disappear, then made his way back down the steps and across the lawn to his horse. Smarting from Yvette's unruffled dismissal, he mounted and turned toward The Green Door.

By two o'clock, he'd enjoyed a lavish dinner with two saucy lasses he'd not encountered previously, serving as his amazingly accommodating waitresses. Later, reclining against the pillow of the shorter one's munificent breasts, he gave himself up to the sensuous delight of her clever hands massaging his temples.

"Ah, Mr. Whittaker, could I interest you in joining me in my boudoir?"

The possibility was appealing and he was tempted to give himself up to her ministrations. Yet, some scrap of good judgement kept him from doing so. He must keep his wits about him and was soon ensconced at a gaming table with Madam Charleen and several of her regulars.

With Yvette away in Cheyenne and Dom trying to tread a more reliable and upright course, an interlude of calm ensued at *Rancha Mariposa.* With Chandler at the helm, the work on the ranch was well organized and following the spring roundup and branding, a bumper crop of hay was harvested and stored in the corrals that had been rebuilt the year before.

Chandler had also seen the need for new cattle barns the previous summer. With the approval of all the stockholders, he'd engineered a major renovation of all the outbuildings. The crude sheds that had sheltered the Herefords in the early years were torn down and new sturdy structures went up.

Now in the autumn of the second year of Chandler's maintenance program, the headquarters had taken on a prosperous, gracious mien. Cattlemen came to see the highest quality Hereford cattle in the world. When they wished to add Whittaker stock to their own breeding program, they were taken to the new viewing arena where venerable old cottonwoods shaded comfortable seating and Dobbs, the newly-hired footman served tea and scones. Bourbon was liberally offered to everyone.

Chandler, Jamie, Luke and Caldwell had begun training prime breeding stock to halter for ease in showcasing the handsome beasts before visiting clientele. Nothing warmed the hearts of Damien and Harper more than sitting with their fellow cattlemen and their wives as their beloved Herefords, scrubbed and combed until their red hides gleamed, their white markings sparkling, plodded around the enclosure as unruffled as carousel horses.

The prices paid for their stock created by decades of precisely refined bloodlines were staggering. After the buyers had departed one evening in July, Harper, and Damien pondered their good fortune.

This is what they'd aimed for and toiled towards all those years of storms, drought and rustling. Catching Harper's eye, he winked, then looked up when Delaney and Finn approached along with Granville from the training ring that had now been built in the open field

"Hi, Pa-pa," Delaney said, kissing his cheek. "Aren't they gorgeous?" Her gaze followed the last of the cattle being led toward the barns.

"Darling." He watched as she sat between him and her mother while Granville and Finn sat in chairs opposite. "Yes, they are. All those muddy spring nights when I wrestled to birth Hereford calves, I always marveled at how pristine they looked the next day capering about their mothers in a green pasture. Now after a bath and grooming, these rugged aristocrats are nearly as pretty as their offspring. Quite extraordinary."

"When the judges at the National Western Stock Show see them in January, they'll all rush to adorn their halters with purple ribbons and haul out the gold trophies," Granville opined. He spoke of the premier stock show that had begun in Denver in 1906 as a rough and tumble occasion and had since grown to a prestigious event that drew the finest livestock from across the nation. *Rancha Mariposa* would be exhibiting their best cattle in every breeding class.

Three-Day-Eventing at the Stock Show would mark, at long last, Delaney's debut, which meant she would ride in Stadium Jumping, Dressage and Cross Country over three days. She'd been training Destino hard for months under Granville's expert scrutiny, with Finn's constant help and support. Centaur was also in training in case some calamity befell Destino.

During previous autumns, the weather had deteriorated by October and training was moved inside to a huge barn where riding rings were furnished with jumps and dressage areas were covered with deep sawdust. This year, the weather held, with clear warm days continuing with no change in sight and Delaney's training took the same course.

By the end of the summer, Dom had fallen back into his obsessive gambling. The emotional rollercoaster of winning large sums was like an opiate to his senses. While he remained devoted to Yvette and was determined to give her the time away from him she claimed she needed, he was desperately lonely and vulnerable without her.

His state of mind was hardly improved by reports that whenever Chandler chose to visit Yvette, he was welcomed and allowed to spend entire afternoons and evenings with her. This state of affairs refueled Dom's insane jealousy of his brother.

Chandler still could do no wrong in his father's eyes. He'd labored all summer, making changes and repairs at the ranch headquarters and by autumn, *Rancha Mariposa* had been transformed into a rural showplace reminiscent of the most revered old estates in Europe. During the balmy days of fall, wealthy cattlemen and their wives came to inspect the grand herds from carriages and motorcars before retiring to the shady viewing arena where they drank cocktails, while the finest bulls were paraded before them. When they'd chosen which of the beasts they wished to take home in the hopes that one day they would own Herefords of the same superiority, they departed, happier for the chance to have rubbed elbows with the aristocracy.

Dom watched the genteel promotion of *Rancha Mariposa* with amazement that he hadn't come up with the idea himself. He'd witnessed enough of this kind of schmoozing with the wealthy when he visited the Thoroughbred farm owned by Caldwell's parents. He'd attended endless open barns and afternoon socials where horses were trotted out in all their highly-polished glory while champagne bubbled in crystal fountains and buffet tables groaned with delicacies.

If he'd only known this sort of thing was what his father wished to pursue, he could have outdone his little brother and garnered some of the idolatry for himself. As it was, he'd missed his opportunity in this so kept his eye out for other ways to build his standing.

It also irked him no end that Chandler had appointed himself along with Finn as Granville's aides in preparing Delaney for her inaugural horse show in Denver. In light of his greater experience in English horsemanship, it galled him to have been passed over because he wasn't Delaney's full brother. Indeed, his shoddy ancestry on his mother's side continued to plague him.

Because Chandler was his superior at the ranch, Dom saw no reason to put forth more effort than was strictly necessary. When he was in charge, he'd found the work challenging. Now that he'd been demoted, he was bored and uninspired, and craved more and more time in the gaming parlor.

After the fall roundups were completed, the very best calves, yearlings and two-year-olds, both heifers and steers were selected for the Denver Winter Stock Show. Dom had entered another period of bad luck.

While he was in nowhere near the dire straits of years back, he was desperate to recoup his losses any way he could. He redoubled his efforts at the tables and left the additional autumn work that year to Chandler and the other men.

The forty head of Herefords bound for the Stock Show were confined in indoor pens where they were fed a special diet and exercised daily. This activity added hours to the usual winter routine of caring for the rest of the cattle. The men were aided in this by the excellent weather ushering in winter.

To keep up appearances, Dom turned up at the ranch a few days every week but concentrated most of his attention on his activity at The Green Door. After one particularly discouraging evening of gambling, he retired with Charleen to her boudoir.

"I believe I may know of a means for you to recoup some money," she said at some point during the night. "You doubtless know Bob Williams."

"Of course, he owns a feed store in town."

"One that provides most of the feed for your cattle."

"That's right."

"Well, before you ride back to your ranch, you must speak to him. I believe you will be very interested in what he has to say."

When Dom stopped at the feed store the next morning, he learned that he could not only make some money for himself, he could make greater strides toward undermining Chandler. He left the store with the promise to see Williams again at the end of the week after he'd had the chance to think over what the man had proposed.

As he rode towards the ranch, he was at battle with himself. Not so long ago, he'd resolved to repair his tarnished relationship with his father, and to do that he'd concluded he must endeavor to treat his brother with greater respect and goodwill.

But Chandler hadn't made this pledge easy or even feasible for Dom to carry out. He'd proven once more that he was his father's golden son who could do no wrong. Everything he'd undertaken on behalf of the ranch and his family had been completed with admirable skill and dispatch that'd made Dom weary watching it.

He couldn't fathom how he could ever best Chandler on an even playing field. He was clearly out of his league and the sole means he possessed for undercutting him was by guile.

By the time he joined the work in the cattle pens, he'd made up his mind. He would join Bob Williams in bilking whatever *Rancha Mariposa* funds they could manage. What other choice did he have?

*Rancha Mariposa* had bought feed at Bob William's store for the better part of twenty years. During Dom's ride back to Cheyenne two days later, he could have wept for the money he'd lost because he'd been unaware of the merchant's true character. Up until Chandler recently took over, Jamie had been in charge of buying feed. If he'd known the opportunity he was missing, Dom would have assumed responsibility for buying grain the minute he became a stockholder.

Once he arrived at the feed store and tied Acer outside, he walked through, finally stopping outside the shabby office at the rear. "Afternoon."

"Anything wrong with your last order, Mr. Whittaker?" The fat, sweating man behind a disordered desk inquired.

"I've considered you proposal!"

He snickered. "You don't say." He jumped up and rounded the desk in such haste, he knocked a stack of papers to the floor. He slammed the door, then rushed back to his chair where he collapsed, staring at Dom who attempted to gather the scattered papers. "You in then?"

Dom straightened. "I am. I believe we may be able to do business together with both of us profiting."

"You'd best bear in mind your brother buys the grain and he ain't gonna skim the bills and you know it. He's too much like his pa who's straight as ol' Robin Hood's arrow." Williams' face took on a pugnacious frown. "I don' want no trouble. I've got to trust those that work with me."

"Well, just jack up our bills and I'll come by from time to time to collect half the proceeds."

Williams shrugged. "I'll keep an eye out fer ya."

As Dom departed, he decided it was important the padding went on for some time for it to have the desired impact on his father when he eventually learned of it. He was more than happy to wait while he collected the ill-gotten money that would give him working capital for gambling.

Because more and more autos were purchased throughout Wyoming, many Good Roads Clubs were organized during the autumn, providing voluntary labor to make the crude trails more accommodating. Rocks were removed, ruts filled and bridges were either repaired or built for the first time. Dom and a crew of *Rancha Mariposa* men joined the workers erecting a substantial bridge at the Lodgepole ford that had served the Whittakers for decades.

Dom and most of the ranchers harbored an intense dislike for the noisy machines that frightened horses and appeared to hog the most-traveled routes. But gradually as legislation dealt with the problem, the disapproval began to wane.

While Yvette still lived in Cheyenne, Dom had his own Chalmers Touring Car sent out from Detroit. After taking possession of the smart convertible at the depot in October, he managed with some difficulty to maneuver it to Mrs. Foxe's boarding house to show Yvette.

She was less than impressed when he invited her out on the porch to look over the shiny machine at the curb. "It's very bright," she allowed at last, taking in the brilliant yellow shade of the paint.

"Don't you think it's beautiful?" He urged her to go closer down the steps.

She reluctantly approached the car. "Much too flashy for my taste," she said with a deflating lack of enthusiasm. "And what happens when it rains?"

He darted forward to point out the cover folded neatly behind the two luxurious seats. "It's very easy to raise this on a moment's notice. Come take a ride," he pressed. "You'll see how nice it is. So much more comfortable than a carriage."

She shook her head and turned back. "No, thank you. I'm quite busy and it's going to take me some time to grow accustomed to this fancy machine. Perhaps next time you drive to town, I'll be more receptive to the idea."

He'd learned by this time that when she made up her mind about something, she wouldn't budge so he abandoned further tactics to convince her. Nonetheless, she'd once again managed to puncture his bubble of happiness. He couldn't bear the same reaction at the ranch so instead, drove his prize to The Green Door for the night.

The following week Yvette received her teaching certificate. Her parents traveled to Cheyenne to attend her graduation and bring her home. Since she was now ready to take up her duties as teacher of the girls at the ranch, it was decided she would live in a suite of rooms at the *Mariposa.*

Damien and Harper hosted a congratulatory dinner for her the first night she was back. Eliza's twins Helene and Harkin were only six weeks old so they stayed at home with their nurse.

Mrs. Mildred Blanchard originally from Sussex had been hired after Mrs. Goodeve died during the winter. Mildred had come from England in 1888 to work for another family from Europe who had returned there the previous year so she was happy to come and work for the Whittakers. Though most of the family had favorites from Mrs. Goodeve's bill of fare, they soon found their new cook and housekeeper could duplicate most any dish.

Harper looked about the table, taking in the families that now made up the guests. What changes had been wrought over the past decades. Arthur and Laura sat opposite. Their youngest

Mercy who was ten was the image of her mother with the palest skin and hair. Their two sons Ashley and Aaron were home from their early study at the University of Wyoming. Testing in history had shown them both so far ahead of their high school classmates, they were allowed to become college students years ahead of schedule.

Caldwell and Anne sat holding hands. Further along the table, Luke and Ivy's family sat in a jolly line, three-year-old Sally beside Sawyer who'd come home to celebrate Yvette's graduation. Next to her, Doreen, twenty years old, fair and lovely, held one-year-old Jesse. Finn and Delaney sat with his sisters Cassidy and Caitlyn. Jamie and Eliza looked on with pride.

Aunt Pris managed to attend in her wheeled chair pushed by her nurse, Colleen, who'd been hired after a stroke left her unable to navigate on her own. John and Audra sat with Millie and her young husband Sam, a *Rancha Mariposa* groom, holding their two wee daughters Della and Winnie, endearing in matching lavender dresses, their pale curls dressed with green grosgrain ribbons.

Delaney looked fondly at her old friend and her handsome family. She still harbored a bit of pique over Millie's decision to abandon their plans to ride horses together forever for marriage and children. Now that a few years had passed, they were once again each other's greatest champions.

Studying the cheerful group and all the beautiful children, Harper's heart surged with gratitude and the greatest sense of accomplishment. How marvelous that the quest, begun so long ago, had reached fruition in this circle of friends and family around the table. Reading the direction of her thoughts, Damien gave her a wink, squeezing her hand beneath the linen.

She took note of those missing, most notably Dom whose rudeness at missing dinner sent an ache of regret through her. How much she would love to always be able to depend on him. She couldn't really remember the last time that had been the case. Olivia, Bethany, Willa and their families were also absent but only because of the short notice of the celebration.

Her attention settling on Delaney and Finn, she idly wondered when they might decide to marry and have children. With the goals her daughter had set for herself, she knew it might be some time before she blessed her parents with grandchildren.

Considering all that Delaney had already accomplished, her mother was content to wait. Her girl's talents caused her heart to swell with pride.

Seated together, Yvette and Chandler appeared gleeful at her return. After dinner was completed with champagne, they were desperate to be alone. Since the gathering broke up early, Chandler invited her to sit with him in the piazza.

It seemed perfectly natural for her to settle into the familiar circle of his arms as twilight came down around them. "I've missed you so much," she said softly.

"Thank God, you're back now. Were you able to sort things out while you were away?"

"I've thought of little else. I can say for sure, I can't imagine my life without you."

"So you've made your choice then?" He asked, his pulse hammering at the possibility. His eyes darkened with his love as he looked into her exquisite face.

She lifted her arms around his neck, kissing him with all the vehement ardor that had built while they were apart. After a long time, she wrenched her mouth from his. "Oh, my darling, Chandler. I love you so," she breathed against his neck.

"You haven't answered my question?"

Sighing, she gazed at him helplessly. "Let me end things properly with Dom."

He groaned. "I was under the impression that had already happened."

"I still must speak to him. He's very tenacious."

"That's one word for him."

She traced one finger along his jaw. "Please give me a bit more time. We do have time now that we'll be living in the same house. As I told you and Dom last year, I truly want to teach. Now that I have my certificate, I'm anxious to take over for my mother in the girls' classroom here. But you and I will still have time to enjoy each other's company." She burrowed her head into the valley between his throat and shoulder. "I want to be courted again."

A smile lifted the corner of his mouth and he gathered her close. "Are you telling me I now have exclusivity in that regard?"

She straightened so she could look at him squarely. "Yes, that's what I'm saying. I'm no longer interested in being shared. I want to be loved and cherished by you alone."

Passion drifted into his eyes, lending them a silvery hue. "Lord, I don't know how much more I could bear of this peculiar game we've been playing. I cherish you, Yvette, and I want you with me forever."

Abruptly, tears overtook her and he found a handkerchief in his pocket and tenderly wiped at them. "I must speak to Dom," she added.

"I know that and I want our new status made very clear to my brother. Perhaps this will help convince him." He reached into his pocket for the filigreed sapphire ring she'd refused the last time he'd given it to her.

Smiling as she watched him slip it onto her finger, she slowly lifted her eyes to his. "Darling, it's so beautiful."

"As are you." He kissed her for a long interval, then drew her to him once more and they continued there in the cool of the thickening darkness. He savored the reality of her recommitment. Was it possible that at last, his brother was no longer a threat to their future?

Yvette settled into her suite at *Mariposa,* cherishing the new peace in her life since she'd made her choice between the two Whittaker brothers. The sole source of lingering unease stemmed from not having had the opportunity to tell Dom of her decision. Perhaps sensing the turn of fate, he didn't return to the ranch for over a week after she came home to stay. She longed to have the matter finished and remained at loose ends until a startling development girded her resolve and removed the last doubt about her choice.

Early the next week, Chandler rode to Cheyenne to do the usual errands that were his responsibility as ranch foreman. Upon his return in the afternoon, he sent Dobbs, the footman, to summon his parents, John, Jamie, Luke, Granville and Yvette to his father's study which he now also used for his own business.

As Yvette entered, taking in the group, she was at a loss to know why they'd been convened. Adare arrived with bourbon on a tray and set to the task of serving.

Yvette settled into a chair next to Chandler and immediately picked up his nervous energy. He caught her hand, kissed her cheek and offered her a smile.

"I'll get right to what I need to say," he began once everyone was present. "As you know, when I go to Cheyenne every month, I personally pay all the invoices that have accumulated. Last night, I looked over the bills and wrote out the checks I would deliver today. I thought something didn't look just right. Prices for feed had gone up substantially which didn't make sense because we've had good moisture and no hail or anything else that would cause a shortage." He looked steadily at his father, his mouth twisting in thought.

"Perhaps it was hasty of me but the first thing that came to mind was Dom. I thought perhaps he was involved, intent on getting his hands on funds illegally again. The more I considered it, the more it made sense that he was guilty of something. So I went to see Ted Meyer."

Damien's gaze narrowed. "You went to the sheriff with nothing more than your suspicion?"

"I know it was risky and could have turned out badly. But as it is, I was right. As soon as Ted and I turned up in his office, Bob Williams became very agitated and told us the higher prices were due to a greater demand for feed."

"I told him I wanted to see his account books and by that time, he was already through arguing. He'd bothered to make a duplicate copy of the orders Dom had made so it was all very clear. The amount of feed ordered was clearly noted, then multiplied by a percentage he evidently thought he could collect from us without any questions. I also inspected Williams' record of written checks and found those written directly to Dom." He rested elbows on his knees.

"What is truly astonishing is just how sloppily this was all pulled off. My brother isn't stupid by any stretch of the imagination, yet this was a very amateurish scheme. What do you make of that?"

"He's been drinking a great deal for some time now," Yvette said. "I'm certain you know that is one reason he spends so much time in Cheyenne lately. He's simply not in any condition to ride home or to work when he gets here."

All eyes settled on her.

"I actually wasn't aware that he's sunk to that level," Damien allowed. "As has happened so many times in the past, I daresay, my love for him has muddled my good sense. I've been blind to much of his deception. Now, I can no longer trust him in any capacity." He let his eyes slide between Chandler and Yvette. "Do either of you have any idea how we should deal with him at this juncture?"

Yvette twisted her thin hands together in her lap. "I, too, harbor a soft spot in my heart for him. He's so sensitive to everyone's opinion."

"I know that," Damien concurred, "but it's done no good continuing to let him have a free rein."

"Perhaps he would benefit from a period away from *Rancha Mariposa,"* Jamie ventured presently.

"I'm thinking along the same line," John agreed. "It seems to me, he needs a jolt to get his attention."

"And prevail upon him to stop taking his life here for granted," Granville added.

"I don't wish to leave him without means." Damien turned his gaze around the group.

"He's far from being without means," Chandler interjected. "I daresay he's doing rather well for himself at the gaming tables. If not, there's likely a message to be learned in that."

Damien pondered this, reaching for Harper's hand. "Well, I do know one thing for sure. I will no longer tolerate his behavior. So I need to speak with him as soon as he can get himself home." His sipped his bourbon reflectively.

"I shall be pleased to fetch him," Granville offered with a sudden twinkle in his eye. "It's a splendid afternoon for a drive."

Everyone smiled at his enthusiasm for taking out the blue Flanders Coupe he'd recently purchased, stunning everyone at the ranch. Indeed his unexpected capitulation to the rising trend toward automobile ownership had inspired the Whittakers, Carrolls, Horncastles as well as Arthur, Caldwell, Finn and Luke to follow suit. Shiny autos now graced hastily-constructed garages at each home.

Granville soon departed for his apartment while the rest filed out into the courtyard where shortly, they watched his handsome little coupe speed past along the driveway. He wore a driver's cap and goggles and a gay orange neck scarf fluttered jauntily behind.

Because the new transportation by automobile speeded up the trip to Cheyenne and back, Granville returned by six o'clock with Dom's flashy yellow convertible close behind. By this time, the rest of the party had come in from outside and gathered in the parlor where Dobbs served more bourbon and lemonade.

When Yvette heard the men arriving in the rear hall, she excused herself to wait in the drawing room for her own meeting with Dom. She sat near a window, looking out past the piazza where evening draped dark over the front garden. Ravens circled in the gloaming.

Huckleberry and Rumor settled on either side of her on the settee. She idly rubbed their ears, her thoughts turning to what Chandler had divulged earlier. Helpless to comprehend how Dom could have continued sabotaging Chandler when his earlier deceit had been discovered with the resulting repercussions, she felt ill.

She knew how vulnerable and afraid he was. Yet, she was also keenly aware of her mounting rage. She felt used and doubted she could ever trust him again.

Slowly impatience intruded on her reflection. She wanted an end to the indecision that had dogged her for over a year. Her heart now belonged fully to Chandler and she wanted the last impediment to their love removed.

Apparently, brevity had attended Dom's session with his father and the others. No more than fifteen minutes passed before he approached Yvette. She was quite unnerved by his disheveled appearance. As he lowered himself beside her, dislodging the beagles, she was appalled by his unwashed odor. She couldn't remember a time when she'd been near him when he wasn't perfectly groomed.

Now she looked into his bloodshot eyes, nearly weeping with her worry for him. "Dom, what has happened to you?"

He appeared in shock, running his hands back through his uncombed hair. "They've sacked me," he said, seemingly unable to grasp this reality.

"Did you believe you could go on with your deceit with no one the wiser?"

He stared at the floor during a long pocket of silence before lifting haunted eyes. "I didn't know what else to do."

"Whatever do you mean by that?"

"I've wanted you to be my wife from the time you were just a little girl. But once Chandler came home from college, he was so perfect. And you decided to become a teacher instead of marrying me." He considered her bleakly. "I thought if I made it look like my brother wasn't so honorable after all, you might love me again. And my father would see I could run *Rancha Mariposa* the way I did when *I* came home from Harvard."

Heartsick, she could only stare at him. "Right now, you disgust me," she said at last. "I am so furious with you! You've always been so blessed. You had every advantage, yet you've squandered it all. I can't fathom what the matter is with you."

"I was always damaged goods."

"Oh, please. You had everything anyone could want. You were gifted with stunning good looks and a brilliant brain. You had money and privilege."

"I had a dreadful mother despised by everyone . . ."

"Oh, spare me, you ridiculous ingrate! You had a father who loved you to the depth of his soul and a step-mother who couldn't have loved you more if you were her own child. *My* family adored and sheltered you; every one of us was bewitched by your charm and sweet nature." Her periwinkle eyes snapped with anger. "You've never had a single moment in your entire life when you lacked for anything!"

He gave no answer to her harsh words, only sat with shoulders bent.

"I hope at this pitifully late date, you take your family's rejection as a sign that you must seriously change your ways! You're still young and if you begin anew from this day on, you can become the man we all know you are capable of being." She testily waited for his reaction.

"If I had you by my side, perhaps I could . . ."

"It's far too late for that, Dom. I belong to Chandler now."

Tears glittered in his beseeching gray eyes as he lifted his head. "Oh, Yvette…."

"No one can give you the strength you desire. You must find that within yourself."

"I can't . . ."

"You're disgusting. You've no choice now but to be on your way and get yourself settled. There's nothing at all left for you here just now."

Fumbling a handkerchief from his pocket, he wiped his face and stood up. Without speaking or looking at her again, he strode toward the back hall. Shortly, she heard his auto in the driveway and then he was gone, swallowed in a haze of dust.

# CHAPTER FOURTEEN

## October 1915 – November 1915

In the face of the hard work that occupied all their days now, Delaney and Finn still hadn't made their relationship official. The matter came to the forefront for them in November when they both entered a bewildering period when constant agitation dogged them and despite the good weather, they weren't putting the finishing polish on either Delaney's performance or that of her mount. With all their bumbling, Granville concluded they looked more like beginners than a seasoned pair ready for competition.

They both had difficulty concentrating on the training. Finn tended to drift off into flights of imagination, losing track of what was happening in the schooling ring.

For her part, Delaney was far from her customary disciplined self. She lost her way in the midst of dressage drills that were so familiar she could've managed them while asleep.

Granville watched their mutual anxiety manifest itself in all manner of odd behavior until he came to the end of his patience barely half an hour into their customary morning schooling session. He motioned them to the edge of the ring where he sat in his usual chair.

When they stood before him, he studied them for several minutes while they grew more nervous and ill-at-ease. "What am I to do with the two of you?" He finally asked.

They could only wait, unable to figure out what was amiss. He presently looked directly at Delaney.

"My dear, you have been totally inept for the past week, longer actually if we're to be strictly honest. If this continues, we may as well cancel the trip to Denver. At this rate, Miss Delaney, the spectators would laugh you out of the ring."

Her face crumpled and she was instantly fighting tears. "I . . . I know. I can't figure out what's wrong." Her thin shoulders slumped. "I'm so tired . . . I can't even sleep anymore . . . ." She glanced at Finn, who she now saw looked as exhausted as she felt. He reached a hand toward her and she grasped it like an anchor .

"Well, my friends," Granville said, frowning at them. "What I think we should do is give up on working today. We're getting nowhere. And I believe the two of you should try to sort out what's wrong."

They looked at him numbly until a knowing glint crept into his wise appraisal. "Let's send Destino to the barn, shall we, while we have a bit of a heart-to-heart." He beckoned to a stable lad who led the horse away, then rose to put an arm around each of them, guiding them to a bench along the rear edge of the garden.

"Now then," he said when they were seated, "you're likely wondering why I'm being so presumptuous as to propose speaking so openly to you. The reason is it just now occurred to me why the two of you have been behaving like ninnies." He grinned, apparently quite proud of himself. "Before I married my beloved Angela, we were both behaving much the same way."

Delaney stared at him, wondering what on earth he was talking about. Glancing at Finn, she saw he was equally nonplussed.

"You two have been close as conjoined twins for years now. I daresay everyone has long since taken your bond for granted, assuming that it will be the same between you until you're ninety years old. The same is apparently true of the two of you. At least, I am unable to see another reason why you're behaving so oddly." He spread his hands, lifting an inquiring eyebrow.

Digesting his words, Delaney suddenly understood what he was getting at. He knew what was happening. At least, he knew what was happening to her. She couldn't be sure about Finn, but lately, she certainly hadn't been thinking that they would continue forever as just friends.

Her nights had become fraught with amazing scenarios where she often found herself imagining in great detail what it would be like to share a bed with Finn in the same way her parents shared theirs. Even on nights when she was completely worn-out from training, she was helpless against the provocative pictures. Her heart raced and perspiration soaked her nightgown.

"In any case," Granville continued. "Back so many years ago, Angela and I had been courting for four years and we behaved very chastely as was expected at the time. On the few occasions when I gathered the courage to kiss her, we were thrown into paroxysms of passion that shocked us to the depth of our souls. For myself, I often thought I might die if I couldn't have her. Our families and friends had expected us to become engaged months before we did. For some insane reason, Angela and I thought we must continue as we were. It was only after Angela's maiden aunt asked her the reason for the delay that we realized we were free to marry and express our love for each other in whatever way we wished." He laughed, slapping his leg at the memory. "What a revelation! We married within days and spent thirty-one lusty years together."

Delaney felt warmth creeping into her cheeks. She looked at Finn standing so close, seeing him as she never had before. Abruptly, she began to see what Granville was getting at. She knew with absolute certainty she never wanted to be apart from Finn for as long as they lived.

Granville noted her blush. "Oh, my sweet girl, don't be embarrassed by an old man's frankness. I wouldn't expect you with your delightfully forthright nature, of all people, to be caught in this muddle of misunderstanding. If you two wish to be married, I say, get on with it as quickly as possible. We have work to do and short time remaining to do it. So we cannot have you mooning about like love sick adolescents. You are both old enough and wise enough to follow your hearts." He sat appraising them with satisfaction. "Now, I believe you have some matters to settle between you."

Delaney threw her arms around him, kissing his weathered cheek. "Thank you! Thank you so much, Granville."

"You two are as precious to me as though you were my own grandchildren. I've loved working with you and look forward to seeing Delaney win in Denver." He squeezed the hand Finn offered, then waved them away.

Remaining in his chair, he watched them walk off along the drive, Delaney's arm tucked through Finn's. She moved with the physical grace that made her such an extraordinary rider; she and Harper were cut from the same cloth in that regard.

Delaney suddenly began to tremble. Finn stopped, gathering her close. "I always want to be near you."

"I know." He considered her tenderly, smiling. "Come, let's sit."

They were soon settled on a bench in a patch of sunshine that warmed the grass around them.

"Why haven't you been able to sleep?" Finn asked after a time.

"Because even when I'm exhausted, all I do is think about you." She met his gentle blue eyes looking at her with such concern.

"What sort of things do you think about me?"

Warmth suffused her face at his sweet rueful grin. "Like I wonder what it would feel like lying in your arms in my bed."

He stroked his eyebrow with the tip of a finger, still studying her. "I wonder about that most every night."

She stared at him. "You do?"

"I do," he said with a roguish grin, reaching his hand to stroke the side of her face. "And I wonder about a lot of other things as well."

Her heart was beating like the wings of something wild and she had the shivery sense of time moving without restraint, out of control. "Such as?"

"Like how it would feel to hold you so close, our bodies would fit together like pieces of a jigsaw puzzle."

She laughed at the image, then went absolutely still again. The air was practically vibrating with emotion and he offered his love to her in a tender smile before he lifted his hands to cradle her face while his mouth found hers.

Shaking, she pulled his kiss deeper into herself, the feeling vibrating into her core. Abruptly, she convulsed with the overwhelming intensity and he tightened his arms, rocking her gently.

"My God," she breathed at the wonder of it. "You've always been my best friend and now you love me." She tried out the words. "I love you, Finn."

He gently settled her against him, stroking her hair he released from the scarf she'd used to tie it back while she was riding. She relaxed in his arms as the sunshine fell around them in a circle of contentment.

Being so weary to begin with and then being released from their self-imposed prison of confusion, they soon fell asleep, leaning together there in the winter garden. They had no idea how long they'd been there when someone chuckled nearby.

Delaney opened one eye to see her father regarding them from where he stood, a bucket of birdseed in one hand. After a moment or two, he shrugged and stepped toward a bronze bird feeder suspended from a post. Stephen had started feeding the many species that either made their home at the ranch headquarters in summer or stopped by during their migration south. Now a flock of chickadees swooping about impatiently while Damien dumped the bucket into the feeder, then settled in to devour the new offering.

A commotion in a crab apple tree some distance into the garden drew Delaney's attention and she lifted her head to see a great bunch of cedar waxwings descending on the laden branches. With much raucous high whistling, they fluttered about while efficiently stripping the branches of the dried fruit.

Finn, too, was awakened by the ruckus and straightened to watch the show. Before long, the tree was bare and the showy birds were fading away into the brilliant sunshine.

Damien stepped closer and sat beside them. "I love it when I see those lovely birds attack a fruit tree."

"Me too," Delaney agreed.

He glanced at her and Finn. "Why aren't you two at work in the training ring?"

"Granville told us we needed a day off."

"Ah." He sat still, contemplating them with a puzzled look.

"Pa-pa." Delaney covered his hand with hers. "We want to get married."

A grin surfaced through his bafflement. "Well, your mother will say, it is high time."

"Why is that?" Delaney asked.

"You know your mother. She's known you were to be married, likely before you knew it yourselves." He leaned close and kissed her. "I am delighted, sweetheart, and I know your Ma-ma feels the same."

"Oh, Pa-pa." Sudden tears made her eyes starry.

"What's all this?" He asked, looking into her face. "Aren't you happy?"

"Oh, yes . . . but we have to get married right away."

His eyes darkened. "You aren't . . . ?"

"Of course not! Pa-pa, how could you think that, even for a moment?" She considered him, aghast.

"Darling, I'm sorry." He drew her against him. "It's just that I so keenly remember how I felt about your mother before we were married. At times, I thought I'd go quite mad with my longing for her. We both had a devil of a time keeping our thoughts pure so I completely understand what you've been up against."

Delaney glanced helplessly at Finn.

"Sir, it seems, the depth of our love has caught us unawares. We've both been carried along by it for some time now but didn't think to talk with each other about what we were feeling . . . ."

"We've became quite discombobulated by the whole thing," Delaney went on. "We've not been sleeping and I've been having an awful time with my riding lessons, making all sorts of silly mistakes. Finally, Granville lost patience and had a heart-to-heart with us. He told us we were behaving like he and his wife Angela did before they were married . . . ."

"Really? A heart-to-heart, you say."

"He advised us to get married very quickly so we can get our minds back on ensuring Delaney and Destino are ready for Denver," Finn declared.

A smile tilted Damien's mustache. "A wise man, indeed, our Granville." He reached for Delaney's hand and gave Finn a wink. "If my behavior when Harper and I fell in love is any indication, I don't doubt your concentration suffered recently. I was quite out of my mind as I recall."

"Were you really?" Delaney inquired. "All I can think about lately is Finn and some of the things I've been thinking are quite shocking."

Her father laughed in delight at this. "I doubt that very much. I'm rather certain whatever you've been thinking is very typical for someone wildly in love with the man you want to spend the rest of your life with."

She thought about that for a time. "Oh, I'm so glad," she blurted at last. "I thought I was being very sinful."

"Darling, I thought you were smarter than that." Her father's eyes were merry and kind.

"That's what Granville said."

"I believe the problem came up because we've been working so hard side by side the last few years," Finn ventured. "We were always together but didn't have much time for wooing. So when we fell in love, it was something of an avalanche of emotion."

Damien reached across and gripped his hand. "I believe you're exactly right. You've just missed a huge part of your courtship."

Delaney sat upright, lifting her hands to her face. "Now, there's no time for it. We start working the horses very early and don't stop until dinner. By that time, all we want to do is sleep but lately we haven't been able to do that."

"There's always time for courting," Damien insisted.

"No." She vehemently shook her head. "Granville said we must get married soon so we can start thinking clearly again. But then we have to get back to work because we only have six weeks before we go to Denver."

"Ah, I see what you mean." He stroked long fingers along his chin. "Well, I think we must speak with your mother. She's so smart, I know she'll have some good advice. Let's go have lunch with her."

A few minutes later, upon entering the *Mariposa,* they climbed the staircase to consult Harper in her studio. "Well, what a nice surprise." She abandoned the half-finished painting on an easel and plunged her brush into a jar of turpentine, then came forward to enwrap Delaney and Finn in a hug, kissing them both.

"We need your wisdom to deal with a bit of a dilemma," Damien explained.

"Oh my, I feel very privileged to have my advice needed."

"I'm quite desperate," Delaney said, still fighting tears.

"Darling, I can hardly believe anything can be that bad." She slid an arm around her thin shoulders to guide her to a sofa.

"It is."

"My sweet girl, you look so weary and sad." When she was settled beside her, she studied her carefully. "Have you been working too hard?"

"No, I can't work at all anymore."

Harper lifted worried eyes to Damien who sat opposite and attempted to sort out the situation for her. When he'd explained most of it, she wrapped her arms around Delaney.

"Oh, sweetheart, I'm so sorry I didn't speak to you when I realized you and Finn would be married." She hugged Delaney again and reached a hand to Finn seated on an ottoman, giving him a smile.

"So what are we to do?" Delaney asked shakily.

Harper took a few minutes to collect her thoughts, finally giving her full attention to the misery filling her daughter's lavender eyes.

"First of all, we're going to banish all this gloom right this minute. Good heavens, my darling, you are about to embark on absolutely the most fabulous adventure of your life, your marriage to this lovely young man we've all known and loved since he was born! You've really no idea what's in store for the both of you, but I can tell you from firsthand experience that marriage is the ultimate means to enjoy a truly brilliant life."

Delaney straightened, daring to look at her mother, a little smile surfacing. "I know you and Pa-pa have been ever so happy. That's what I want for us."

"And that is what you shall have! Now we must decide how to proceed. But first, let's have lunch!"

By the time, they'd trouped down to the dining room, Granville emerged from his suite as he usually did at lunchtime. Constance was ready to serve Mrs. Blanchard's chicken pot pie.

At Damien's instruction, Adare broke out three bottles of champagne.

Yvette had already begun her teaching duties with the girls in the school room so she ushered her charges to the table and was soon joined by Arthur and his school lads. As the meal progressed amid many toasts by Damien, Arthur, and Granville the gloomy mood was dispelled by an atmosphere of frivolity and happy hope.

Delaney drank so much champagne she grew quite tipsy. At the meal's end, Harper dispatched her to her bedroom for a nap while Granville and Finn went to the stable.

In Delaney's absence, Finn took Destino out for a long canter, then did the same on Centaur. By the time he finished, the winter twilight settled over the ranch headquarters and he delivered the sweating horse to the stable lads waiting to cool him off.

Granville had already retired to the *Mariposa* so Finn headed home. When he joined his family after bathing and dressing in fresh clothes, he was met by Caitlyn and Cassidy, his serious blonde sisters, eleven and eight. They settled on either side of him with books they'd been reading and now wished him to read to them.

He managed to beg off with the excuse he was fagged. Jamie and Eliza arrived with the twins, Helene and Harkin who were fat little cherubs with dark hair like their mother.

They settled in rocking chairs and Eliza began feeding Helene with the forthright lack of shyness that had influenced her approach to motherhood from the time Finn was born. After a few minutes, Jamie rose and deposited Harkin on Finn's lap. "Please excuse me. I need to fetch something."

He headed upstairs and was soon back. "Granville came by this afternoon."

Finn and his mother waited for him to elaborate.

"He told me you and Delaney are about to be married."

"We are."

"It's marvelous news," Eliza said. "We adore Delaney."

"We certainly do," Jamie agreed. "I can think of no one I'd rather have become your wife. We're truly blessed."

"Thank you, Da."

Jamie stood and approached to take Harkin from him, then handed him a small jewelry box. "Your Mum and I thought you might like to give this to your fiancée."

Finn opened the lid to reveal an elegant antique ring; two perfect emeralds flanked by one exquisite diamond. "It's grand. But far too extravagant for my budget, I'm afraid." He raised his eyes to meet Jamie's.

"Well, I wasn't planning on selling it to you," he said with a chuckle. "That ring belonged to my mother. My father inherited it from my grandmother so it has an impressive provenance. I believe it was created in 1746."

"How extraordinary."

"It would be my great honor if you would give it to Delaney to mark your engagement."

Finn leapt up to embrace him, jostling the baby who protested with a little squeak. "Thank you so much! Delaney will adore it."

"Let it be a symbol of your enduring love for each other."

"It will be." He was filled with euphoria at the prospect of putting such a gorgeous ring on Delaney's finger, sealing their commitment. All the unease and confusion of the morning was already swept away. "But why isn't this *your* engagement ring?" He asked, glancing at his mother.

"Dearie, your da wanted to use his own money to buy this lovely piece he gave me. Said it made him proud." She extended her hand to show him the large diamond on her ring finger. "I've cherished it every day since." She smiled adoringly at Jamie. "His Gran's ring is the one for you to give to your love."

"Oh, I must go speak to Delaney now!" He said with sudden purpose, bending to sweep up Cassidy and waltz her about the room while she laughed and Caitlyn clung to his arm as she danced beside him.

Heading toward his mother, he swooped down to kiss her cheek. "I'm so happy, I can't stand it!"

"Off with you then!" Eliza laughed, clutching Helene with one hand while she waved Finn off. "Oh, you should have your supper first . . . ."

"Who could eat when they're in love," he said, bestowing a kiss on each of his sisters' cheeks as well as Harkin's. "Thank you so much, Da and Mum. You're the very best!"

With that he bounded into the hall to fetch his coat and was out the back door. Making sure the ring was snug in his pocket, he sprinted toward the *Mariposa.*

He raced through the piazza and tapped on the front door before dashing inside. The Whittakers and Granville gathered around the dining table, looked up, startled by his entrance.

"Good evening," he said, bending to kiss Delancy before grabbing her hand. "Come with me, I must speak with you." With a small bow of apology, he gave the rest a little wave before he drew her with him into the rear hall, then bundled her into a coat and hurried her outside.

"Finn!" She suddenly protested, lurching to a stop. "What's gotten into you? Have you lost your mind?"

"I'm in love!" He threw his arms around her, lifting her off her feet as he kissed her soundly.

When he finally put her down so she could catch her breath, she stared at him, still at a loss to understand what had gotten into him. "Where have you *been*? You've been gone for hours."

He guided her to a bench. "I was doing what you would've been doing if you hadn't been catching up on your rest. I took both of our equine pupils out for a long canter. I only got back an hour ago."

She considered him, quite astonished. "Weren't you exhausted? Lord, I slept like I was drugged. You should have gotten some sleep as well."

"I was much too excited. After talking to Granville and your parents earlier, it finally dawned on me that we're about to be married." He rested his hands on her shoulders, looking at her steadily. "Isn't it wonderful?" He cocked an eyebrow when she remained still. "You do want to marry me, don't you?"

She smiled and he was sure there was a twinkle in her eyes if he'd been able to see it in the dim light from a nearby lamp. "Oh, darling, you know I do. More than anything in the world."

"Well, then, I have something for you you're going to like very much." Putting his hand in his pocket, he managed to separate the ring from its resting place in the box, then brought it out to slide it onto her finger.

With a little gasp, she brought it close enough to see. "Oh, Finn, how lovely. But I can't see it very well."

"We'll go in soon but take it from me, it's stunning. It belonged to my great-grandmother."

"Oh, my. How can that be?"

"My da gave it to me."

"How darling of him." She hugged her hands to her chest. "But why didn't he give it to your mother?"

"She said he wanted to spend his own money on the ring he gave her. Said it made him proud."

"Finn, my darling." She buried her face in the warm hollow of his neck. "I love you. Let's go show Ma-ma and Pa-pa, and Granville . . . ."

"What a good idea." He lifted his hands to frame her face so he could kiss her again before they went inside.

Upon entering the hall once more, they found everyone settled near the fireplace. All heads swiveled in their direction as they came closer.

Unable to stand a moment's more suspense, Delaney ran forward, dropping her arms around her parents sitting on a sofa. Leaning over their shoulders, she held her hand so they could inspect her ring.

"Oh, darling!" Harper twisted about, taking her hand in both of hers, closely inspecting the setting. "I can't recall ever seeing anything so lovely."

"Except perhaps your gorgeous amethyst ring Pa-pa gave you," Delaney said with a giggle.

Damien winked at Harper. "Very wise and diplomatic, our daughter." He leaned back to inspect her, then reached up to cradle the back of her head to tug her down so he could kiss her. "I'm so delighted for you, honey."

Finn led Delaney with him around the sofa so he could kiss Harper and shake hands with Damien. "My kind Da gifted me with that magnificent ring that belonged to my grandmother. I'm so very proud that I can give it to Delaney." With a wink, he pulled her down next to him on a nearby bench.

Chandler and Yvette came to offer their congratulations. "What brill news!" Chandler said, pumping Finn's hand, then embracing his sister, holding her close for a long interval.

"We'll leave you now," Yvette said. "You must have lots to discuss." She dropped a kiss on Harper's hair, then took Chandler's hand as they headed into the drawing room.

Granville left his chair and the betrothed pair rose to hug him. "I'm so pleased we had that talk this morning," he said so quietly only they could hear him.

"You're a genius," Delaney said gaily.

"Now I'm off to my bed. I'll be most intrigued to learn what developments have unfolded by the time I arise tomorrow." With a fond chuckle, he raised his hand in farewell and strode toward the stairs.

As he disappeared, Harper's gaze fell on Delaney. "So have you two decided when you will be married?"

"Soon," Finn said.

"Tomorrow?" This from Delaney.

"I don't know that we can arrange a wedding quite that quickly," Harper allowed.

"I think we can," Delaney speedily interjected. "We don't care about all the hoopla, merely to be married so we can get past feeling like we're being pulled in a dozen directions . . ."

"We wish to get back to work preparing Delaney and the horses for Denver," Finn interposed.

Harper considered them thoughtfully. "I forget how sensible you both are. When I think of a wedding, I picture lovely dresses, extravagant food, pomp and dozens of guests. Now that you've steered me back to our present state of affairs, tell me just how we should proceed."

Delaney smiled, reaching for Finn's hand, meeting his calm gaze. "Tomorrow is Saturday so I'd like Granville to marry us. I have lots of gorgeous dresses so any one of them will be fine for my wedding. Adare can make me a bouquet from the roses blooming in the greenhouse and I'll be set. I'd like Millie to stand up with me." She consulted Finn again. "How about you?"

"My needs for my wedding are even simpler. I could use a rosebud for my lapel and Chandler as my best man."

"Well, then, tomorrow will be an exceptional day for a wedding," Harper said.

"If you and Pa-pa wish to have a big celebration, it can happen later on, after we've returned from Denver."

"We shall have a marvelous celebration when the time is right," Damien agreed.

"I've been thinking about your honeymoon," Harper said. "You must have a honeymoon, short as it may be."

Delaney grinned at Finn, then turned to Harper. "Ma-ma, for weeks now, all I've been able to think about is having Finn with me in my bed upstairs. That's all I want on my honeymoon. Maybe sometime down the road when we're no longer working so hard, we'll go away to someplace lovely but for now, it's not what we need to do."

Harper relaxed back against Damien, cherishing his arms about her. "How are we blessed to have such a sagacious daughter?"

He pressed his lips to her temple. "I can only conclude that we've managed to impart some of the good sense and integrity of our forebears to our delightful young Delaney."

"Oh, please Pa-pa, you make me sound like some hopeless goody-two-shoes," Delaney protested with a scowl.

He chuckled. "We both know that would never be the proper label for you, my dear."

She grinned at him, then sat still for a time, pondering what he'd said. "We must go tell Aunt Pris about us. Is it too late?" She asked, consulting her mother.

"No, you should go ahead. With her covert network of maids and Roddy, I'm sure she's already heard and is waiting for you to come."

"We'll do that then." She went to kiss her parents good night before she and Finn headed to the staircase.

As predicted, Aunt Pris, splendid in a jade green bed jacket of brocade, sat propped up with a mountain of pillows. "Ah, my dearies, I'm so pleased you've come to say goodnight."

Delaney sat next to her on the bed, hugging her arms around her corpulence. "Have you heard our spectacular news?"

She gazed at her placidly over her spectacles. "I did hear a rumor about a wedding."

"Silly Aunt Pris, who told you?" She asked with a playful frown. "I so wanted to surprise you."

"You know me," she replied with no apology. "I just adore romantic intrigue. Roddy knew how much I'd enjoy the news. So I've just been here all evening, thinking about you and your handsome young bridegroom." She reached up to tug Finn down so she could kiss his forehead. "You're such a lucky boy."

"I know, Aunt Pris. I adore Delaney."

Smiling broadly, she set her triple chins ajiggle as she drew them to her bounteous chest. "I wish both of you all good luck and happiness."

"Thank you," Delaney offered. "Now we must let you go to sleep. Do you think you can manage to attend the wedding?"

"I wouldn't miss it. I've already made arrangements with Roddy for him to transport me to the event in my wheeled chair."

"We're so happy you'll be there," Delaney said. "You're one of my very favorite people, you know."

"I feel the same, lovey. Now I want to give you your gift while I have your complete attention." She plunged plump fingers into her cleavage, coming up with a slightly damp check that she patted into her hand.

Delaney unfolded it, gasping at the amount. "Oh, Aunt Pris, this is too much!"

"Nonsense. I'm quite well off as you may know. And, the chances are nil that I will pass on to my ultimate reward while I still possess most of my money. So I choose to spend it extravagantly while I'm still in custody of my faculties."

Delaney kissed her. "You're too kind."

"And you and your handsome fiancé are very dear to me."

After saying goodnight, Finn and Delaney climbed the stairs and he walked her to her bedroom door. "Only tonight and then you can come in and sleep with me," she observed. "Can you bear one more night alone?" She quirked a crooked smile at him.

"I shall gird my loins and be strong."

She laughed outright at that. "Take care, you don't hurt yourself . . ."

He put his arms around her, cutting off further talk as he covered her mouth with his, kissing her with great enthusiasm.

Losing all sense of time, she clung to him as his love poured over her, reconfirming his commitment, his desire for her as a woman, as his wife. She trembled as his hands roved over her back and then lower, pressing her to him. She longed for his kiss to go on forever, wanting never to be separated from him or escape from the avalanche of sensation and longing.

Abruptly, he stiffened, frantically pulling away, his breathing ragged. "My darling." At her frenzied attempt to move back into the wild eddy of arousal, he reached up to unwind her arms from his neck. "Please . . ." he drew her to him, rocking her tenderly until they'd both regained a semblance of control. "I must go home. If I don't make haste out into the cold, it won't bode well for us remaining unsullied . . ."

Delaney teasingly nipped at his earlobe. "You sound like some dandy in a dime novel. Actually, I'd just as soon be sullied . . ."

"You've become positively wanton, my dear." He tapped the end of her nose, then turned her about and opened the door of her bedroom filled with warmth and lamplight. "Now be off, you wench." He swatted her bottom to propel her inside.

Twisting back, she clasped him to her once more and kissed him with all her pent-up desire. "Sleep well," she said at last.

"I doubt I'll sleep at all," he allowed as she started to close the door.

"I love you, my husband-to-be," she added, gazing at him demurely from where she leaned seductively against the door jamb.

Groaning, he headed downstairs with the fervent hope that the walk home in the cold would alleviate his acute arousal.

# CHAPTER FIFTEEN

## November 1915

Mrs. Blanchard was up before dawn the next morning to begin making the wedding cake. Harper set Adare to the task of creating a festive setting in the Great Hall for the wedding at seven o'clock. Afterward, dinner would be served to what guests could be gathered on such short notice.

Granville went to the stables to instruct stable lads to take Destino and Centaur out for limited workouts so they didn't get off schedule in their conditioning. He was back at the *Mariposa* to join Harper, Yvette and Delaney for lunch. "Where has everyone gotten off to?" He asked at the nearly empty dining table.

"Damien and Chandler had pressing business with Finn in town so they drove off right after breakfast," Harper said. "I've been busy myself spreading the word to the Carrolls and the rest. It's going to be astonishing what a beautiful wedding we're going to host." She smiled and reached out to wrap Delaney close for a moment.

Granville took in the butler placing the sumptuous arrangements of roses, hydrangeas and daisies he'd cut in the greenhouse and arranged in porcelain bowls. "It's surely to be splendid affair. You're all so clever."

Delaney left the table and came to hug him, leaning over his shoulder to lay her cheek against his. "So Finn asked you to marry us?"

"He did indeed. He came by the stables earlier. I must say, he's positively walking on air."

"Just as I am," Delaney said, reaching for his hands to drawn him to his feet. "And dancing on clouds."

Unable to resist her infectious high spirits, he waltzed her about the dining room until LuAnn called repeatedly that she was serving lunch.

"Oh, my," Delaney said, fanning her cheeks as she collapsed into a chair next to her mother. "Will I be able to stand this much frivolity?"

"I'm sure you will manage, dear," Harper said, laughing at her as LuAnn began ladling soup into their bowls.

"None for me," Delaney said, "I'll have something later. Were you as happy as I am when you got married?" She asked, resting her chin in her hand with her elbow propped on the table.

"That depends on which marriage you're asking about. The first time, I was positively heartsick because I wasn't marrying your Pa-pa. And, he was half out of his mind with disappointment and rage. I was so agitated the morning of my wedding day, I took Embarr out for a ride and came across your father who'd gone for a walk. He tried his best to talk me out of marrying his brother. I was so bewildered and torn, I nearly did as he said. Yet, I couldn't face seeing him come to America without me so I defied his wishes."

"How could you bear marrying someone you didn't love?"

"It was the hardest thing I've ever done. The only thing that allowed me to get through that awful time was my faith in your father, knowing he and I would one day be together as man and wife."

"So how did you feel the day when you and Pa-pa finally married?"

Remembering, Harper clasped her hands together beneath her chin. "Oh, my darling, I felt exactly like you do right now! All my love for your Pa-pa filled my heart and all the pain of the time we were forced apart, seemed like a distant memory. From that day forward, we've known such delight and happiness. There have been other dark times but because we always depended on each other, our love endured just as yours for Finn will. I can scarcely imagine the happiness you two will find together."

Delaney still gazed at her wistfully. "It's going to be so lovely."

"You have no idea, my dearest girl." Harper leaned closer to smooth the dark hair back from Delaney's face and to kiss her cheek. "Now, if you feel at all the way I did on my wedding day, I think you should go take a leisurely ride on Destino. It will clear your head and by the time, you come back, we'll have everything sorted here. Now, off you go."

Half an hour later, Delaney guided her horse along a bridle path beside the Aspen. The day was warm and still with sunbeams slanting through the bare aspens and cottonwoods, such incredible weather for late November.

Delaney delighted in Destino's smooth and fluid canter that he could maintain for miles. What a joy to her he was. He felt like a coiled spring beneath the saddle and arched his neck playfully against the bits.

She tipped her face to the sunshine, thinking of the competition in Denver. What would the weather be like by January? While excellent conditions had graced the Denver Stock Show during most of the years it had been in existence, the Cross-Country competition had been cancelled twice due to heavy snows.

Dressage and Stadium Jumping would always go on because they were held in roofed arenas. Only Cross-Country might be stymied by weather. Delaney said many prayers each day this wouldn't happen as it was the long, rugged outdoor course that she most wished to complete, besting all other comers against Destino.

Two hours had gone by before Delaney returned to the *Mariposa* that had been transformed by Adare's lavish bouquets of roses. Amassed candelabra and candle sticks held waiting tapers that would create a lovely ambiance for the wedding ceremony.

"Oh, Ma-ma," Delaney cried, skipping about the hall. "How positively charming. Our wedding is to be *enchanting*! Thanks to you!" She hugged her happily.

"Thanks to Adare, actually. He's the one with all the tricks for creating magic with roses and cello concertos."

"No cello concertos tonight," Delaney said with a hint of regret "but everything else is perfect."

She gave her attention to the lunch of squash cassoulet Constance set before her. Harper sat beside her, offering fresh bread from a loaf freshly baked that morning.

"When do you think Pa-pa and the others will be back?"

"Before long, I'd say so it's time you had your bath. Jill will be up to do your hair."

Finished eating, Delaney bestowed a kiss to her mother's cheek and headed to the back hall where Roddy helped her off with her tall boots. She asked him to bring her up a glass of wine, then humming, ran up the staircase.

She found her bedchamber also transformed by roses and candles ready to be lit. A warming fire burned in the fireplace.

The maid, Jill, waited in her dressing room where she'd already prepared a tub. "How much time do we have, Miss?" She asked gaily.

"As much as we need. The wedding will be at seven when it's dark enough so all Adare's candles can be enjoyed to best advantage. Can you think of anything more romantic than a candlelight wedding?"

"I surely can't. It will be so pretty as will you."

Observing her, Delaney stripped off her riding clothes and submerged herself in the warmth of the tub, the water delicately scented with primrose bath oil. After Rachel retired a few years earlier, Jill had been hired to serve as lady's maid to Harper and Delaney, neither of whom used her services with the regularity of previous years. A plump and plain girl, she had a happy and accommodating personality everyone appreciated.

Delaney heard Roddy's tap on the door and Jill went to answer and was quickly back with her wine that she set on a small table within reach. Lying back, she swallowed some, relishing the mellow warmth oozing along her veins.

Presently finished with her bath, she wrapped herself in a thick robe and sat before the mirror. Jill toweled her hair until it was only slightly damp, then employed a hot iron to form large curls. Finally, she swept the entire glorious dark mass of it back, securing it with a wide headband encrusted with emeralds. She finished by plaiting loose braids from the curls and securing them in an elegant fall down her back.

Next, Jill reached for the various forms of makeup spread in the top drawer of the dressing table. For several years, Delaney and

Harper had been enhancing their natural beauty with the latest products that had become available.

Now, loving being pampered, she watched Jill skillfully apply kohl eyeshadow and mascara to her huge lavender eyes, drawing out their remarkable shade. After sweeping circles of pale rouge on her cheeks, she drew a perfect cupid's bow with rosy lipstick.

Surveying her reflection, she loved what she saw. Jill was always a magician when she prepared her for a special event and today was no exception. "Thank you so much," she said, smiling at the girl in the mirror.

"You look splendid. Now let's get you dressed as it's nearly six."

Delaney heard voices in the piazza and ran to a window to look down at the men getting out of Granville's auto. She wanted to rush downstairs but knew her mother thought it bad luck for her to see Finn before the wedding. Jill was waiting with her corset so she turned back to her.

When Jill prepared to help her on with the foundation garment but she abruptly waved a dismissive hand. "No corset tonight." She spun to look at her profile in the long mirror, taking in her svelte young body.

"Very well, miss." The maid carefully placed the velvet gown over Delaney's head and let it fall past her lacy underthings. Delaney stepped back to the mirror. The pale gray fabric embellished with a black mesh overlay was a favorite because it was such a daring counterpoint to the nearly-black shade of her hair.

"You look ever so pretty," Jill declared with a grin. "Will you be warm enough?"

Delaney considered the dress's plunging neckline and cap sleeves. "I should think so," she decided with a toss of her head and a wink.

A tap on the door preceded Millie who entered, wearing a provocative velvet gown in brilliant red. She curtsied before Delaney. "Am I dressed to your liking?"

"Oh, indeed. I've always loved that dress."

They stood side by side, looking into the cheval mirror. Nearly the same height, they made an elegant picture in the contrasting fabrics of their gowns. Each wrapped an arm around the other's waist.

"Your father will be here soon to take you down," Millie said, turning to catch her in a hug. "Good luck!"

Delaney lost track of her surroundings as Damien arrived, his eyes brimming with love and pride. "Darling, you are exquisite." Smiling, he kissed her cheek, then reached for her hand that he tucked into his arm. "Shall we?"

Nearly overcome with excitement and her eagerness to see Finn, Delaney stepped with him to the top of the staircase where Adare bowed and presented her with a bouquet of red roses. They paused there as Millie accepted an arrangement of white roses. Delaney was suddenly aware of soft music wafting up from below and she looked at her father in surprise.

He smiled. "Yes, my dear, we managed to get Jane here in time."

With a little gasp, she hugged his arm. "Oh, Pa-pa, how lovely."

The music swelled and the couples prepared to descend the staircase. As they proceeded, Delaney took in the hall below where hundreds of candles created a fantasy of soft radiance amid the profusion of multi-hued roses. She reminded herself to thank Aunt Pris for the lavish ambiance because it was she who'd purchased the greenhouse and roses years before.

As they reached the bottom, she nodded to Jane Lamb, seated at her cello, before her gaze settled on Finn and Chandler, so handsome in a black tail coats. Finn's narrow features lit with delight and soon enough, he'd stepped forward to take her hand, leading her to a spot before Granville.

She took Finn's hand, looking up at him. "I so love you."

He winked at her before giving full attention to Granville who'd begun speaking.

Struggling to concentrate on what he was saying, she couldn't recall when she'd ever felt so emotionally scattered. Maybe she shouldn't have had the glass of wine earlier.

Squaring her shoulders, she redoubled her efforts to hear Granville's message. Seeming to read her thoughts, Finn squeezed her hand and gave her a smile.

Somehow she managed to get through the remainder of the ceremony and she and Finn were caught in the crush of congratulatory hugs and good wishes. She hardly saw all the faces until her mother was suddenly before her, dabbing at tears as she looked at her probingly.

"Are you all right, dear?"

"Of course. I'm wonderful!"

"Bless you, darling. And you." She turned to embrace Finn.

The remainder of the evening passed amid a flurry of frivolity. Mrs. Blanchard had created Delaney's favorite dinner of roast chicken that ended with the pretty wedding cake she'd created from Mrs. Goodeve's recipe and written instructions. Delaney felt a pull of nostalgia when she thought of the former housekeeper who'd often spoiled her with favorite treats and meals.

While the staff began clearing up after dinner, Jane managed to play music for dancing and Damien swept Delaney out onto the floor near the fireplace. "I can't tell you how much I've loved this evening," he said.

"Pa-pa, it's been so splendid. Thank you for bringing Jane. What a nice surprise."

"You're welcome, my lovely daughter. Now I give you to your husband." He turned to Finn who'd come to wait his turn to dance with Delaney.

It felt so right to be held in Finn's arms as they took up the waltz. And then others came to claim a dance with her—Granville, Arthur, Caldwell, Chandler, Luke, John and Jamie. When the gathering started to break up, she and Finn stood near the front door with their parents, Millie, Yvette and Chandler, and said goodnight to their guests as everyone departed.

When the last one was gone, they collapsed on a sofa before the fire. "What a splendid time," Finn said, putting an arm about Delaney's shoulders. "Was it as nice as you hoped?"

"Even more so," she said dreamily, snuggled against him. "I feel like a princess." She noted the pile of wrapped gifts piled on a table by the bank of windows. "Do you think we've been given can openers and mixing bowls and flat irons?" She asked.

"I hardly think so. I'm certain we've received quite lovely items that won't be of use in the kitchen," Finn replied with a mischievous grin.

"I'm so happy this will always be our home," Delaney presently declared.

"Your father has told me we can move into the empty apartment whenever we wish."

She straightened a little to consult him. "Really? Is that where you want to live?"

He nuzzled her neck. "I really have little preference where I hang my hat as long as it hangs close to yours."

"What a nice thing to say."

"It's exactly how I feel. This will always be your home and I'm content to continue working for your father as long as he wishes."

She laughed with something akin to relief. "Oh, I'm so glad. Earlier, I began wondering about our future, thinking maybe you'd insist on making your mark somewhere else."

"Ye woman of little faith. I could never do that because I must continue to train you and your fine steed for competition. If when you're eighty and decide you wish to write the greatest novel ever to be published or paint a masterpiece for the *Louvre*, I will help you in your new venture in any way I can."

"You're a marvelous husband. I'm so lucky I didn't marry a greedy tyrant intent on making buckets of money and dragging me away from my home and what I've always known I want to do with my life."

"Greedy tyrant, indeed." He grasped the back of her neck and tugged her close so he could kiss her. "One thing I am not is a greedy tyrant."

"Thank Goodness." She abruptly looked at him intently. "I didn't know you work for my father."

"What did you think? That I devoted my life to you from the time I was five years old just because I was hopelessly in love with you?"

"I didn't think about it, actually," she said, suddenly worried. "I guess I thought you did it because it was fun for you. That was very selfish of me. I'm sorry."

"Don't be, you silly goose. It was fun and I've always loved you. So I was perfectly happy to help you every day and not be paid. But eventually, your father said it was time he hired me officially. Not as your trainer at first because I was still a boy but as a stable lad in training to be a groom."

Delaney still looked sad. "I truly took you for granted. How awful of me. I can be very obtuse. Will you mind that?"

"You are the least obtuse person I know, my love. And now I want to take you to bed."

Looking around for the first time since they sat down, she saw that all the candles had been extinguished and the house was quiet. Even the noise of washing up in the scullery had subsided. Only Dobbs stood by the windows at the opposite end of the hall, apparently waiting to bank the fire for the night.

"Where did my parents go?" Delaney whispered.

"I think, perchance, they wished to give us privacy so they took the back stairs to their bedroom."

She considered him with wonder at their sensitivity. He soon rose, bent to gather her in his arms and carried her up the staircase. The door to her bedroom was ajar and he shouldered it open carrying her to the bed that had been made up with fresh linen and strewn with rose petals. Firelight bathed the room in a golden light.

Delaney wound her arms about Finn's neck as he lowered her on the bed, then went to lock the door and hurriedly removed his coat, tossing it on a chair. "I should have asked Jill to help me out of my dress," she said when he was back.

"I'm sure we can manage," he said hoarsely, stretching out next to her, trailing kisses down the creamy expanse of her plunging neckline while his fingers worked at the silver buttons of her bodice. When the fabric gaped to expose a filmy chemise, he gasped as his fingers tugged the fabric aside, baring her breasts.

When his mouth settled over first one, then the other, she sighed with longing. He continued his exploration of bare skin once he'd pulled her dress over her head and divested her of her chemise. His lips edged along her ribcage as he tugged at her bloomers, then moved across her flat stomach and lower.

Once he'd belatedly raised himself on elbows, he gazed down at her, his blue eyes going dark with his arousal. "My darling, Delaney . . ."

She reached up, opening the buttons of his waistcoat, and then his shirt beneath, pulling the layers back so she could strew kisses across the hard planes of his chest while her hands roved down to unbutton his pants. Her fingers moved inside, stroking his arousal, eliciting a long groan before he suddenly heaved himself away from her. Standing up, he yanked off his pants and the other garments that he tossed on the floor, then remembering, he dove to grab his pants again and pulled an envelope from a pocket that he laid on the bedside table.

Curious, Delaney picked up the packet, discovering it held condoms. She glanced up at him as he lay beside her once more.

"We can't have you getting pregnant just now."

"I know but I have something better than these." She tapped the envelope in her hand.

He studied her musingly. "Do you really? What would that be?"

"A sponge."

He stared at her, at a loss.

"Last time I was in Cheyenne, I paid a visit to Belle Henning."

"Ah, yes, Aunt Pris's friend. Isn't she older than God by this time?"

"Probably," she agreed with a grin. "But she still knows how to keep someone from getting pregnant."

"So do I." Finn took the packet from her.

"But, according to Ophelia, what Belle gave me is so much nicer. Let me fetch it."

"Not quite yet," he protested, sitting on the edge of bed and grabbed her legs that he laid over his thigh and began unlacing one chic little boot, then the other. After nuzzling each shapely leg from ankle to calf, he shifted her back on the linen and knelt to remove her silk hosiery. He leisurely unhooked the left garters, then very slowly rolled the stocking down and off before concentrating on the other side.

When her muscled legs were bare, he hoisted them to his shoulders and began thoroughly kissing the silken expanse of her inner thighs. She writhed under the intimate attention and grasped his head when his mouth settled on her center, licking and teasing until she could bear no more and rolled away from him.

"I'll be right back," she gasped and quickly scrambled out of bed and ran to the dressing room.

While she was there, she stripped off her bloomers then retrieved a square box from a drawer. When she arrived back at the bed, she found Finn naked, leaning on the headboard, laughing at her. "You'll thank me later," she said breezily, sliding in next to him.

He watched, fascinated, as she opened the box and took out a round and flat circle of sea sponge. "How does it work?"

"Keeps sperm from moving to a place where an egg can be fertilized," she divulged with perfect candor. "Needless to say, it has to be put inside me. Your fingers are longer than mine so that's going to be your job." She smiled at him with a quizzically lifted eyebrow.

"That seems rather straight-forward."

"We need a bit of water to moisten it first so the soap in it will work . . ."

"Work? Ah, I see. Work to kill all those pesky sperm."

"Exactly." She gave him a teasing punch on the arm.

"I'll bring some water." He sprang up and rushed to the dressing room where he poured some water from the pitcher on the washstand into a cup he found on a dresser.

Delaney grabbed the cup with such haste, the water sloshed on the linen. "Oh, damn." With a frown, she took the sponge and placed it in the cup where it floated. "Do you think that's what it's supposed to do?" She asked Finn, watching with great interest.

"Never having seen such a thing in my life, I wouldn't know. But I'm certain it will work." He took the cup from her and held it steady while he squeezed the sponge with the fingers of his other hand. "Aha!" He held it up so she could see that it was covered with suds. "We're in business!"

"Thank Goodness!" She scooted down and lifted her knees so he could attempt placing the device where it was supposed to go.

As he worked at the task, his befuddlement was clear on his tense features. Yet, soon enough, he relaxed and gave her a smile before gathering her close. "Quite a stimulating little exercise," he allowed with a chuckle.

Delaney laughed at his goofy look and draped her arms around his neck, pulling him down so she could kiss him with all the longing that had built in her all day. Slowly, with greatest care and tenderness, she entered the expected enchantment of kissing, caressing, soft endearments that he reciprocated, drawing them both toward the ultimate consummation. At last, they lay in languid euphoria, holding tight to each other, talking softly, laughing, rejoicing in their love until they both drifted into sleep.

Much later, Delaney awoke, wondering for a second where she was. The lamps had been extinguished and the candles snuffed, leaving the room lit only by the fire still burning on the hearth.

She glanced at Finn sleeping beside her, listening to his quiet, even breathing. Just as she'd longed to have him in her bed, now he was there, her husband.

She whispered the word, hugging her arms around herself at the wonder of it. She was Mrs. Finn Horncastle

# CHAPTER SIXTEEN

### November 1915 – January 1916

Delaney awoke in the cool perfection of sunrise. She rolled over so she could look out her bedroom window at the rear garden where Stephen, the gardener watered plants with a hose. Lifting her hand, she inspected her antique engagement ring. A pair of sparkling emeralds nestled among diamonds in an intricate Victorian gold setting that had belonged to Jamie's grandmother.

Delaney adored the ring even more because it had come from Jamie. Now she caught the facets in the first rays of sunshine, smiling as the fractured light danced about the room. As she'd grown up on the ranch, hardly anyone had been kinder to her or more interested in her pursuits.

Excitement pushed her from bed. She was filled with heady anticipation of getting back to the routine of training with Finn.

As the weather remained dry and fair, they'd taken up the habit of riding in the cool after dawn and again when evening brought bracing temperatures to the ranch meadows. She was eager to keep working Destino hard as the time grew closer to his debut in the show ring.

Hurriedly, she dressed in breeches and a knitted heavy fisherman sweater. Stepping to the cheval mirror, she tied back her wavy black hair and grabbed her helmet, smiling at her image. Bending close to the glass, she examined the sprinkling of freckles dotting her nose. Aunt Pris deplored the spots she thought unladylike but Delaney had always liked them.

Minutes later, she'd skipped down the staircase with Huckleberry and Rumor capering behind and entered the dining room where her parents sat at the table. "Good morning!" She threw her helmet on a chair and paused to hug and kiss each before she sat beside Damien and began eating the oatmeal Dobbs placed before her.

"You look very chipper, this morning."

"Marriage agrees with me. It's such a pretty day; I can't wait to work Destino over the cross-country course."

Damien's gaze narrowed. "I wasn't aware we have a cross-country course."

"We don't but Finn and I have been jumping both horses over natural obstacles like the Aspen and fallen logs. We ride together so it's a bit like a competition, gives them practice in one striving to get ahead of the other without getting sloppy on the jumps."

"You all are becoming very proficient," he remarked with a wink. "I'd love to ride out with you today and watch you ride. Do you think Granville and Finn would mind?"

"No, they love showing off their pupils," she said with a grin, carefully spreading a piece of toast with marmalade.

"Could I interest you in riding out with us, my dear?" Damien asked Harper who'd left her chair to lean on the back of his so she could rest her chin on his hair.

"I'd love to. The weather is truly beguiling for November so a ride will be perfect."

Delaney scraped up the last of her cereal, then put down her napkin. "I'm off then!" She hugged her parents, adjusted her helmet on her head and headed into the back hall where Roddy waited to help her with her tall boots.

Amused, her parents watched her disappear out the door. Harper gazed happily at Damien. "I shall always thank God that our beautiful, talented daughter has chosen to love Jamie and Eliza's tall, handsome son who shares her fearless passion for Thoroughbreds and her desire to be a champion."

"I share your gratitude, my darling." He leaned his head to rest it against hers. "And now if we're to keep up, we also must be off."

When Delaney arrived at the stables, Finn was helping three lads groom Destino and Centaur in the breezeway.

An orange cat wove himself around Delaney's boots, purring with enthusiasm until she scooped him up.

"Darling," Finn approached to wrap his arms around her from behind.

She burrowed her head into the curve of his shoulder. "Isn't it nice out this morning?"

Squashed, the cat jumped down and Finn turned Delaney around, regarding her musingly. "It's a beautiful day in wonderful Wyoming."

"How corny is that?"

With an arched brow, he hauled her into an empty stall and began kissing her hungrily. She wound her arms around him, parting her lips as he pressed the thin length of her to him. As always, she was engulfed by his passion that stunned and overwhelmed her. Soon enough, she was possessed by the familiar answering hunger in herself. For some unknown reason, her muddled thoughts tracked back to her former experience with other men.

She'd been held close to the bodies of men and boys during endless balls at *Mariposa* and Trail's End during her adolescence and teen years. There'd been plenty of stolen kisses and she'd always been an eager player in these youthful games of exploration.

Yet, nothing had prepared her for the ardor of Finn Horncastle that ignited in her a shocking response that often left her reeling. She loved him to the depth of her soul.

At last, he set her away from him a little, regarding her with the impish fascination that always lay twinkling in the depths of his clear blue eyes and constantly made him look on the verge of laughter. His easy goodwill invariably reminded her of his father.

"How are you feeling this morning, Mrs. Horncastle?"

"I'm as happy as I knew I'd be when I had you sleeping in my bed."

"So having me sleeping next to you has had the effect Granville anticipated?" He inquired with a roguish tilt of his chin.

"It has. Though it wasn't precisely your *sleeping* that inspired me, I can assure you that I'm ready to pursue my training with renewed dedication." She smiled wickedly. "Now I can keep my mind on my work instead of daydreaming about you because I know you'll be in my bed tonight and tomorrow night and the night after that."

"Well that sounds like an extraordinary arrangement to me." He drew her against him, holding her while they lingered there a bit longer.

From the time she knew she and Finn were destined for each other, she'd been thankful that he was Jamie's son, and had inherited his character and day to day delight in *Mariposa.* After being reared with the integrity of her own parents, she knew she could never have settled for a man with any less respect for the land and the animals.

With a mischievous grin, Finn presently let her go. "And now we must get back to business." He guided her from the stall and they continued outside where Luke and the lads waited with the horses.

As he boosted her into the saddle, Delaney gave silent thanks for this lovely man who now belonged to her. Her parents were already mounted on Jasper and Avalon and waiting along the drive. Granville climbed into a trap pulled by a carriage horse and picked up the reins. He preferred the conveyance for tooling about the meadows in lieu of riding. Soon enough, the little procession proceeded down the driveway, then took up a trail that traveled alongside the Aspen.

Delaney cantered Destino in wide circles to warm up his muscles in preparation for harder work. After some minutes of this, she spotted a hay wagon with a broken wheel abandoned a short distance ahead. As the stallion neared it, Delaney gathered him with pressure from her knees and hands on the reins, then unable to resist the challenge, she gave him his head, leaning forward so her weight rested over his withers.

Exhilaration rushed along Delaney's every nerve as he tucked his front legs and soared over the wagon with plenty of room to spare. "Woo-hoo!" She pumped her arm in the air as Finn rode toward her. "Did you see that?"

He laughed at her exuberance. "I did, you reckless girl!"

"I couldn't resist," she said, patting Destino's neck. "Wasn't he amazing?"

"You were both extraordinary!" He leaned over to kiss her as Granville arrived in his little wagon.

"How astonishing, my girl!" He said. "I see you are back in top form."

"Indeed!" With another whoop, she turned Destino toward the arrangement of jumps that had been constructed two years back in a flat area of meadow land a half mile further on. She put the stallion over all fifteen obstacles without touching any cross-beam, which in actual competition would be a penalty.

"A clean run," Granville said with satisfaction when she stopped by his trap. "Now perhaps you should go along the Aspen and see what you can find there."

She turned Destino toward the stream where they jumped a series of five downed trees before continuing over flatter terrain. Finn followed suit on Centaur before drawing even with the stallion to give him the illusion of being in competition. Delaney urged Destino to a faster pace and within a quarter mile, they'd left Centaur well behind.

They continued in this way all morning, Delaney and Finn playing off each other as they sent their horses back and forth over the stream, ditches, up and down steep banks and over ponds. Their mounts were soon lathered with sweat but never winded.

Astride their horses, Damien and Harper had kept pace with the others throughout the conditioning exercises. The weather was ideal, comfortably warm but not hot. Near mid-day, they'd pulled up beside Granville's trap, watching as Luke approached on his horse from the direction of the ranch headquarters.

"Have you had an enjoyable morning?" He inquired.

"It has been delightful seeing how proficient Delaney and Destino have become," Harper allowed. "I think her chances in Denver are excellent."

"They're a formidable team," Damien agreed. "I hope the competition is prepared," he added with a droll look.

Delaney and Finn rode up, happy to learn that Luke had brought lunch. Harper dismounted and unpacked the meal from saddlebags and set everything out in the rear of the wagon. Luke took up the job of keeping the Thoroughbreds from becoming stiff by walking them in a circle around the group while everyone else ate the chicken, biscuits and wine that Mrs. Blanchard had packed.

After they finished eating, Harper and Damien rode back to the *Mariposa* with Luke, and Granville soon followed. Delaney and Finn rode their horses a few miles further from the headquarters, then turned and returned to the stables at a slow, collected canter.

The next two months passed in concentrated preparation geared to deliver Delaney and the horses to Denver at the peak of their ability. The challenge of getting fifty head of Herefords, the two Thoroughbreds and additional mounts and equipment to Colorado had been addressed for months. Three trucks capable of hauling animals were ordered from England. Yet, when the time came to get the entrants to Denver the last week of January, the conveyances had not arrived.

Since there was no other means available to transfer such a large number of cattle and horses it was decided the men would lead the beasts to Cheyenne, then send them on to Denver by rail.

To keep their coats as sleek as possible for the show, the horses and cattle had worn heavy blankets in the barns since October. Their special diet had given them a show bloom that amounted to an extra layer of fat.

On the morning of their unorthodox departure for Denver in mid-January, the well-mannered beasts were haltered and blanketed and lined up along the driveway, half of them led by mounted riders, the rest left to follow their companions of their own volition. Delaney and Finn rode Destino and Centaur behind the cattle as the cavalcade began the trek along the road across the prairie. A stable lad drove Granville's trap which he would need during the cross-country competition.

Bringing up the rear in the handsome autos most had acquired in recent years were the Whittakers, Carrolls, Horncastles, Arthur, his family and in-laws, Caldwell and Anne. Yvette and Anne rode Avalon and Jasper because Harper and Damien wished to have their own mounts while at the competition in Colorado.

Gazing about as they headed out, Delaney was filled with hope and exhilaration. She felt confident in her chances in the three phases of Eventing. Granville was of the opinion that she performed best in Dressage, the highest level of the contest and she did love all the pomp and spectacle, the precision of the movements. She and Destino had been a team for so long, they could read each other and that was a great advantage because obedience of the horse and its harmony with the rider was one of the criteria the judges looked for.

She glanced at Finn beside her, a striking figure astride Centaur. She loved his easy grace on the horse, his poise and self-assurance. He was truly a superb rider and for several weeks, she'd harbored the thought that he should be riding in competition. "I'm going to speak to Granville about you," she said.

"Whatever for, darling?"

"So he can arrange for you to enter a stadium jumping class on Centaur."

He stared at her for perhaps a minute. "Centaur is going to Denver as a backup mount in case Destino should go lame," he said at last. "And I am one of your trainers."

"I know," she said hurriedly. "I'm not talking about Eventing. There must be open jumping classes on days when I'm not riding."

"I don't want to tempt fate. From the start, we've planned all this down to the last detail so you will have the best chance of placing well." He shook his head, looking into the distance. "Why would we deviate from that now?" When he glanced back at her, tension deepened the lines in his tanned face.

"Because you're such an extraordinary rider and would do so well."

He pondered this for a bit while she waited.

"Wouldn't you just adore trying?" She urged, noting his hesitation.

A grin slowly curved his mouth and seeped into his eyes. "It would be a lark."

"Then you'll do it?"

He raised a gloved hand. "Not so fast. I'll consider it but only after your competition is finished. I won't hear of anything detracting from you and Destino."

"Oh, Finn, thank you. You're going to do so well!"

He reached for her hand, pressing it to his mouth. "Now let's think no more about it. We have a lot to deal with next week."

"I must talk to Granville," she reminded him.

"Only that, then I want all your attention back on your work."

"Yes, sir." Laughing at his sober demeanor, she saluted him.

Progress was steady and uneventful and the group reached the Union Pacific depot well before noon. The three converted stock cars that had been reserved by Chandler waited on a siding. Inside each, sturdy stalls of various sizes had been built to accommodate huge bulls as easily as weanling calves and all ages in between.

The horses were led into the third car. Once fitted with blankets, thick leg wraps, hoof boots for traction and cross-tied, they were as secure as was possible to be on the lurching train. Nonetheless, Delaney, Finn, Damien and Granville stayed in the car during the ninety mile ride to Denver, soothing the horses whenever they grew fractious in the jolting noise. Chandler, Luke, Caldwell and the hired men assumed the same guard duty in the cattle cars.

Baskets of food had been packed by Mrs. Blanchard to feed everyone caring for the animals. The autos and Granville's trap were rolled into two additional railway cars for the transfer to Denver.

Upon reaching the Denver depot, Damien and Granville supervised the unloading of cattle and horses, vehicles and equipment. As soon as his trap and carriage horse, William, were ready on the siding, Granville climbed in and with Damien sharing the seat and holding the map he'd procured months earlier, they set out for the show grounds and more specifically the Hereford barns and horse stables. Harper rode Avalon alongside.

The animals had been placed in the same formation that had delivered them to Cheyenne and now fell into line behind the wagon, bound for their lodging for the next ten days. Meanwhile, Arthur handled the transfer of the remaining group into their automobiles, then guided them to the sumptuous Brown Palace where a block of rooms had been reserved.

The sights greeting Delaney and the rest as they traversed the show grounds to the barns prepared for their animals made her head swim. She'd never seen so much livestock and so many different varieties of each breed being led by men in frock coats, women in elaborate gowns and hats—hundreds of cattle, horses, sheep and goats, of all ages, shapes and colors, every one so docile, they suffered the jostling of the crowds around them unperturbed.

At one point, they were astonished at the spectacle of a man wielding a cane, gently herding six huge pigs along the route. Further on, they found themselves in the midst of a herd of longhorns driven by several shouting cowboys. At another juncture, a half dozen huge longhorns with the longest horns she'd ever seen had been hitched to a wagon filled with children and several barking dogs. Stagecoaches rattled past, hordes of Indians in native dress and performing intricate dances gyrated in and out of the spectators, automobiles and horse-drawn fire engines with bells clanging sped past.

When they'd finally emerged from the chaos, they had come to the *National Amphitheatre and Livestock Pavilion*, the recently-completed facility offering steam-heated livestock stalls beneath the spectator seats. Granville informed Delaney that the Dressage and Stadium Jumping would be held there. Seeing the vast size of the arena, she acknowledged a thrill of anticipation.

Show officials approached to speak with Damien and Granville and shortly, the cattle and handlers were escorted to the proper section of pens where the *Rancha Mariposa* Herefords were bedded down on shredded green tanbark. Chandler, Delaney, Finn, Granville and several stable boys continued to the opposite end of the building where Destino, Centaur and the other horses were rubbed down, blanketed, fed and watered.

Leaving the boys to care for the horses overnight, they returned to the Hereford area, seeing the weary beasts had collapsed onto the bedding, already taking their ease. "They're very pleased with the accommodations," Damien remarked with a grin. "I daresay the rest of us are also anxious to eat and find our beds."

"I could sleep for days," Delaney said, laying her head on Finn's shoulder.

Harper came to slide her arm about her waist. "Our carriages await." They filed out of the barn, finding that John and Audra, Arthur and Laura had arrived in their automobiles to ferry the group to the Brown Palace.

After dinner and a good night's sleep, Delaney was ready to ride very early the next morning. Granville had found a large paddock they could use for final practice and she put Destino through the Dressage routine before they went to a practice ring where jumps had been erected.

Once Destino had made two clean circuits and Centaur one, Granville called a halt, not wanting to overwork them since the Dressage competition would be run tomorrow. Delaney and Finn rode the horses to the wagon where Granville watched from the edge of the course.

"No more hard work today. Now it's a matter of keeping Destino relaxed and limber for your debut tomorrow morning." He consulted Delaney. "Do you feel rested?"

"I'd like a nap later."

"Excellent idea. In the meantime, I want you and Finn to take the horses out beyond the edge of the show grounds and ride at a leisurely pace for a couple of hours. Mostly, I'd like them walked as though you're out for an amble along a bridle path. A few intervals of collected cantering would also be helpful in keeping their muscles supple. When you return, we shall retire to the Brown Palace for a lavish lunch and a long nap."

"Have you gotten Centaur and Finn entered in a jumping class next week?" Delaney inquired.

"Yes, I did. They'll compete on Thursday." He smiled broadly. "I'm so pleased you came up with that suggestion as I, too, will adore seeing them in the spotlight. After training as understudies all this time, you both deserve your chance to shine."

Finn smiled tentatively. "I must say, I do look forward to trying competition as I feel I could ride a Stadium Jumping course with my hands tied behind my back. I just want to be very certain my participation will have no bearing on Delaney's." He directed a concerned glance at her.

"No worries there," Granville declared, "and you will be grand in your own right."

"I'll do my best."

"And that will be very good indeed. Now, you two go have a ramble on the prairie while William and I go see how our Herefords are performing in the show ring." He picked up the reins and clucked to the chestnut who moved out smartly. With a jaunty wave, Granville sped toward the show area where the cattle conformation classes were underway.

Delaney and Finn rode in the opposite direction, passing among the huge network of paddocks until they reached the edge of the show grounds and continued out onto the prairie beyond the city. The day was much the same as yesterday with brilliant sunshine and endless blue skies filled with occasional drifting white clouds.

When they had left the bustling show grounds, the Rocky Mountains came into view, a sharp blue rampart to the west, so striking, Delaney rode in awe for some time. "When Eliza taught us about those mountains, I had no idea how extraordinary they are."

"Makes me wonder what sort of dynamic upheaval in nature caused that splendor. It's almost like glimpsing the face of God."

Delaney stared at him. "That's exactly right." She looked back at the distant layers of blue that stair-stepped from the prairie floor to create the astounding mountain range. The shadows of trees covered the nearest foothills that faded into the solid blue of interim ridges. Ultimately, snow-covered peaks pierced the cloudbank capping the entire faraway bastion.

Sunshine reflected off the snowy slopes like moonlight on diamonds. As they continued on, side by side, Delaney and Finn were mesmerized by the glorious sight.

"I wonder how it is to live in the midst all that splendor," said Delaney.

"Lovely, I'm certain." Finn opined, leveling his inquiring gaze on her. "Shall we leave *Rancha Mariposa* behind and come live in the Rockies of Colorado?"

She returned his look, appalled. "Of course not, you ridiculous man! I would *never* leave our ranch." Sulking briefly at the idea that he wasn't fully aware of her loyalty to the land in Wyoming, she shook her head at the notion.

"I know that," he said, laughing at her. "I merely thought perhaps you're becoming besotted by this splendid landscape."

Scowling at him, she urged Destino closer so she could wrap an arm around Finn's neck, jostling him in the saddle. "There is no more beautiful scenery anywhere in the land than at our very own *Rancha Mariposa.*"

"Amen." He twisted his head toward hers so he could kiss her. "Shall we canter on, milady?" He presently asked and they increased their pace.

Once they finished their ride and returned to the horse stalls, they joined Granville in his trap for the ride to the Brown Palace for lunch. Afterward, Delaney and Granville retired for naps while Finn returned to the Amphitheatre to bathe Destino and Centaur in preparation for tomorrow's Dressage competition.

When they'd been rubbed dry and blanketed, he fetched a farrier to check their shoes to be sure they were totally ready to perform on the shredded bark bedding in the show rings. "All this primping isn't for naught, my friend," he told Centaur as he began employing clippers to shave any excess hair with special attention to his ears and nose. "Come Thursday, you and I are going to show how we can jump hurtles. You must look your best for your unveiling."

The horse craned his sleek black neck to snuffle his nose against Finn's coat.

"I'm happy you agree." Once Finn was finished with the trimming, he turned to the task of braiding Centaur's mane and tail.

Meanwhile in her bedroom at the Brown Palace, when Delaney awoke, she gave the remainder of the day to mentally preparing herself for the first leg on the Eventing roster. Seated by a window, she looked out over the show grounds that were still a hub of frantic activity with parades of the same kind of astonishing exhibits she'd seen yesterday, traveling through the milling spectators from one end to the other. Aside from this odd entertainment, countless men and boys along with a smattering of girls and women led animals of every description to unknown destinations throughout the grounds.

Delaney smiled at the melee, never having seen the like in her entire life; she'd seen only a few of the animals on display. She'd never realized there were so many varieties. She directed her thoughts to the Eventing competition. At a tap on the door, she rose to let in her mother, Yvette, Millie and Sawyer. "We're going to the dining room for tea," Yvette said. "You must come with us."

Delaney clapped her hands, delighted. Once she'd waved them inside and saw them to a sumptuous sitting area, she excused herself and ducked into the dressing room to remove her riding clothes. She hastily donned a simple wool dress in green that she accented with a smart little black velvet bowler with a green ostrich feather, and draped a creamy cashmere shawl about her shoulders.

"I'm ready for tea and scones," she announced when she returned and they were quickly off to the dining room.

"Are you prepared for tomorrow?" Sawyer asked when they'd been served tea and assorted scones and pastries.

"I will be by the time, Destino and I enter the ring. I don't believe we could do anything else that would improve our chances. Granville and Finn have been very thorough."

"And you have worked very hard," Yvette pointed out. "I must say, I'm positively ecstatic that Centaur will have his chance to show what a magnificent horse he is! He's grown weary of always being the alternate."

"Has he? Then I wish I'd thought of it sooner." Delaney said teasingly. She dabbed at stray strawberry jam at the corner of her mouth. "It's only fair. We began training him in case something kept Destino from competing but in the end Centaur has proven to have amazing ability in his own right. I've no doubts, he'll be incredible in Stadium Jumping."

"I'm so excited!" Yvette hugged her arms about herself.

"Damien shared some more exciting news," Harper divulged. "Back when the show officials were planning this year's show, they wanted to do something out of the ordinary to stir public interest after not having a show last year."

"Why was it cancelled last year?" Sawyer asked "I forget."

"Some ranchers were dealing with a hoof-and-mouth disease outbreak among their cattle. Thank God, it didn't affect us. But it was far too risky to gather cattle together on such a large scale under those conditions. Hoof and mouth disease can be devastating when it spreads. So after that unfortunate situation, the show lost some of the momentum it gained since the first one in 1906. To rekindle some of that excitement, whenever he is chosen this week, the Grand Champion steer will walk a red carpet here at the Brown Palace and be on display every day at High Tea."

"Oh, Ma-ma, how marvelous!" Delaney exclaimed. "Imagine a *Rancha Mariposa* steer strolling on a red carpet."

"Wouldn't that be something?" Harper had a wistful sparkle in her eye. "However," she added, lifting a cautionary hand, "we mustn't let our hopes overpower our good sense."

"What does Pa-pa say?" Delaney asked.

"Your father is the ultimate pragmatist," she said, touching her arm. "But in this, he is guardedly optimistic. And Chandler believes it's a certainty."

"Me too," Delaney declared, serving herself an apple scone.

# CHAPTER SEVENTEEN

## January 1916

The following morning, Delaney mounted on Destino passed the inspection by veterinarians, then waited beside the Dressage ring in the Amphitheatre. Seven horses had performed so far and they were up next. She walked Destino in a circle, testing his mood. She'd cantered him for a mile earlier and now, he seemed relaxed and eager.

She'd thought that he looked very handsome after Finn had groomed him to fastidious perfection. And she assumed she appeared appropriately put together in white jodhpurs and ascot, black coat, boots and top hat. Glancing at Granville and Finn waiting in the trap at the edge of the show ring, she acknowledged their waves with a nod and checked the progress of the current rider.

When that horse left the ring, she glanced at Granville, waiting for his sign to put Destino into position to enter. As he presently raised his arm, she urged the horse to a spot just inside the ring entrance where they paused for the judges' bell. When it rang, she rode forward at a canter, saluting the judges and keeping in mind they were looking for suppleness, balance, rhythm, with obedience. Destino's harmony with her was perhaps most important.

Granville had already worked out the judges' perspective in the test and told her where she could, if necessary, cover up mistakes. Delaney appreciated the tip but hoped she wouldn't have to use it. She'd been trained to always be precisely accurate, aiming to execute each movement a fraction before the appropriate marker that would most often put the rider exactly on target.

When she reached the spot in the test for canter serpentines, she recalled Granville's instruction. She rode so Destino was broadside to the judges at the moment of crossing the center line to avoid making points of the turns instead of curves. Points are so sharp they would encourage Destino to change legs instead of moving smoothly into a counter-canter. As they executed the movement while she softly talked Destino through, he managed it with flowing, rounded turns. With a sigh of grateful relief, she urged him into the next of the twenty total movements in the test.

At one point near the end, she was hazily aware of distant applause that served to refocus her attention. She thought Destino may have heard it also because she felt him react with a new keenness, responding to her cues eagerly and precisely. "Yes, darling, that's the way," she whispered, smiling when his ears flipped back toward her.

They finished the test with a flourish in a serpentine in three loops and a canter before coming to a stop as Delaney saluted the judges, then guided Destino from the ring on a loose rein. She rode toward the wagon where Granville and Finn were clapping furiously. As she drew near, Finn leapt down, catching her in his arms as she slid from the saddle.

He spun her around, kissing her mouth, then both cheeks. "You were simply beyond reproach, my love. Right now, you rank first."

Granville had also alighted from the trap and stood nearby, leaning on his cane. A tear ambled down his kind face. "Ah, my dear, dear Delaney, you were simply grand!"

"No more than Destino," she cried, burying her face against his tweed coat. "He was so incredible."

"Yes, he was. I'm so proud of you both. You remembered everything I taught you. And were brilliant," he added, causing Delaney to smile. All during the training, he'd harped on that she and Destino must be brilliant, a description she found hard to grasp until this morning when she'd sensed they had reached that state.

"I concentrated on doing what you said." Tears ached in her throat and then she was in Damien's arms.

"My darling girl," he said, hugging her so tight. "Did you know you're on top?"

She nodded, glancing around for Finn.

"He's taken him to his stall to cool him out," Granville explained.

"Oh, good." She turned as Harper appeared, running toward them with Yvette and Sawyer close behind.

"Darling!" She threw her arms about Delaney, rocking her. Pulling back a bit, she looked at her intently. "How was it? Did you love every second?"

"I did, Ma-ma! And Destino was just so good. He did everything I asked so flawlessly like he knew what he had to do to impress the judges."

"I am certain he did know," she said with a smile.

Millie stepped forward to speak to Delaney. "You are truly the most amazing rider," she declared. "I was on the edge of my seat."

"As were we all," Yvette interjected, extending her arms to Delaney. "Do you have one last hug in you, or do you feel like a squeezed orange?"

"I always have a hug for you." She wrapped her arms about her.

"And for me?" Millie asked.

"Always, always." She looked at her beaming friend, then drew her close.

"You're doing what we planned we'd both do," she said, raising her head. "But you're so much better than I ever was. I could never have gotten this far. But I'm so happy you have!"

"Thank you, Millie. I love you so."

"Now shall we have an early lunch?" Harper asked, realigning her large lavender hat that had been tipped askew in all the hugging.

"Yes, I'm starving. But what about Finn?"

"I'll escort him to a wonderful lunch when he's gotten Destino bedded down for a well-earned rest," Damien said. "Now you ladies go along and enjoy yourselves rehashing Delaney's victory."

"I shall be your escort," Granville said. "Ah, perhaps we can hitch a ride to the Brown Palace," he added, observing the arrival of Arthur's automobile. He beckoned to a lad to take William.

Always the gentleman, Arthur left the driver's seat and came to congratulate Delaney. "We're all so happy for you. Now, come along as the rest have reserved a table for us."

The group trouped forward and began settling into the plush auto. Delaney turned back to her father who gave her a pleased smile as she tucked her arm into his.

"Oh, Pa-pa, I'm so happy." She laid her head in the hollow formed by the curve of his shoulder.

"Darling, you did so well."

Looking up, she studied him. "Is our steer going to walk the red carpet?"

He smiled, then pressed his lips to her forehead. "We will know by Thursday. Chandler and I are quite discombobulated by the whole thing. There's little doubt that our entries possess the quality to win the championship. Now we must see if God wishes to bestow another huge blessing."

"I'm sure he will. And by Thursday, I will be finished and can walk the red carpet with you."

"I'll look forward to that, my dear."

"Good luck." She kissed his cheek, then hurried to the auto where Arthur held a rear door for her.

When Delaney reached Destino's stall the next day, he was already saddled and Granville sat waiting in his trap. "All set?"

"We are," Finn came to kiss her. "I took him out for a walk, then washed him and rubbed him down with liniment and put on his boots. He's very calm so I think he's ready to go without more exercise. Now, we should head out."

Granville clucked to William and proceeded out of the barn while Delaney and Finn walked, leading Destino. Outside, Delaney joined Granville in the trap so he could advise her about the course that he'd walked that morning. She pulled on her gloves before taking the drawing of the cross-country route he'd sketched.

"We'll get to the course early so we'll have time to go around again so you will know what to expect. I don't believe there is really anything out there that will give you any trouble. But you must keep your wits about you and ride smart. You know how to do that."

"Yes, I do." She returned her attention to the diagram.

They soon left Finn walking a blanketed Destino and began their tour of the competition sites. Presently, they bypassed the roads and tracks, and steeplechase portions of the course, these tests to be run within time limits before the cross-country.

Once they reached the beginning of the cross-country course laid out in a grassy field, they inspected the twenty jumps placed around the four mile course. Delaney looked out across the picturesque meadows; when the trap dipped down into a shallow hollow the silhouettes of massive cottonwoods and other trees stood as sentinels on the horizon.

As they continued at a fast clip in order to finish well ahead of the first riders, she took note of the natural obstacles. Relieved to see she'd trained over worse at the ranch, her confidence rose.

When they returned to where Finn waited with Destino, he showed them the starting lineup. Because Delaney had finished in first place in Dressage, she would start today close to the bottom of the roster.

Granville pulled out his pocket watch, checking the time. "So I would guess you will start close to two o'clock. I'd prefer you go much earlier before the sod gets trampled into the mud." He raised his hands in a gesture of surrender. "But that's the rule since you had such a fine dressage test so it's all fair."

"Shall I continue walking him?" Finn asked, having stopped nearby.

"I'd like to give him a couple handfuls of grain for lunch but we must stand firm at that. He'll have to be happy with a few swallows of water. Then, yes, more walking to keep him limber. We must bear in mind the Ten Minute Box vet check after the steeplechase."

Half an hour later, they watched the first horse depart. "Ah, good, they're off then," Granville said.

After another hour watching the horses enter the course, Delaney began to feel impatient. She jumped down from the trap seat and began pacing a small circle.

"Are you getting nervous?" Granville inquired with a questioning look.

"Not nervous, just eager. I want to *go!*"

"You will, shortly now," he said, chuckling. "In the meantime, why don't you go get a hug from Finn, then spell him. Walking will calm you and before you know it, you'll be off."

"You're very wise." She adjusted her helmet and secured the straps, then pulled on her gloves while she approached Finn.

He studied her, then wrapped an arm around her as they continued walking. "You're going to be magnificent, you know," he said softly.

"I hope."

"I have no doubt."

"Granville wants me to walk him now."

"That's good then." He gathered her close, holding her a moment before kissing her and smiling into her face. "I'll see you in the Box."

She took the reins and started off, Destino walking eagerly, a slight bouncy spring in his gait. "You're so brave," she told him, resting a hand on his shoulder.

He whickered, lifting his head to put his nose in her hand.

"We're going to be magnificent, you know," she said, laughing at him.

Soon enough, Finn came to tell her she was up and after tightening the cinch and adjusting her stirrups, boosted her into the saddle. "Does everything feel right?"

She stood in the stirrups and leaned flat over the horse's neck. "Yes."

"I love you, darling." He rested his arms on either side of her. "Now, go give 'em hell!"

She heard the bell and raised her arm to salute Granville before she entered the start and was on her way. Granville had drilled her about the purpose of this phase, telling her to ride with utmost concern for Destino, trying at all times to save him unnecessary effort to conserve his energy for the Cross-Country. Riders had discretion in how they covered the terrain in the time allotted.

She and Granville had decided the best option for Destino was to cover the ground at either a canter or trot, taking care to finish the course under time. She kept him on the flattest ground available and nearing the end of this phase, she glanced at Granville who'd managed to keep pace in the wagon and gave her a sign to speed up.

Once they entered the Steeplechase section, they jumped the first two fences at a fast pace they maintained for a time, Delaney, thankful Destino had been trained to jump at speed, never checking his stride. Nearing the end of the phase, she consulted Granville again and he signaled she could walk into the Ten Minute Box with two minutes to spare.

This timing was ideal because the slow pace would give the gelding time to recover and slow his panting breath; the extra two minutes would also be welcome in the Box where so much was required to refresh him before the Cross-Country.

Delaney arrived at the Box at a trot so the examining panel could see that her mount moved straight and sound. The second they passed him, she hastily slid off, turning him over to Finn and the three stable lads who'd hitched a ride on the trap. Their job was to use the next twelve minutes judiciously to prepare him for the grueling Cross-Country. Delaney listened to Granville, Jamie, Damien, Chandler and Caldwell, who'd been stationed around the course as fence inspectors, tell her all they could about the course conditions. The lads leaped on the heap of equipment that had been unloaded from the trap, brought pails of lukewarm water and scrubbed Destino from nose to tail.

After he was scraped and toweled dry, they covered him with a sweat rug, and cleaned his feet with a pick. His shoes were checked to see that the studs were still in place. Minor cuts were treated and globs of Vaseline were plastered thickly down his legs from belly to hoof over boots and bandages. This messy practice was necessary to help him slide over if he should hit the top of a solid fence.

Lastly, Finn soaked a sponge in clean water and washed out his mouth, then walked him some more to finish drying him. They watched Granville approach the panel to see if they wanted to check Destino again. When they waved him away, they brought a clean pad to place under the saddle they cinched halfway before giving Delaney a leg up. Finn came to watch her tighten the cinch from the saddle and gave her a quick kiss as they waited for the call to start. Once the countdown began, she rode into the starting box.

And she was off, settling into a strong, relentless canter she was determined to maintain to ensure she would finish in time. As they headed into the Rails and Brook Jump, she was delighted with Destino's performance as he seemed totally in tune with her. Approaching, he looked intently into the drop, crouched and lowered himself carefully, his hocks tucked and his belly close the ground. As he moved through the water, his fast, compact action made her heart sing. "You are such a smart, careful boy," she told him.

Because it remained dry, the course was in relatively good condition and covered four miles with twenty obstacles, a mixture of solid jumps, banks, ditches and water hazards. Delaney was vigilant in keeping Destino pushing boldly ahead because she'd learned early on, that this was the sole means to cover the miles efficiently. In the early days of training, she'd learned how much it slowed an overall time to let the gelding lag into periods of slower speed when he'd then struggled to get back on pace.

Today, he made few mistakes and his strong, steady canter ate up the miles and jumps while preserving his energy. The first trouble came when they least expected it. As they approached the Fish Hatchery, they were both confident and the gelding's approach was perfect. But when he leaped, his legs dropped on either side of the rail, and he was left straddling the large log below.

Delaney threw her weight back to help him on landing and impelled him forward with tightened legs and loose reins. With great effort and courage, he dragged his body over even as his hind legs caught the rail. Delaney was thrown forward by the impact on touchdown but recovered quickly and with the help of the thick grease on his legs, they were off again, vastly relieved, happy and with their poise restored after their remarkable save.

Their progress continued uneventfully until the final fence when disaster struck again. Destino dropped a foreleg against the rail with a crack that sent a chill through Delaney. He attempted a quick save and managed to free his foreleg as Delaney shifted her weight backwards.

And when a crash into the water seemed inevitable, they managed an amazing recovery as Delaney shifted her weight back over his center of gravity. He easily jumped free of the stream and they headed to the finish line where her parents, Finn and Granville waited.

All Delaney could think about amid the flurry of hugs and congratulations was the injury to Destino's foreleg. "He's hurt," she told Granville and Finn who immediately understood the gravity of the situation.

He was still blowing from the strenuous exercise and Finn pulled off the saddle and buckled on a sweat rug before starting the walk back to his stall. Delaney rode with Granville. Her parents followed on Avalon and Jasper.

"In all my years of watching Eventing, I've not seen better riding than what you did today," Granville observed. "I thought you were in huge trouble at those two obstacles but between the two of you, you survived. It did my heart good to see such excellent teamwork."

"You prepared us well."

"You were truly amazing," Damien said.

"Where's Chandler?" Delaney asked.

"He couldn't get away from showing Herefords this afternoon. We're getting very close to winning the coveted Grand Champion Steer trophy."

She was so weary as they continued, she hardly heard him and dozed against Granville. Soon enough, they reached Destino's stall where Finn had already washed him down and was walking him to cool him out completely.

Delaney joined Granville and Damien when they carefully examined the bruised cut that had begun to swell. He had begun limping and this sent stark fear through Delaney. She was also filled with such anguish that he was suffering after such a courageous Cross-Country.

Granville stood up after running his hands up and down the leg. "It's on the surface and that's good. We may have a chance of keeping him fit enough for tomorrow." He wrapped his arms around Delaney, causing her to burst into tears. "I can't promise but we're going to do our damnedest." Peering into her desolate face, he produced a handkerchief he pressed into her hand.

She wiped her face and took a deep breath, determined to be strong and see Destino through. She squared her shoulders and blew her nose. "I'm going to stay right here with him," she said with renewed resolve.

Harper hovered close and didn't argue or protest. "Then I'm going to go fetch you some blankets and hot soup." She squeezed her hand and was gone.

Granville dispatched Damien to bring a large supply of ice and an inner tube from an automobile tire that he would fashion into a sleeve around the injured leg. By the time the supplies were procured, Finn had removed the studs from Destino's shoes, medicated his other cuts and bruises, and bandaged his sound legs with hot kaolin poultices that, left on overnight, would relieve the strain in the bones and tendons after the strenuous day's work.

When the ice arrived, Granville filled the rubber envelope then considered the others. "Let's pray this works and our boy is good to go in the morning. I'm going to go have a bite and a nap, then I'll be back to see how he's doing."

Harper delivered the blankets and soup. By this time, Delaney and Finn were quite shaky with hunger and fatigue and gratefully drank the bracing broth before crawling under blankets in a corner of the stall. Damien and Harper stayed with them, settling in their own corner, leaving a lantern burning.

Nestled in the security of Finn's arms, Delaney slept immediately. Much later, she was awakened by Destino breathing in her face. Opening her eyes in the dimness, she reached up to put her hands on either side of his face. "Are you all right, big guy?" She asked.

He snuffled and moved off to the other side of the enclosure. Delaney's worry had slid away and she was now certain he was going to be fine for Stadium Jumping tomorrow. Sliding down a little, she drifted back into sleep.

Finn, disentangling himself from the blankets, woke her just before dawn. He turned to appraise her, then leaned back to kiss her. "It's time we see if you're going to ride today."

She watched him leave the tent, then got up, seeing Destino cross-tied in the breezeway with Damien and Granville examining his leg. Donning a heavy cape as she went, she rushed toward them.

They had already cut the sleeve away and peered at the gaping wound on the long pastern bone. The exposed flesh over the bone was pink which Granville deemed a positive sign. "Now we need to dress it and bandage the leg. We can use the same salve Finn used on the cuts and bruises."

"Wouldn't Bag Balm work better?" Delaney asked, thinking of the salve made in Vermont over a hundred years ago to keep dairy cows' bags comfortable. Lucinda, the current jersey cow at *Rancha Mariposa* had benefitted greatly over the years from Bag Balm as had all the other milk cows at the ranch over the years. "When Destino cut his fetlock last year, I bandaged it with Bag Balm and it was totally healed in a week."

"It is an amazing product," Damien concurred. "I've used it often enough, myself. Not only on the milk cows but the Herefords and horses as well. I believe Delaney is correct and it would keep this wound soft and comfortable."

"I agree," Granville said, "but I don't think we brought any with us."

"I shall pay a visit to the Dairy Barn and see if I can find some," Damien said. He gave Delaney a smile and a hug as he departed.

While they waited for him to return, Finn fed Destino. Outside the barn, the sun had edged up from the horizon, sending streaks of brilliant orange across the grounds. Delaney paced around the stall, thinking about the final veterinary inspection that would take place in an hour. While she walked, she prayed Destino would be fit.

When Damien returned, he carried a green can of Bag Balm. Granville moved in to watch as Finn slathered the salve over the wound and wrapped the leg with a cotton bandage before buckling on a white leather boot. He then set to the task of removing the sticky kaolin from his other legs and applying the other three boots.

"Now we can see if he's sound," he said to Delaney.

"Let's take him out" Granville caned his way to the door.

Once outside, they found a vacant paddock and Finn let their patient loose. He trotted away, delighted to be out of the stall. Everyone watched intently for the telltale bobbing head of a lame horse but he betrayed no sign of pain.

Delaney dared breathe as Damien pulled her close. "He's sound, Pa-pa."

"It appears so although we won't know for sure until you jump him. As you know, we can't risk a permanent injury by putting him in Stadium Jumping if he isn't one hundred percent."

"I know," she said. "I want to ride him now so we'll know before I take him to the vet exam."

"I'll get him ready." Finn snapped on the lead to take him back inside.

Within minutes, Delaney had mounted, feeling stiff and sore in the saddle. If she was in this much pain, how must Destino feel? She rode back into the paddock and walked him around the edge until she felt him relax, then pushed him into a canter that was smooth and straight. Glancing at Granville by the gate, she caught his nod, then turned toward a schooling fence.

Destino cantered forward, gathered himself and soared, then landed perfectly and took up the canter again. "Woo . . . hoo!" Delaney pumped her fist in the air as she rode toward the gate. "We're ready to compete!" She called when she neared the others. "How long until the vet exam?"

Granville checked his pocket watch. "Half an hour. Ride him for a while slow, then canter a little to keep him flexible."

She guided him to a grassy area behind the Amphitheater where they walked until he moved with confidence and comfort before cantering the length of the plot. Certain he would pass the exam, she rode back to the barn.

She soon headed to the waiting area for the vet exam where she practiced trotting him back and forth. When she was summoned, she led him in and stood him squarely so the panel could look him over carefully, then walked him away and trotted him back. Despite knowing he was fit, she was relieved when they were passed and they headed back to his stall.

Leaving Destino with Finn to be fed his noon grain and groomed, Delaney and Damien went with Granville in the trap to drive around the course. She was pleased to see it was very straight-forward as Granville had already told her. Because the purpose of the competition was only a test of obedience to determine if a horse was still willing to work for his rider after a grueling day at Cross-Country, tall and tricky obstacles were absent.

When they finished, Damien suggested Delaney go to the hotel for a bath and a nap before the time for her to begin the Stadium Jumping. Since she was in first place, she would start late again, after four that afternoon. Finn would spend the interim hours massaging Destino with liniment and walking him to keep him supple. Damien and Granville returned to the cattle competition to see how the quest for Grand Champion Steer was coming.

An hour before Delaney left the hotel, Harper and Yvette came to walk over with her. Sawyer had arrived earlier to style her hair beneath her black top hat and tie her ascot. When the others got there, Delaney considered herself one last time in one of many huge mirrors. She wore white breeches and black boots, topped by a long red coat. Satisfied, she turned to embrace her mother.

"You look wonderful, my dear."

"So do you." She took in Harper's purple brocade coat and white hat lavishly decorated with white feathers.

When they reached Destino's stall, it was empty but Finn soon led him inside and buckled on his saddle and bridle. Granville arrived shortly with final instructions for Delaney.

He guided her to the collecting ring where she put the gelding through some dressage maneuvers to further loosen his muscles, then did a series of small jumps to get him into rhythm and willing to use his entire body even if it was still a bit painful. But she soon realized just how stiff and fatigued he was. Tears flooded her eyes as she picked up each hit when he failed to clear a rail.

She soothed and encouraged with her voice but he continued to falter.

Suddenly she saw her father watching her, his face tense with concern. She pulled up next to him and he was quickly holding her hands, then reached up to cradle her head a moment before tugging it down so that he could look at her intently.

"Oh, Pa-pa, it's hurting him to go on. And he can't jump clean."

"Darling, he's a big strong jumper who's been training for this for a really long time. It's a bit tough just now but he can finish. Don't give up on him now!"

Granville arrived on foot, furiously stomping across the lot, beckoning furiously at Finn. "Let's take off his boots and bandages!" He ordered, not bothering with his usual courtesy. "We need a miracle here! He can't feel it when he touches a rail so he's liable to knock down every one. Particularly since he got accustomed to banging into the solid cross-country jumps yesterday. Now then," he said when Finn had removed the three expendable boots. "Try him now."

The change immediately improved Destino's performance. When they went over a few more jumps, he sat back on his hocks properly and his concentration was much better.

Delaney took him back to the collecting ring and put him through dressage moves for a short interval, then turned to the practice fences again. Once his mind was back on his work, he lifted his legs high enough to consistently clear the rails.

Delaney smiled in relief. She realized they were as ready for the Stadium Jumping as they would ever be and got in position to enter the ring.

He jumped well and clean. An hour later, Delaney stood with Finn, Granville and her family to accept the 1916 Colorado Livestock Show Trophy for Eventing. The group pressing close around her erupted in joyous celebration, clapping so long, Delaney finally told Finn he must take Destino to his stall.

With a final kiss for Delaney and a wave for the rest, he lead the Thoroughbred away, still blowing, his dappled hide wet with sweat. Delaney longed to go after them.

"Shall we go have a glass of champagne before dinner?" Damien asked her.

She shook her head. "Not until Finn can join us. And I want to see Destino settled. He's so tired and he did so well." Tears ached in her throat when she thought of how hard he'd worked.

"Of course," Damien said. "I'll come with you and we'll join the others later."

"Thank you, Pa-pa."

Granville started to come with them but they told him to go with the rest.

"He did such a wonderful job, training us," Delaney said as they continued to the Amphitheatre.

"Yes, he did. He's an extraordinary horseman."

Delaney hugged Damien's arm. "I still can't believe we won."

"You did, darling. We are so proud of you. Do you know who is rejoicing in heaven tonight?"

"My Granpa-pa, Moreton?"

"Precisely. He must be hosting a huge party in your honor."

She laughed at the idea as they stepped into Destino's stall where Finn worked by lantern light. He rubbed him down after his bath. "I thought you went to dinner."

"We wanted to wait for you," Damien told him. "You've been doing a wonderful job keeping Destino fit. You and your wife make a powerful team."

"Thank you, sir. I'm very proud of what we accomplished this week."

"As are we all."

The weary gelding was finally dry so Finn applied a heavy blanket and turned him loose, then brought in a full hay bag that he hung from a hook. "He's had his mash so he's ready to have his hay and relax." He checked the water pail, then came toward Delaney and Damien. "We're off, then."

He and Delaney stopped off in their room at the Brown Palace so they could change. Damien continued on to the suite where he and Harper entertained everyone who'd come with them from *Rancha Mariposa,* as well as a contingent of Hereford breeders whose acquaintance they'd made since arriving in Denver.

Once she'd washed in the adjoining bath, Delaney inspected the gowns she'd brought but hadn't made a selection before Sawyer arrived to help her dress. "Oh, please, you must wear this one," she said, grabbing a snugly-fitted dark green satin from the closet.

"I do love it," Delaney allowed, lifting her arms so it could be slipped over her head.

"It's simply gorgeous," Sawyer said, taking in the close fit over her slender hips; the long sleeves ending in points at her wrists.

Delicate gold trim edged the deep vee of the bodice, and circled the hem in several tiers. When Sawyer had done up the tiny buttons at the back, Delaney studied herself. "It's a bit risqué," she said of the plunging neckline.

Sawyer went to the closet, looking over the scarves and other accessories on display. "This will be perfect." She snatched up a red silk rose that she pinned to camouflage some of the revealing slash of flesh.

"Perfect," Delaney concurred, turned to embrace her. "We must talk about you becoming a designer."

Sawyer laughed with a toss of her tawny mane. "I've been thinking a lot about that, actually."

Finn appeared in the door and came to look Delaney up and down. "You're looking stunning tonight, my love." He gathered her close, pressing his lips to her forehead.

"Thank you, kind sir." She executed a little curtsy and took his arm as they headed out. They and Sawyer presently arrived at the suite where Damien and Harper were hosting their party. Granville served champagne with Arthur's help. A staff of the caterers' girls circulated with trays of canapés.

Eventually, the lot was invited downstairs for dinner. As they walked by the area where the Grand Champion Steer would make his appearance, Delaney watched Chandler and their father for a hint as to whether their steer was to win the great honor. Neither gave anything away but she already knew they thought their chances excellent.

She skipped a little along the corridor. How amazing would it be if a *Rancha Mariposa* Hereford should win this great honor?

She breathed a little prayer that it would happen, a symbolic reward for all the years of grueling work and careful breeding that began with Moreton Whittaker. The dream was now coming to fruition in the superb consignment of cattle that'd walked across the prairie last week to be judged against other beasts bred with a similar vision of greatness.

Finn studied her with a grin. "You look like the cat who ate the goldfish."

She gripped his arm. "I'm just excited to see what tomorrow brings. I know you're going to be spectacular on Centaur. And then perchance our steer will go to tea."

He hugged her against him. "That would be grand!"

The next morning, Delaney sat with Granville in the trap, watching Finn compete in the Open Jumping class. Considering that neither he nor Centaur had had the concentrated and lengthy training program that prepared her and Destino so well for Eventing, they both comported themselves admirably. At the end of the first round, they were sixth in the standings.

Delaney and Granville followed Finn back to the barn and helped him bathe Centaur and walk him until he was cool. When he was resting in his stall, Delaney went to check on Destino who lay stretched out flat on the straw.

"Is he all right?" She asked Granville beside her.

She knelt beside the horizontal beast, running her hands over him.

"Is he cool?" He asked when she stood up.

"Yes, and he's breathing steady."

"Then he's right as rain, just taking the opportunity to rest and recover. Smart boy."

Delaney bent to remove the boot from his injured leg, seeing the wound was healing nicely. "All is well with you, my big wonderful friend." She replaced the boot and with a parting pat to his shoulder, followed Granville outside.

A couple hours later, Finn finished the Open Jumping competition in fourth place which was a first-rate victory for a pair of novices. Delaney stood with Finn beside the course.

"Did I not tell you that you would be superb?" She asked him when they were finished caring for Centaur and left him in his stall to rest.

Finn laid his arm across her shoulders. "You did and thanks to you, I discovered I have the ability to compete without falling on my face."

"That would never happen to you, my darling," she said, laughing at him.

"I was relieved to learn that, in this contest, in any case."

"You weren't really worried about falling off?" She was incredulous.

"I was a bit."

"After all the wild riding we did in training?"

"Ma'am, I'm but a mere stable boy," he rejoined with an exaggerated scowl.

She socked his arm. "I'm ready for a nap. How about you?"

"What a good idea. Like Destino, I believe it will require some time before I'm fit again."

"Luckily, we have time now to get both of you back to normal."

Once they reached their bedroom, they lost little time curling up together and falling asleep. Sometime later, something woke Delaney and she lay still, listening, finally recognizing the sound of the telephone ringing.

Disentangling herself from Finn, she ran into the next room to answer it. "Yes."

"Delaney," Harper said, "darling, your Pa-pa called and said we must go to the cattle judging right away."

"Oh, Ma-ma, I think our steer must be about to win!"

"Yes, yes, I think so too. Arthur will pick up you and Finn very shortly. Be outside."

"Yes, Ma-ma." She put down the phone and went to wake Finn.

"What!?" He asked when she sat on the edge of the bed.

She told him again what Harper had said. "Come, we must go." She wore a muslin dress that looked fairly presentable in the mirror so she retrieved the chic little straw hat she'd worn earlier, laced up her boots and shrugged into her red wool coat.

Finn raked his fingers through his disheveled hair, grabbed his coat and they hurried outside where Arthur's auto waited near the entrance. Once they were mashed into the car with Harper, Yvette, Millie and Sawyer, they were off and arrived at the Amphitheater in a matter of minutes despite the constantly roving crowds.

Damien and Granville sat at the side of the ring where Chandler showed a *Rancha Mariposa* steer among a group of some twenty other steers, all sporting championship ribbons on their halters. They had each been judged best in the various breed classes and were now competing to be named best among all the winners.

Tiered seats stood all around the outer edge of the ring. Delaney and Finn found a place near Damien, and Harper who'd edged closer to sit with her husband. Once seated, Delaney gave her full attention to the cattle and the judges pacing up and down before the long line. She was amazed at the huge, blocky shape of the beasts. Most appeared quite square and in top condition.

After a long time, the steers were each led before the judges for close inspection before the entire line circled the ring. During this segment, the judges began eliminating the animals one by one. Delaney was surprised that she could see why each was dismissed. Apparently, though her interest had always been with horses and riding, she had also absorbed many of the specifics of cattle breeding.

Presently the field had been reduced to six steers, including *Rancha Mariposa's* Hereford. Delaney studied the six in turn—the massive red Santa Gertrudis, the somewhat lighter red Limousin, the immense Black Angus, the unique Belted Galloway with its wide white band against a black body, the creamy white Charolais that was her favorite aside from the Hereford who she'd named Fat Fred when he was a newborn calf.

Each champion was led forward for final intense examination by the judges, then either waved back into line or dismissed from the ring. Delaney found she wasn't breathing as the Angus and Santa Gertrudis were sent away.

Gulping for air, she glanced at her mother who held up her thumbs. Smiling at her, Delaney did the same before she dared look back, where the Belted Galloway was exiting the ring.

She threw her arms around Finn when she realized only Fat Fred and the Charolais remained. At the very worst, Fat Fred would be Reserve Champion. Do they also get to have tea at the Brown Palace? Before she could ask Finn, a great cheer went up from the crowd and she saw that her parents were dancing in the aisle.

Wrenching her head around, she stared at the two steers now wearing ribbons. Fat Fred had the purple and the lovely Charolais the lavender. "Oh, my, gosh, we won!" She shouted at Finn who spun her around and led the way into the walkway where Damien and Harper still danced a merry jig. She flung her head back, laughing like she'd lost her mind until her parents came to hug both her and Finn before they all took up their frolicking again.

Several photographers had set up cameras and gestured for the owners to get into their shots for the newspapers. After this was finished, the crowd, realizing the steers were leaving the barn, trickled out of their seats and surged forward, pushing the Whittakers ahead of them.

Like the Pied Piper, the steers with their ribbons fluttering gaily, marched resolutely toward whatever awaited them. While the crowd formed a celebratory parade behind, Chandler led Fat Fred while Damien, Harper, Delaney and Finn followed and the remainder of the Whittaker entourage trailed further back.

When they neared the rear entrance of the Brown Palace, the Reserve Champion veered off while the Whittakers and their Grand Champion took up the red carpet that had been rolled out to welcome them. Everyone inside and out clapped as they negotiated the corridor that led them to the site of High Tea where the diners rose in a frenzied ovation.

A short distance from High Tea, the hotel workers and Stock Show officials scurried about, ushering the exalted Fat Fred into his bunting-draped pen already bedded with straw in preparation for his stay.

Once he was settled before netted bundles of hay, munching contentedly, the Whittakers posed for more photos. Finally, a waiter in livery came to usher anyone who had any connection whatsoever to Fat Fred to tables reserved for them at tea. Settled with her parents, Finn, Yvette and Chandler, Delaney looked out over the sea of faces, feeling huge pride. Their success in Denver was greater than any of them could have predicted when they set out from *Rancha Mariposa* last week.

She watched Chandler open a satchel at his feet and draw out a great bundle of purple and lavender ribbons shot through with blue and red. He laid them out among the teacups.

"I thought everyone would be interested to know how our cattle fared in the show rings," he said. "Our success was quite astonishing." He slid a small notebook from his coat pocket. "We brought fifty head of Herefords here, ranging in age from weanling calves to mature bulls, cows and steers. We were awarded fifteen grand championships, including Fat Fred's as Delaney christened him when he was only a baby."

The crowd laughed and Delaney acknowledged warm appreciation for Chandler's teasing. She clapped and threw him a kiss.

"We also garnered ten reserve championships and twenty-seven first place wins," he continued.

Delaney scanned the tables around them, seeing the enjoyment and pleasure of the people she'd known all her life, all of them either family or dear friends who had helped in the quest for success in Wyoming. She reached out to take her parents' hands, feeling as though she might burst with joy.

Only one thing marred the perfect moment, the absence of Dom. She wondered if he was at the Show or had been earlier. Had he seen her and Destino win the Eventing? More importantly, had he seen their triumphant walk on the red carpet, the ultimate victory of the Herefords he'd worked with for so many years? She felt ill that he wasn't there to celebrate with his family. A chill crawled up her spine when she remembered how much Dom hated Chandler. How bizarre was that?

The trucks that hadn't gotten there in time for the journey from *Rancha Mariposa* were delivered in time to take the Stock Show entries home. Everyone who'd been to Denver returned to the ranch exhausted but elated by their victories.

# CHAPTER EIGHTEEN

## January 1916

The fine weather that had blessed the Stock Show in Denver continued briefly and ushered the *Rancha Mariposa* contingent back home but didn't hold longer. During the following week, the wind escalated until it was a howling monster raging across the prairie. A sense of foreboding spread as Damien and others with long experience dealing with Wyoming's unpredictable weather realized a dramatic change was imminent.

The men rushed to get the Herefords into shelter, gathering them in from the meadows along the Aspen. With the exception of Fat Fred who'd sadly gone to auction on the final day in Denver, all the show animals as well as a good part of the breeding stock were settled in the barns. The rest gained sanctuary from the frigid gale among the towering trees that had grown into substantial shelter belts among the network of sheds and pens that had provided protection for the herds for just under forty years.

The wind blew for three days without slackening. To ease their transition to days of rest in their stalls, Finn and Delaney took Destino and Centaur out for short rides every day.

By the time it started to snow the evening of the fourth day back home, most all the cattle, horses and other livestock had been secured in the barns and stables. The hired men retired to the bunkhouse while everyone not living at the *Mariposa* and Trail's End holed up in the cottages.

Mrs. Blanchard had cooked a pot of beef stew that LuAnn and Constance served early. Weary from the hectic days in Cheyenne and the frantic work since coming home, everyone who'd worked out in the cold was exhausted.

Damien and Harper, Granville, Chandler and Yvette, Delaney and Finn settled near the fireplace after dinner to have a cup of bourbon-laced cider before bed. No one could ward off their drowsiness as they listened to the wailing wind that was becoming a full-blown blizzard.

Soon enough, they all headed off to bed. Finn and Delaney hadn't yet moved into their apartment so settled into their bedroom, Finn poked up the fire that wasn't really keeping the cold at bay. Delaney quickly put on a flannel nightgown and crawled into bed that had been nicely heated with the bed warmers the maids had passed between the sheets. As Finn got in beside her, she curled close. "Ahh, I think I'll sleep until noon. What a blessing to have such a cozy nest in our lovely house."

He leaned over to kiss her before turning down the lamp. Delaney listened to the wind for a few minutes, savoring the feeling of being so protected within the walls of the mighty old home.

Within the space of seconds, she was asleep. She awoke to complete confusion sometime later. When she heard people running and screaming, she sat bolt upright, staring into the hall through the door that stood wide open.

Finn appeared and grasped her shoulders, shaking her. "Come, hurry! There's a fire!" He struggled into his clothes.

Suddenly starkly awake, Delaney rushed into the dressing room, snatching a long fur coat off a shelf and collapsing onto a stool to tug on boots. She wrapped a wool scarf around her head and raced into the hall where thick smoke now made it difficult to breathe. She pulled the scarf up over her mouth.

Finn, dressed in a coat now, grabbed her hand and dragged her along with him as they headed downstairs to the hall where Damien and Harper ran toward them. Shortly, Chandler and Yvette appeared.

"Come, help us with Aunt Pris!" Damien shouted and he, Finn and Chandler headed to her apartment.

When the women looked up, they saw smoke billowing from the ballroom. Something inside glowed red.

The three men emerged from Aunt Pris' apartment, pushing her in her wheeled chair with Granville and Colleen running behind with an armload of blankets. The group careened into the back hall where the servants had come down from their quarters.

"Stay here," Damien instructed everyone except Chandler, Finn and Arthur who'd just arrived with his family from their apartment. After donning wraps, they all headed outside.

Mrs. Blanchard shuffled into the kitchen and added wood to the cook stove, then stood wringing her hands for a minute or so before she burst in sobs. "Oh, what are we to do!" She wailed.

Harper darted forward to clutch her shoulders. "Mrs. Blanchard, good heavens, you must buck up! We have a fire burning in the west apartment but it's hardly the end of the world! Even as we speak, the men will be battling it. And they will need hot drinks. So make yourself useful and have a quantity of tea and coffee ready."

"Yes, milady." With a great quavary heave of breath, she set to the task at hand.

Harper tied a scarf about her head and pulled on heavy gloves. She took Delaney's arm and then Yvette's. "Come, I'm going to go batty if I don't see what's happening this minute! Let's go out!"

The wind hit them broadside as they left the protection of the entryway and made their way down the steps to the courtyard beside the rear garden. The three of them held tight to each other as they leaned into the gale and shuffled towards a bench in the haven of the brick wall edging the garden to the west.

Once they'd collapsed on the seat, they had a vantage of the fire as well as the frantic activity underway to extinguish it. Every hired man was there, either dragging garden hoses up ladders that had been placed against the adobe walls, or hauling up buckets of water to splash on the flames. Indeed, every man on the ranch had joined the force, coming from Trail's End and all the cottages. A great pile of sand behind the barns had been applied to small fires that broke out in the stables and other outbuildings over the years. This too was rushed to the *Mariposa* in wheelbarrows and raised to the roof with ropes and buckets.

Several men had gotten up to the front gallery and from there to the roof where they managed to make much greater progress. From that perspective, they directed their efforts nonstop on the licking flames at their source that appeared to be somewhere on the small balcony attached to the apartment's second level.

Staring through the blowing snow, Delaney identified the various workers—Jamie, John, her father, Finn, Caldwell . . . . Gradually, she realized the blizzard itself was beginning to put out the fire, the sheer volume of snow was piling up now, drifting over the steps to the rear entrance.

She found Chandler some distance from the activity with the ladders, hoses, sand and water. He seemed to be hunting for something among the trees and shrubs planted before the entry to the apartment. Peering into the vegetation, he bent down several times, searching beneath the evergreen limbs nearly touching the ground.

She pointed him out to her mother and Yvette who also stared at him in confusion. Suddenly, another man appeared to stagger out from the cover and stood confronting Chandler who slammed his fist into his face, knocking him into a snowdrift where he lay, unmoving.

"It's Dom!" Yvette screamed and wrenched herself free, running toward the brothers.

Harper and Delaney followed, meeting Chandler who'd wrestled Dom up into his arms and carried him toward the door of the *Mariposa.* Yvette ran beside him, weeping and trying to touch him.

"Let me get him inside," Chandler pleaded, bearing him up the steps and into the rear hall where he put him down on a cot someone had set up in the scullery.

"Why did you hit him!?" Yvette shrieked, kneeling beside him.

Chandler just shook his head. "Why did I hit him? Well, my dear, if you'd found his pile of sticks and kindling, all saturated with gasoline so it would burn hot and quick enough to catch the wood of the door trim because he'd chopped it loose with an axe, what would you have done?" He looked down at Dom with such a look of disgust, Harper reached for his hand.

"Are you saying, he set the fire?"

"Oh, dear," Granville sighed from his seat by the fireplace.

"That's what I'm saying. When I first woke up, I went to the end of the hall and looked out the window. I saw him on the balcony of the apartment, then when I got outside, I ran up there and watched the flames going up the edge of the door and catching the facia of the overhang. He'd soaked every bit of wood with gasoline and whenever the fire touched it, it exploded. Earlier, he'd apparently broken into the ballroom and splashed gasoline on the drapes and carpets . . . ."

Harper looked closely at her step-son, hardly recognizing him. He'd usually been very slender but now he'd lost so much weight he was nearly cadaverous. Once he'd begun drinking heavily, he'd become very bloated but that poundage had now disappeared as well.

Yvette was attempting to remove his woolen coat and Harper proceeded to help her. Despite his dead weight, they managed to free his arms and pull the wet and smelly garment free. Chandler gingerly picked it up and deposited it in a heap on the floor somewhere in the back of the hall.

"Back in his cups by the smell of him," he observed when he returned. "Or, more precisely, *still.*"

Harper looked at Dom's bony white features and felt the same hopelessness she'd felt so many times where he was concerned.

"What are we going to do with him?" Chandler asked presently.

"We must talk to your father about that."

"I'll go see how things are going outside." He replaced his gloves and ducked back out into the storm, disappearing in the swirling white.

Yvette hugged her arms around herself, staring forlornly at Dom. "He's really done it this time, hasn't he?"

"He's in serious trouble," Harper agreed, sadly shaking her head as she consulted Granville.

"Might he be sent to prison?" Yvette asked.

"Why *wouldn't* he?" Delaney said. "He tried to kill all of us in our beds."

Harper touched her arm. "It does appear quite bad for him, darling. But we don't know at this point, just what he was trying to do."

"We must find out more of exactly what he's been up to lately," Granville opined.

"You're right. I shouldn't be jumping to conclusions."

Yvette folded her arms and paced close to the cook stove, then came back and stood looking down at Dom. "Too bad, he's out cold. At this moment, I could kill him myself."

"We've all had those feelings toward our incorrigible Dom," Harper allowed, bringing a blanket to spread over him.

Within minutes, Damien, Finn, Chandler and Arthur came inside, stripping off their wraps that they left in the hall. When they were seated at the dining table with hot drinks and bourbon, Damien looked at Chandler. "You seem to be the detective in our midst, so what do you think?"

"We were apparently so busy since we've been home we didn't notice when he dumped a big heap of wood and kindling by the second floor door of the balcony. Then he came back in the middle of the night and splashed gasoline over it all, and set it afire. He'd already broken into the apartment and gone up to the ballroom where he'd splashed gasoline about."

"When exactly did he do all this?" Damien asked.

"While we were all out preparing for the snow, I suppose," he said. "Then he waited until we were all in bed and started the blaze."

"Well, I don't know about the rest of you, but I'm bloody tired of his insanity. He could have killed some or all of us tonight so." He threw up his arms. "What the hell am I do with him now?" His gaze leveled on Chandler again. "Do you have any clue about where he's been since he was dismissed from the ranch?"

"I daresay, he's still thick with Charleen at the brothel."

Damien nodded slowly. "Well, just as soon as the snow moves out, I'm going to go have a talk with Charleen, then send the sheriff out here to arrest him. As far as I'm concerned, they can throw the key away as I never want to lay eyes on my son again as long as I live."

Harper's eyes betrayed her grief and worry as she listened but she said nothing. Yvette wept silently, gripping Chandler's hand.

Delaney looked angry enough to do something rash but shortly, said good-night and started up the stairs with Finn.

"I'm going to my bed, myself," Granville declared and headed after the others.

Soon after they left, a great crash was heard in the rear hall. Those still at the table rushed into the kitchen where Mrs. Blanchard stood next to the cot with Dom hanging onto her arm, swaying as he tried to remain standing.

Damien intervened between them, twisting Dom's arm behind him, eliciting a sharp cry of pain. "I should kick you out in the snow and pray to God, you freeze to death! What the devil is wrong with you?"

Dom's head bobbed and weaved while he tried to focus his gaze. His black eye was fast becoming deep purple, and the spot where most of the force of Chandler's fist had connected had grown to a sizable knot.

Damien abruptly shoved him back down on the cot and strode into the hall where he grabbed the half-empty bottle of bourbon. Upon returning, he threw the alcohol down next to Dom. "Drink up, my boy! Drink yourself into a coma!" Then he stomped back into the hall and slumped onto a chair.

Unnerved by his uncharacteristic rage, Yvette and Delaney as well as Arthur had left for bed, leaving only Chandler and Harper. Damien brought a new bottle from a nearby cupboard and once he'd uncapped it, poured a large measure into his cup and downed it in two gulps.

As the alcohol seeped into his blood, warming him and calming his agitation, he looked at Harper, and then Chandler. "I have made my opinion where Dominique is concerned, pretty clear, I think. What do you two have to say?"

"I've spoken to Belle Henley about Dom," Harper said. "How he drinks far too much alcohol and can't control the amount anymore. She told me there are experts who have tried to understand all this. One thing they did find out is that certain people have an allergy to alcohol."

"An allergy? Like what happens when some people are stung by a bee?"

"Perhaps. In any case, some people should never touch a drop of alcohol, according to Belle."

"That would be our boy but I doubt he's going to be delighted to hear that, or put it into practice."

"And what do you think?" Damien asked Chandler.

"That at the moment, Dom is a complete and total wastrel with absolutely nothing to offer to anyone. Actually, in my opinion, he's dangerous to himself and everyone near him."

His parents glumly considered him. "You are absolutely correct about that," Damien said at last.

"I have an idea," Chandler said. "Quite radical but it might work."

"Let's hear it," Damien said, a testy edge in his voice.

"Dom and I and the cowboys always enjoyed the days on the upper range when we stayed in the line cabins at night. We were comfortable and had plenty of good food so it was a nice way to spend our time when we weren't working." He traced circles on the table for a moment, then met Damien's eyes. "Why couldn't we put Dom in one of those cabins instead of jail?"

Both his parents merely gazed at him at first. "Are you asking if we could lock him in a cabin and leave him there?" Harper inquired.

"Why not?"

"He might freeze to death." This from Damien.

"We'd have to make some repairs and cover the windows with something strong enough to keep him in. And provide him with plenty of food and fuel. After we take those basic measures to keep him comfortable, I daresay he would benefit greatly from a lengthy term of solitude."

Harper reacted first. "You may have come up with a plan that might be of great benefit to him."

"Why do you believe that?" Damien asked, turning his head toward her.

"Because it won't make him angrier. If he went to jail, it would just inflame his rage and send him further along the hopeless road he's on. If we put him where he's safe and comfortable and self-sufficient, I think he might gradually come to his senses."

Damien nodded, digesting what she'd said. "Well, as for me, I've reached the end of my patience with him so he is going somewhere. I will not have him anywhere near this house or the people I love. I'm all for him going to jail but if you two think locking him up at some remote spot in the foothills is a better plan, then we'll do that."

"So do I have your permission to take a sledge loaded with food, fuel and any other supplies he'll need up to the first cabin I find? I'll fortify the outside and see that the stove and chimney work."

Damien waved his hand in dismissal. "Yes, of course, go as soon as you can. The wind's laid so perhaps you can leave once the sun's up." He glanced at Harper. "Are you really on board with this, darling?"

"Yes. It's the only hope we have just now."

He rose and placed his hands at either side of her shoulders. "Then we'll talk more in the morning before we put this plan into action." With that, he selected another bottle of bourbon and strode into the back hall.

Dobbs and Mrs. Blanchard sat near the cook stove, drinking tea. They both rose when he entered and Dobbs came to stand next to him when Damien went to a coatrack and took several silk scarves from the assorted wraps hanging there. "Dobbs," he said, "just the man I want to see. You've no doubt gotten the gist of what happened here tonight."

"Yes, sir."

"Dom is responsible and he will be dealt with tomorrow. But we have to keep him here for tonight and that's where I need your help. He's very drunk and I wish to keep him that way so here's a bottle you can use to that purpose. I want you to be on guard. Whenever he comes around, please see if you can get him to use the chamber pot you'll find in a cupboard at the bottom of the stairs to the servant quarters. Then have him drink a measure of bourbon which he'll do readily enough, I should think. Now I'm going to secure him to the cot with these scarves. You'll have to untie him partially perhaps. Just be sure, he's secure again." He studied the footman. "Can you handle that?"

"Yes, sir."

"I'm going to bed but I'm sure I won't sleep long so I'll be back soon enough."

"Goodnight, sir."

Harper and Chandler still waited at the bottom of the staircase and joined him as they climbed to their bedchambers. Despite the earlier chaos, the maids had kept the fires burning.

As she moved toward the abandoned bed, Harper appreciated the warmth. Sliding under the covers, she watched Damien stir life into the crumbling logs on the hearth until flames flickered up.

"Well, Dom certainly knows how to turn a night of rest into pure terror," he said when he'd joined her.

"Oh, my, gosh! In my wildest imagination, I couldn't have thought Dom's treachery would come to this. Do you believe he was trying to murder us with the fire?"

He drew her close with her head on his shoulder, stroking her hair. "I truly can't bring myself to believe that. Nonetheless, the facts speak for themselves. If he'd just wanted to destroy the *Mariposa,* he'd have set the fire while we were in Cheyenne for ten days. Besides, adobe houses don't burn so well."

"He knew when we would be home." She shivered. "It terrifies me to think he watches us."

"Well, that will end once he's in the cabin." His hand rubbed her chilled skin. "Try to sleep now, darling. I'll hold you."

Chandler was up only an hour or so after he went to bed. He went to a window to look out over the front garden where the snow had been whipped into drifts, leaving much bare ground. The storm had moved on so wouldn't hamper him in his unsavory duties today.

Some minutes later, he descended the stairs and found his father sitting with Dom in the rear hall. His brother looked poorly after the events of the night before and being in the throes of what must be a colossal hangover.

He slumped against a pile of pillows with his eyes closed and managed to swallow with a grimace when Damien brought the glass of bourbon to his lips. When he started to choke, he shot upright, spitting liquor down the front of his shirt and over his father's arm.

"Damn it!" Damien shouted.

"Sorry," he mumbled, leaning back again.

His father grabbed a towel and began frantically wiping up the splatter.

Mrs. Blanchard passed by them from the stairs to the servants' quarters. "I beg your pardon, sir," she said when she stood near Damien, "but it's getting mighty cold upstairs from the hole in the roof of the ballroom."

Both Damien and Chandler gaped at her a moment. "I'll be sending men up there to cover the hole," Chandler said, coming back to the moment. "Just as soon as I get outside, I'll get things started."

"Thank you, sir." She began bustling around the kitchen, getting the cook stove started so she could prepare breakfast.

Dom had opened his eyes again and noticed Chandler. "Hullo, li'l brudder," he slurred, dislike dull in his gaze.

To Damien's great relief, Chandler didn't answer him but soon turned out the backdoor to dispatch some men to the roof. Within half an hour, he'd sent a crew of ten up the ladders under the supervision of Jamie and Luke.

When he returned inside, Constance was serving breakfast. He joined Granville, Finn, Delaney and Yvette who were already seated. Once Chandler had told the others what they planned to do with Dom, Yvette began to weep and Granville volunteered to go to the cabin with him.

"Well, then, I will go load the sledge and come back to pick you up as soon as I'm ready," Chandler said to Granville, then went back out of the rear door. The banging of hammers already echoed in the stillness as he walked along the edge of the garden toward the barns.

He set another group of hired men to the job of loading the huge sled with boards to cover the windows and strengthen the cabin walls. By this time, lads had harnessed two huge Shires to the sledge and drove it to the immense pile of chopped logs near the bunkhouse where they loaded as much of the fuel as the vehicle could hold.

Chandler climbed onto the driver's seat and guided the team to the courtyard beside the back entrance of the *Mariposa.* Inside, he found Granville dressed in a heavy coat and wraps, ready for the trip to the cabin. Dobbs and other servants rushed to load the supplies from the storage area beyond the scullery—cartons of canned fruit and vegetables, bags of flour, potatoes, butter, rice and oatmeal, bacon, coffee, tea, salt, baking powder and baking soda, sugar and an assortment of bowls, pans, silverware, and a skillet. Finally, several stacks of blankets were piled atop the rest to prevent the liquid from freezing on the trip through the cold.

Chandler went to the girls' school room to say goodbye to Yvette before speaking to his parents in the kitchen. Harper handed him a packet of art supplies and a Bible.

"Do you really think any of this will help him?" He gave her a questioning look.

"It's worth a try." She leaned up to kiss him. "Take care, darling."

He hugged her and his father, then followed Granville out to the sled. They were immediately underway, presently turning along the Aspen and finally headed up the trail toward the upper boundaries of the *Rancha Mariposa* ranges.

Chandler had happy memories of the general location of a cabin perhaps ten miles from the ranch headquarters. He and Dom and some of the cowboys had spent a few weeks there while they built fences and patrolled the prairie, looking for rustlers. He didn't have any recollection of battles with Dom perhaps because they'd only been together at night when they were mostly interested in sleeping.

"What do you make of this latest betrayal by your brother?" Granville inquired as they proceeded along a high ridge where the view in all directions was spectacular.

Chandler shrugged. "I've actually never been able to figure out why he hates me so much. To me, he was always my big brother. I thought him remarkably handsome and quite brilliant."

"His attitude during his entire life has mystified us all."

"He always blamed his mother," Chandler observed.

"And well he might. She was evil to the bottom of her heart. But I can't fathom how hating his mother had anything to do with Dom feeling the same about you."

"He's caused my parents so much heartache, I'd have thought Pa-pa would've reached the end of his patience a long time ago."

"I believe he did when he sent him away from the ranch."

"Perhaps. My mother sent along a Bible and some art supplies. Do you think he'll look at them?"

"It's hard to say what a person will do after a time being totally alone. Dom has never struck me as a man particularly comfortable in his own company." He glanced at Chandler. "How long do you intend to keep him up here?"

"We haven't talked about that. My personal choice would be to have no contact with him for a few months at least."

Granville mulled this over. "If indeed it turns out to be that long before anyone familiar sees him, I know someone who would like to speak to him, catch him while he's feeling forsaken, so to speak."

"Who would that be?"

"Well, while I still lived in England, I enjoyed attending mass at a cathedral in London."

Chandler stared at him. "Are you telling me you're Catholic? Why'd you never tell us?"

"Because neither John and Audra, nor your parents have participated in organized religion, it was never a subject that came up."

"My mother is a believer," Chandler interjected. "I'd say, we all are actually. My grandfather, Moreton, was the one who became disillusioned with organized religion and Catholics."

Granville chuckled. "Ah, yes, Moreton and I had many discussions on the subject. We each thought the other very foolish and tried our best to convince him of the error of his ways.

Neither was successful, yet we remained fast friends until Moreton's death."

"Because my mother is so matter-of-fact about her faith, I never felt bad about not going to church. Ma-ma always made it seem like anywhere we were was as blessed as any church."

Granville laughed again. "Your mother just makes my heart sing when we talk about her faith in the Lord and her Sight. When she first showed me the painting she did of Eddie's death, I was stunned. That was pure genius and I believed her when she said she couldn't have done it without God's help."

"That was a miracle," Chandler agreed. "Still, whenever as a boy, I heard the story behind that painting you sold to the *Louvre,* I wondered why Jesus hadn't saved Eddie."

"Because your mother wouldn't have been inspired to paint the exact moment when Eddie passed into the afterlife. His passage from the horror of his own death into the arms of Jesus was the miracle."

Chandler spotted the cabin hazily visible perhaps a mile ahead, some distance below the horizon.

"The reason I brought up my own faith is because I've been friends with a young priest in a little country parish not far from here actually. Father Richard is a delightful young man who ministers to many of the ranch families in the area. I'm frankly surprised he hasn't knocked on the door of the *Mariposa*."

Chandler snorted. "If he does that, he better hope it's my mother who answers and not my father."

"Oh, I don't know," Granville mused, "he's very engaging and it would be my guess that soon enough, he'll be breaking bread with us at the *Mariposa*."

"Why would he want to do that?" Chandler asked, incredulous.

"Because I have a strong feeling, he will decide he can help our Dom."

"Why is that?"

"He's managed to overcome his own alcohol problem, as bad or worse than what Dom's dealing with."

"Has he really?" Chandler asked, very interested now. "How do you know this?"

"He told me. He and I have talked often about his life when he still lived in England and what has happened to him since coming to Wyoming. He claims he's helped others with this problem and managed to stay sober himself for the past five years."

Chandler studied him without further comment for a time.

"So at the proper time, I will introduce them," Granville said. "In the meantime, if your parents wish to talk with him, I'm sure he'll be delighted by an invitation to dinner."

They approached the cabin a short distant ahead and rode the final way in silence. Once they'd stopped before it, they both sat looking at it.

"Not so grand, eh?" Granville ventured.

"It will do." Chandler jumped down from the seat and collected the heavy blankets he spread over the team and buckled in place. This done, he walked to the front door that opened at his shove. He ducked into the dim room and Granville soon followed.

The interior wasn't in particular disrepair but had never been more than a crude shelter. A wooden bunk was attached to the log wall. A basic stove meant for cooking stood in the center, the pipe threading into a rustic chimney at the edge of the roof. A rustic fireplace stood along the back wall.

The men passed on to the rear where a door opened into a porch that would do as a storage area for the food, and fuel for the stove and hearth. Another egress passed out into a second small room along the outside wall. A crude privy occupied one end.

Back inside, they inspected a table below a small window. Chandler went closer to examine the wooden frame and glass panes. The entire opening was too small for a man Dom's size to crawl through so this eliminated any need to make it more secure.

With the door open, there was enough light to see everything clearly. They gave their attention to the log walls, searching for any spot where Dom might escape by somehow getting through to the outside. But all appeared strong with no way out.

"Well, I'll unload the sledge," Chandler commented, heading outside. Within half an hour, all the supplies were stacked on the table or on the scattered crude chairs furnishing the room. Twenty ten-gallon metal cans of water were lined up against the back wall.

While Chandler turned his attention to the split logs that he piled in the porches, Granville swept the floor with a tattered broom he found in a corner. Chandler piled some of the fuel inside the cabin and found a metal pail and shovel he employed to remove ashes from the stove as well as the hearth of the fireplace. He checked the flues and chimney to see that everything was working properly. Finally, he laid crumpled paper and kindling in the stove and on the hearth so fires could be lit quickly once Dom was brought to the cabin.

After making one last inspection, Granville climbed onto the sled seat. Chandler soon appeared and once he'd closed the door, locked it with the heavy padlock he'd brought with him. He removed the blankets from the Shires and handed them up to Granville to be used as lap robes on the drive home.

Chandler picked up the reins and the horses turned in a large circle before heading back along the trail they'd traveled earlier. The warmth of the morning had given way to a cold wind, sharp and biting now in the fading light near twilight.

Chandler pushed the team into a brisk trot that swiftly covered the miles. Granville had spread the blankets over their legs and held them in place as they descended toward the ranch headquarters.

# CHAPTER NINETEEN

**January 1916 – June 1916**

Dom spent the day following the fire in a drunken stupor. By afternoon, everyone dealing with him was eager for his transfer to the cabin. By the time Chandler and Granville returned from preparing the cabin, Dom had been transferred to his old room at the *Mariposa* where Dobbs oversaw a bath in the dressing room and provided him with clean clothes. The footman finished his ministrations with the suggestion that Dom confine himself to the room and his bed for the remaining of the evening.

"I'm feeling a bit better," Dom announced, "so I believe I can manage to join my family for cocktails and perhaps dinner."

Dobbs considered him with a mixture of amazement and trepidation. "That won't be possible, sir."

Dom stared at him, agape. "Why ever not? I know I had rather too much to drink yesterday but it certainly wasn't the first time. I'm sure all is forgiven now."

"I think not. You're to stay here until your father comes up. He wishes to have a word."

Dom's features narrowed. "I'll just wait for him downstairs." He stepped toward the door.

"I can't allow that, sir." He insinuated himself between Dom and the door and held up a key.

"You're going to lock me in? Not bloody likely!"

Dom lunged for the door but Dobbs knocked him sideways so he sprawled onto the floor. "Then I'll go this way," he said, scrambling to his feet.

Dobbs stood over him, nodding toward the French doors leading to the balcony fronting the second floor. Outside, a huge black hulk stood against the doors and the windows on either side. "No way out, sir."

Dom peered blearily out as he pushed on the doors that were already locked and barricaded. "What've you put out there?"

"Bags of corn. I believe. Luke said a thousand pounds."

This set off a tantrum in Dom who put his fist through a pane of glass in the unmoving door. "Damn the lot of you!" He screamed, jumping forward with the apparent intent of hitting another pane before Dobbs landed his fist in a blow to his arm.

"Give it up, my man." Dobbs shoved him down on the bed despite the squirting blood pumping from a gash on Dom's hand. Stripping off a pillow case, he wrapped the wound. "Now lie still unless you want to bleed to death which is fine with me!"

There was no more protest from Dom as the footman let himself out the door to the hall and locked it behind him, then sprinted down the stairs. Damien and Harper looked up from where they sat before the fireplace.

"So is he settled?" Damien asked.

"Not likely, sir." As Dobbs hastily explained, they both followed him to the rear hall where he gathered bandages.

"What the hell!" Damien yelled, heading up the staircase with the others close behind.

He'd already unlocked the door and sat on the bed beside Dom by the time, Harper and Dobbs entered.

Amazingly enough, Dom had ripped off the makeshift bandage and sat staring at the fountain of blood flowing over the linens. "Have you lost your mind?" Damien shouted at Dom, wrenching his arm close enough so Dobbs could begin wrapping the wound with gauze.

Harper had the presence of mind to bring a bottle of bourbon and now offered Dom a portion. "Drink this!"

He gripped the glass with his good hand and gazed at it. "Why's everyone so angry?" He asked before draining it with an exaggerated grimace.

"Is your memory so short?"

The look he turned on her held nothing but bewilderment.

"You don't remember trying to burn the *Mariposa*?"

His eyes were blank. "I'd never do that." He glanced from her to his father.

"Whether you remember it or not, that's exactly what you did," Damien declared with deadly calm.

Dobbs had finished wrapping the bandage and fixed it fast with tied strips of gauze.

Dom sat still as the liquor calmed his rage until Dobbs pointed to a chair. "Please, sit there so I can strip the linens."

He made no attempt to move until Damien jerked him up by one arm. "Do as you're told before I knock you out."

Slumping into the chair, Dom lifted the empty glass in his hand, peering into it.

"Oh, do let me serve you," Damien said with elaborate solicitude. Grabbing the bottle, he sloshed bourbon into the glass. "Why don't you finish this off?" He asked, leaning close to peer into Dom's face as he brandished the bottle. "Drink it all! Perhaps you'll die! I am so enraged with you at this moment, I do believe, it would be a relief to be rid of you. Do you know why that is? Do you comprehend why I can say something so dreadful about my eldest son whom I've always loved more than my own life?"

Dom gazed at him darkly, appearing on the verge of tears but said nothing. He drained his glass and reached for the bottle to fill it again.

"I loathe you right now because I have no idea what insanity you're going to be involved in next. Last night, you put every one of our family in mortal danger. I simply refuse to let you get by with this lunacy any longer. You are going to find your freedom strictly limited for a very long time, my man."

Dom raised his chin with a shadow of his pugnacious attitude in the past. "I'd like to see that."

"Well, you can rest assured it *will* happen."

The beagles who'd come upstairs cocked their heads, then rushed to the door. Dobbs moved to open it and they dashed out, barking as they headed to the stairs.

"Dobbs will be staying with you now," Harper said, approaching Dom and kissing his battered face.

She and Damien descended the staircase, finding Chandler and Granville removing their coats and other wraps in the back hall. Yvette arrived to greet Chandler who drew her into his arms before they went to sit before the fire.

Granville soon followed, rubbing his hands together before the hearth. "Quite wintry again out there," he observed, accepting the bourbon Roddy served from a tray.

"Well, how did it go at the cabin?" Damien asked when he and Harper were seated opposite.

"We found the building I remembered, about ten miles up," Chandler said. "It will serve our needs nicely. If the winter continues to be mild, Dom should have enough fuel to see him well into spring. How long do you plan on leaving him up there?"

"Until hell freezes," Damien said, his grin rueful. He glanced at Harper. "We haven't discussed how long he should be left there initially."

"If I may offer my opinion," Granville said, "I believe our Dom will benefit from an extended period of solitude before anyone rallies to his cause." He sipped his drink and sat down. "Actually, Chandler and I discussed this in some detail today." He went on to tell them about Father Richard.

"You truly believe this priest friend of yours can be of some help with Dom's obsession with alcohol?" Damien inquired when he fell silent.

"I'm quite certain of it, judging from his own experience. He's managed to stay sober for some years now."

Harper clasped her hands together beneath her chin. "Perhaps we should invite him to dinner and ask him what advice he can give us."

"Just what I was thinking," said Yvette.

"When I see Richard on Sunday, I shall tell him what we have in mind, and also give him a key so that he can visit Dom," Granville said.

Damien chuckled. "So you've been harboring a secret life while living in our midst."

Granville laughed. "I merely enjoy my faith and feel the need to indulge myself by attending mass, or visiting my friend who's a priest, from time to time."

"If we'd learned of your Catholicism earlier, we wouldn't have disowned you," Damien observed drily.

"Well, after being friends with your father for so many years, I wasn't certain of your reaction. Moreton repeatedly advised me not to practice such a *fabricated* religion."

"Yes, he gave me the same advice," Damien said. "He preached to Brendon and me about how the first Pope perverted the word Jesus used to enlighten his followers."

Both the fear of Dom somehow managing to escape, and his father's continued rage at being anywhere near him convinced Chandler and the others to transfer him to the cabin the following day. Dobbs approached him after serving him breakfast in his bedroom.

"Your brother and father will be up shortly," he announced after he'd poured him a large measure of bourbon to cap off his meal.

"What the devil do they want with me now?" Dom demanded upon emptying the glass.

"I believe they'll be moving you to a different location." He lifted the tray with most of the food remaining to a table by the window. "It's some distance so I must get you dressed in some warm clothes."

Dom watched with suspicion when the footman brought long underwear, a thick sweater, heavy wool pants and socks and lace-up boots. He became impaired by the liquor straight away so didn't offer any resistance when Dobbs pulled on the items of clothing as if he was dressing a small child.

"Now then, let's get you downstairs," he said when he was ready. "Let me get ahold of you so you don't fall down the steps." After they'd haltingly traversed the hallway and stood at the edge of the staircase, he held tight to his arm and they started down.

It soon became clear that Dobbs needed help. Dom stumbled and nearly lost his balance three times in the time it took for Chandler and Finn to race up the steps. With them on either side and Dobbs behind, holding tight to Dom's belt, they made it the rest of the way down and soon had Dom balanced precariously in a chair before the fire.

Damien appeared, looking down at his son for a time. "Are you ready?" He asked curtly.

"For what?" Dom blearily tried to focus on him.

"A ride."

Dobbs brought a heavy coat, cap and mittens from a closet in the hall. Once he'd gotten Dom into them, he wrested him up by one arm and propelled him to the front door.

Harper and Yvette came to tell Dom goodbye. He could only gaze at them while he swayed from side to side in an effort not to keel over. "Goodbye, darling," Harper said at last, embracing his emaciated form.

Yvette refrained from touching him, only studied him for a while. "Try to get yourself back on track," she said at last.

Delaney merely sat next to Finn at the dining table and watched him depart, staggering between Chandler and Damien.

As they made their way to a sleigh in the piazza, Dom looked around in confusion but climbed meekly into the rear where he collapsed on a pile of lap robes. Chandler covered him with a buffalo hide before sitting beside his father and taking up the reins.

Neither felt like talking for the first few miles along the trail. A peculiar set of circumstances marked the situation in which they found themselves. Neither of them could have visualized themselves participating in the strange banishment that was now underway.

Chandler could find no sadness in himself at doing this to his brother. Dom had always treated him with such utter disrespect and dislike, if not, outright hatred, the only emotion he could identify was relief.

He let his uneasy thoughts track ahead as he dared wonder what would happen in the future if this radical remedy affected no permanent change in his brother. Would he end up in prison or a mental facility like his mother?

He thought of the few people he knew who'd become empty and helpless within the ravages of alcohol. A couple of fellow students at the university had been robbed of any promise of a useful life by their descent into constant drinking. Everyone at

*Mariposa* had watched the pitiful decline of Mrs. Quinn, Arthur's mother-in-law. Was it to be the same for Dom?

Only time would tell. He prayed that Granville's friend, the priest, would have whatever was necessary, be it skill or wisdom to turn Dom around. He, himself, had no conception of the scope of whatever force could create such havoc in the life of one person, while leaving the next unscathed. He'd never had much of a taste for alcohol and couldn't wrap his brain around any obsession with it.

"Having some deep thought, there," Damien observed.

Chandler grinned. "Just trying to comprehend what's going on with Dom. But having very little luck."

Damien nodded. "I'm as baffled by him as I always was with his mother. Neither of them ever made much sense to me. I so adored Dom, I thought I understood him." He spread his hands. "Now, I see I never did, while he had a bead on me from nearly the day he was born. He knew just how to pull at my heart and I could never stay angry with him for long. I daresay, I felt sorry for him having such a mother, so I continually made allowances. I perhaps should have taken a firmer stand with him years earlier."

"Hindsight is always much clearer," Chandler offered.

"So it seems."

Chandler was relieved that the weather had warmed considerably since the day had dawned cold and still. With the supply of food and fuel they'd provided for Dom, he should be fine at the cabin for several weeks. This certainly calmed the nagging question in the back of his mind. What if they were putting his brother in danger?

"Do you have qualms about what we're doing here?"

Damien continued staring off into the distance. "It is certainly not what I would choose to do with my son. But considering his total lack of good sense and disregard for the rest of us, I can see no other way. I'm grateful you came up with this plan as I'm not sure, I'd have had the courage to lay it out in such straightforward terms. And now that we have Granville's wise input, I feel rather confident, this may turn out well. Your mother and I are very interested in meeting Father Richard."

Chandler nodded. "It would seem he's our best hope," he said with a chuckle. "Granville continually comes up with plans of action that succeed on a large scale. Think about what he's done to promote Ma-ma's art in Europe. And he said he could coach Delaney to victory in Eventing of all things. Who would have believed that was possible in the midst of ranching country? So if he says his friend Richard can help Dom, I, for one, believe he can."

Damien smiled. "Our Granville does inspire confidence."

They had covered the distance from the *Mariposa* at a fast pace and within an hour, the cabin came into view ahead and Chandler soon pulled up before the door. In the back of the sleigh, Dom still slept with no awareness of their arrival.

Chandler alighted, blanketed the horses and unlocked the cabin door. As he stepped over the threshold, Damien followed, scanning the interior.

Chandler quickly lit the kindling he'd prepared yesterday and soon, fires were crackling in the stove and in the hearth. Damien headed back to the sleigh and soon enough, Chandler went to help with Dom who'd sat up on the blankets and groggily looked around him.

"Why are we up here?"

"You're going to stay here for a while," his father explained, steadying him as he nearly keeled over.

Dom stared at him, a nervous light making his eyes large and imploring. "You would leave me here?"

"At this point, it's a matter of leaving you here or putting you in jail. You're in a great deal of trouble in case you've forgotten."

He struggled to make sense of that. "What did I *do*?"

"You'll have time to think about that. I'm sure you'll remember soon enough. Come along now."

A new depth of fear came into Dom's gaze but he allowed them to pull him up and out of the sled. His dread made him unsteady on his feet and they ended up half-carrying him into the cabin where he collapsed onto the makeshift bunk.

"Listen up, now!" Damien ordered, sitting nearby. "You have everything you need. If you use your head, you'll be fine for however long you're here. Now watch Chandler and he'll show you where everything is."

His gaze settled on his half-brother and followed him as he moved through the cabin, indicating the fuel, water, food and blankets. When Chandler presently approached from the porches, Dom covered his face with both hands, leaning his head against a post supporting the bed.

"Do you have any questions before we go?" Damien asked.

"How long must I stay here?"

"We don't know that yet. The reason you are here at all is because you've completely disregarded any common sense you ever had. You've disrespected your brother and tried to turn his family against him in an attempt to make yourself look better. Not once but several times. I've taken measures to discipline you but those were utterly ignored. And you've become completely besotted by alcohol, to the point where you can't even remember setting the *Mariposa* afire in an attempt to murder your family." With that, he stepped toward the door, then turned back once more. "I don't want your death from alcohol withdrawal on my conscience so I'm leaving you two bottles of bourbon. If you have a lick of sense left, you will taper yourself off in the next several days and survive. If you choose to continue drinking to salve your guilt, then I have no pity for you. When you're out of bourbon, you may very well die for the need of it. The decision is yours. Good luck."

He stepped past Chandler who locked the padlock in place and approached the team. Uneasy silence settled around them as they took up the trail for home. Yet, when the ranch headquarters came into view soon after noon, they were both possessed by a great sense of relief.

Indeed, during the next months, *Rancha Mariposa* was held in the grip of unprecedented serenity and happiness. Everyone at the ranch had the opportunity to fully savor their huge success at the Stock Show.

Chandler and Yvette could cherish their romance free of Dom's disquieting influence. Though everyone acknowledged some concern about his well-being in the cabin, Granville remained optimistic and promised that with spring, he would arrange a meeting between Dom and Father Richard.

True to his word, Granville announced at dinner in May that Father Richard had accepted his invitation to come to the *Mariposa*.

"When will we do this?" Harper asked.

"Perhaps next Sunday."

"Oh, good. We shall look forward to that. What do you suggest we serve for dinner?"

Granville waved his hand dismissively. "Oh, his tastes are quite humble so I'm sure he will love whatever you serve."

"Shall we have brandy in the parlor?" Damien asked.

"Lovely." Harper took his hand as he helped her up.

Yvette and Chandler followed Delaney and Finn as they trailed after Granville. Dobbs served brandy as soon as everyone was seated. The beagles arrived to sit in a row on a rug, looking longingly at the basket of tea cakes waiting on a table. Unable to resist their beseeching demeanor, Delaney broke a cake into pieces before putting them through a short routine of tricks that she rewarded with the morsels.

The rest applauded and satisfied with the treat, the dogs collapsed into slumbering heaps. "Father Richard owns a very clever terrier," Granville observed. "His name is Filbert and he travels everywhere with him in his automobile."

"Oh, how marvelous!" Delaney said.

"I believe we can look forward to a visit from Filbert when his master comes for dinner. He is very well-mannered so we have nothing to fear in that regard."

"Will we be expected to set a place for him?" Harper asked with a cocked eyebrow.

"I expect he will be happy dining with our merry trio. By the way, Dom has become very fond of Filbert."

All eyes turned on him. "How long have they known each other?" Finn asked with a wry grin.

"A month or so, I believe. Father Richard thought it prudent that he initially meet Dom one on one. He's the expert here so how could I argue."

Harper was fast losing her patience and sat on the edge of her chair. "How *is* he? Is he all right?"

"He is, apparently. We'll soon be able to judge for ourselves but Father Richard is of the opinion that he's benefitted greatly from being solely in his own company for a time. He reports that he has gotten in touch with his soul again and deeply regrets the terrible things he's done in the past."

Harper sagged against Damien, tears wandering down her face. "Thank, God."

Damien put his arm about her shoulders, nestling her against him. "This is very good news, Granville. Thank you."

"It's still too early to know yet how it will turn out. But it does look positive. I'm so eager for you to hear what Father Richard has to say. The way he speaks about Dom. He truly is the most inspiring man. He's just so grateful to be delivered from his obsession with drink that he sort of glows with it. You'll understand when you meet him. It's really not easy to describe it."

"Does he still have enough food and such?" Chandler asked.

"He had plenty on hand when Father Richard first saw him and he's since taken him some fruit and vegetables and fresh water."

"That was kind of him," Harper said.

Granville nodded. "He's a very kind man."

Father Richard picked up the basket of food from the table in his kitchen, whistled to Filbert who raced out of the bedroom and the two of them went outside to the battered sedan in front of the rectory. Filbert stood on the passenger seat, madly wagging his tail as he tried to lick his face when Richard finished cranking and slid behind the wheel.

"Now, then, my incorrigible companion, we are off to see our new friend, Dom."

Filbert yipped in delight, then propped his front feet against the edge of the window to watch the world go by. Leaving the stone church behind, they took the road to *Rancha Mariposa* as Richard's thoughts turned toward the invitation to dinner at the ranch in three days.

After having spent several hours with Dom, he was very curious about his family. According to Granville, his parents were the most ethical, loving parents any child could hope to have. Since the elderly gentleman had begun coming to mass at St. Matthew's, Richard had come to trust him implicitly so he had no reason to doubt his assessment of Dom's people.

He'd gathered from the beginning of his friendship with Granville that Dom's mother had been a profoundly depraved influence in his young life. Yet, he couldn't believe the woman was solely responsible for his untoward behavior as an adult.

From his associations with fellow drunks and more importantly, his own history of intemperance, he'd come to certain conclusions. A life-threatening compulsion to drink alcohol, such as Dom's resulted from a physical predisposition rather than one's childhood environment.

This knowledge had come from the Almighty ten years earlier. Richard had finished his study for the priesthood in Boston. When he should have been on top of the world, he was on the verge of suicide. When he'd called out to his God, he'd been delivered from his desperation, and filled with the need to help others who suffered as he had.

He had no doubt this same God had sent Granville to him at St. Matthew's and he was up to the challenge he now faced. "Before we're finished with Dom, he'll be a new man," he told Filbert, reaching a hand toward the dog who patted it with his paw. "Good man!"

They soon sped past the ranch headquarters and headed along the trail toward the cabin. When they parked, Filbert recognized where they were and began barking happily.

"Hush!" Richard reprimanded, stepping out and catching the terrier when he leapt into his arms.

They approached the door that opened before them. "Hello, Dom."

Dom stood in the doorway. His beard had grown so it touched the middle of his chest. He reached out to embrace the priest; Filbert licked his face when he could reach it. "I'm very glad to see you. I was at loose ends. Come in and I'll make tea."

Richard put Filbert down and he scampered to the rear door and disappeared.

"He's after the squirrels again," Dom said with a laugh as he dipped water from a can to fill the tea-kettle. He poked the fire to life in the cook stove and placed the kettle on to heat, then beckoned and led the way out through the first porch to a crude table and stools he'd built at the edge of an aspen copse next to the cabin. Filbert stood with front feet braced against a nearby cottonwood trunk, barking at a squirrel calmly observing him from a branch high above.

The men sat on stools in the shade next to the table. The afternoon was agreeable around them, still and warm.

"Have you been tempted to break out yet?" Richard asked after a time.

Dom vehemently shook his head. "I've not the slightest desire." He looked somberly at his friend. "What if I just stay here forever? Would you continue bringing me food and water for the rest of my days?"

Richard's chuckled. "I hardly think that will be necessary."

"I don't know. I think I've transferred my reliance on drink to this cabin. As long as I stay here, I won't have to worry about what I might do if I leave. It seems like a good way to protect me from myself."

Richard considered this for a few minutes. "I can certainly comprehend why you feel that way, just now," he said at last. "It must be such a comfort to be off the merry-go-round your life had become. I felt much the same when I first became sober. My life was so pleasant in Boston, living in a rectory with some friends with whom I'd attended seminary. Several of us hadn't yet been called to a church and there was little pressure to do so. As a result we worked in the community and waited to be inspired to begin our real work."

"How long did that take?"

"It took me almost a year. I simply could not force myself to move on before that. Yet, when the time was right, I was suddenly ready, excited to find where I belonged. Very shortly after that, I was called to St. Matthew's."

"So you're telling me, one day, I'll be inspired to get back to my life?"

"Oh, I don't believe you'll ever want to go back to your life as it was. But yes, there will come a time when you're ready to leave this place and decide where you wish to live the rest of your days."

Dom studied him. "I don't have to go back to my family?"

"Not unless you want to. I rather think it will happen but it's totally your decision."

Dom considered him with something akin to amazement. "I didn't know I had a choice."

"Well, of course you do. Perhaps in the past, you behaved in the way people expected you to. In my opinion, that sort of behavior often comes about after one's reputation is compromised. But today, you are a new man, sober, and in complete possession of your faculties. You must give careful thought to how you wish to proceed from here."

"Sometimes at night, I miss my family so much I want to run into the night and not stop until I reach the *Mariposa*."

"Yet, I doubt you'll ever take such a drastic action. When you are ready to reunite with your family, you will welcome them here, or you'll go to them in broad daylight and beg their forgiveness for all you put them through in the past."

"They would send me to jail." He gave Richard a dismal look.

"Perhaps. Perhaps not."

"Ah, the tea . . ." Dom stood and rushed back into the cabin.

In a matter of minutes, he was back with a teapot and cups on a tray he set between them on the table. "Sorry, I didn't get my baking done today," he said with a grin.

"If you like, I brought some cake. Look in the basket."

"Oh, brill!" Dom leapt up again and went to fetch the treat. "Thank you so much!" He said when he returned with the wrapped cake and a butter knife. He sighed with pleasure once he'd eaten two slices. "Marvelous!"

Richard smiled. "I've had quite a special invitation to dinner."

"That so?"

"Filbert and I are invited to the *Mariposa.*"

"How did that come about?" Dom appeared a bit dazed.

"Our mutual friend Granville arranged it."

"Why would he do that?"

"Oh, you know Granville. If he meets someone new whom he thinks would enjoy the company of his friends, he takes it upon himself to see that they are introduced. I'm very much looking forward to meeting your family. And Filbert is very keen for making the acquaintance of the resident beagles."

Dom smiled in spite of himself. "I'll look forward to hearing all the details."

# CHAPTER TWENTY

### June 1916 – February 1917

Harper turned from the mirror in the dressing room to face Damien, dapper in a black cutaway frock coat. "My, but you look handsome."

"Why, thank you, ma'am. It's not every day that I have the good fortune of having dinner with a priest." He raised a droll eyebrow. "My father must be whirling in his grave."

"I doubt that. Moreton Whittaker was the most level headed man I've ever known. I have no doubt he would see the irony in our present circumstance."

"I can't argue with you on that point," he said, sliding his gaze down her narrow green silk that adhered to the new Edwardian simplicity. "Are you wearing that new-fangled invention?"

"It's called a brassiere," she said, turning to inspect her silhouette. "And I rather like it as it does wonders in contouring my bosom that has begun to drift a bit south."

"Well, I for one, prefer you uncontoured," he said, bending to kiss the lowest area of her exposed décolletage.

"Perhaps next time we entertain someone other than a priest, I'll forego my brassiere," she rejoined breezily, picking up a hand mirror to examine her loose chignon.

Shortly, her nonplussed husband offered his arm and they headed downstairs to the drawing room where Chandler, Yvette, Delaney and Finn were already seated.

Dobbs soon arrived with a pitcher of lemonade and scones. When the doorbell sounded, he hastily put down the tray and went to answer it.

The beagles had gathered in front of Delaney as though aware they too had company coming. The footman soon ushered in Father Richard, followed by the pompous Filbert.

Damien rose to shake hands, then introduced the others. Father Richard greeted everyone warmly before sitting beside Harper.

She took in his elegance in the black robes. He was very slight of build and disconcertingly handsome. Light brown hair set off his olive complexion. His smile was very disarming.

When Delaney crumbled a scone for distribution to the dogs, Filbert agreed to join the party, lying down happily among the beagles.

"I've been looking forward to coming here today," the priest said presently. "The longer I'm friends with Dom, the more of an enigma he becomes for me."

"He's been that to us most of his life," Damien said.

"I visited him a few days ago. He's becoming much more interested in life apart from the cabin. Still, he seems to have a way to go yet before he's ready to break free."

"He's locked in so he really can't break free in any case, can he?" Chandler asked.

"Actually, I took the padlock off the door two months ago."

They all stared at him.

"Then why hasn't he come home?" Chandler inquired.

"Because he can't just yet. You must remember he had reached the absolute end of his endurance when you put him there. He'd come to a place of such despair that he had to get help. After so many years of deceiving his family and living such a despicable life, he couldn't bring himself to ask for help. So he was intent on getting your attention by whatever means it took. He tried to burn this house but he still has no memory of that. He readily admits that he did it but can't remember because of his state of intoxication."

He paused to drink half his lemonade. "I'm sure this is all very difficult for you to grasp."

"Indeed," Damien said, suddenly glancing at the liquor bottles stored on a shelf near the fireplace.

"Please have a drink if you wish," Richard said, reading the direction of his mind. "It won't bother me in the least because God has totally taken my taste for alcohol from me."

Everyone gazed at him as though he'd said Filbert had taken up poker playing. "I know it sounds unbelievable but it's true. I fully expect Dom to undergo the same spiritual awakening in due time.

When that happens, he will be as immune to alcohol's call as I am."

"How do you know this?" Harper asked, longing to believe what he said.

"Because I was once as helpless to the compulsion to imbibe as Dom when you hauled him off to that cabin. Now I can pour each of you a serving of bourbon without the slightest longing to join you." To prove his point, he rose and crossed to the small bar where he set out six glasses before reaching for a bottle.

"Thank you, sir, but I can do that," Dobbs said, hurrying to his side.

"Very well." Richard returned to his seat and watched with obvious satisfaction as everyone was served and quickly drank from their glasses. "You see there is absolutely no reason you shouldn't have alcohol if you like. Unlike Dom and me, you do not possess the unknown part in your body or soul, wherever it resides, that drives you to insanity when you ingest liquor."

After quickly downing most of their bourbon, the gathering appeared somewhat more accepting of what he'd been telling them. "What do you recommend where Dom is concerned?" Damien eventually probed when LuAnn announced dinner and they made their way to the dining table.

"That depends on how he chooses to proceed," Father Richard said when they were seated.. "Right now, he is very reluctant to leave the cabin . . . ."

"How is that possible?" Chandler demanded. "Why on earth could he prefer to stay locked up when he could come home."

"As I mentioned, he is no longer locked up. Except within his own mind. What he fears most just now is what he might do once he returns home. So I believe he must be given time to come to terms with his new circumstances. He is now a sober and sane man who can think again. And he recognizes that to remain in such a state, he must proceed very carefully, moving forward only when he feels safe doing so. And he realizes for the first time in his life that he can choose what he wants to do. He no longer is expected or compelled to be a part of *Rancha Mariposa.* If he decides that he wants to be a rancher, he can be, or if he decides to become a preacher or teacher, he can do that."

"I see I've been quite presumptuous where my sons are concerned," Damien allowed, passing the roast beef.

"Only because you didn't know any better. You assumed your sons would be eager to join in your dream that began with your own father in Herefordshire. And this one did." He nodded toward Chandler with a smile.

"You're telling us we must sit back and wait for Dom to decide what he wants to do with his life?" Delaney ventured.

"Yes. I doubt it will take too long but I'm determined that he have the time he needs to follow his soul wherever it leads."

"May we visit him?" Harper asked.

"When he's ready. If you like, I will talk to him and let you know when he wishes to see you."

"Yes, please do that," Harper said.

They continued talking like old friends. Once they had consumed Mrs. Blanchard's blackberry cobbler, Richard looked from one to the other around the circle. "I can't tell you how much I've enjoyed being here and meeting all of you. I hope I haven't shocked you. I believe the future will be very bright for our Dom. He's a wonderful young man and I predict the day is quickly approaching when you will find him quite delightful."

Harper sighed with the fervent hope this was true.

"And now, Filbert and I must be off."

They all rose to see the pair out. The terrier marched to the automobile with his usual aplomb.

Once Damien had cranked his auto for him and they had said their goodbyes, Father Richard turned about in the courtyard and headed along the driveway with Filbert happily barking as they disappeared. "Well, that was remarkably illuminating," Damien observed as they filed to the front door.

"I can't tell you how much better I feel now," Harper said. "You've no idea how worried I've been about Dom."

"Oh, my darling, I have been sitting in my own little corner of hell ever since Chandler and I left Dom at the cabin."

She stopped, looking searchingly into his troubled face. "Have you really? You were so silent all this time. I thought you had washed your hands of him. I couldn't blame you because he had behaved so disgracefully. But my heart simply broke for both of you."

He took her in his arms. "Perhaps if Father Richard is to be believed, we will be close again one day."

"I'm sure of it. I've never trusted anyone so much on such a short acquaintance."

"I agree. He is extraordinarily wise for one so young."

"Why else would Granville have gotten us together?" Harper observed, linking an arm through Damien's.

He smiled. "Exactly." He kissed the end of her nose before they hurried to catch up with the others.

Granville continued to visit Father Richard on Sundays, and at other times when the spirit moved him. Although during the remainder of 1916, Father Richard didn't approach the Whittakers again. Granville reported that Dom was making good progress and had even gone to Cheyenne a couple times, once with him and another time, with Richard. On both occasions, they had eaten dinner at The Plains which Dom seemed to enjoy. During his own meal with Dom, Granville had declined alcohol as a courtesy to his guest and afterward, been thanked profusely by an agitated Dom.

When told of this incident, Richard had appeared quite concerned by Dom's behavior. As for himself, Granville couldn't comprehend his worry.

On a windy and frigid Sunday in November, Granville, returning from a drive to visit Richard, parked in the piazza and then came inside to join the Whittakers drinking tea at the dining table. They all looked up questioningly as he settled into a chair to remove his scarf and gloves. A new kitchen girl called Lynda scurried in to pour his tea.

"Anything new with Dom?" Damien asked.

Granville shook his head. "Richard says he's well and very happy. He started painting some months back and gave some of his work to Richard to have framed in Cheyenne."

"So what did you think of it?" Harper asked.

A smile played with his mustache while he stirred his tea. "Rather brilliant work, I must say. It reminds me of what you did back after Eddie died."

"Truly?" She searched his kind eyes and took the hand he reached toward her. "It sounds quite profound then, what he's managed to do?"

"Indeed. Richard is positively gleeful, I might add," he said with a smile. "He believes Dom has sorted much of his trauma through his painting."

"I can completely understand that," Harper agreed. "That is how it worked for me." She held his hand in both of hers. "All my suffering went into my art."

"With remarkable results," Granville said.

"You created work that was accepted at the *Louvre*," Damien remembered fondly.

"How did you know to send those canvases and paints with Dom?" Delaney asked, resting her head on her mother's shoulder a moment.

"It must have been my mother's instinct. He was in such trouble and I'd prayed so much for him, I couldn't think of one thing more I could say to Jesus. So perhaps sending along the art supplies was just one more prayer, one more piece of my hope for him."

"He's very lucky you did that for him," Yvette said from the other side of the table.

"I wish I knew when he'll come home," Chandler observed. "The way things are going, Finn and I may be gone before he gets back." He referred to their plan to enlist for service in the war that'd been underway in Europe since 1914.

In the years since the war began, Wyoming had enjoyed unparalleled prosperity as the demand for beef increased. During the initial two and a half years, the fighting had seemed remote, especially because President Wilson had stuck to a policy of neutrality even after the British unarmed ocean liner, Lusitania, was sunk by German submarines. Now with the New Year just ahead, the United States teetered on the brink of war and there was already talk of conscription in Wyoming.

"Whatever happens with the war, we will arrange for you and Finn to see Dom before you go," Granville declared.

As always happened when anyone mentioned the war, Finn looked positively ill. Harper reached out to pat his arm, knowing he was paralyzed with fear whenever he thought of leaving Delaney. He gave his mother-in-law a weak smile and straightened his shoulders to put an arm around Delaney who nestled close.

*How cruel was the world,* Harper thought. Dom would likely have welcomed going to war where he'd have had a reason to play out his reckless quest for self-destruction. Yet, Chandler and Finn were the ones chosen by circumstance to go. They would leave behind two women whose lives would never be whole again should they not return. She said a silent prayer of thanks that she and Damien had never faced the horror of being separated by war.

Harper was so intent on her private thoughts that she didn't notice the others leaving the table, until she was left alone with Damien.

"You look very sad, darling,"

She gave him a smile. "I was just thinking about how it will be when our young men leave for Europe."

He placed his hand over hers. "I wouldn't worry too much as yet. President Wilson still appears quite adamant about keeping us out of it."

"My sweet husband, naiveté has never been one of your traits. You know as well as I do, we're going to be in the war by spring. And Wyoming boys, including Chandler and Finn, will be sent to Europe. To have our honorable son going to battle tears at my heart, I'm so afraid. But, I'm even more terrified for Delaney. If she should lose Finn, it will destroy her. He's like the other half of her. We both watched them working together at the Stock Show. They share Delaney's passion for Thoroughbreds and competition but it's only with Finn's help that she can realize that dream. Without him, I'm afraid she would be utterly lost to herself and to us."

Damien's gaze focused on her more closely. "You haven't . . . haven't had one of your . . ."

"My premonitions?"

He nodded.

"No, darling, nothing as definitive as all that. I'm just uneasy, hating the thought of them going away."

He reached up to cradle her face, kissing her tenderly. "We've made our way past many awful times, Harper, my darling. Yet, together, you and I, we've always come through stronger for the experience whatever it was." Smiling, he traced her throat with one finger. "The same will be true for us now. We must trust God to bring them back to us."

Christmas at the *Mariposa* that year came and went with barely a ripple. Aunt Pris and Roddy were both ill with influenza and the household was paralyzed with worry and fear.

Dr. Alex Ritter came to the country twice in a matter of days. This was the son of the original Dr. Sheldon Ritter who'd seen those at *Rancha Mariposa* through all manner of medical scenarios from scarlet fever to childbirth until he'd retired and turned his practice over to Alex at the turn of the century. Though it would perhaps require a few more years for those at the ranch to love and appreciate him the way they had his dear, straight-forward father, he'd already gained their trust.

Two days after Christmas, Harper answered the door when the young Dr. Ritter called at the *Mariposa.* "Oh, hello, Doctor. Do come in."

With a smile, he stepped inside out of the light snow blowing about the piazza. "How are my patients today?"

"Aunt Pris seems to have rallied a bit while Roddy still has that awful cough."

"Well, lead on, and I'll have a look."

When they'd climbed the staircase, Harper glanced around the ballroom that had been put to rights after the fire. In fact, while the carpenters and masons from Cheyenne were at it, they'd done quite an extensive refurbishment of the huge room. The work did much to exorcise the ghosts of memory left by Dom's treachery.

Harper guided the doctor to the spacious room in the servant's quarters where Roddy had lived for over forty years. Despite his age, the valet was still handsome, his thin features reflecting his aristocratic bearing.

Catching sight of them, he managed a smile before he was convulsed with a fit of coughing that lasted for some minutes. Dr. Ritter quickly opened his nightshirt and rubbed his chest with the latest treatment available—Vick's Vaporub. This ointment concocted from menthol, cedarleaf, camphor, eucalyptus and turpentine had become a widespread treatment for coughs and congestion of the lungs.

It soon calmed the spasms of Roddy's cough and he could breathe normally. "Ah, better . . ." He leaned back on the pillows. "Thank you."

"You are welcome, my good man. Now perhaps you'd like some of Mrs. Blanchard's chicken soup."

When he nodded, Harper dispatched Jill down the back stairs to fetch some. Once the soup arrived, they left the maid to spoon feed Roddy.

"Now, let's see how your aunt fares." They headed down to her apartment where she lay propped in her usual splendor of an extravagant cerise brocade bed jacket among heaps of silk pillows.

Upon seeing them, she raised the arm that was still working and hugged Harper to her chest that was much less bountiful than it'd been even five years back. Now folds of excess flesh hung from her face and chin. It sometimes hurt Harper to look at her now. Back when they'd first come to Wyoming Territory from England, Aunt Pris had been such a vital force to Harper.

Indeed, since Harper was four years old, her guardian had been her mother after her own parents' sudden death. Life with Aunt Pris at her estate, Laughlin, in Herefordshire, had been happy and secure. Harper soon made the acquaintance of the Whittaker twins for the very first time, and later met her nemesis Peggy, Dom's mother.

She brought her thoughts back to the present while Dr. Ritter listened to Aunt Pris' chest with his stethoscope. When he finished, he lifted his eyes.

"Quite good today. Much clearer." He brought a jar of Vick's Vaporub from his bag and presented it to Harper. "Nevertheless, she also will benefit from an application of this. But you should have the maid apply it. Not so embarrassing that way," he added with a wink, standing up. "I must be off, Harper, as the Carrolls have also suffered casualties from the influenza. If you need me, send word."

Harper saw him out and watched him crank his Model T for the drive to Trail's End. She went to the rear hall and asked Mrs. Blanchard if the soup had been sent up to Aunt Pris.

The *Rancha Mariposa* contingent to the Stock Show in Denver during ten days in January was much smaller than the previous year. Chandler and Damien took ten head of Herefords. Delaney and Finn took Destino and Centaur. Delaney placed in the top five in Eventing and Finn won third in the Stadium Jumping. They and everyone at the ranch were happy with the results, considering they hadn't trained nearly as hard as they had the previous year. All realized their lesser victories indicated the consistent ability of the Thoroughbreds as well as the lasting fitness of the riders.

Harper remained at home because Aunt Pris and Roddy were still not totally recovered from the influenza. Most of the others living at *Rancha Mariposa* chose not to go to Denver. None of the ranch's steers came close to winning the coveted Grand Championship this year.

Indeed, a rather large scandal surrounded this most prestigious portion of the show. Owners from Iowa had entered an Angus steer that won the Grand Championship, yet immediately stirred up talk of something untoward having gone on. Fearing for the future of the show, officials hastily began an investigation. In the end, it was discovered that the victorious Angus steer was actually a Charolais that had been dyed black.

Upon returning home, Damien, Chandler and Granville could only laugh at the ridiculous nature of the scandal. They shook their heads at the foolishness that had prompted the illegal entry.

By mid-February, Harper could wait no longer to see Dom. Father Richard was coming to get her before driving to the cabin on Sunday afternoon. Dressed in a long fur coat and hat, she sat at the dining table, awaiting his arrival.

Damien approached, placing his hands on her shoulders before kissing her hair. "I'll miss you."

"I won't be that long I shouldn't think. Do you have any message for Dom?"

He lowered himself on a chair next to her. "Tell him, I'm rooting for him as I always have, and I love him."

Harper pressed her gloved hands together. "I'm so excited! It seems ages since we've seen him."

"I'm so hoping you will find the engaging young man who so often enchanted all of us."

"That is my fervid hope as well. Ah, here is Father Richard," she added, rising as the priest's auto stopped in the piazza.

Damien took her arm and walked with her outside where he greeted Richard who'd hurried around to open the door for her.

"Hello, Damien. So good to see both of you again." He offered his hand.

"Have a pleasant afternoon." Damien said, kissing Harper before he shut the door and raised his hand in farewell.

Richard guided the car to the driveway while Filbert leaned his front paws on the back of his owner's seat, barking merrily.

"Hush, my friend!" He said, tousling his head. He smiled at Harper when Filbert retired to gaze out the rear window. "I'm afraid, I tend to indulge him."

She laughed. "Oh, don't apologize to me about indulging dogs. Our beagles live a better life than most kings."

"I can't fathom those who dislike animals."

"Well, we certainly don't subscribe to that policy at *Rancha Mariposa.*"

"Granville told me all the details of your success at the Stock Show last month."

"We didn't give it the huge effort we did last year but we were still gratified by the results."

"It would appear your daughter has a marvelous future on the horse show circuit."

"She is very talented and tenacious. Her new goal is to join the U.S. Olympic Team. I understand that can't happen until the European War is over."

"We must pray the War is short-lived for any number of reasons."

"Yes, it quite terrifies me because both our youngest son and son-in-law will doubtless be called into service."

"Granville has spoken to me about that. All of you will be in my constant prayers."

"Chandler is concerned that Dom won't be home in time to see them before they go."

"We'll hope that will resolve itself very soon now."

# CHAPTER TWENTY-ONE

## February 1917 – June 1917

As Father Richard and Harper approached the cabin, Harper thought it appeared quite like a snug little cottage, set as it was against the backdrop of snow-bedecked woods. Smoke spiraled up from the chimney.

Richard helped Harper to the door that opened before them. Filbert hopped about when Dom appeared.

Harper stopped, appraising him as his thin face lit with a smile. "Darling . . ." she then stepped into his outstretched arms, treasuring the interval when she was pressed so close to him. He hadn't hugged her with such open delight since he was a young lad. Leaning back a bit, she saw the glimmer of tears in his eyes.

"It's marvelous to see you," he said. "I've missed you so very much." He turned back to the door. "Come in."

She followed him into the warmth of the cabin, a bit taken aback by the enticing aroma of freshly-baked bread. Glancing at the table where four loaves had been dumped out of their pans to cool, she felt a new awareness of hope.

Dom grinned and helped her off with her coat. "Yes, I've taught myself to bake bread. Sit and we'll have some."

Father Richard took a chair and winked at Harper. "Necessity is the mother of invention, you know."

"I had to get very hungry for fresh bread before I built up my courage to try making some myself." Dom lifted a hand with an apologetic look at the priest. "That's not to say I didn't love the fine bread you and Granville brought me. But I kept thinking about the wonderful bread Mrs. Goodeve used to make and how amazing it would smell just out of the oven."

He set out some small chipped plates and battered butter knives, apparently the only utensils available. After he'd spread out a sheet of brown paper, he centered the loaf and deftly sliced it. When he'd placed thick pieces on the saucers, he hurried to bring butter and preserves from a crude cupboard.

"Ah, heavenly," Harper declared after a bite, chewing slowly. She leaned forward to squeeze his arm. "You are so clever, my dear."

Grinning as he used to do when he was small, he sat beside her and tackled his own thick slice of warm bread. They all sat without talking for a time, enjoying the solace of the bright room and comforting food.

It was only after they'd eaten all they wanted, that Dom's demeanor changed. He sat still, staring at his hands clasped together atop the table. New tears wandered from his eyes as he finally looked back at Harper. "I'm so sorry."

She remained still.

"You were always so good to me." He sniffed and fumbled a handkerchief from a pocket, pressing it to his wet cheeks. "I always knew Pa-pa loved me a great deal and the same was true of you. You made sure I was included in things. Right after Eddie died and Pa-pa told me my mother was going away, I was so afraid. The maids left me alone in the nursery because everyone was busy getting ready for the funeral . . ." He choked to a stop, frantically wiping at the tears streaming unchecked now.

Harper fought the desire to wrap him in her arms. Instead, she waited for him to continue.

"I was all alone in the nursery, terrified. And then Audra came and said you wanted me to come to your bedchamber. When I got there, you gave me food and comforted me. And you smelled so good. My mother never smelled the way you always did. Sitting on your lap, I wasn't so sad and frightened. And from then on, you kept me with you as much as possible. You were my protector and I could be stronger even when the fear came back . . . but then I had to go stay with the Carrolls in the winters!"

"Didn't you like that?"

"I did, but I missed you and Pa-pa so much." He fell silent for a long interval, still blotting up his tears. "I'm just so sorry for the way I've let down my entire family," he went on at last. "Pa-pa wanted me to run *Rancha Mariposa* and I wanted that so much."

He leveled a desolate look at Harper. “But all I could think about was making money for myself and soon enough, I didn’t care how I did it. I stole from Pa-pa’s business associates, I cheated at cards, I stole more money and made it look like Chandler had done it. And by that time, I couldn’t stand the guilt so I drank more and more because I had to deaden the pain . . . .” He floundered into silence again that lasted for several minutes.

“Aft . . . after Pa-pa sent me away, I thought I’d die because it hurt so much. I stayed dead drunk at Charleen’s place for days and then, a long time after that. Eventually, even she got weary of my drunkenness and cheating at cards in her gaming parlor so she kicked me out. I took rooms for the night here and there after that, always moving on before I got evicted. I tried to get sober but I couldn’t pull it off. I’d get so sick, I’d have to drink so as not to have convulsions. And so I carried on like that until I heard you all were going to be at the Stock Show in Denver so I went there. I watched Chandler showing the Herefords and followed along behind when the Grand Champion Steer walked the red carpet into the Brown Palace. I was still filled with pride somehow but then I was weeping so I could barely see and stumbled outside before any of you saw me.

“I ended up crawling into an empty cattle car that night. I must have figured out the train was headed back to Cheyenne. The weather was fairly warm when I got back so I bought another bottle and crawled into a culvert for the night.

“I repeated that general behavior many times in the next several days during which I drank so much I was half out of my head. And that’s when I somehow got myself to the ranch and started the fire. I have no memory of any of it.” He fell back into silence, weeping again. This time, he remained still while he was totally consumed by his self-revulsion. At some point, he stretched one arm out on the table and pressed his face in the crook of his elbow.

Harper sat frozen in her grief for him but couldn’t bring herself to reach out. She was somehow certain he was beyond any help she could offer. His state of mind was far worse than she’d believed possible.

At last, Father Richard stirred from where he'd sat still, seemingly absorbing the gravity of Dom's condition. He got to his feet and circled the table to sit in a chair he drew close. Bowing his head, he began praying silently while he hugged one arm around Dom's shaking back.

"Father God," he presently said out loud, "I beseech you to take away Dom's suffering. Remove from him the last vestiges of his desire and dependence on alcohol. Free him of his bondage. Let him live again and with your help, repair the damage he's done. He is your willing servant, Dear God. Let him show you his goodness. In your son's most holy and precious name, I pray. Amen."

He still clung to Dom with his eyes closed. After a while, Dom's trembling began to wane and his breathing calmed. When he finally moved, pushing himself up from the table, he looked about him, still slightly dazed.

"How astonishing," Dom breathed. "I felt the Holy Spirit move through me in the most amazing warmth. It started here," he said, pointing to the top of his head, "then floated down until it left through my feet."

Harper stared at him, seeing his gray eyes had cleared and humor tugged at the corner of his mouth. There *had* been a remarkable transformation. *Praise the Lord.* She gave in to her own onslaught of tears. "Oh, darling."

Richard smiled at both of them. "How do you feel, Dom?"

"So happy. I could almost fly." He suddenly twisted toward Harper, pulled her up from her chair, then waltzed her about in the small space available.

"Dom." She framed his face with her hands, happiness shining in her violet eyes. "I'm so glad!"

"Now I can make up for all the horrendous things I've done. And I will! I promise." He pressed his lips against her forehead, ardently willing her to believe him. By tiny degrees, his loosened his arms. "I know I've lied so often but now I'm not. I've been delivered from all the pain and doubt that's held me back. Now I can repair the damage." He stared hard into her face. "But I can't do it if you doubt me, if you don't believe I'm a new man, washed clean in the blood of Jesus."

She saw the pleading in him and knew this wasn't the clever manipulation he'd been so good at over the years. So many times, she'd believed what he said, only to find out later he'd misled her. And it wasn't only her he'd fooled. Over and over again, he'd garnered second and third chances from his father when not even one more opportunity was deserved. Yet, she was certain of him now. Any doubt had been swept away by Father Richard's profound prayer. There were holy forces at work here even she hadn't experienced before, nor completely understood.

The God who walked with her each day had answered the pleas of her heart. She said a short prayer of fervent gratitude.

She suddenly reached out to the handsome young priest who'd given Dom back to her and the rest of his family. "Thank you," she said, gripping his hands.

"Thank, Jesus," he said, returning her rapturous smile.

Despite the holy revolution within his soul that had utterly turned Dom's life right-side up again after all his years of debauchery, he was not immediately ready to rejoin his family at *Rancha Mariposa.* As spring came to Wyoming once again, the weeks spooled out in still warm days that compelled him to set up his easel beneath the tree beside his cabin. His new joy and hope poured from him onto canvases that glowed with passion for life. He often became quite lost in the act of creation and only realized an entire day had passed when his light faded beneath the descending curtain of twilight.

While Chandler and Finn watched the developments in Europe with growing unease, Dom was completely ignorant of the political climate. He'd been so impaired for so long, he had paid attention to little going on in the nation, let alone the world.

Few in Wyoming had given much thought to the European War during the first three years. Only in the spring of 1917 did the matter become less remote. The nation abruptly teetered on the edge of war after German submarines sank five American ships during March.

April 6, on President Woodrow Wilson's orders, Congress declared war on the Central Powers. Having gotten confirmation for what they'd expected for so long, Chandler and Finn lost no time enlisting in military service.

Dom was past forty now so there was no thought of him fighting in the war. But with Chandler and Finn scheduled to leave for training in New York in June, he was finally ready to return to the *Mariposa.*

Granville and Father Richard drove to the cabin the last Sunday in May to bring Dom home for a celebratory dinner for everyone at *Rancha Mariposa.* They arrived in early afternoon and were greeted by Damien and Harper at the front door.

"How splendid to have you home," Harper said, hugging Dom and accepting his kiss.

His smile revealed his own happiness at being there after so many long heartbreaking months. "Ah, Harper, I cherish you so!"

His father approached and he turned into his arms, laying his head on his shoulder. "I'm home, Pa-pa."

"Yes, you are, my dear son. I can't tell you what it means to have you here where you belong."

"I promise my life is going to be very different from now on. You used to be proud of me, and you will be again."

"I know that Dom." He pulled him close for a second time, hugging him violently.

"Now, you're probably eager to have a bath and dress for dinner," Harper said, threading her arm through Dom's to walk with him toward the staircase. "Are you hungry?"

"No, I'm too excited to eat just now."

"Well, we've prepared your old room," she said as they started up the steps. "Your father bought you some new clothes you'll find in your closet. Why don't you take your time. Have a nap if you like and we'll see you when you're ready to come down."

"Thank you so much." He gave her a smile before going on to his bedchamber. Inside, he looked around at the familiar furnishings. He hadn't often slept there since he'd returned from Harvard, yet, his memories were strong.

Although he had loved sleeping in Damien's dressing room before he married Harper, he'd still felt secure and loved after he moved into this room further along the hallway. He moved to the French doors and looked out past the balcony into the courtyard below. He acknowledged a new awareness of everything he saw and realized he'd been sleepwalking through his life for the past fifteen years at the very least.

Breathing a prayer of thanks for his deliverance, he lay down on the bed, relishing his new appreciation of everything he encountered. The terror and worry that still possessed him only a few weeks ago had now lessened its grip. When he considered this reality, a vague fear invaded his thoughts.

He realized with utter clarity that he must never lose touch with that black place now consigned to the far reaches of his mind. To be certain he would never return there, he knew he must remember what a dark and hopeless place it was.

Shortly, he drifted into sleep. Upon waking later, he had no idea where he was. He jolted upright, staring outside, then collapsed back as he remembered.

Someone moving around in the dressing room reminded him of his need of a bath. He got up and ventured to the door. Bill, a recently-hired hall boy looked up from pouring hot water into the tub.

"Just getting your bath ready, sir," he said with a little bow.

"Wonderful. Thank you very much."

Within half an hour, Dom was dressed in a handsome black suit he'd found among the clothing in his closet. When his father selected the items in his new wardrobe, he hadn't taken into account the thirty pounds Dom had lost recently. Studying himself in a tall mirror, he smiled at the sagging fit of the coat and trousers. With a shrug, he turned into the hall and descended the staircase, pleased to find Yvette seated before the fireplace below.

With a little gasp of delight, she bounced up from the sofa and rushed to him. "Oh, my goodness, it's so good to see you!"

She accepted his chaste kiss on her cheek, then stood, smiling at him. "You truly are transfigured. Harper said I'd hardly know you and she was right."

He put a hand over hers resting in the crook of his arm, guiding her to sit with him. "I must say, you're not transfigured. You're just as beautiful as ever."

She found him very confounding. Not only did he look like a different man from the one who used to send her into frantic storms of emotion, there was an unfamiliar calm about him.

She hardly knew what to make of the change but sensed it was profound. For a long space of time, they sat still, reacquainting themselves with each other.

In years past, when Dom was still held prisoner by his addiction, his physical appearance had deteriorated. Unlike the slender young man who beguiled her from the first time he caught her attention, he'd gained weight, taking on a dull and bloated appearance.

This outward decline did nothing to lessen Yvette's love for him. Other factors had brought about the demise of their romance. Still, taking in his serene demeanor, she felt a fluttering of the old attraction that had kept her unsettled for years.

His face had again taken on the finely-detailed features of his father. He was divinely handsome as he'd been at twenty and she could scarcely believe he was now twice that old. Instead of the perpetual sneer of belligerence she'd become so accustomed to, his face was now lit by mischievous good humor. Indeed, she'd never seen this version of him and her heart swelled.

"How are you liking teaching by this time?" He inquired, his gray eyes warm with laughter.

"I love it as much as ever. I'm very good at it, I think, which I knew I would be when I set out on this quest."

"I'm so happy for you."

She studied him closely. "You look so much better, even better than you did in photos when you were very young."

His eyes crinkled. "Well, the truth is, I've had a spiritual epiphany. I don't understand just what that means, but I've been crying out to the Lord for a long time now. And finally, Father Richard prayed for me and I felt Jesus transform me." He leaned closer, patting his hair. "I felt a lovely warmth that started here and flowed down through my entire body. It was truly astonishing and with one great surge of emotion, I was happy like I've never been before."

Yvette clapped her hands, laughing at his blissful demeanor. "Oh, Dom, I'm so happy for you! You've gone through absolute hell!"

He chuckled softly. "Right now, I can scarcely recall any of that although I realize I behaved abominably and hurt so many people, including you. I'm truly sorry, Yvette."

She could clearly see the deep remorse in his eyes and reached for his hand. "I know you are and I forgive you. What are your plans now?"

He turned his gaze to the dancing fire on the hearth. "I'm not certain. Because Chandler and Finn will be away for some time, perhaps years, I will certainly help run *Rancha Mariposa* while they're gone, if that is what Pa-pa desires." His gaze grew rueful. "All the years that was my job, I was so hell bent on making money and throwing my weight around as though I was bedazzled by my own inflated opinion of myself. What an insufferable bastard I was." His eyes smiled into hers. "Was I not?"

"I found myself weeping over your behavior rather often," she agreed. "And I'm positively over the moon that the part of you we all adored is back."

"No one is happier about that than I," he said.

"I saw some of your paintings Granville brought home."

"What do you think?"

"Oh, Dom, they are amazing. You must be stunned to learn you have that kind of talent."

"Painting became my obsession this year. I no longer craved alcohol but was addicted to sitting before a canvas with my brushes and paints. Somehow the shadowy dark images in my brain broke free and poured out over the course of weeks and months."

"Granville says your art should be marketed in Europe like Harper's."

"Likely not as long as war is going on," he said mildly. "My art's value in money isn't what's important in any case. It served to free me from my demons and open the way for God's grace to alter my heart."

"Don't you want to keep painting?"

"Oh, certainly I do, but not for money. Not now at any rate."

"Well, perhaps you'll want to be part of the artists' colony in Harper's studio," Yvette suggested. "Caldwell is up there every moment he can spare from his other work. And Delaney still joins them when the spirit moves her."

They grew silent, sitting together in the pleasant quiet of being in each other's company again after so long. Soon enough, others arrived for dinner, everyone greeting Dom.

When Chandler stood nearby, contemplating his brother, Dom leapt from his seat and drew him into a bear hug. When they stepped apart, he thrust out his hand. "It may take a while but I swear to you, I'm going to make up for all the godawful things I did to discredit you. I apologize from the depth of my soul."

"A sincere apology goes a long way toward mending wounds," Chandler finally said with a wink. He drew Dom's thin frame close once more. "Let's make the most of the years remaining to us, shall we?"

They both sat again as LuAnn arrived with a plate of cheeses while Dobbs served bourbon. Yvette excused herself to confer with Jill who headed down the back stairs, soon returning with a cup of tea on a tray that she presented to Dom.

As he sipped from the cup, he watched the Carrolls file through the front door, Audra and John and those of their daughters who'd been able to make it to dinner. Yvette lingered beside him as her family approached; she greeted each of them before they reached him. For the first time in years, there was a genuine ease among Dom and the family who'd been an important part of his young life.

Audra smiled and cradled his face in her hands to kiss him. "Darling, I've been so worried about you but you look wonderful. Welcome home."

"Thank you, dear." He kissed her cheek.

As she moved on, John shook his hand. "Good show, my man." He pounded him on the back before pulling him close for a moment.

To Dom's great relief, once dinner was underway, attention shifted from him to Chandler and Finn who would be leaving for army training in early June. He was keenly aware of the sadness about the table and shared it. It seemed terribly unjust; when the time was right for him and Chandler to appreciate each other for the first time, they were to be separated. No one could say how long the European War would last, or if Chandler would survive.

The reality of their situation saddened Dom greatly. How could he have wasted so much precious time, just frittered it away as if there was no end to it? Now when he wanted that time more than he'd ever wanted anything, he had no idea if there was any left.

Perhaps he and Chandler would part in a week or two, as much strangers as they'd ever been and with no chance ever to become close as brothers should be. He felt renewed dejection that he was responsible for their continued estrangement. It was entirely his fault, his lack of judgment.

Father Richard picked up on Dom's regretful mood and came to join him after dinner; Dom had left the others and sat alone beside the fireplace where he and Yvette had lingered earlier. "Are you rather overwhelmed by all the attention?"

Dom spread his hands in a futile gesture, nodding. "Fate can be a cruel judge of a man's character."

"Indeed." The priest settled onto the opposite end of the sofa. "What is troubling you?"

"Father, my brother is going to war in a matter of days. Thanks to my stupidity, we'll part for God knows how long, still as estranged as we've been for years. He may never return."

"Or he may. The way you've been in God's favor of late, I can't imagine he would be that unfair." He continued regarding him carefully. "You are perhaps feeling all the guilt that has surely accumulated over the years . . . ."

"I felt nothing but guilt for so long."

"You have been forgiven," Dom. "The Lord does not provide forgiveness retroactively. Once you're forgiven, it's forever."

"Nonetheless, I have squandered all my time. Now that we've come to this point where we want . . . I want to truly know my brother and love him as I should have all these years, there's no time left . . . ."

"You'll have all the time you need," Richard said with the absolute certainty that even now sometimes took Dom by surprise.

"I hope so," he said doubtfully.

"Dom, you've come to possess a phenomenal faith. Hang onto it now with all your strength."

The few days remaining before Chandler and Finn departed were made sadder by Roddy's imminent death. Harper had made arrangements with Dr. Ritter to come stay with his patient at *Mariposa* while she and Damien went with the others to see the future soldiers off on the train in Cheyenne.

Though everyone had prepared carefully for this inevitable time of parting, the tension gripping the group in the automobile couldn't have been thicker. Although Dom and Chandler had managed to talk at length, they both realized, they hadn't sufficient time together to even properly begin bridging the gaping gulf between them.

Nevertheless, they were both on their best behavior as they approached the Union Pacific depot and made every attempt to treat each other with courtesy. Chandler and Yvette were caught in their own sphere of grief and love with little attention to spare for anyone but each other. As they all waited next to the passenger cars, Yvette clung to Chandler, weeping, her heart breaking.

Watching them, Dom wondered why he'd ever lusted so for Yvette, suffering spasms of jealousy as she'd turned from him to his brother. Now he was filled only with concern for them both and pleasure that he was and would likely always be close friends with Yvette.

With her innately well-grounded and straight-forward approach to life, Delaney seemed to be weathering the approaching separation from her young husband with much greater equanimity than Yvette. She clung tightly to Finn's arm but shed no tears. And when it came time for him to board the train, she gave him a brave smile and a lingering embrace, then let him go.

After confiding in Father Richard his pain over having little time to set things right with his brother, he'd been reassured that all would happen in its own good time. Now after watching Finn disappear into the passenger car, he saw that the few bags had been loaded and everyone pressed toward the lowered steps to say final goodbyes to Chandler.

Dom waited his turn after Harper and Damien, then returned to the waiting auto where he settled in the rear seat with Delaney who'd finally succumbed to tears and sat crying quietly. "It's awfully hard, seeing him go, isn't it?" He asked.

"I don't know how I'll stand him being so far away." She raised her tear-streaked face as she searched in her bag for a handkerchief. "Oh, darn, I'm such a mess," she moaned when she couldn't find one.

"Here," Dom offered, presenting a pressed one from his shirt pocket.

"Oh, thanks." She daubed at her reddened eyes, sighing as she noted from the sound of the engines the train was about to move out.

Damien soon approached and handed Harper into the car before he employed the crank, then slid into the driver's seat. Yvette had dared follow Chandler onto the train in order to have a few extra minutes with him.

Now she rushed down the steps, looking a bit sheepish from being evicted by a porter. A moment later, she hopped in beside Delaney and seeing her tears, was soon weeping again herself.

"Shall we stop for lunch?" Damien inquired when they were underway.

Aware that he was frantic to get home to Roddy, Harper declined. "I would prefer to go right back."

"Is that agreeable with the rest of you?" Damien asked.

"Fine with me," Dom said and the young women murmured accord while trying to get their emotions under control.

Relieved, Damien put the auto in gear and they were underway, each lost in private reverie. Damien was possessed by melancholy when he thought of his old friend so near death. At nearly ninety, his valet had remained loyal to his duties until illness had sidelined him.

Damien was further saddened by the inevitable changes to the *Mariposa's* grand lifestyle in general. So many beloved servants had died or been replaced—Mrs. Goodeve, Adare, Rachel, Julia, Amos, Kendrick, Gwen, and Ivy who'd retired years earlier to raise her family.

Now Roddy would soon be gone as well. This loss more than any other was acutely painful to Damien, as his valet had been his friend, tutor and confidant for nearly sixty years. Harper and their children, too, had loved him as part of the family and comprehended what a large vacancy his death was going to leave.

"I'll not be able to bear it if Roddy is gone when we get back," he said presently. "On any other day perhaps but not this one."

Harper slid closer and laid an arm across his shoulders as she leaned her head against his. "My darling, he will be there. You'll have the chance to say a proper goodbye."

He lifted a hand to hold the side of her face, comforted by her assurance. Dom reached forward to place a consoling hand on his shoulder. His father turned his head to offer a smile of acknowledgement.

As Yvette watched the intimate interaction between Damien and Harper, new tears flooded her eyes. Their devotion and ability to sense each other's thoughts and moods without apparent effort had enchanted her from the time she'd first noticed it as a small girl.

Her own parents' marriage was filled with love and open enjoyment and she'd always been thankful for their frankness, yet the Whittakers' knew a passion that went well beyond this. Yvette had resolved as a girl to settle for nothing less when she married but now realized this was not to be.

"There has been so much sadness at the *Mariposa,*" Harper murmured. "So much death."

"There has been huge joy as well," Yvette said, causing them both to glance back at her. "I've always loved it there and felt safe and warm."

"Yet, the last several years have been difficult for you. Deciding what you wanted from your life, which of my sons you would marry." Damien looked back at Dom for a second. "Sorry to be so frank."

"Oh, don't apologize. One of the biggest reasons, I was left lacking in Yvette's heart was my own shoddy behavior. For far too long now, my ethics and honor have been dreadfully lacking while Chandler has comported himself with the greatest integrity. I could not be prouder of my brother and my heart aches at the very thought that he might not come back to us. After all the turmoil and due to Yvette's good sense, she's chosen to spend the rest of her life with Chandler. I don't resent that decision for one moment and I thank God that Yvette and I remain good friends."

Yvette reached out to squeeze his hand with a smile as they all grew silent for several miles. "Doesn't it ease the painful times like what's happening now, to recall the happiness?" She eventually asked. "Your wedding day, for instance? Or when your children were born?"

"I never tire of remembering those times," Damien said, smiling at Harper who was gradually over taken with tears, the indirect mention of Chandler shattering her control.

Appalled that she'd added to her agony, Yvette scooted forward to wrap her arms around her. "I'm so sorry. It was thoughtless of me."

"Yvette, sweetheart, he will always be close in our hearts though it causes us pain."

Once Yvette had settled back, Delaney took her place, embracing her parents with an arm around each. "We're all together so we'll get through this until Finn and Chandler get home."

"You're absolutely right," Dom offered with a little pat to her thin back.

They arrived at the *Mariposa* within half an hour and gathered in the drawing room. LuAnn and Jill immediately appeared with trays of fresh apple fritters and tea.

"How are Roddy and Aunt Pris?" Harper asked.

"No change with Miss Begbie, milady," Jill said. "I'm afraid Mr. Roddy's failing real steady. It's lucky you got home as Dr. Ritter had to get to a birth." After a stiff little curtsy, Jill departed for the kitchen with LuAnn on her heels.

"I'm going up," Damien said and hastily turned into the hall.

"I'll be there shortly," Harper said.

Dobbs appeared with bourbon but no one accepted and Delaney soon went to change before she went to the stables to ride Destino. The rest also headed up the staircase. At the top, Harper turned to the footman. "I doubt any of us feel like coming down to dinner so please send trays up later."

The others went to their bedchambers as Harper continued to join Damien in Roddy's room in the servant's quarters. As she passed through the deserted ballroom, she felt the expectant, empty waiting of the house. She already longed for the time when Chandler and Finn would be home to stay. She yearned for the birth of children, many, many children to fill the *Mariposa* with love and laughter for many, many generations to come.

# CHAPTER TWENTY-TWO

**June 1917**

Harper paused in the doorway of Roddy's sickroom. The chamber was dimly lit by a lamp by the bed; a fire burned in one corner. Damien sat looking down at his friend who lay ghostly white on the linens, his breathing labored, his body shaking with fever despite the warm day and the heavy covers

Damien glanced up. "Darling."

"Is there any change?"

"No. His pneumonia has returned. Dr. Ritter rubbed his chest with Vapo-Rub again before he left. I can't see it's helping much anymore."

"Probably nothing will."

Nodding, he reached out to pull another chair close to his. They still sat there when Delaney, dressed in riding clothes, arrived. "How is he?" She asked, her voice trembling.

"He's dying, sweetie," Harper said, catching her hand.

Delaney blinked back sudden tears. "I'm so sorry. He was always such a lovely man."

"He was," Damien said, reaching to squeeze her shoulder.

Delaney looked from him to Harper. "Millie's visiting the Carrolls. We're going to go riding, then she's invited me to their house for dinner and to spend the night."

"That's just what you must do then. Go have a nice time."

Delaney hugged both her parents before departing. Harper turned to Damien to say she was going to check on Aunt Pris. Soon after she stepped out, Yvette knocked softly.

"Yvette, my dear," Damien watched her sit next to him. "How's Aunt Pris."

"I didn't see her yet. Is Roddy any better?"

"No."

"Shouldn't we send for the doctor again?"

"No. Roddy is an old man, almost ninety-one. It's time for him to die. I'm merely going to stay here with him so he won't be alone when he passes over." He smiled when Rumor jumped onto the bed and snuggled down against Roddy's back. "Ah, someone else has come to wait with him."

Yvette cupped the beagle's head in her fingers. "It must feel strange to have known someone for so long."

Damien nodded. "He came to Willow Rook when Brendon and I were ten. He tutored us until we went to Oxford, then became my valet. When we eventually came to America, he left his homeland so he could continue serving me and the rest of the household."

"He loved you."

"I daresay but I sometimes felt guilty about that kind of devotion. I wonder what sort of life he might have had if he'd stayed in England. For instance I'm sorry he never knew the love of a woman like Harper."

"I'd think he's known his share of women," Yvette ventured.

"There were a few liaisons through the years. He and Rachel were close for a time though they never expressed an interest in marriage. Harper and I would've welcomed such a request but it wasn't meant to be."

"I think he preferred devoting his life to those in this house. I remember how nice he always was to me. I'd sometimes ask him to bring me hot chocolate and he always seemed delighted to spoil me."

Damien smiled. "He was very kind to me and Brendon as well. My father called him a soft touch, but then it took one to know one."

"I love to hear you talk about the past. I wish I'd lived with you back then."

"But then, you wouldn't be with us now when we need you even more."

"You're so sweet to me. I can understand why Harper has always been so wild about you."

"I daresay you'll have the good luck of that kind of love from my son."

"Of course, I will." Smiling, she inclined to kiss his cheek.

He considered Roddy again. “I’m sad to think how people’s expectations are changing; few in the future will know the same loyalty we’ve known here from Roddy or Adare or Mrs. Goodeve. And so many others. Neither Dom nor Chandler will have valets. Perhaps that’s best. I sometimes think Roddy has been little more than a slave. I often couldn’t discern a great difference between our life and that of the plantation owners in the Deep South before the Civil War.”

“No, Damien,” she said softly. “Roddy was no slave or indentured servant. He came to Willow Rook and then to Wyoming because he loved you and Brendon.”

“Of course, you’re right. I’m just a despondent old man.” Turning his head, he studied her thoughtfully. “I’m sorry so much sadness must come at one time. I remember how I felt as a young man when Harper had to go off to Paris. I’m sure you must be suffering in much the same way. I wish I could offer you and Delaney more comfort.”

“I’m going to hold tight to a picture of the time when Finn and Chandler will be home with us. I promise we’ll all be happy then. You’ll see.”

He reached for her hand and pressed it to his lips. “I shall cling to the optimism of youth.”

“You must.” She rose and kissed her fingertips that she pressed softly to Roddy’s forehead. “I’ll go now.”

“Thank you for keeping me company, my dear. Good night.”

Perhaps another half an hour passed before Dobbs arrived with a supper tray he placed on the edge of the bed. Rumor roused herself to look over the food but then, after turning in a circle, flopped down and went back to sleep. Footsteps in the hall preceded Dom who carried plates of food to the chairs where he sat beside his father. “I thought you might enjoy some company.”

“Thank you.” Damien accepted the plate of food Dom lifted from the tray. He lifted a cover to inspect the cold salmon, potato salad and rolls. “Ah, this looks good.”

Just then, Dobbs came to deliver a pot of hot tea.

“I can’t begin to tell you how much I appreciate being here,” Dom said when he’d accepted a cup.

"I feel precisely the same. I doubt you have any idea how I suffered after I kicked you off the ranch. Nothing I've done in my entire life prepared me for the pain of that decision. I have no conception of how many nights afterwards, I was jolted awake by nightmares where you were lying somewhere cold and ill, trying to find me."

Stark pain etched his lean features, lending his eyes a hollow depth that unnerved Damien. "Despite my happiness at my current state-of-mind and my desire to somehow correct all the damage I've wrought, I truly doubt I'll be able to express how much I regret hurting you."

"Dom, I believe we must settle something between us once and for all. I cannot tell you how happy I am you're back where you belong and I completely forgive you. Yet, I sense you don't fully believe that. Our friend Richard labels that sort of thinking, borrowing trouble. We don't need any more trouble, Dom. So can we please, put this whole thing to rest right here, tonight? If either of us starts getting off track, let's promise to talk about it so we can resolve whatever it is and get on with life." He considered Dom for reaction.

"You sound like Father Richard."

"I must confess, we've talked quite a lot. Do you agree with what I'm saying?"

"I do. I will do my best to remember I'm forgiven."

"Good man."

They fell into companionable quiet then as they finished their meal and Damien enjoyed a glass of bourbon. As twilight settled down beyond the window, Colleen came from downstairs to check on Roddy.

She brought a basin of warm water to the bedside and wrung out a cloth that she used to bathe his face and hands, then the rest of his upper body. After she had dried him with a towel, she proceeded to remove his cotton trousers. With Dom and Damien's help in lifting him, she pulled off the soiled pants and replaced them with clean. Next, she asked them to roll him to one side of the mattress so she could place fresh linen beneath him. Rumor, who'd been displaced by the activity jumped back up, curling close to Roddy.

Once she'd covered both with a newly-laundered sheet, Colleen stood back to inspect him. "Oh, I must comb his hair."

"I can do that," Dom said, rising to select a comb from atop the dresser. He gently pulled the teeth through the sparse hair, finally straightening to check his work. "I always remember how handsome and well-groomed he was."

"He was stiff competition when he began instructing Brendon and me in such matters. He always insisted our ascots and waistcoats be spotless and our pants and frockcoats perfectly pressed."

"No wonder you two were such dandies." Dom smiled and returned to the seat he'd occupied earlier.

"Is Harper still with Aunt Pris?" Damien inquired as Colleen prepared to leave with the armload of laundry.

"Yes, Aunt Pris had quite a lot to say for herself tonight."

"I daresay." He watched the nurse disappear down the back stairs. "Have you given thought to what you may want to do with your future?"

"Yes. I have thought a great deal about it but all I seem capable of doing just now is paint."

"Nothing wrong with that. Your work is brilliant."

"That's what Harper and Granville tell me and I hope I can live up to their faith in me. I must say, though, I still feel guilty that I just abandoned my work at *Rancha Mariposa*. Particularly since you were so generous and gave me so much responsibility."

"I thought we'd decided you've been forgiven."

Dom shrugged. "Yes, I suppose we did."

"Then you must relax and become accustomed to your new life. I, too, have been giving much thought to your future. When you're ready, I believe I've arrived at a decision you'll find much to your liking."

Dom stroked his chin, absorbing what he said. "Ah, that sounds intriguing."

"Indeed. We must talk again soon!"

Damien's eyes were abruptly riveted on Roddy and Dom jumped up, following his gaze. Then they both bent over him as his face contorted and his breathing stalled in his throat.

His eyes stared fixedly into the middle distance and as they watched, his anxious features smoothed into the most peaceful mien. He appeared to be looking at something that brought a smile even as his chest rose with the ragged intake of air. And, then his breathing stopped and this time it didn't begin again. Still his face betrayed the greatest serenity.

Both men saw the small ethereal mass that shot from Roddy's body and flew across the room and through the wall. During the spectral departure of Roddy's soul, Rumor threw back her head, howling in a thin, tremulous spiral of haunting sound that hovered above the bed for a parade of seconds.

Moments later, running feet approached up the stairs; the other beagles bounded into the room and onto the bed where they joined Rumor in her mournful song.

"Holy, God . . ." Damien breathed, sitting again to carefully close Roddy's eyes.

When he looked at Dom, his eyes shone with tears. "Pa-pa, I'm sorry." He stepped closer and put his hand on his shoulder.

Harper abruptly stood in the doorway, clasping her hands. Tears streamed down her face and she staggered inside and into Damien's arms.

"Did he go easy?" She asked. "We heard the beagles."

"They just sang him home," Dom said, smiling at her. "Caldwell once told me wolves do that. Whenever one of the pack dies, the rest gather and howl to guide it into the afterlife."

"How absolutely lovely," Harper said, sitting to gather the little dogs close.

"I'll go alert Dobbs," Dom said presently, walking along the corridor to tell the footman about Roddy's death.

Yvette awakened the next morning to the sounds of Debbie, the chambermaid, kindling a fire on the hearth. Glancing toward the windows, she saw the June morning was gray with a drizzling rain.

When the maid left with the pail of ashes, Yvette soon got out of bed and approached the fireplace where she drew a stool close the fire. She often lingered there for a time of a morning, sometimes ringing for her maid to bring a pot of tea but today, she soon hurried to dress herself.

When she'd donned a shirtwaist and cotton skirt, fastened the endless buttons on her boots and tied back her hair, she headed downstairs to the dining room. She met no one on the way and found the hall deserted. Downstairs, she summoned LuAnn, then stepped to a window to watch the rain.

"Miss Yvette."

She turned to face the plain little maid who inspected her through spectacles. Her personality was sharp and her smile always evident.

Yvette had always found her to be an engaging girl. "How is Roddy?"

Dark curls bounced above each ear as she shook her head. "Gone. Poor dear Roddy's gone to the Lord."

"Oh, dear."

"Yes, he was such a fine man. So kind." She swiped at tears on her cheek.

"Where is everyone?"

"You know Granville visited Father Richard yesterday and he's stayed the night at the rectory. Mr. and Mrs. Whittaker and Dom are sleeping. They was up with Roddy 'til four. Now I hope they'll sleep for a good long time."

"I hope so too. May I please have some breakfast?"

"You just sit, honey, and I'll bring it right out."

Yvette sank down at the table, feeling remote and disoriented. She yearned to have Chandler sitting in his usual chair, easing her mood as he always could. When he wasn't preoccupied with his own thoughts and perhaps problems at the ranch, he was every bit as sensitive as his father, able to make Yvette feel better even when she was certain her world was about to fall in around her.

She imagined Chandler and Finn together on the train. What thoughts must be circling through their minds as they looked toward the long months of training ahead. They were traveling to war, though they wouldn't be at that final destination for some time yet.

Yvette had no doubt of their bravery. They would not shirk their duty to fight against the forces intent on such destruction in the world.

Still, she loathed what would surely happen to them in the course of their duty. They would encounter things no human should have to deal with or witness. They would stare into the face of evil and be forced to annihilate it.

A chill crept along her spine and she reached for the cup of tea Jill had poured. By the time she'd stirred sugar into it, boiled eggs and toast were placed before her.

Her appetite was faltering but she made tried eating. Rumor came to sit next to her chair, longingly eyeing her food. Unable to resist her imploring gaze, she tossed her a bit of toast.

The rear hall bustled with activity as the maids, Bill, the hall boy, and Dobbs tended to morning chores. A stable boy arrived at the back door with pails of fresh milk that a scullery maid took to place in containers bound for the ice box.

Restless, Yvette soon wandered back along the hall and decided to visit Aunt Pris. Colleen sat beside the bed, feeding her patient porridge. Yvette greeted her and took a chair nearby.

Her first memories of Aunt Pris were of a woman huge and kind who smelled of lemon verbena. Picking up clues everywhere, she'd known from the start Aunt Pris was a true lady, meaning she strictly adhered to the rules of society, to the point of sometimes being thought stern and unbending. Yet, Yvette soon realized she wasn't so rigid in her convictions but rather jolly and overflowing with love for Harper, her adopted daughter, and the rest of the extended family making their home at *Rancha Mariposa.*

Yvette suspected that the years when Damien and Harper lived with her without benefit of marriage, even though their relationship was above reproach, had caused the woman untold distress. Still, she'd remained faithful to them and became matriarch of the entire clan.

When she'd eaten all she would, Yvette sank down on the vacated chair and straightened the covers. The once massive woman was now thin; skin that had been stretched tight with fat, hung in great folds, her vacant eyes peering from sunken sockets.

Yvette took her hand, smiling. There was no reaction, no recognition but she began telling her of the trip to Cheyenne anyway. "Chandler and Finn are on their way to become soldiers, Aunt Pris. It's hard to think of a Whittaker and a Horncastle fighting in a war, isn't it? Harper says that Chandler will be the first military man the family has known since the days of King George III. But I'm certain he'll be a fine soldier as will Finn. When they come home, we'll be married and begin a new generation of Whittakers."

Harper entered, pausing at the door to call up a smile, then came to kiss Aunt Pris' cheek.

"I've been telling her about Chandler and Finn, becoming soldiers."

She turned to give her a quick hug. "Thank you, love. What would we do without you?"

Yvette left the chair. "Sit here. I've been so keyed up this morning, I'm going to go visit my mother."

"Oh, that's a good idea. Please tell your parents about Roddy. The funeral will be tomorrow afternoon."

Yvette soon let herself out the front door and walked through the piazza and courtyard and finally, the front garden. She waved at Stephen who knelt by a bed of roses near the wrought iron fence. The garden stood in all its June finery and Yvette would have loved to sit on a bench in the shade beneath towering oak and elm trees.

But she was eager to see her family, so soon hurried on toward Trail's End. The elderly maid Loretta limping with arthritis answered the door, her wizened face twisted into a huge smile.

"It's our Yvette." She reached out to tug her inside. "How fine to see you, m'dear."

"Hello, Loretta, is anyone home?"

"Oh, goodness, yes," her mother called, striding into the hall. "Yvette, what a nice surprise!"

"I wish I had better news. Roddy has died."

"Oh, dear . . ." her hands drifted to her throat. "I know this was expected but nevertheless, I'm so sad."

"I know, Mother." She kissed her cheek. "I feel just the same."

"I must go to Harper and Damien," she said absently, "but not just yet as I want to enjoy your visit." She hooked her arm through hers to lead her into the parlor. "Come, sit."

Audra, still straight and regal at seventy, sat on a sofa and patted the seat beside her. "Oh, Yvette, it's so good to see you. This is the day for visits from our children. Millie came yesterday . . ."

"Did she bring her family?"

"Not this time. She wanted a bit of time away and also to see Delaney. They're out riding again just now. Delaney has such a heavy heart and riding always helps her." She smiled. "They should be back shortly." She studied Yvette closely. "And how are you bearing up?"

She lifted her hands. "I haven't grown accustomed to them being gone even as I already miss Chandler terribly."

"It must be so hard for you. I've always thanked God that your father and I never had to be separated for any length of time." She suddenly brightened. "Oh, I have the best news. Our Dom came to see me this morning. Your father was already out with the cattle but Dom said it was me he wanted most to see, in any case. I must say, I'm so relieved after talking with him. As you must know, I've been so confused by his behavior. I've wondered for so long, how I went wrong with him since he spent so much time with our family as a boy. I tried to instill in him the same values I managed to give you girls but he became an absolute wastrel for far too many years."

She clapped her hand together. "But I needn't have worried, as I tell you, Yvette, he's positively transformed. This morning, he was every bit as charming and polite as he was as a boy. But it was far more than that. Now, he's filled with a serenity that I've never seen in him or anyone else for that matter. He exudes it and is so comfortable in his own skin. I was quite stunned and have been saying prayers of thanks ever since he left." She peered at her daughter. "Have you seen in him what I saw?"

She nodded. "It's truly astonishing."

A commotion in the kitchen alerted them to the arrival of Millie and Delaney. They soon hurried in and collapsed side by side on the opposite end of the sofa. "How is Roddy?" Delaney asked Yvette.

"He died."

Her face crumpled. "Oh, dear. Are Ma-ma and Pa-pa all right?"

"Yes. The funeral will be tomorrow even though it's Sunday."

After they'd digested this, Yvette soon returned her attention to Audra, marveling at her elegance with her snowy hair piled high. "Have you had recent letters from our sisters?"

"I have! My, with all that's happened, I've forgotten the best news. Bethany and Olivia are both having babies in the winter. Isn't that grand? I only wish they lived closer."

"Denver's not that far," Yvette pointed out.

"That's what your father tells me. He says I can visit whenever I like. And, of course, I have Ophelia closer."

"What do you hear from Willa?"

"She's still happy teaching at the University and has a most peculiar marriage. Neither she nor Ben appear to have the slightest desire for children. Willa will doubtless still be teaching college in forty years, it never having occurred to her and Ben that they would have been happier with a more normal marriage. And Anne has simply hasn't had any luck conceiving."

"She and Caldwell haven't been married all that long."

"Well, when I married your father, Ophelia was on the way in very short order."

"We've not all been blessed with your effortless gift of motherhood," Millie pointed out.

"Evidently not." Despite her age, she still had her imperial bearing with not an excess ounce of flesh covering her fine bones.

Audra, Delaney, Millie and Yvette presently walked back to the *Mariposa* where they found Granville and Father Richard had arrived and Sawyer had come for lunch. Everyone sat at the dining table where LuAnn served chicken soup.

While Damien and Harper discussed Roddy's funeral with Audra, Granville and Father Richard, Dom and his daughter were in the midst of a lively conversation about her future as a dress designer. Yvette sat around the corner of the table from them. "So you've decided to pursue your dream?" She asked her friend.

Sawyer's freckled face was animated with enthusiasm. "Yes, I am!"

Yvette considered her with avid interest. "That's wonderful." She spotted Sawyer's portfolio and pulled it closer, lifting a brow for permission to open it.

Sawyer nodded eagerly and she sorted through the sketches and elaborate drawings of dresses she'd created in recent months. Some were astonishingly fine images of formal wear wrought in colored pencil to show the delicate details of lace, appliques, sequins, beading and embroidery.

"Who is going to make these?" Yvette asked.

"*Miss Patsy Patchett's Fine Clothiers For Ladies* has seamstresses that will fashion patterns from my drawings and then sew the dresses. She wants to do a dozen and then have a private show to introduce me. After that, we'll see where we go from there."

"Oh, Sawyer, you're going to be a sensation," Yvette predicted.

"I've little doubt of that," Granville declared, having looked at the portfolio and listened to Sawyer's eager talk. "In wartime, ladies look for something new and exciting to take their minds off their men going away to fight."

Yvette glanced at Sawyer with a wink and reached out to squeeze her hand.

Dom sat still, absorbing the proceedings. "If you should need some working capital, I'd be interested in making an investment in your company."

"I too, would very much like to invest as I can see you're going to have a profitable future," Granville interjected. "Your work is fresh and exciting. The demand will be brisk, I have no doubt."

Yvette considered his enthusiasm with delight. He was such an amazing man who had to be nearing ninety, yet remained lean and handsome. His mind was still young and insightful. She recalled how he had guided Delaney to victory at the Denver Stock Show with his eager passion to help her realize her dream.

Sawyer beamed at all the praise and good wishes. "Finally, I know what I want to do with my life," she said with wonder.

"May I pre-order a design before your show?" Delaney asked.

Sawyer looked at her in surprise. "I suppose so. I never thought about anyone wanting to do that."

"You must grow accustomed to all sorts of innovative ideas," Granville said. "Once word gets out, you will have orders coming in at an overwhelming rate. So you must be prepared."

Sawyer suddenly looked unsure. "I don't want to let anyone down. What if I can't keep up?"

"You will," Dom assured her. "We'll help you."

"Indeed," Granville said. "In fact, when you can spare a little time, I'll be happy to go over some basics with you."

"Thank you so much," she said gratefully.

"My pleasure. It's unfortunate that Aunt Pris isn't still in fine fettle. In her prime, she would've snapped up every new design the moment you finished it."

"I daresay there are many Aunt Pris's out there, just waiting for your dresses to come on the market," Dom said.

"Oh, I hope you're right." She hugged him happily.

That night, Yvette slid into bed early. Stretching out, she felt her muscles relax. That morning, she'd been torn in a dozen directions. Yet, the afternoon had passed happily in spite of the grief in the house.

It'd been a wonderful surprise seeing Millie and visiting their mother. And once she'd returned to the *Mariposa,* she had been delighted to observe the caring rapport between Dom and his daughter. Because they had never enjoyed any particular warmth between them, their affection today indicated to Yvette, as nothing else had, the huge change in Dom.

In the past few weeks, he'd been totally unlike the capricious man who'd caused such turmoil for Yvette. Now he was kind and even-tempered, his zeal and passion replaced by an unaccustomed prudence.

Having become so used to his impulsive personality, she found his new calm and consideration confusing to say the least. And while she would've been appalled if he had made overt advances as was his constant habit in the past, she found herself missing the keen longing that'd always lain in his eyes when he looked at her.

She was quite amazed at herself. Now that she'd freed herself from the tangled web of emotion when she had been unable to decide if she would marry Dom or Chandler, she felt somehow adrift. Ashamed, her thoughts turned to Chandler whom she loved so dearly. She should be rejoicing that her destructive liaison with Dom had gentled into friendship.

So why the return of her untoward fascination with him? He had certainly not shown any improper interest in her since she'd decided to marry Chandler.

It was curious the tumultuous, distorted images and emotions, she'd kept at bay so many nights since Dom had been out of her life, came tumbling back tonight. She had been on guard all the time she and Chandler had been engaged but was helpless to banish Dom now. He was there at the edge of her mind, his bottomless gray eyes mesmerizing.

Turning restively beneath the covers, she couldn't escape, nor did she want to as his gaze slid down, undressing her with a deliberate ease that was both loathsome and enthralling. He'd been an enigma since she first noticed him when she was perhaps three.

Over the years, he was more handsome than any boy or man she knew. As she matured, he'd looked at her with an all-knowing expression that convinced her he knew every secret thought that had ever passed through her head. He had known she loved him before she did. Yet, as well as he knew her, and after their rocky romance, he still remained a mystery.

It had always been insanity to love him, now more than ever. Still, she was helpless to dismiss her renewed feeling. All she could do was keep it buried deep within her, hidden from everyone else. As long as she never allowed herself to be alone with him, she would be safe from the treacherous passion.

It was cruel irony that Chandler didn't stir in her the fervor she felt whenever she stared into Dom's laughing eyes. Chandler would be a good husband, yet she was unable to dismiss the suspicion that her marriage would lack something vital. She knew with growing despair what Dom had always kindled in her was the same overwhelming passion that had bound Harper and Damien for over forty years.

With Chandler, she would never know the total melding of body and spirit and this filled her with regret. Nonetheless, she loved her fiancé and was confident of their happiness; they were bound by a heritage and an understanding that would sustain them as passion never could.

She slowly brought to a halt the dangerous, headlong rush of longing. As she pushed Dom away, thoughts of Chandler remained.

She'd once more buried Dom under reason and practicality. Eventually she fell into sound sleep, as exhausted as if she had battled a physical foe rather than one sleeping a short distance along the corridor.

Roddy was laid to rest in the *Rancha Mariposa* family plot the next morning. Damien eulogized his friend. Much to the surprise of most everyone at *Mariposa*, he asked Father Richard to handle the remainder of the funeral held at the graveside due to the hot weather. Roddy's body had been wrapped and placed in the ice house over-night.

Soon after noon, everyone who'd attended the burial walked back to the mansion for lunch. "Do you think my father is spinning in his grave because I asked a Catholic priest to hold Roddy's funeral?" Damien asked Granville as they neared the rear entrance.

"Oh, I hardly think so. Considering the help Richard has given us, I believe Moreton would be very pleased."

# CHAPTER TWENTY-THREE

**June 1917 – March 1918**

With Chandler and Finn moving to New York from California, and Roddy gone, a deep melancholy settled over the *Mariposa.* Since her school girls were on summer vacation, Yvette didn't have her day to day work to keep her focused and busy. She sought ways to pass the time, taking up riding again.

She and Delaney took out Centaur and Destino most every morning or afternoon. Whether there was any significance attached to his behavior or not, Dom also began riding again. When the women passed through the meadows along the Aspen, they often came upon Dom astride his horse Acer. He always appeared deep in thought and barely acknowledged them as they passed.

After a few weeks, he tired of his aimless wanderings and asked Damien if he could use his help with the cattle. His father happily accepted his offer and he was soon working most days with the hired men, repairing fences and doing maintenance on the irrigation network. When the crews began haying, Dom eagerly joined them in that as well. After years of little or no activity, he welcomed the chance to work hard and become physically strong again.

Sawyer was particularly excited about life during this time as she gave full attention to her budding career in fashion design. Yvette agreed to help her and the two visited Patsy and her daughter Mary who'd joined in the running of *Miss Patsy Patchett's Fine Clothier For Ladies.*

The two of them spent several days in Cheyenne conferring with the ladies and discussing Sawyer's sketches. When they finally returned to the ranch, they brought back three finished dresses that had begun as vague ideas in Sawyer's mind.

Patsy and her staff had been so eager to have some of Sawyer's styles in her store that she'd instructed her seamstresses to begin working. By the time Sawyer and Yvette were ready to go home, they were given the finished garments to show to the investors who had grown to a rather long list—Dom, Granville, Damien, Harper, Luke, Ivy, Delaney and Yvette.

Everyone had gathered in the drawing room where Yvette and Delaney modeled the dresses. Having listened to Granville's prediction that fashions were becoming less sedate because of the dismal mood brought on by the war, Sawyer had created an outing suit of blue *moire* with slender ankle-length skirt and short fitted jacket. On Delaney's slim curves, it had a smart look that any lady working in an office would love.

Yvette appeared in a short black lace dress embellished with beads and embroidery. She wore silk stockings and the skirt barely covered her knees. As she moved about the room, she felt a bit abashed to have so much of her skin showing but after a few minutes, she found she loved the daring style and couldn't help seeing the admiration in Dom's gaze.

The third was a beaded cocktail dress in a bold pattern of red and black with fringe swishing along the bottom of the straight skirt and edging the deep V neckline. It fit Delaney snugly and presented a young and chic flair.

"Well, what do you think?" Sawyer asked with a bow when their impromptu exhibition was finished.

Everyone applauded heartily. "I believe you're on your way to great success," Granville concluded. "I do have one suggestion. It's clear to me that the demand for your designs will increase dramatically in a very short time. I should think you may need help keeping up. Perhaps Delaney would enjoy trying her hand at creating some designs. Few women have the panache and bravura she possesses. And she has as well a masterful grasp of fine art."

Delaney stood close by and he reached for her hand, drawing her into the chair beside him. "Perhaps I'm being presumptuous. Or is this something you'd like to pursue just now?"

She sat with her hands clasped under her chin. "I don't know how good I'd be at it but I'd be willing to try for a while. Of course, when the war is over, I'll be back in training for the Olympics."

"Yes, of course you will," Sawyer said. "But I'd love to have your help now." She hugged her.

"Then you have it."

The gathering soon broke up and Yvette started up the staircase to her bedroom.

"You make a beautiful model."

She turned to find Dom just behind her.

"Thank you. Helping Sawyer with her new enterprise was nothing I ever thought I'd enjoy. But, I've always loved pretty dresses. Aunt Pris was eternally generous and kept all of us girls and ladies well stocked with all the latest styles and fabrics. It was so much fun when she decided it was time to order us all the latest frocks for whatever dinner or ball she was planning." She leaned back against the stair railing.

Dom smiled. "I do remember the beautiful colors and styles all of you wore whenever the *Mariposa* was filled to the rafters for some amazing entertainment. I wonder who will step in to take Aunt Pris' place as fashion expert."

"Oh, if Sawyer ends up living here after she marries, I'm sure she'll be the one to keep us all well-dressed."

"How exciting."

Yvette still wore the short black dress and she ran her hands down over the ornate decoration. "Well, I must change out of this."

"It looks wonderful on you."

When she glanced over her shoulder, she saw a familiar hot light in his eyes. "You're too kind," she said in a rush and ran up the stairs.

In her room, she collapsed on the bed and appraised herself in the long cheval mirror pulled close, unnerved to see the pink suffusing her cheeks. What was happening with her? Last night, she'd thought about Dom in the same sexual way as she had before she'd committed herself to Chandler. And today, he'd looked at her with more of the old sensuous interest than he'd betrayed since coming home from his exile.

She jumped up and flounced to the French door she flung open. Rushing out onto the balcony, she leaned her elbows on the railing, fighting to bring her riotous thoughts under control.

Yvette fought to bring some order to her days by spending much of her time helping Sawyer and Delaney as the three of them worked toward the keenly-anticipated fashion show at *Miss Patsy Patchett's Fine Clothier For Ladies.* When the date of the event in March drew near, an extravagant newspaper ad announced that during the following week, one hundred women living in Cheyenne would receive hand delivered invitations. No one would be admitted without the highly-coveted summons. A spirit of intrigue quickly spread and lively discussions ensued as ladies speculated on who would gain entrance into the extravaganza.

When the day arrived, only the most wealthy and influential ladies gathered in the vast showroom for a lavish high tea. The spectacular menu, including a dozen varieties of scones, tea sandwiches, English trifle, breads, cakes, candies, puddings, bars, lemon curd, strawberries and Devonshire cream had been ordered from a Denver catering company and arrived fresh on the train, an hour before it was served in late afternoon.

While the clients partook of the feast, Delaney and Yvette modeled Sawyer's line of fall fashions, gliding among the tables. Miss Patsy, herself, stood at a podium and described the finery, encouraging the ladies to make their selections.

Sales were brisk during the hour after tea when magnums of champagne were uncorked and young girls circulated with receipts on which they could conveniently record their choices. When the inventory of Sawyer's designs was quickly depleted, the ladies were encouraged to put in orders for any of the styles they'd been shown, or make selections from the catalogue offering a line of spring finery.

Finally, the last client departed, carrying her purchases in the smart bags decorated by an elegant logo drawn by Delaney. The weary hostesses sat about a table, finishing off the remnants of food and nearly-empty bottles of champagne. They congratulated one another on their tremendous success.

"Well, we certainly have our work cut out for us now," Miss Patsy observed. "This was such a coup, I feel certain business will be booming for as long as we can provide the product our customers obviously love so much." She glanced around the table. "Are we all in agreement that we must work harder than ever?"

Yvette shook her head. "This was all wonderful fun but now, I must get back to my students. After all, I am a lowly school teacher. This was a very temporary fling for me."

"Oh, dear, but we make such a well-oiled team," Miss Sara protested.

"I promised Yvette that her participation would be temporary," Sawyer admitted. She looked Delaney. "What about you?"

"I can stay on for a while. At least through the summer and maybe longer. It will help keep me from worrying about Finn. But, I want to work from home so I can ride every day. It can't be too long until I can get back into training and I don't want to have to start from scratch getting into condition."

"Well, then," Miss Mary said, "we'll count on the two of you. We must put some advertisements out in Denver and see if we can find some additional designers." They continued talking for a while before Yvette, Delaney and Sawyer hugged the two intriguing fashionistas and departed for home.

While they'd been occupied with the extravaganza, Dom had taken part in the spring work with the cattle, working in the calving sheds. Having trained a competent crew of midwives from among the cowboys, he spent much of his time with the cows and newborn calves.

He was reporting on the work to Damien at the *Mariposa* dining table when Sawyer, Yvette and Delaney filed in through the rear entrance. They collapsed onto chairs, and LuAnn appeared with tea and cookies.

Delaney saw Harper descending the stairs from her studio and ran to meet her. "It's so good to see you," she said as her mother hugged her.

"How was the big show?" Granville asked, strolling in from his apartment.

When they were seated, they all began talking at once in their enthusiasm to relate what a triumph they'd had. But soon enough, Sawyer took over and explained it all to everyone's satisfaction.

"How grand for you," Damien said. "Now Harper and I have some news for Yvette. We all miss Chandler and Finn so much and their letters tell us how homesick they are. So we are going to go visit them in New York. You and Delaney are coming with us."

Yvette's heart leapt at the news but then she remembered her responsibilities. "I shouldn't leave my pupils again so soon after this time I've been away."

Harper put an arm around her. "Darling, we've taken care of that. Your mother is going to fill in while we're away. It'll only be for a week or two because I can't leave Aunt Pris for long."

Yvette felt warmth spreading through her. This was the answer to her prayers. She needed to be with Chandler to regain her perspective. While she'd been staying in town helping Sawyer, she'd been able to free herself from her conflicted feelings for Dom. But now that she was home, she feared she might give in to her destructive fantasies again.

Now she was saved. She jumped up and draped her arms around Damien's shoulders. "Thank you for this. There's nothing in the world I'd rather do than visit Chandler." She kissed his weathered cheek, catching Dom's eye.

He smiled and gave her a thumbs up, yet she couldn't help catching the depth of sadness in his gaze.

She quickly turned to Harper. "I'm so excited! It will be such fun!"

Those bound for New York planned to leave the first week in April. A few days before, Yvette went to see her mother about taking over her duties in the school room.

Audra answered her knock and led her into the parlor. "How is Aunt Pris doing?"

"Not so well. Harper's on pins and needles, hoping that she can still go with us to New York as planned."

Audra frowned as she took a seat opposite Yvette. "Oh, I hope she can. Being away from Chandler has been very difficult for her. I'm sure she knows I'll be happy to keep a close eye on Aunt Pris while she's away."

"Of course she knows that. But I don't think she could bear it if Aunt Pris should die while she's gone."

Audra nodded glumly. "One's mother is the most difficult person to lose in anyone's life, I think."

"Was Aunt Pris truly as close to Harper as a mother?"

"Oh, indeed. Her real mother died so young, she hardly knew her at all."

"What about your mother?" Yvette asked. "You've never talked much about her."

"She died when I was sixteen and I went to take care of Harper at Laughlin the very next week. My mother had been a widow since I was a baby and we weren't well off. She supported us by taking in sewing. I had no talent for that sort of work so I realized early on, I'd go into service. I was a good student though so that's how I escaped being a servant and became a governess."

"How splendid that you met our father when you came here with Harper."

A dreamy look came into her mother's green eyes.

"Oh, it was as though, my fairy godmother had found a divine man to fall in love with me. I shall never stop thanking God for that blessing. I sometimes imagine what my life would've been like if Aunt Pris hadn't hired me. I believe I would've lived a very lonely life as most governesses do."

Yvette considered this. "I hope I'm as happy with Chandler as you've been with my father."

"I pray for that."

She caught the hint of doubt in Audra's voice and waited for her to explain.

"Darling, you needn't take your old Ma-ma for a fool. I've watched you and Dom these past weeks. You've both done an admirable job concealing it but I've seen how he adores you. As much as ever, I'd say. When he underwent his spiritual awakening, he didn't become a priest."

Yvette was aghast that she knew her secret. "I love Chandler".

"Of course you do but it's altogether different from the way you love Dom."

"Ma-ma, Chandler is right for me. He's so much like his father that I'll have as fine a marriage as Harper's."

"I'm afraid your marriage to Chandler will be more like Harper's marriage to Brendon. And they loved each other. But it was never close to the passion she's always felt for Damien."

Yvette was perplexed to hear her mother speak so practically, playing Devil's advocate.

"You are right, my darling," Audra went on softly. "There would be amazing ups and downs with a man such as Dom. Great joy tempered by times of doubt and pain. As Chandler's wife, you will know a gentler pleasure without the wild swings of passion." She sat still, regarding Yvette for a time. "But, it's awfully hard, isn't it? Knowing how Dom feels and wanting to give in to him because you feel the same way. Yet, knowing you mustn't."

"Oh, Ma-ma!" She cried. "I had no idea anyone knew what I'm feeling."

"Your secret is safe with me, my gentle little Yvette. I promise that you will know a very special happiness with Chandler."

"If only we'd been married before he left."

"That would have made little difference I'm afraid. You will always have to be on guard against your love for Dom. For all the years of your life, he will doubtless invade your most private emotions at vulnerable moments."

Yvette knew she was right and was comforted to know her mother was aware of the battle continually raging within her. She sensed she would likely need her counsel in the future. "Should I break my engagement?"

Audra observed her with concern. "It seems to me you answered that question when you chose Chandler over Dom in the past. And I believe it would be very unwise to break your engagement just when Chandler is going off to war."

Yvette nodded, knowing she had no choice but to continue on the course her life had taken. "I'll do what's right," she assured her mother.

Audra rose and came to embrace her tenderly. "I know you will. Now, tell me what your pupils are studying just now."

The days following Yvette's heart to heart talk with her mother passed in a fever of impatient waiting. Aunt Pris' condition neither improved nor deteriorated. Colleen tended the old woman around the clock with Harper and Yvette spoiling her as much as possible. The hovering threat of death once more seeped into the house.

Yvette was grateful she saw little of Dom who was working long hours in the calving sheds. March and April in Wyoming were customarily violent months of transition between two seasons. Spring evolved through erratic birth pangs. Intermittent flashes of sleet, snow, rain and calm sunshine made one never certain from one minute to the next what sort of weather was imminent. Only the wind was nearly constant.

Yet, this year, there came a tranquil span of days near the end of March. The days were still and mild, melting the remains of dirty snowdrifts and swelling the buds on trees and shrubs in the gardens. Nights were nearly as warm and held the ranch headquarters in the soft glow of a waning moon.

Curiously, Yvette became increasingly edgy during this time. Letters from Chandler promised lovely warm conditions in New York and she could hardly wait to arrive there to see him.

She suffered from insomnia and invariably, walked down to check on Aunt Pris well after the rest of the house had retired. Back in her bedroom two nights before departing for New York, she stepped out onto the balcony. It was soothing standing there in the quiet; when she eventually made her way to bed, she hoped to sleep as she usually could albeit for a very short time.

The night prior to their leaving, she'd gone through the early part of her odd ritual and stood out on the balcony. She lingered there for nearly an hour, a bit chilled but reluctant to leave the deep hush of the night. The moon had shrunk to a silver sliver that hung in the trees along the stream. A breeze stirred her dressing gown around her legs. In summer, there would have been the dry rustling of the cottonwoods. Now there was only the occasional melancholy lowing of a cow in the pens.

A small noise caused her to look back into her bedroom, dark since she'd put out the lamps. Dom spoke before she could make out his silhouette in the doorway. "Don't be frightened, Yvette."

Her heart quickened as he stepped closer. She had no time to be shocked by his invasion of her bedroom and gave not the slightest protest when he tenderly drew her into his arms. Embraced against the lean planes of his body, she was helpless not to press still closer, overcome by mindless hunger. Lifting her mouth to his, she returned his savage kiss, trembling with her need of him, carried toward the forbidden, unseen place where she'd never been.

Her dressing gown had fallen open and his fingers worked open the top buttons of her nightgown. His demanding touch wandered over her, stroking, taunting and she could only tug frantically at him, struggling to draw him closer.

Why reason returned so abruptly, she had no idea, yet she suddenly shoved herself back from him. They stood slightly apart for an interminable span while control returned, their breathing slowing. Yvette pulled her dressing gown together and tied the belt.

"Yvette," he whispered hoarsely, reaching out an imploring hand.

She pushed her way past him through the door but he caught her just inside and held her at arm's length. She was unable to pull free now that he chose not to let her go. She realized if he was determined to have her, there was nothing she could do to stop him. That reality filled her with both revulsion and raw desire. He reached behind them to close the door.

"Why did you come here!?" She demanded, welcoming her anger because she knew it would protect her as nothing else could. "If your father knew you were in here, he'd throw you off the ranch!"

"I daresay," he agreed amiably. "You may be interested to know I've tried to resist coming here. Every night for the past month, when I came back from the barns, I saw you standing there on the balcony. Tonight I could no longer fight my obsession to visit you; I must say, I received a much warmer reception than I dared hope."

"This is insanity! From now on, my bedroom door will be locked!"

"How long do you think you can douse the fire in your veins? You wanted me just now. I could have carried you to that bed and taken your maidenhead and you wouldn't have stopped me. If you've convinced yourself you're going to feel differently once you're married to my brother, you're mad. You'll only want me more." He drew her close again and she held herself rigid, not allowing the earlier glorious melding.

He suddenly stepped away and slumped onto the edge of the bed, leaning his elbows against his knees as he stared at the floor. "I daresay you think I'm not playing fair now but actually, since I've returned to my right mind, I haven't agreed to give you up. We were split apart during the upheaval when I finally got banned from the ranch. My pain acted as an anesthetic of sorts and since we were apart for nearly two years, I'm sure you believed that I'd accepted the situation. Darling, Yvette, I haven't." The dim illumination from the gaslights outside brushed his handsome face with gold.

She squeezed her hands into fists and whirled to look out into the night. "Do you really believe you can just rewrite the story whenever the notion comes to you?"

"I hardly think that's how matters stand between us. I might ask how you can do this, Yvette? How you can marry Chandler? How you can go off to be with him in New York? What a hypocrite you are."

"I wouldn't toss about such labels if I were you."

"You haven't explained to me how you can do this to us," he persisted.

"Because I must!" Tears stung her eyes and her voice broke. "Even if I might have changed my mind earlier, I can't now. It's much too late."

"Why? I can't see that it's ever too late to change something so important."

"I have given my word, my promise. Chandler's going to war; it's possible knowing that I'm waiting for him will mean the difference between him living or dying. I'll not go back on my word . . . I won't . . . ." She broke off raggedly and turned to move into his open arms, burying her face against his chest. "Please," she sobbed, "please, if you love me as you say, help me instead of tormenting me this way. I can be strong enough for myself but I can't be strong for both of us. That . . . that is all that saved us earlier . . . . You were kind enough to stop . . . if you hadn't, I couldn't have either. Please . . . stay away from me . . . ." Her plea gave way to a tortured wailing.

He cradled her, so very gently now and found his handkerchief to wipe her face. "My darling little Yvette, you are so naïve; you've no idea what you ask." The words were a groan of agony against her hair. "Nonetheless, I'll do as you ask, if only to prove to you I'm no longer the selfish brute you believe me to be. I'll stay away from you until Chandler comes home. But then, I doubt very much if I'll be able to let you marry him without putting up a fight."

"I will marry him."

"We'll see, my love. For now, I'll play by your rules." He kissed her forehead, then released her. "Have a pleasant trip to New York. I doubt I'll have the stomach to see you off. Good night." He passed through the darkened bedroom and into the night.

She went to the closed door and though she knew it was no longer necessary, lifted the key from where it hung from the knob and rotated it in the lock. Feeling a deep chill throughout her body, she glanced at the windows where a cold wind now gusted into the room. She went to lower the sashes at either side of the French doors, looking into the shadowy garden where the black ghosts of trees and shrubs gyrated.

Shivering, she pulled back the covers and got into bed. She remained awake for a long time, listening to the gale moaning about the mansion.

# CHAPTER TWENTY-FOUR

**April 1918 – September 1918**

Though brilliant sunshine spilled into the dining room when Yvette joined Damien and Harper the next morning, she immediately sensed the gloom. She hung her light coat over the back of a chair and laid her reticule on top.

"Yvette, my dear." Damien hastened around the table to seat her. "You're looking very pretty this morning."

"Thanks." She kissed his cheek, studying Harper who appeared on the verge of tears. "What's wrong?"

Harper forced a smile, reaching across the table to squeeze her hand. "I can't go with you to New York. Aunt Pris took a turn for the worse during the night. I must stay with her."

"I'm so sorry." She felt suddenly desolate.

"It can't be helped," Harper said. "Chandler and Finn are due to sail in two weeks so you three must go as planned."

Yvette steepled fingers beneath her chin, observing both of them tearfully.

"Darling, don't look so sad." Damien rose to approach her chair, resting a hand on her shoulder. "We will have a nice time and bolster Chandler and Finn. Now we must be off or we'll miss our train. Is all your luggage ready?"

"Yes, in my bedroom. When I looked in, Delaney was just finishing packing so she'll be down in a thrice."

"All right, I'll send Dobbs shortly. Now perhaps you and Delaney will want to see Aunt Pris. I'll meet you two outside, shortly, dear."

Delaney came rushing down the stairs. "I'm so happy we're off today! Are you ready?"

"Nearly," Yvette said. "Let's go say goodbye to Aunt Pris." Numbly, she abandoned the toast she couldn't stomach in any case, and with Delaney close behind hurried toward Aunt Pris' apartment. Colleen rose from where she leaned over the old woman. "She's still hovering on the edge like she's done time and again."

Yvette sat next to the bed and lifted a claw-like hand from atop the counterpane, holding it in both of hers. There was no reaction so she presently kissed her sagging cheek and stood to go.

Delaney hastily squeezed the old woman's hand. "I love you, Aunt Pris," she said, wiping at unexpected tears.

"Take care, Miss Yvette and Miss Delaney," Colleen said as they hurried out.

Yvette left with the groping feeling that she was leaving something important undone, yet she knew that wasn't true. After collecting her belongings from the dining room, she and Delaney stepped outside where Harper waited beside the automobile where Damien and Dobbs loaded bags into the trunk.

Harper came to pull Yvette into her arms and held her close for a long interval. "You have a lovely time, darling, and hug Chandler for me. Tell him how much I love him."

"I will." Yvette drew back, blotting at her tears with the back of her hands. "I'll send postcards."

Delaney rushed up to say goodbye to her mother and they succumbed to another round of tears before Damien announced they must be on their way and helped his daughter into the car next to him. After he kissed Harper and saluted her with a jaunty wave, he slid behind the wheel and Dobbs cranked the engine to life.

Settled in the back seat, Yvette waved at Harper and Dobbs and they were on their way to Cheyenne. During the drive, she had the first chance to think about the interval Dom had spent in her bedroom the night before. And once they were aboard the train, she was intermittently bombarded by the memory that brought exhilaration as well as sorrow.

The following morning, while they breakfasted, Damien abruptly hauled her back from idle musings on the secret visit. "I must say, Chandler is a lucky man," he observed, having misinterpreted the telling look that'd crossed her face.

She felt a hot flush creeping over her cheeks as he observed her with amusement. "Yvette, my dear, there is no reason for embarrassment." He gave her hand a fatherly pat. "You may be interested to know that I have always had to police my thoughts of Harper when I'm in public."

She managed a smile.

"I can't tell you how pleased I am that my son will know the passionate love of a delightful young woman. My love for Harper has been the driving force of my life for so many years. Until I could have her, I was a very unhappy man."

"Were you truly miserable with Dom's mother?"

His eyes went a shade darker. "You have no idea. Our marriage was a disaster for all concerned. If circumstances had been different, we might have made a success of it for a few years as Brendon and Harper did. As it was, it was doomed from the onset."

"Harper told me that after her son Eddie died, she could no longer live with Brendon as his wife. But what came between you and Peggy?"

"Harper. Though she made no conscious attempt to do so. In fact, I believe she was rather happy with my brother for a time. Yet, I was so preoccupied with her that I'm afraid I didn't give Peggy a fair chance."

Yvette wondered which circumstance would attend her marriage. Would she find contentment with Chandler as Harper had with Brendon, or would she hunger for Dom and make Chandler miserable?

"You only married Peggy because your father insisted?" She concluded, meeting his calm gaze.

"Yes."

"Would you still do the same thing?"

"You can't imagine how often I've asked myself that question. Much as I'd like to believe that I would put my devotion ahead of practicality, I'm afraid we're all destined to behave a certain way. Given the same ghastly circumstances, I'm convinced I'd make the same decision."

Again, Yvette found herself looking ahead. If only she could see the consequences of her marriage to Chandler. Perceiving the future not being within her grasp, she had to content herself with the knowledge that marrying him was the right choice while a life with Dom would be disastrous. "I wonder if it's ever possible for the right choice to be wrong?"

"I'm afraid so," Damien replied. "We all have only our best instincts to guide us." He observed her thoughtfully. "What troubles you, sweet Yvette?"

She forced a smile, unwilling to increase her confusion by confiding in him, yet groping for his input. "I'm a bit at-sea with Chandler and I facing such a long separation. After all, we've hardly been apart since we were children."

"It's only natural that you feel lost. Still, seeing Chandler this final time before he goes away will make all the difference, I should think."

"I hope so," said vaguely.

Smiling, he cupped her chin in his hand. "I am quite certain it will."

Damien's belief that Yvette's uneasiness stemmed from the insecurity of the coming months did serve to push Dom further back in her mind as the trip continued. Nonetheless, she doubted, once she returned home if she could keep Dom isolated from her thoughts or her life for that matter.

Upon reaching New York, Damien, Yvette and Delaney settled into a suite at the Algonquin Hotel. The city was cold and rainy. Chandler phoned from Camp Upton to say he and Finn were coming to the hotel on a weekend pass.

When the two soldiers arrived Friday afternoon, Damien went to let them in. As they strode inside, Yvette and Delaney rushed to greet them.

Yvette was reminded anew how much she'd missed Chandler as warmth surged through her. Dressed in his uniform, he looked divine—fair, lithe, a smile matching the amusement in his eyes. They stood still, his gaze gently holding hers.

She had often marveled that he and Dom were half-brothers. Both possessed Damien's finely-sculpted bone structure and granite gray eyes, yet beyond that, they were opposites and the shadings of emotion in their eyes were seldom the same.

Even now, there was a reserve in Chandler's regard while her last interval with Dom had been rife with tempestuous feelings that still stirred in her three days later. She was thrust again onto the mental see-saw, roughly shoved back and forth between them.

Chandler reached for both of her hands, drawing her back on firm ground. "How splendid you look. It seems ages since I left." Holding her face in his long fingers, he kissed her leisurely—her forehead, her eyelids and at last, her mouth. "Perhaps I shouldn't have been so stubborn about not marrying you before I left," he murmured after a long time, laughing softly. "I'd like nothing better, just now, than embarking on a tumultuous, two-day romp with my wife."

Aware of Damien and the others in the next room, Yvette blushed in-spite of knowing he would be anything but shocked by his son's remark. Misreading her discomfiture, Chandler grinned, drawing her close. "I apologize, my dear. I'm afraid my priorities have been rearranged a bit in the last weeks. I'm sure you'll have me back within the bounds of decorum by Sunday night."

"I daresay," she said, taking his arm as they went to join the others gathered about the grand fireplace opposite a floor-to-ceiling bank of windows overlooking Central Park. "I must say, you two look very fit and handsome." She appraised Chandler and Finn, lean and toned from hard work.

"They've been putting us through our paces," Finn agreed. "I'm certain that when we reach France and begin working with the teams, it'll all be a bit more tolerable, or at least, we won't be performing with no idea what is expected of us."

Sitting with Chandler, Yvette leaned her head back on his arm, concentrating on the weeping glass window. "You wrote that you thought you were to be artillery drivers. Is that certain now?"

"Yes. There're so few of these New York boys who know one end of a horse from another so the army was impressed that Finn and I grew up on a ranch."

Yvette snuggled closer, draping an arm over his shoulder. "Oh, Chandler, that is good news, isn't it?"

"It is, and even better, it looks like Finn and I can drive together."

"What does that mean exactly?"

"The artillery guns are hauled on batteries pulled by four horses. The drivers ride the left two in the team."

"Over the centuries, that arrangement has proven to be most effective in keeping the big guns on the move," Damien observed from a nearby chair. "And it's one of the more coveted branches of service."

"Why is that?" Yvette wondered.

"Keeps a soldier out of the trenches with the doughboys."

"The doughboys are the infantrymen, correct?"

"Yes." He touched the end of her nose. "From what we hear, the trenches are really horrible, full of mud and lice and rats and Lord knows what else."

Not wanting to dwell on that picture, Yvette asked when they would leave for France.

"Sometimes, we hear it will be tomorrow, then next week. I do think we'll go before the end of the month." He tightened his embrace.

Yvette continued staring out into the vivid green of Central Park. "Is it rainy this time of year in France?"

"So they tell us. But drier weather will be coming soon. Perhaps it will have arrived by the time we're out driving the guns to wherever the hell they're supposed to go. Oh . . . sorry." he pressed a finger to his mouth. "Sorry."

"Are they teaching you to swear along with everything else?"

He grinned with a little shrug. "No, we've sort of picked that up on our own. Sometimes, it relieves the tension, I guess. But, I promise, I'll do my best to leave the habit in France when I come home."

"I don't care if you swear if it helps you."

His eyes smiled into hers. "It doesn't really. It's just a habit and a bad one at that. Like smoking. I tried that also but I discovered pretty quickly, I didn't care for it."

"I'm glad because it's not good for you."

"True enough." He lifted his hand to tilt her chin toward him, kissing her. "I promise we're going to have a wonderful time while you're here."

"I'm already having a nice time."

"Yes, but tomorrow we'll go walking in the Park. Perhaps we'll visit the Bronx Zoo."

"Oh, I'd love that. Maybe we can all go, if the sun comes out." She looked doubtfully at the city shrouded in rainy fog, lights reflected in a whimsical glow off the gloom.

She shivered and Chandler tightened an arm around her. "It looks so cold but like a fantasy—other-worldly."

"We'll surely have sunshine tomorrow. The gods wouldn't dare disappoint us and we shall have a spectacular adventure."

Laughing softly, she nestled into the hollow of Chandler's shoulder, acknowledging her happiness and feeling delicious contentment while she watched the traffic moving along Fifth Avenue. "I had no idea there were so many autos in the world, let alone one city. Cheyenne still has so many carriages."

"Cheyenne is a far piece from New York. And the Easterners will always be a jump ahead of us, I expect." He nuzzled her neck, then studied her. "Are you hungry, my dear? Pa-pa has invited all of us to travel out for a concert, then go to dinner after."

"Oh, that sounds lovely."

Some hours later, their party left by taxi for *The Metropolitan Opera* where they saw Mozart's *The Magic Flute.* Afterward, they proceeded to Delmonico's for dinner.

Back at the hotel, it was well after midnight before Yvette retired. Lying in bed, she recalled with something akin to joy that she hadn't once thought of Dom since he fleetingly passed through her mind when Chandler first arrived. This told her how much easier it would be to fight Dom once Chandler returned home. Only the threat of the months just ahead filled her with returning dejection. Still, she clung to the comforting memory of the day with Chandler; their bond was as comfortable and supportive as ever and as long as she kept him foremost in her mind, she could push Dom ever further away.

Her thoughts tracked toward Delaney and Finn together further along the corridor. She was both envious of their married status that allowed them to share a bedroom suite, and relieved she could still enjoy the privacy of her own room.

True to Chandler's prediction, the rain clouds had cleared by morning. Soon after ten, they walked into Central Park and found a bench in a splash of sunshine.

"How will you spend your time while I'm away?" Chandler asked.

"Much the same as I've spent the last several years, I expect. I can't imagine what I might do to prepare myself to be a wife. Since we'll continue living at the *Mariposa,* I daresay I already know most everything I need to."

"I should think," he agreed with a grin. "My mother trained you well to be lady of the manor and yours has taught you the more practical skills. I've never seen my mother wield a needle in her life, yet, I seldom recall Audra without some sort of needlework in her lap."

"If you expect the same from me, I'm afraid you'll be greatly disappointed. I can sew a straight seam but can think of nothing more boring. I much prefer teaching or riding Centaur."

"How is old Centaur?"

"Fit as ever. I've promised myself I'll ride him every single day this summer." She noted his sudden sadness. "What is it, darling?"

"Yvette, this is no game America is playing. After the training we've had, I've some idea of what we'll be up against in France. England and France have lost most of their young men." Bringing up his hands, he held her face. "I must say something to you I've thought about night and day since you wrote you were coming to New York. I love you and look forward to our life together. But, if I don't return, you mustn't grieve too long. You must make another life for yourself, different from what we would have had but a fine one even so. And you mustn't let my death destroy my parents."

"We will be able to face whatever we must!" She gave him a tiny smile.

He sighed. "I'm free then to do whatever I must as a soldier." His mustache lifted with his smile. "That said, we'll not talk of it again. We'll savor every minute we have."

Sunday dawned as a mild spring day in New York, yet seemed from the beginning to be on a reckless rush toward its end. Afterward, Yvette remembered little of the details, only how she and the others struggled toward afternoon when Chandler and Finn were due back at training camp while the rest would catch the evening train.

Thousands of soldiers mobbed Grand Central Depot as they arrived. Yvette was astounded by the numbers of wives, sweethearts, children, parents and friends bidding farewell to hordes of men in uniform.

At last, she found herself in Chandler's arms, looking searchingly into his face one last time. His kiss was swift, then he hugged Damien and Delaney and was gone, swallowed by the crowd.

Chandler and Finn charted a resolute course through the throng but once they'd gained seats on the train bound for Camp Upton, Chandler could scarcely restrain himself from bolting back out to find Yvette. The men around them sat in dazed silence for the brief span before the train lurched into motion.

Chandler was possessed by mindless jealousy of the faceless soldiers hailing from the various boroughs of New York who might have one or more additional chances to visit their families before sailing for Europe. For him and Finn, there would be no more respites from whatever awaited them on the other side of the Atlantic.

His thoughts turned to the last two days. Despite the uncertainty of the coming months, the time with Yvette and his family had left him with a new resolve and sense of peace.

His time with Yvette in New York had reinforced his love of his fiancée. Dear little Yvette who looked so defenseless but was actually, daring and stalwart. He couldn't imagine how he would make it through the coming months without his helpmate at his side, their happy camaraderie and her talent for making him laugh.

He and Yvette had never known the forthright passion he'd found with a few obliging girls, yet they were bound by familiarity and love that had held them in gentle joy and understanding since they were children. Because they'd grown up in homes so close together, they had practically been reared as brother and sister. Chandler thought this accounted for their subdued ardor; their bond was strong as blood, yet lacked some of the lust of most lovers.

He was far from concerned by this lack and was determined to get back to Yvette as quickly as possible to commence their marriage. He foresaw their years after the war as a serene life at *Rancha Mariposa,* well away from the accelerated pace that appeared to be taking over the world as a whole.

He looked fondly towards the far-off time when his hard work with the Herefords would be priority. He anticipated as well the gentler hours to be spent in the company of Yvette and his parents as well as others residing at the ranch headquarters.

As the train presently neared Camp Upton, he was filled with agitation that hadn't bothered him until now when nothing stood between him and the passage. He was at a loss to figure out what made the difference. Perhaps the explanation lay in him having the goal of seeing the visitors in New York before, while now, he would only be biding time.

During the following week, he and Finn and the rest of the men gave their attention to their departure. Possessions were rolled into cumbersome ninety-pound bundles, ready to be carried out quickly when the word came.

His nearly-constant battle with lice was now his only diversion, a complaint shared by everyone in camp. Vigorous scrubbing, application of the prescribed blue ointment and a clean uniform just before he departed for New York was all that prevented his usual companions from accompanying him to the Algonquin. Back at barracks, they had attacked with new enthusiasm and it was an uphill struggle to gain even a few hours of peace each day. The tiny tormenters were particularly active at night, frolicking relentlessly and keeping sleep at bay.

In typical military style, the news that the soldiers would be leaving for France came suddenly the night of April 25. There followed a march over muddy roads to the train station and by morning, they were on a Brooklyn ferry making its way to the piers.

The city appeared in silvery brilliance in the sunshine and the men were in high spirits. The lot of them gave up repeated cheers as the boat passed under the Brooklyn Bridge. Eventually the hull of the *Von Steuben* loomed ahead and Chandler and Finn found themselves pushed along in the line of troops filing through the gangway the remainder of that day and the next. Women of the Red Cross rushed back and forth along this line, dispensing food and cigarettes. Once aboard, the men went directly to the sleeping quarters, each furnished with two hammocks.

Standing on deck the following two nights when the ship remained in dock, Chandler looked back at Manhattan Island veiled in the eerie glare of the city lights. Already, it seemed he was far removed from Wyoming. Just as he had been filled with great expectation when he'd come across from Brooklyn, he was now swamped by homesickness. Sometime between midnight and dawn the second night, the great ship got underway.

The two weeks of passage proved to be extremely unpleasant. Finn was wretchedly seasick throughout so was confined to quarters, yet, spent much of his time at the rail.

Seasickness also affected Chandler but not to the same degree as Finn, so he managed to get through his various required tasks in a nauseated haze. He fell out with the rest at six in the morning and joined his neighbors in a common race to get fully dressed before all the clothes were gone. Occasionally, he started the day in an especially aggravating manner by getting one leg wrapped with a puttee, only to discover that someone else had been industriously bandaging their leg with the other end of the same strip.

Meals aboard ship were customarily followed by a general stampede to the rail. Chandler and Finn soon came to realize they were better off eating very little of the poor food.

For those well enough, days were spent watching impromptu wrestling and boxing matches or playing cards. An abandon-ship drill was also held every evening.

No lights were allowed on deck so all but the guards retired early each night. The hammocks provided a bit of much needed levity as the men, unaccustomed to these contraptions, performed various acrobatic stunts, trying to swing into them without losing their blankets or life preservers. These antics were amusing for a time but after being repeatedly sent scrambling out to retrieve their scattered covers or being flipped onto the floor themselves by the contrary lengths of canvas, tempers flared and there was much shouting and swearing before all were settled for the night.

Some days out, the danger of submarine attack increased and a torpedo-boat destroyer escort steamed alongside and stayed with the *Von Steuben* until it reached Brest on May 4. Once ashore at their destination, the men hiked through town, the ancient buildings and narrow streets reminding Chandler and Finn of scenes from *Oliver Twist.*

They eventually camped in a field where they remained for barely two days before boarding small, inefficient French trains for the transfer to training camps. Packed in a box car with thirty-eight other men, Chandler and Finn got their first taste of the acute discomfort known by a soldier of war. The men could neither sit nor lie down and because the trip lasted two days and three nights, they were eventually so exhausted, they slept standing, swaying together much like the cattle the cars were originally designed to accommodate.

They passed through some of the finest French wine country during this initial journey, the landscape dotted with castles, windmills, rustic villages and stone houses that peculiarly sheltered a farm family in one end, their livestock in the other. Only the faces of the people reflected their misery. Women worked in the fields, plowing with aid of a bony cow or horse.

Their desolation made the symbolic hope of the backbreaking work all the more admirable.

The soldiers staggered with fatigue once they reached the training camp near Bordeaux where they were to be molded into artillery drivers. Yet, they'd soon recovered and settled into a routine initially little different from what they had left in Camp Upton. Real work only began in earnest when the horses arrived later in the month.

While the majority of the men watched the influx of the first transports of horses with trepidation, Chandler and Finn observed the unloading of the massive draft animals with near glee. For the first time in months, they were on familiar ground with beasts that each weighed more than seventeen hundred pounds.

The clash between the uninitiated recruits and the towering draft animals resulted in untold skirmishes and many would-be driver found himself flat on his back, contemplating the belly of a long-suffering gelding. Even harnessing was beyond the city boys' immediate grasp, the tangle of bits, buckles, and endless strips of leather, an unfathomable puzzle. Many were kicked for their clumsy effort but the actual driving was the real challenge.

Chandler had never ridden the Shires at the ranch and now, found it odd to drive a team from astride the forward left horse, yet mastered the practice straightaway. Finn didn't master the unaccustomed means of horsemanship as quickly as Chandler but soon enough, the two of them were old hands at tacking up their team, hooking up the battery on which the guns would be transferred, mounting and rushing off at top speed.

Once comfortable with their impending duties, they turned attention to helping others who were getting nowhere fast. They had observed a particularly hapless pair of Manhattan natives battling with their assigned steeds for three days before Finn suggested they lend a hand.

As they approached the unfortunate duo, the taller one who declared his name was Reed had just dragged himself into the saddle. Once his partner, Gene, had managed to do the same, the horses apparently decided it was time to be on their way and moved out. The two riders swayed precariously from side to side as their mounts picked up speed, then both toppled head first to the ground. While they hauled themselves out of the dirt under the noses of their resigned beasts, Chandler and Finn approached, leaning down to pull them up.

"I'm never going to get the hang of this," the lanky one called Gene observed with a wan grin. "I'd sell my soul to the devil right now if I could ride like you two." He eyed them narrowly. "Where did you learn to ride so well?"

"We grew up on a ranch in Wyoming and have been riding since we were about two."

"So you're cowboys?" The stockier one inquired.

"I guess one could say that. Yet, Finn here is also a champion in stadium jumping."

The two gaped at them, then Reed threw up his hands in frustration. "We are neither cowboys nor stadium jumpers so it's just a matter of time 'til we're sent to join the doughboys." He raised his hand in a grim salute.

"Good luck to you."

Before they left, Finn stepped forward. "Perhaps we can be of help."

They both continued to stare until Chandler and Finn began beckoning and nodding their heads behind them where the team still waited for whatever peculiar thing the men might try to do to them. The natives finally followed to stand before Chandler and Finn.

"Riding one of these grand beasts is not all that challenging," Finn presently observed. "It's a matter of finding your center of gravity. Instead of trying to stay in the saddle by jabbing your feet down in the stirrups while you're flopping around, you must get your balance first. Let's see you up on this guy without using the stirrups."

Reed threw back his head, laughing like he'd lost his mind. "I surely can't do that if I can't stay on with the stirrups."

"Well, just humor me here. Let's get you up on this big boy, and we'll see what happens." Once he'd given him a leg-up, he looked up at him. "Now balance on your tailbone and get in rhythm with his motion." He nodded to Chandler who grabbed the lead horse's neck and propelled himself nimbly into the saddle before gathering the reins.

After they'd made a half dozen large circuits around Finn watching in amazement as Reed repeatedly keeled to one side on the verge of falling off, only to right himself and continue with more stability on each revolution. Chandler pulled up. "Well, my friend, what do you think?" Finn asked.

Reed grinned, moving his boots to capture the stirrups, then leaning down to rub his hand along the horse's neck. "I think, me, and this bonny big boy can haul the guns all over France."

"I think so too. Now we must give Gene a lesson."

By the middle of June, the drivers were confident in their newly-learned skills and quite bored with the endless drills but the monotony was eventually relieved with the delivery of the guns. During the remainder of the month, the soldiers were engaged in a general polishing of the interaction of men, horses and the great guns they were to move with dispatch.

The transition between the training period and the advance to the front lines included an exhibition parade through the city of Bordeaux on July 4. The city was draped with Allied flags and cheering crowds lining the parade route did much to bolster the men's spirits and put them in the proper frame of mind to enter combat.

Their elation on that stirring day of celebration was short-lived as after another tedious train trip, they were at the front. The clock was turned about for the drivers whose main task after the guns were in position was the care of the horses that were kept several miles back from the lines. The feeding, grooming and watering was a monumental task, yet helped pass the excess of idle time. Getting the beasts to water was often a matter of taking them to a stream three or four miles distant. The men did all the work at night and slept during the day.

Chandler and Finn shared a tent and their riding students Reed and Gene had another nearby. The four soon became fast friends as they worked together. They filled ticks with dry leaves and lay these on boughs to make serviceable, though hardly comfortable beds. The main drawback was the length of the tents that hadn't been designed to accommodate the six-foot frames of Chandler, Finn and Reed. Gene, a short, spare fellow fared better but the other three invariably had at least a foot and a half hanging out, and when it rained, it was a matter of shrinking up as best they could.

They were seeing the sordid side of war now. The food was disgusting and in short supply; the lice remained a constant vexation. Reed and Gene were likable, enterprising sorts who adapted to whatever detestable business came their way and along with Chandler and Finn managed to find some sport in their situation for a time.

Once they'd grown accustomed to the drill, Reed and Gene were more than capable riders and took great pains with the care of their horses. They all managed to give their frequent letters home a positive flavor, concentrating on the shared experiences of the four of them, not particularly exciting stuff but also not altogether depressing. Their new friends provided fodder for many amusing anecdotes. The first letters from Wyoming to catch up with Chandler and Finn in France brought the anticipated news of Aunt Pris' death. They all read their letters aloud in an effort to lend what comfort they could to one another.

By August, they'd moved through what had been exquisite farm country before it was blown to hell by the shelling. Craters marred the fields. Shattered stumps and bare skeletons were all that remained of once proud trees. Women still stoically worked their ravished land and just as gas masks had become standard equipment for the soldiers, they were also worn by these drawn, bitter phantoms, the sight utterly bizarre. Since all the horses had been requisitioned by the army, a scrawny milk cow was usually employed to pull a plow.

They advanced under heavy shelling all month. Behind the lines, the drivers had constructed dugouts next to the tents as protection from the shrapnel. The Germans were in retreat and as they went, they abandoned stores of supplies and ammunition as well as German rifles and sabers. Helmets hung on the crosses marking German graves.

The big guns boomed all night and day, reminding everyone of fierce thunderstorms. The drivers weren't greatly bothered by the shells when they were laid up behind the lines. It was when they moved the guns that they engaged in their own battles of nerves, traveling the roads at night. On more than one occasion, shells burst all around, often digging holes of sufficient depth to bury a horse.

They had suffered no casualties until their corporal was killed in an artillery duel near the end of August. From that point, their misery increased almost daily as the push accelerated and the conditions deteriorated. September brought rain that turned the roads into slimy expanses of deep mud that mired the horses and gun wagons.

It became a wretched struggle to keep the guns moving through the darkness. Sleep was scarce on the roads because they drove all night and spent most of their days caring for the horses.

There was no great improvement once the guns were laid and they retreated behind the lines. The lice were a constant menace and the soldiers rarely had a dry bed with the rain seeping into the dugouts where they were forced to sleep now that they were under unceasing fire.

None of the four friends grew accustomed to the decaying corpses occupying the trenches along with the living. The sickening smell never abated from the flesh that'd been partially eaten by the hordes of marauding rats on both sides. One of the most appalling sights was the boots still on the legs gnawed to bare bones.

After a short span under these conditions, Chandler, Finn and several of the other drivers were suffering from various stages of influenza. They sometimes had difficulty staying upright in the saddle and slept like the dead every chance they got.

"I'm lousy as a pet coon," Finn commented one morning as they prepared to retire after riding through thick fog most of the night in search of water for the horses.

"I haven't had my clothes off for six months so I share your pain. I remember running the Herefords through a dipping pit when the flies and such were particularly bad. If that pit was here right now, I'd dive in for a swim."

Finn was seized by a fit of coughing that had been the primary symptom of his influenza for the past several days. Now when he had haltingly recovered after Chandler brought him a cup of water, they both dropped into stuporous slumber.

# CHAPTER TWENTY-FIVE

**September 1918 – November 1918**

Chandler's final night on the battlefield began two evenings hence when word came that advance was imminent. As so often happened when the men were told to prepare for immediate movement, the final order was often delayed for hours. Tonight the command came shortly before midnight and they took the horses forward.

The stench of mud, rotting flesh, high explosives and sewage had become more overpowering as the rainy season continued. The night was cold, damp and foggy but the Germans had pulled back in recent days so the shells hit well ahead of them, creating remote, rumbling flares on the horizon much like sheet lightning.

The men were always grateful for such times of relative calm. Though the roads were black, the drivers had acquired remarkable night vision and could chart their course over the most treacherous terrain. The mud was not so deep as to cause great problems and only the sucking sounds of hooves and wheels moving through the muck accompanied the jangling of the bridles and harness.

The guns grew silent with first light and the drivers took cover in woods, then proceeded to unhitch. A scout arrived to tell them of a stream less than a mile ahead and by the time they returned from watering the horses, grain and mess had been delivered. It was well into the afternoon before they finished grooming and could think about sleep. The drizzle continued and the wet had gone through all layers of Chandler's clothing, but this was nothing new and he soon stretched out beneath a tree and slept.

The advance would continue and after only two hours, he was up and working with Finn to prepare their team for the hard nights work ahead. As soon as darkness fell, they mounted and set forth with the others to move the guns closer to the front.

The rain intensified and once they'd covered a few miles, they steadily drew closer to the shelling that had been far off the previous night. The stormy darkness was not so densely black because it was more frequently lit up by bursting high explosives. Peculiarly, though the noise and flashing light made men and horses alike more nervous with each hour, the drivers welcomed the occasional illumination.

The narrow, muddy road grew treacherous as it neared a precipice rising from the edge of the stream where they had watered the horses earlier, and was at this point, a torrent roaring along the rocky bed. In the periodic shell fire, Chandler could clearly see the raging white foam far below the incline. It was impossible to gain any space on the opposite side as they already passed within inches of a sheer hillside.

The road along this shelf was barely wide enough to accommodate the teams and wagons. Chandler led the procession, and at times, he seemed to be floating out over the foaming water. His mount Oscar suddenly slipped in the mud, causing Chandler's racing heart to lodge in the back of his throat while the horse struggled.

Chandler spoke calmly to Oscar, applying gentle pressure on the reins to bring him to a halt. "Good man," he said, rubbing a gloved hand along his trembling neck. "Steady on."

"What the hell's up?" Someone shouted from behind.

"We're fine! Let's just stay calm. I'm going to walk awhile," he said sliding into the sliver of space between Oscar and the cliff.

"Good plan," Finn answered, following suit before quietly passing the word back.

Chandler sidled forward until he stood in front of Oscar, then took his bridle and proceeded with caution. The mud went over his boots, soaking the puttees halfway up to his calves.

The battery moved forward along the shelf and had perhaps gone half a mile when a scout approached from the front. "Road's caved off ahead!"

"Can we get past?"

"But barely by crowdin' the bloody cliff like 'ell! If your team starts going down, get away from 'em and let 'em go. Sergeant says there's no choice so carry on." With that, he warily turned around, keeping his arms braced against the muddy wall until he could find his balance and make his way out of sight through the mud.

"Did you get what he said?" Chandler asked Finn.

"I got it and have passed it along."

"Pray like you've never prayed before and let's get on with it."

"I'm right behind you."

Praying every second, Chandler took a new hold on Oscar's reins, placed his other hand on his neck and began edging sideways with his back shoved against the slippery cliff. He took care to walk as close to the wall as possible to give Oscar and the rest every bit of available space.

When they reached the cave-off, Oscar instinctively slammed himself broadside into his harness-mate, shoving the two of them hard into the escarpment as they squeezed past the gaping hole at the edge of the road. Chandler collapsed against Oscar in relief, grateful for the good sense of his lead horse.

Some of the other drivers had drawn one or two fractious or stupid beasts as part of their allotment but he'd been fortunate in that regard. All of his team had performed well and he had yet to lose any.

As they were underway once more, they rode through utter darkness along the same precarious road; they periodically held their breath, waiting for the sound of wheels sliding over the edge. When disaster failed to materialize, they collectively exhaled as the rocky shelf gradually widened out.

Not all the drivers were so fortunate and the final wagon stalled with one wheel cast in the hole. The panicked screams of the thrashing horses brought the entire column up short. Because of the perilous state of the muddy road none of the forward horses could be transferred back to the incapacitated caisson; it had to be left there until a scout sent reinforcements. As Chandler remounted, his thoughts remained with Weaver and Jack, the ill-fated drivers, perfect targets for the shells.

Still, at the end of the night, any drivers who'd thought themselves fortunate to continue, would have gladly traded places with the two left behind. As the road presently broadened out and descended from its precarious height, the shelling escalated, some explosions so close that even the most steadfast mounts shied. Chandler could not remember a time previously when they had moved through such heat, the reflection of the flares off the rainclouds creating a strange purplish hue. It struck him that the color was the precise shade of angry bruises, appropriate somehow with the nauseating smell permeating the dank air. For all the days of his life, he knew he'd never forget the odor of bodies left lying in the mud for weeks.

This was his last thought before he was hit. A shuddering percussion rocked through Oscar's flesh beneath him and time was suspended in agonizing fragments as he fell. Yet, gradually, he realized it was Oscar that was floundering, struggling, screaming whilst Chandler lay in the mire beside the road.

Something was radically wrong with him but he couldn't decide precisely what it was. He floated on the fringes of consciousness, weak and unable to concentrate on anything. The terrorized team still flailed about above him, their shrill neighing like a siren in his mind. Something huge rolled against him and he reached out a hand, discovering with a jolt of dread that it was Oscar, his last breath rattling in his chest. His fingers found a warm, sucking hole; a slippery mass pushed rhythmically back at his probing hand for a moment, then was still. When he touched a sharp edge protruding from the dripping cavity, he knew shrapnel had pierced Oscar's heart.

The sobbing cries of injured men penetrated Chandler's bewilderment, mixing with the strident noise from the suffering horses. The metallic smell of blood sickened Chandler and he vomited. Whatever beasts were still alive breathed in sighing, shuddering gasps. He tried to gain his feet to do what he could for them but fell back, his strength leaving his body at such an alarming rate he wondered again what his injuries entailed. There was no pain, only the overwhelming weakness.

Someone loomed above. "Chandler, you're hit." Finn knelt beside him, running his hands over him, along his arms and torso; his fingers slid lower, over his left knee when his breath caught.

"Wh . . . What is it . . . ?"

"Your leg's hit. I'll have to stop the bleeding . . . ."

Chandler pulled himself up a little, still leaning against dead Oscar while Finn proceeded to tie a handkerchief around his leg, chattering madly while he worked. "Hell of a mess. Three of our horses are dead and the rest won't make it, I think. Reed and Gene are dead along with their team. Henderson's got a chunk of shrapnel in the neck . . . ."

"How'd you get through?"

"After we came down off the cliff, I was so sick from the smell, I stepped off into the brush a bit to throw up. That's when the shell exploded."

"Thank God for nausea, I suppose," Chandler ventured, reaching down to rub his leg that had begun to ache something fierce. His hand found a splintered mass of flesh and bone just below his knee and with growing comprehension and horror, he felt his entire calf swing to one side when he pushed against it, pain spiraling through it in a suffocating jolt. "Holy, Jesus! My leg's all but gone . . ." he sobbed, clutching Finn's arm as he shoved his back against Oscar.

"Chandler," Finn said, peering into his face. "You're going to make it, old boy. I've stopped the bleeding so we just have to hang on here until the medics come for you . . . ." A shell burst some distance behind them and Finn flattened himself over Chandler, sheltering him with his own body.

The hellish quality of the night deepened as Chandler began to lose contact with his surroundings. His hallucinations sharpened the images around him, making the flashing light and colors blinding. The groaning of the men and horses echoed endlessly in his head. It was only Finn's constant ministrations and encouragement that kept Chandler battling the threatening void that had drawn ever nearer since he was thrown into the mud.

"Don't leave me, Chandler! Damn you, stay awake and talk to me!" Finn's constant ranting sawed into his brain as though he was jabbing him with a stick.

All he wanted was to let the hovering black cloud engulf him, snuffing the agony, but Finn wouldn't let him drift away. He listened to his blustering with detached fascination and haltingly crawled further back from the void. Machine guns chattered somewhere far ahead.

"Poor old Oscar's getting c. . .cold," Chandler said softly, the injustice of such a faithful animal being thrust into this hell and dying so violently stabbing through his confusion. He was suddenly weeping for Oscar and himself and the rest of the thousands and thousands of men and horses that were dying in the bloody mud.

His hand drifted down past his knee where the nerves of his severed leg were on fire. "Wh . . . what will I do without my leg, Finn?"

He cradled the side of Chandler's face in his hand, leaning his own head against his. "A good many doughboys would say you're damned lucky. There's been more than one who got a wound worse than yours by shooting themselves in the leg. Now you've got a sure ticket home and I'm not so certain I don't envy you. You'll find Yvette will merely be happy you lost part of one leg instead of some part that's a lot more important. You can still hold her in your arms and love her."

"It . . . h . . . hurts like hell . . . ."

"It's going to be light soon and they'll come for you."

"I doubt it's past three . . . ."

"It's within an hour of sunrise, old man, so trust me, they'll be coming. Can't you see it's getting lighter in the east?"

"All I can see are the bloody shells . . . ." The entire length of his leg felt as though it had been set afire. Gradually he could make out the various indistinct forms of the men and horses. His team had flung themselves into various grotesque positions as they died. Gene lay off to the right with Reed sprawled across his legs.

Chandler had drawn close the waiting abyss again when an officer arrived to size up the situation. Within half an hour, soldiers from another battalion came with enough horses to move the caissons. He shifted away from Oscar so the harness could be removed, then leaned back against the now cold, hard flesh.

"I have to go with the rest now," Finn said when the new horses had been hitched to the wagons. "You take care of yourself." He brought a stack of blankets to spread over him, then clasped his hand in farewell before following the others.

As Chandler watched the teams and guns disappear into the trees, he was filled with a strange, fleeting regret. He would miss the mates and would've liked to see the job finished. He forced his eyes down to his legs. Both rested in a great red circle that'd soaked the blankets. For the first time all night, he saw he'd been sitting in Oscar's blood that had poured out around him, the added wet having gone unnoticed in the rain and mud.

Only an inch or two of skin connected the severed part of his leg with the rest. Finn had used a grimy handkerchief as a tourniquet, securing it with a twig.

The pain now forced Chandler to grind his teeth together and his breath came in great tearing gulps. He felt close to screaming. Instead, he finally lost his battle and tumbled into the waiting darkness.

He was awakened by the sensation of motion and opening his eyes, realized he was being carried between two men, his damaged leg roughly jostled with each step. He heard his screams erupting through clenched teeth. The stretcher bearers appeared oblivious to his suffering and he soon lost consciousness again.

He lost all track of his surroundings and time as he was transferred from the front lines. The only certainty was the constant gnawing pain whenever he surfaced, then someone plunged a needle into his thigh and he was gone again.

At some point, he awoke to see a huge white plaster column soaring above him. As his gaze followed the length of it to a frescoed ceiling, he took in archways, paintings, towering piles of rubble and realized that he lay inside a shelled church. Turning his head to one side, he saw nothing but other moaning, writhing, weeping men and the medics moving among them. A man stopped to loosen his tourniquet and the harshness when he retwisted it was sufficient to knock him out again.

When screaming brought him around again sometime later, he haltingly discovered that the grating noise came from him. He was in an ambulance and the lurching stirred agony like a saw blade just below his knee. Someone grabbed his arm and peeled back the layers of his clothing to jam a needle into his flesh just before a cloud of euphoria settled over him.

He didn't come fully awake again for a very long time. He was never certain if the surrealistic images of white-clad men and women and other broken soldiers passing through his fevered brain were real or muddled extensions of nightmares. Even when he first saw a pretty nurse who said her name was Ainsley Alda, he was unsure if she was real or hallucination.

"Are you feeling any better?" She asked softly. Her voice was silky and very British; this somehow made it sound very familiar to Chandler. He decided if she was a dream, she was an awfully nice one.

"I really couldn't say." Forcing his eyes fully open, he noted the long room where he lay was revolving at a brisk speed. A huge wave of nausea engulfed him and he knew he would be sick.

Unperturbed, Ainsley calmly positioned a basin and massaged his back while he heaved up foul liquid, acutely embarrassed by his lack of control.

When at last, he laid back, trembling, she took a cloth from a basin and gently wiped his face, then offered water so he could rinse his mouth.

Gradually, the spinning room slowed and he saw his bed was close to the wall in a sizable ward. In fact, a window afforded a gloomy view of a barren garden, gray and misty with rain. He thought in any other season, it would be very pleasant, green and filled with flowers.

He lifted his arm, the effort causing sweat to break out over his forehead as the room began to whirl around him once more. "I . . . I say, I'm fagged . . . ." He was astonished by the look of his arm, little more than bone covered with skin. He'd always been thin and in France, had become downright skinny but now, he was a regular skeleton.

"This is ridiculous," he commented, still inspecting his bony appendage.

"You've hardly been awake in six weeks,"

"Six weeks?"

"Indeed. If you were home, you'd be getting ready to celebrate Thanksgiving."

"Where am I?"

"At a hospital outside of London."

Chandler observed her with surprise. "Why wasn't I sent home?"

"My dear man, you were hardly in condition for a long passage. After the Armistice, you went to a field hospital in France where your leg was amputated . . . ."

"Just a moment," he said, clutching her arm. "The war is over?"

"Oh, yes. It was actually over a week after you were hit."

He could only stare at her in wonder. So the all-out push toward the front had brought about the Armistice. Perhaps Oscar's death and his injury had been worth it after all.

"So in any case, you eventually ended up here where we care only for amputees."

At that, he glanced past her at others in the ward, noting now how many men were short one or both arms. He realized with dismaying comprehension that those who apparently looked whole may have lost legs, their deficiencies hidden by covers.

"I'm to be your nurse," Ainsley Alda said with a sassy smile. "And you are Chandler Whittaker from Wyoming in America. After caring for you all these weeks, I'll wager I know you better than any woman in your acquaintance." As she tilted one eyebrow at him, a wicked gleam invaded the soft green of her huge eyes. Wispy blonde hair escaped the edges of her nurse's cap and he realized it was the precise shade of Yvette's. If they had met in some other time and place, he thought he would've found Ainsley quite captivating.

"You came down with a grand case of pneumonia three days after you came in," she continued. "After that, there were plenty of times when I thought we'd lost you. You were one sick soldier boy, Chandler."

"I rather wish I could've stayed on to finish routing the Huns." Inexplicable tears sprang to his eyes and he swiped at them with his pajama sleeve.

"Curious timing, the Armistice. The eleventh hour of the eleventh day of the eleventh month."

"It's truly over then." He turned his face to the window, clenching his teeth against the torment seeping through his leg. It hadn't hurt so much when he first awoke today but now burned as though the sheets had been ignited.

Ainsley stepped closer, her hand cool on his forehead. "It's bad again?"

"It's bloody damned bad . . . ."

"I'll bring morphine straightaway."

"How much of that stuff have I been getting?" He asked after she'd deftly given him the injection.

"A good deal but so have most of the men here." She sat with him until he slept, then went home.

When Chandler awoke near evening, Ainsley hadn't returned. Instead, a fat, terse woman appeared with a bowl of soup. "Come then, you 'ave t' eat somethin' else you can't 'ave your injection." With great efficiency, she brought a spoonful of broth to his mouth.

The soup was bland, totally without substance or flavor but he swallowed it nonetheless.

"I say, you're eatin' better'n you 'ave since you come here," she observed after a time. "I'd al'ays 'ave t' tie you down t' get anythin' in you."

"I don't remember."

"Nah, you don' 'member nothin'."

When he'd finished the soup, she brought an injection of morphine, not bothering to ask if he needed it. In the end, he might have managed for a bit longer but was just as grateful to escape back into oblivion.

His first awareness the next morning was of Ainsley standing beside his bed. "Well now, two days in a row you're all the way back. I've brought you some porridge." After propping him up with pillows, she fed him the milky cereal. "Tomorrow or the next day, I'll give you a bath and make up your bed with fresh linen."

He was starting to smell a little gamey but he had no idea how she would manage either the promised bath or a change of sheets. “Are you a native London girl, Ainsley?”

“Ah, yes, indeed. Just a bonny English lass.”

He observed her with amusement. Though her uniform was hardly the most flattering garment she might have worn, she was very appealing. She wasn’t an exquisite beauty like Yvette, yet slim and lovely. Her short modern haircut formed a wavy cap about her round, merry face. Like most English girls, she possessed fine, flawless skin but her soft brown eyes were her best feature, warm and caring.

“What I’ve been wondering ever since you arrived here, is why you talk like a fine English gentleman when your papers say you were born in America.”

“My parents moved to Wyoming Territory from Herefordshire in 1876. They sound as British today as they did then so I couldn’t escape their accent.”

“Is the Wild West in America as uncivilized as everyone says?”

“Hardly, anymore. It wasn’t even particularly uncivilized when my parents arrived. In fact, at that time, there were a good many from the English upper class going over and they took their Victorian lifestyle right along with them.”

“Were your parents among those who built great castles in America?”

“No, though we still live in their original house, a very gracious place called the *Mariposa.*”

“I daresay a mere cottage.”

“I believe it has somewhere near twenty-five rooms,” he said drily.

“My stars! If that’s no castle, I’ll eat my shoes. Who all lives in a place like that?”

He suddenly burst out laughing at her incredulous expression. “My family history is quite complicated.” As she set aside the porridge bowl, he sorted it out for her as best he could, drawing further exclamations when he mentioned Trail’s End and how many people lived there.

“I can scarcely imagine such a grand life,” Ainsley said.

"Surely living in London, you've been exposed to the peculiar lifestyle of the upper class," Chandler observed, unwilling to end their talk despite the deep ache invading his leg.

"I only wish. I'm afraid I've always languished down near the bottom rung. Nonetheless, my life has been a pleasant enough romp." Setting the empty cereal bowl on a chair, she studied him quizzically. "I'll rub your leg and we'll see if that helps," she offered, having discerned the pain's stealthy attack. "The stump is healing well now," she said matter-of-factly as she rolled back the blankets and began massaging the skin that'd been sewn over the break in the calf bones.

Staring at her fingers expertly kneading the healing flesh, his breath constricted in his throat. He'd known nothing remained below his knee. The night he was hit, he'd known, yet had not truly believed the truth because even as his leg lay practically severed in the mud, it'd felt like it was still part of him. And later when he wrestled with the terrible torment, it had gone all the way down to his foot, his entire calf aching and burning until he wept. How could it cause him such suffering when it was gone? He must have sobbed this question aloud because Ainsley answered, her voice calm, not betraying the slightest pity.

"There're very few amputees who don't have this bloody pain. That's why we use such a lot of morphine around here. It's not because the missing hands and feet and arms and legs are hurting. Those pieces are mostly lying back in France in the mud but there's something in the brain that doesn't easily forget a part that's gone." Ainsley studied him a moment, then stepped toward the head of his bed and wiped her fingers beneath his eyes.

"It's bloody hard to see it the first time."

"Or . . . feel it," he said ruefully, trying to stop crying but could not.

"You must remember you're healing well now," she continued gently. "It was rough going while you were so sick. The wound was infected from lying out in the muck so long and then it took days to get you to a field hospital where they could do the surgery. But now, you're getting better and will soon be fitted with an artificial leg."

"My peg leg," he said glumly.

"It will be a great deal more sophisticated than that. Once you've gotten accustomed to the inconvenience, you'll find you can get around nearly as well as before." She sat on a chair and rested her arms on the edge of the bed, a smile touching her full mouth reflected in her lively eyes. "I'm going to help you, my friend, Chandler. Didn't my rubbing help?"

He nodded, surprised to realize that it had.

"Good. Now have a bit of nap and if it starts hurting again, I'll be nearby." She adjusted the covers over him, touched his cheek with wink and moved off to tend the other men.

He watched her progress along the row of beds, noting for the first time that most of the men had been sleeping constantly since he'd come around two days ago. Others were at a similar point as he, drifting in and out of drugged sleep. A few had begun wandering out through the ward's far doorway, or if they were missing all or parts of their legs, they were pushed in wheelchairs. A large number of nurses and orderlies along with scattered doctors worked among the beds. Chandler gradually concluded that the various women were assigned to certain sections and he thanked his good fortune at being placed in Ainsley's part of the ward.

By sheer tenacity, she kept his pain at bay until she prepared to leave for the day. After feeding him more watery soup and giving his knee a final massage, she considered him for a time. "You've not had morphine for nearly four hours, my man, so I'm getting you an injection as my good night present to you."

"Thank God." He'd been awake nearly the entire afternoon and on the one hand, was weak and trembling with exhaustion, while on the other, every nerve was stimulated to the point of fraying. An exploding, unbearable need for relief screamed through his brain, a longing for the usual brief euphoria that had become a reliable prelude to sleep.

"Hang on, love." Ainsley headed to a stand where medications were dispensed and was back shortly with the hypodermic, she plunged into his thigh. "There, now."

His final thought before he drifted into sleep was how pretty she was.

Instead of Ainsley, a swarthy doctor was the first person he saw the next day. "How goes it, Whittaker?" He peered at him from beneath bushy black eyebrows.

"A bit better it seems."

"I've told your day nurse that I want you ambulatory by the end of the year. Then we'll start thinking about a new leg." Nodding curtly, he strode off, leaving Chandler trying to process what he'd said.

He hadn't made much headway sorting out the time frame when Ainsley arrived with his porridge. "What date is it?"

"December 12. Why do you ask?"

"A doctor stopped by to say he wants me walking around by the end of the year."

"He told me the same. We can manage that, I should think."

He gave her a forlorn appraisal. "Easy for you to say."

"Right now," she said, letting the spoon clatter into the empty porridge bowl, "it's time to change your bed linens. And you can use a bath and haircut. Perhaps we'll wait on the haircut but a bath you shall have."

He stroked his burgeoning beard. "What about a shave?"

"That can wait as well," she said briskly and soon brought a basin of warm water from a sink on the nearest wall. She proceeded forthrightly with her work. "Now then," she said when he was finally dressed in a clean nightshirt, "to get this bed stripped."

He was already fatigued from the slight exertion of being washed and would've opted to stay in his dirty bed for the next month but Ainsley was having none of that. She was amazingly strong for someone so slight and while Chandler clung to one of her arms, she shoved at him with the other and eventually had him sitting on the edge of the bed.

She panted a moment, grasping his shoulders as he swayed dizzily, then shouted for an orderly who came running and held onto him while she finished the bed. He slumped against the man, never having felt so purely done in. Sweat dripped from the end of his nose and his stomach revolted, the cereal threatening to come up.

"Move him down a little now," she ordered and before he knew what had happened, the burly orderly dragged him to the bottom half of the mattress.

"He's all yours." The man whirled around and rushed off.

"Wonderful bedside manner, don't you think?" She glanced down at him a moment, then gestured toward the head of the bed. "Move back up now."

"I can't move, period."

"Of course, you can and then, I'll let you rest. I promise," she added when he made no move to do as she said.

"You missed your calling. You should've been a drill sergeant."

"That's what they tell me," she agreed amiably.

They remained there in a stalemate of wills for an additional parade of minutes until, at last, Chandler sucked in a breath and using his last dram of energy, hauled himself onto the pillow where he lay shaking and panting for breath.

"I daresay we have our work cut out for us," Ainsley ventured wearily, spreading a fresh sheet over him.

He glanced dismally toward the window. Outside, a flock of crows wheeled past. Shortly, he fell asleep.

"I'm very pleased with you," she observed when he came around in late afternoon.

He couldn't imagine what she was talking about.

"What did I do to earn your esteemed approval?"

"You slept without morphine. I think you'll be off injections altogether in a month or two."

He mulled over this news. Considering the deep ache gnawing at his leg once again, he thought her prediction overly optimistic.

# CHAPTER TWENTY-SIX

## November 1918 – April 1919

By a tedious, constantly-exhausting process, Chandler steadily gained strength. By January, he was able to leave his bed with the aid of a wheeled chair, then graduated to crutches.

He became more and more dependent on Ainsley's cheerful company, despairing on the days when she wasn't on duty. Though his need for morphine remained nearly constant, she refused to administer the drug unless he grew positively desperate. Hefty nurse Benson had no such scruples and never argued when he begged for morphine late at night.

Due to this conflicting approach to dealing with his pain, he remained at the mercy of the opiate. He'd not confronted the reality of his continued addiction until mid-February when the brusque doctor came again to tell him he was ready to be fitted with an artificial limb and measurements would be taken this afternoon.

Ainsley had been waiting at the foot of the bed and when he was gone, she came to sit beside Chandler. "It sounds as though you'll soon be out of here."

"Thank, God."

"What are your plans?"

He observed her without saying more for a time. "I expect I'll be getting orders to return home," he said at last. He seemed to be waiting for her confirmation. "Wouldn't you think?"

She spread her hands, at a loss. "I really don't know just what to think." Coming around the side of the bed, she stood close to him. "Your morphine addiction makes it all rather more difficult."

"I'd hardly take it that far."

"It's the truth. I'm rather an expert on these matters after working here all during the war. It's a rare amputee who doesn't go out of this place an addict and while some defeat their habit later on, most die with it." Her comely features twisted with worry.

"Chandler, I can't bear thinking of you that way. Some of the men who remain impaired are weak and unhappy men at the onset and losing a limb is only an excuse to take on another crutch. But not you." Her face softened, warming. "To hear you talk of that lovely ranch in Wyoming makes my heart break with my wish to get you back there to finish the life you were wrenched away from so unfairly."

"You don't understand the pain. It starts with an ache as though my leg is being crushed by a terrible force of some sort, then it passes all through my body until I'm sweating with every muscle tensed, every nerve screaming."

"You'll only have control of your body again when you stop the injections."

"I'll not be able to bear the pain long enough to stop."

"The pain is feeding off the morphine, Luv." Her gentle voice grew imploring. "I'll help you stop."

"These days, I only need it late at night," he pointed out doubtfully. "You're already home in bed. Benson never bats an eye."

"Benson is a very short-sighted soul who expects men to leave here addicts. She sees nothing peculiar in that, declaring if she lost an arm or leg, she would take morphine herself. Chandler, she's wrong. There are good lives waiting for men like you and I can't bear to have you more crippled by a drug than you'll ever be by your leg."

"I appreciate your fervor and if it was in my power, I'd stop tonight. But I know if I promise, I'll only go back on my word sometime between ten and midnight."

"Well as much as I'd like to, I cannot fight the battle for you." She busied herself folding a blanket, then prepared to go.

"Just how would you help me?" He asked, causing her to look back.

"That is entirely up to you, Luv. If you're planning to play me for a fool and keep getting your morphine from Benson, I'll just wish you luck and save myself a lot of trouble, as nothing I might do will make the slightest difference in any case. If, on the other hand, you want to get the best out of this life and will do your share, I'll rearrange my schedule to help you. I'll trade shifts and stay here night and day until the worst of it's over for you. I can even have you moved to a private room so we'll not disturb everyone. Before you're finished, you're liable to get bloody obnoxious." Her eyes snapped with defiance, throwing down her challenge.

"I'll try," he said at last.

"Truly try?"

"Yes."

"Then we'll begin tonight. I'll go talk to Dr. Hale now."

Watching her disappear, he was convinced he'd gotten into something well beyond him, yet there was no means to back down and he forgot the entire matter until two graying, bespectacled men arrived at his bed that afternoon. They peered at, poked and measured both his legs for well over an hour, and had barely gone when Ainsley came to tell him his room had been prepared. She held his crutches and soon led him along a hall fairly awash with amputees and nurses.

"We say here this is one of our singular rooms," Ainsley observed happily as she led him into a tiny square cubicle. "See, here's a single bed, a single window and a single electric light bulb. Quite lovely, don't you think?"

He smiled at her sarcasm as he hobbled on his crutches to the window that offered a similar view of the garden as he'd gotten accustomed to in the ward. He then peered into the closet that sufficed as a bathroom, finding his image in the miniscule mirror. He hadn't seen himself since arriving in France and was appalled by the pallid, bony face staring back. "I definitely must get some meat on my bones before I head home or I'll surely frighten my family to death," he said to Ainsley as he brushed past her with a shrug.

"I can't do much about the quality of the food they serve here but perhaps I can scour the fruit and vegetable stands and find you some more palatable fare."

"Cold potatoes don't sound appealing," he said, lifting an eyebrow.

"Not what I had in mind, you goofy man." Stepping forward, she gripped his arm to help him stretch out on the bed before covering him with a sheet. "Now try to rest a bit before supper."

Watching her stride into the hall, he thought about being sequestered with her, finding the notion intriguing. He dozed off and had no idea how much time had passed when Ainsley arrived back with his supper and a packet of letters.

She sat with him while he ate, offering at the meal's end, a handful of strawberries she'd scavenged in a ditch behind the hospital and dusted with sugar. "Delicious," he proclaimed when he'd popped the final berry in his mouth. "I haven't had such a tasty strawberry since I left the *Mariposa*."

She flicked a crumb from his cheek. "Well, I shall do my best to find you more delicacies as spring arrives in earnest."

"You're a wonder."

"Who is Yvette?" She nodded at the letter still waiting next to his tray.

"My fiancée."

"I see." A shadow passed over her face as she stepped toward the window, staring out into the gathering darkness. "This Yvette will live with you at the *Mariposa?"* She soon turned back, smiling brightly. "Do you play chess?"

"Yes, but very poorly."

"All the better since I enjoy winning." She snatched up the tray and hurried out.

Chandler reached for the envelopes and scanned the letters that seemed so remote. He couldn't get a grasp on the various subjects Yvette and his parents recounted. Even their horror about his injuries was genuine yet, they didn't know what he'd endured, what still lay ahead.

Ainsley's face when he'd told her about Yvette, reared up from within his scattered thoughts. Now he struggled to interpret her fleeting, painful mien. She'd appeared hurt to learn of Yvette. Could the empathy he'd felt for her from the first moment he saw her hovering over him, be reciprocated? He had no more time to ponder the inviting idea before she returned with a tiny, battered chess set that she set up between them on the bed.

"Do you have a young man in your life?" He asked after they'd played for a time.

She gave a rigid little laugh. "I'm much too busy for such nonsense as that."

"I'd hardly call caring for someone nonsense."

"One has their priorities. Mine happens to be my work and family. You've no idea how hard I worked to get my certification and I'm not likely to trash that for a boring husband and a parcel of young ones."

"I should think the right man might make all the difference."

"Perhaps," she conceded and promptly put him in check, then in short order, checkmate. "Shall we play another?"

"No." He restlessly lifted the board to the side. "My manhood can't stand another assault just now. Perhaps I'll have recovered sufficiently a bit later."

Smiling smugly, she gathered the pieces and slid the board beneath the bed. "Tell me about this Lady you're going to marry." She settled again, leaning against the bed's foot board, hugging her thin arms about herself.

"She is John Carroll's daughter. Remember I told you about John enticing my father and uncle to Wyoming?"

"So Yvette is practically part of the family already?"

"Indeed." He studied her closely. "What about your family?"

"My father died when I was twelve, and I still live with my mother who's elderly."

"How did your father support you?"

"He had a nice little farm. Not so grand by Whittaker standards but a fair piece of ground nonetheless. Now it's all gone as we sold it to pay for my nurse's training. All that's left is a tiny parcel around the cottage where I still live with my mother."

"You still live where you grew up then?"

"Yes, it's only a quarter mile from here. We love the peace of the country. I also have a cottage some distance from London. A patient left it to me in his will." She fell silent, her eyelids drooping shut, then flying open as she started awake.

"Why don't you sleep a little?" He suggested. "It's a while 'til my witching hour. I'll take the chair for a while and I promise I won't go roust Benson while you're out."

She frowned at him but offered no protest when he slid onto the chair with his foot propped on the bed. As she lay down, she repositioned his leg a little against her own before quickly falling asleep

Watching her, it struck him in a rather abstract way that he was falling in love with her. A year ago, he would have found the thought ludicrous in the face of his engagement. He would've run in horror.

Now he realized that Ainsley knew exactly what he was, with or without his leg, while the loss might make him a stranger to Yvette. Besides, he decided ruefully, he wouldn't be running far from Ainsley in his present condition.

The predictable agitation and throbbing ache in his leg increased with each hour. When he could no longer sit still, he dragged himself around the tiny room on his crutches. In her exhaustion, Ainsley slept as though drugged and he struggled to move quietly but the thumping of the sticks eventually woke her near midnight.

She came to pace with him, sometimes touching his arm in a fleeting caress. By one o'clock, he was sprawled on the bed, intermittently drenched in sweat and shaking with chills. Even while he was burning up, he continued to shake so violently his teeth chattered and his words slurred when he tried to speak. Ainsley brought cold cloths from the bathroom to wipe his face and spread over his stump.

"Pl . . . Please rub my leg . . . ," he begged.

Removing the compress, she began massaging the smooth skin below the knee as she'd done so often before.

"No! Damn it . . . my leg . . . the calf and ankle. Jesus, it aches . . . ."

Without hesitating, her hands reached lower, kneading the air an inch or two above the blanket. Though even in his frenzy, Chandler knew there was no sense to be made of it, yet, her touch on his phantom flesh relieved the agony. Still, he couldn't lie still.

The tumult raging throughout his body sent him crutching about the room again.

He had no idea how many hours passed before he gave up his fight against this force that tied his nerves and muscles into hard, bulging knots. Too wretched to keep on, he mumbled an apology to Ainsley, intending to find Benson who'd give him what he so drastically needed. In his distraction and balanced as he was on the unwieldy crutches, it took him some minutes to understand why the doorknob refused to turn. He grasped at it with both hands, screaming his rage while he yanked at it. "This damned thing's locked!" He jerked around, unsteadily meeting Ainsley's impassive gaze.

"Yes, it is. Dr. Cunningham locked it at midnight."

"You bloody meddler! You had no right. Why in hell don't you just leave me alone?" He hobbled toward the bed, nearly falling headlong in his haste.

She caught him, his weight staggering her. He clawed his way onto the mattress, pounding the pillow, sobbing. She knelt next to him, her voice soothing, finally quieting him until he lay shaking beneath a blanket.

Looking at him, she smoothed back his damp hair and for the first time, saw the undisguised love in his weary gaze. "Oh, my dear Chandler." She lay her head in the hollow of his neck, unmindful of the foul odor of sweat and the exuding morphine. "I won't leave you, luv. I'll help you through this. We'll get through it together." She gently closed his eyelids, then continued there with him until he slept.

When she finally walked outside and headed home, the sky was the gleaming opalescence of a pearl beyond the towering trees. Despite Chandler's heart-rending condition when she left him, she was elated with his accomplishment. She felt certain, with her help, he would, in time, come all the way back from the War.

Chandler continued to tremble and sweat and vomit every day for nearly a week. Ainsley tended him with unfailing dedication, continually washing away the putrid poison seeping from his flesh. The sight of her slumped, exhausted, yet victorious, in the chair was the last thing he remembered before he slept each night.

He wasn't returned to the ward once the worst of the battle was over but spent hours moving through the halls with other ambulatory amputees. While Ainsley began scouring the grounds for greens and asparagus and green onions to add some zest to his bland meals, he began eating more and gaining much-needed weight. As the days grew milder, he continued to suffer periodic pain, yet it was never so intense as before, and his bizarre craving for morphine gradually eased its grip.

He and Ainsley hadn't discussed their love further, yet seemed to be waiting until the time was right. February faded into the first weeks of March before his prosthesis was ready. On a customary Tuesday morning, Dr. Cunningham and the two shrunken little men who'd fashioned the thing bore it into his room directly after breakfast.

The sight of the contraption of wood, leather and steel hinges left him filled with cold dread. Ainsley stood close to him, her eyes pleading with him to accept this last challenge.

While he stood in his underwear, propped between her and the doctor, the craftsmen, *if that is what one called these curious people who made such ugly devices to replace whatever the war had blown away, strapped on my new leg.* The lower portion fit snugly against the stump and the entire thing was held in place by a thigh piece attached to the heavy knee hinges.

Staring at it, he could picture, all too clearly, the horror that would surely transfigure Yvette on their wedding night. Not that she would be, in any way, unkind. Indeed, she would try frantically to hide her shock but her heartbreak would be so complete, it was unlikely their marriage would be consummated for some time.

The odd little men were muttering back and forth while they fussed with the straps of his artificial leg. He dared glance at Ainsley, amazed to see her smiling. Though a bit peeved by her overly cheerful stance, he was again grateful for her ready acceptance of the atrocities inherent in her work.

At last the men rose and stood back a little, evidently ready for him to perform. He shuddered, recalling the many sad spectacles he'd witnessed in the ward when the various amputees tried walking on their new legs or feet. Usually the moment they let go of whomever they clung to, they fell straightaway.

He concentrated on the curt instructions dispensed by everyone in attendance, then clinging hard to the arms on either side of him, he focused every sense on moving his leg forward. The device felt like the chunk of wood it was made of and responded just as cleverly. It scuffed deadly along the floor, his leg stiff from the ankle to the thigh.

He tottered precariously while Ainsley wrapped one arm around his back, keeping him upright by sheer strength as they moved haltingly to the door and back. She eventually let him collapse on the edge of the bed.

"You've made a good start and you will find with time, it will get much easier," Dr. Cunningham observed. "You and Nurse Alda seem to make a good team so she'll continue helping you."

"When can I leave the hospital?"

"After another week or so, we'll have done most all we can for you. Do you want me to arrange passage to America on a hospital ship?"

"I plan to stay on in England for a few weeks."

"It will take a while for your papers to come through so I'll arrange for your discharge at that time."

"Thank you, sir."

Once he and the other men had filed out, Ainsley coaxed him to make a dozen circuits of the room before he collapsed on the bed. "It's going to take a while before I get the hang of this bloody thing." He kicked the leg over the corner of the bed.

"We'll get the best of it in due time," Ainsley promised, sitting next to him. "Where will you go once you leave here?"

"I've no definite plans except to visit the estates where my parents grew up in Herefordshire."

"Willow Rook?" She ventured, frowning in thought. "And Laughlin, the two separated by the Layton River."

He grinned. "You remembered what I told you."

"But, of course. I can't imagine anything more romantic than your parents living so close together from the time they were children."

"Nor can I," he agreed. "Hearing them talk of those years and how delightful it was living in the country with their horses and dogs and Hereford cattle. My life on the *Mariposa,* was always such an idyll and I always knew the honor and integrity on which my father based his cattle business in Wyoming had originated in the principles of *his* father at Willow Rook. I wanted nothing more than to follow their example as I became a cattleman myself."

"How fortunate you are to descend from men of such integrity." Ainsley had removed his prosthesis and begun massaging the stump that had become bruised and swollen during his exercise earlier.

"Ah, that feels superb." He lay back, giving himself up to her ministration. "You are a marvel."

"Someone from the *Mariposa* sent you a parcel." She leaned down and pulled something from beneath the edge of the bed. "Do you know what this is?"

He reached for a square can she'd pulled from the wrapping and string, then collapsed back, laughing with more delight than he'd felt in months.

"What's the joke?" Ainsley inquired. "What is it?"

Chandler lifted the torn paper to inspect the return address. "Jamie Horncastle, the *Rancha Mariposa* stockman, has sent me a miracle elixir to heal and toughen up my stump. And it will work, I've no doubt. I've seen it heal all sorts of horrible wounds and rashes in horses and milk cows and anyone brave enough to try it on their own skin afflictions."

Smiling, she read the label before twisting off the lid. "This is used to heal cow's irritated udders?" She lifted her gaze to his. "Why would anyone think it will heal an amputee's irritated stump?" She sniffed the salve, then replaced the lid.

"Because over the years of caring for ranch animals, we've yet to find anything it won't heal. Bless Jamie for thinking of this!" He grabbed the can, kissed it, then tossed it aside.

"What am I to do with it?"

"Once you've finished your heavenly massage, slather on a generous amount and wrap it loosely. By morning, we'll see such an improvement, I'll be able to walk twice as far as I did today. And remind me to write to Jamie and ask him to send a supply to last for some months."

She observed him for a time. "You're convinced that with the help of this magic potion, you'll be up to a jaunt to Herefordshire as soon as you leave the hospital?"

"If not, I expect I'll be required to find a hotel in London until I can walk well enough not to frighten my family witless when I get back to Wyoming."

She continued looking at him steadily. "As I told you, I have a rather nice cottage not so far into the country. Will you come and stay with me there until you're ready to go home? You must have gathered by this time that I'm quite in love with you."

Merriment filled his grey eyes. A smile spread from his mouth and he chuckled. "Oh, my gosh, I've thought so much about that, hoping it might be true but I didn't think it could really happen."

"Well, it's happened." She slowly wrapped her thin arms around his shoulders and laid her head on his shoulder. "You'll come then?"

"Yes." He watched her enter the closet and bring out one of two sets of civilian clothes that she had purchased with money his parents had sent. "We're going to the cottage now?"

"No better time. I'll take you for a proper dinner on the way. I have to continue with my job so it will be good to get you settled tonight."

"You're the boss," he said amiably as she proceeded to bandage his leg. It took all their combined ingenuity to apply a boot over the prosthesis but once it was accomplished, his spirits rose to match her happy mood.

"I daresay it'll be helpful as we proceed through all this, that we're so well acquainted," she declared with a sly wink.

He nodded hesitant optimism. "Now it's a matter of learning to get around without keeling over too often. Must keep up appearances as a gentleman."

"Indeed." She stopped to kiss his cheek. "You are such a lovely man."

# CHAPTER TWENTY-SEVEN

**May 1919**

Settled beside her in Ainsley's battered and temperamental automobile, Chandler stared about him out of the window as they drove into the English countryside outside London. Spring had flowed over the patchwork quilt arrangement of fields, pastures and copses, the varied plots edged by low dry-stone walls and hedgerows.

He identified larks, robins, thrushes, and starlings in the quiet of the afternoon. The flitting birds added to his rising mood. He thought about the meadowlarks that were surely singing in the *Mariposa* meadows by this time. A twinge of homesickness drifted through him.

The fieldstone cottage sported a thatched roof and small latticed windows; dormers and chimneys offered charm. Once Chandler had negotiated the cobbled walk and three short steps before the front door, he saw the place afforded a practical main room and two bedchambers but little in the way of modern updates.

Nevertheless, given its tranquil setting among ancient elms and oaks, he found it inviting from the start. He considered Ainsley who waited for him next to a rough-hewn bench before a stone hearth. "So this is where you and your mother live?" He slid down onto the end of the seat, struggling to catch his breath.

She came to sit next to him, threading her arm through his. "No, she lives in our place close the hospital." She gestured about the room. "A favorite patient left this to me years back. It gives me a place to come to when I get so weary of working and caring for my mother, just when I think I'll lose my mind." She considered him frankly. "That makes me very selfish, doesn't it?"

He reached out to squeeze her hand. "No, it makes you human. And I can't think of anyone more deserving of a respite for your soul. But your mother's able to care for herself then?"

"No!" She shook her head. "That's not been true for a long time. Now when I can't be there for whatever reason, I have an amazing young woman who stays with her. Edith has two small children she must support so I pay her as much as I can and let her have them with her when she's there."

Evening settled outside the cottage windows and Ainsley stirred herself to prepare a simple meal of eggs and new spinach, then announced she was going to spend the night with her mother. Exhausted from the day's activity, Chandler was happy to settle into one of the bedrooms before she departed.

During the first week he was at the cottage, his days settled into a routine revolving around Ainsley's responsibilities in London. When she slept in the country, she drove herself off before dawn in her sputtering auto, leaving him to his own devices. He'd found a narrow path angling off through the meadows and trees that had already provided many solitary hours of exercise.

On Friday of that initial week, Chandler set off along the path as soon as Ainsley had left. He keenly looked forward to the weekend when she would be with him. He'd become quite steady on his prosthesis and his gait had improved as well.

He was able to walk with the barest limp and was convinced the handsome cane his father had sent from Wyoming, lent a certain distinction to his demeanor. He no longer took much notice of the pain that still came on at low moments. The skin covering the stump that had chafed so miserably against the wooden socket at first, had with more walking and application of Bag Balm begun to toughen and heal.

Though clouds usually rolled in later on and he was often caught by a shower before he got back, so far, today, the sun shone brightly in the cobalt sky. He breathed deeply of the clover-scented air. Rabbits poked their heads above the tangle of grass and vines along the path, and a chorus of mixed songbirds serenaded his progress.

Soon enough, he located a profound peace within himself there in the springtime quiet. The final horror of the war had been allotted to its proper place in the far corners of his mind. Had other considerations not been part of his life, he would've been ready to go home.

Because Ainsley had been part of Chandler's life for months, he realized his transition back to his family would be anything but simple. Recently, he'd found himself puzzling a great deal over the bond that had formed between him and Ainsley during the winter. Was it possible to love two women at the same time? Was he now caught in the same turmoil of confusion that had held Yvette in limbo for so long?

Or had his love for Yvette been altered when he'd been shoved unawares into the death and senseless destruction of war, and was only able to find his way out of the terror and pain with Ainsley's help? Whatever the reason, he adored his personable young nurse. How easily he fit into her orbit beyond the hospital.

In her grace and loving support, she reminded him so much of Yvette. Although their understanding had flowed constantly between them in an intense current of emotion, they had barely touched each other as lovers.

She'd given him a small bedchamber on the opposite side of the cottage from hers, and for six nights, he'd slept peacefully there, exhausted from the strain of meeting yet another challenge as he struggled to regain his strength. Now, with the weekend nearing when they would have two days together, it was time for him to claim her as they both knew he would.

He reached a fork in the meadow path, his anticipation of the evening, lightening his step despite the cumbersome devise dragging at his knee. He turned in a direction he hadn't explored and presently came onto a stream, a narrow expanse dotted with ducks and swans. He stopped at the edge, seeing a small battered rowing boat tethered to a small tree.

A bit further along the bank, a stone wall was positioned within inches of the water and a dilapidated stile offered access to the other side. He was abruptly tired and the steps looked like an inviting spot to rest a little.

Sunshine flooded the bank, playing delicately off the water where the various birds cavorted. He'd come further today and his knee ached a little. Stretching out his leg, he rested his hands and chin on his cane. He'd been there, nodding drowsily for some time when a shout brought him awake.

"Chandler? Where the hell are you old top?"

He watched with some amazement as Finn emerged from a stand of willows near the stream. "You're a hard man to find."

Chandler stared at his humorous face, his heart hammering. "Finn, what on earth are you doing here?"

"Searching for you." Dressed in trousers and linen shirt, he appeared altogether different than he had in his muddy uniform. Seeing him was like looking into the past, or perhaps more accurately, the future.

"I say, it's good to see you. How'd you track me down?"

"Your girl gave me directions after I found that hospital."

"Where've you been all the time since we got separated?"

"Turns out, I wasn't in such great shape myself after our wreck. Had a whole pile of shrapnel smashed into my stomach and back. And a concussion. I actually didn't come around for a couple months after they got me to a hospital."

"Good Lord," Chandler said. "Sounds like you got the worst of it."

He shook his head. "No, I still have all my limbs." He inspected Chandler a moment. "Looks like you're near good as new."

"I'm getting there."

"If you make it all the way out here every day, you must have the hang of your new leg."

"The two of us have made peace. For a time, I was convinced it was going to get the best of me."

Finn seated himself on a log a little in front of Chandler, considering him quizzically. "What's going on with you and your nurse?"

"I've fallen in love with her. She's wholly responsible for bringing me back from the brink. I got hooked on morphine and she managed to get me off the stuff when I was more than willing to let it have a big piece of my life for the rest of my days."

Worry had seeped into Finn's gaze. "I'm so sorry you had to go through that. Morphine is an amazing blessing when men are riddled in battle but it exacts a huge price when there's addiction."

"I'd never had to deal with anything like that and it was a bloody nightmare. I couldn't sleep at all unless I had it but then when I came around, every nerve was strung so tight, I could do nothing but shake while the pain was so bad I thought I would die from that alone."

"And . . . this girl . . . nurse brought you back from that?"

"Yes. Ainsley is one stubborn lady and she's strong as a steer so I didn't have a prayer once she made up her mind to save me."

"Thank, God. At my hospital, I saw some amputees just fade away into their dependence on the drug. It broke my heart . . . ."

"I daresay," Chandler said. "In any case, after fighting my way back with Ainsley's help for so many weeks and months, we found ourselves in love. We didn't plan on that but there it is."

Finn mulled this over for a time. "Rather complicates things for you, doesn't it?"

"More than you can imagine."

"Is she going to be Mrs. Whittaker instead of Yvette?" He ventured, voicing the question that'd lain in the back of Chandler's mind since the autumn.

"I can't see how that's possible though I also can't imagine how I can bear leaving her behind when I go."

"When will that be?"

"Not for a while yet. I'm going to go to Herefordshire first and see where our family came from."

Finn's eyes widened with keen interest. "How brill for you. I'd love to do that."

"You can if you want. I'm taking the train Monday and you're welcome to join me. I won't be gone that long."

A smile drifted from Finn's mouth into his eyes. "I would really love that but I'd love to be back with Delaney more." He chuckled amiably.

"Well, I can't argue with you there. How is my little sister?"

"Longing to have me home if her letters can be believed."

"I've no doubt you can believe her," Chandler said with a grin.

Clouds had scudded across the sun and Finn caught a raindrop on his hand. "We're going to get wet if we don't start back, old top."

"Ainsley should be home and will make us supper," Chandler said as they walked.

"She's a rather gorgeous girl," Finn observed.

"I've noticed that." He winked. "Your health has kept you in England all this time?"

"My road back has been beset by many detours. Once I reached the field hospital, I was soon suffering another round of influenza which I still had when they transferred me to a little village where I nearly coughed my guts out. I was determined I wouldn't leave for home until I found you."

"I'm so happy you did!" He reached out to hug Finn, teetering a bit on his crutch.

"Lord, home seems such a long way from here. During those final couple of weeks at the front, I was so sick I doubted I'd make it through."

"We were both as sick as dogs," Chandler recalled.

"I said a lot of prayers for you while we were lying out in the mud or I was slogging through the muck looking for the stock vegetables I used to make that delicious soup we survived on when the mess wagons weren't getting through."

Finn laughed. "That was delightful stuff, a mixture of mud and turnips boiled in a tin can as I remember."

"At least we didn't starve but we got damned close before the big boys got around to signing the Armistice."

Finn watched him closely as they traversed the meadow before the cottage. "Let me tell you, Chandler, I'd never know you have a wooden leg. A wound of some sort perhaps but that's the size of it."

"Thanks for that, my man. I've worried a great deal about giving the family a nasty jolt when I show up with this gizmo but I daresay, I'll look normal enough by the time I get there. That likely shouldn't be important to me but it is."

"You may be the lucky one in the end as you won't have to deal with these bloody headaches." He pressed his hand to his temple.

"They're bad, then?"

"At times. So far, all they've given me are powders so I'm hoping when I get home, Dr. Ritter can give me something with more punch." He frowned. "We're both damned fortunate, old top," he said with a wry grin. "I can't even work up much pity for you in your dilemma with your women."

"You've no idea how lucky you are to be married to my lovely little sister, and are finished with all the agonies of the heart."

"You're correct in that. I can think of nothing I'll enjoy more than pulling our rockers close the fire." He cocked a brow. "Of course that may not be Delaney's choice after my homecoming. Both she and Pa-pa have mentioned how anxious she is to try the European show circuit now that the war's over."

"I daresay you'll be ready for that soon enough once you get rested up."

Ainsley appeared on the cabin steps, waving both arms at them before dashing to meet them. "Oh, I'm so glad you're here." Without a second's hesitation, she threw her arms around Finn. "Come in. Our supper will soon be ready." Looping an arm through his, she turned to catch Chandler's hand, walking between them into the cottage where a cheery fire burned on the stone hearth and the enticing aroma of frying chicken wafted from the kitchen.

"Oh, my lord," Chandler breathed, collapsing onto a battered sofa, "this is absolute heaven." He rotated his head to consider Ainsley who'd flopped down next to him.

Moving close, she wrapped him in her arms and gave over the next minute or so to thoroughly kissing him. Opening her eyes at last, she looked at him closely. "You've got some color in your face. How are you feeling by this time?"

"Like I could sleep from now 'til next Christmas but otherwise excellent. Fresh air and the good company of my friend and brother-in-law, Finn, did wonders for me."

"I sacrificed one of my laying hens to the cause of providing us with roast chicken for supper. I think you should have a bit of a nap while it finishes cooking." Her gaze fell on Finn sprawled on a nearby bench. "You look a little peaked as well. I prescribe a nap for you as well."

"Bless you, my lovely," Finn said, saluting her.

Ainsley's chicken was delectable and the three of them consumed it with the relish of those in need of nourishment after exercise in the bracing springtime air. "That was marvelous," Finn declared after daubing up the last of the gravy from his plate with freshly-baked flatbread.

"Was your mother a good cook?" Ainsley asked, settling back into the curve of Chandler's embrace on a daybed.

Finn discarded his napkin. "I couldn't say as we always had a cook and a maid to prepare meals."

She glanced between the two of them with something akin to wonder. "I never cease to be amazed by what your life must've been like at your great *Rancha Mariposa*."

"As we grew up, I never realized we were unique, especially in that part of the world," Chandler said. "All the effort it took to provide our family with such a comfortable way of life. But like here in England, all that is passing away now." He stared into the fire. "I'll never fully comprehend so much that our father and other men from his background and position, took for granted all their lives. I sometimes wish I could go back fifty years as that life was indeed an ideal. I don't relish the thought of progress and the way the world seems to be speeding up. I'm going to love my drowsy life on the ranch."

Finn nodded knowingly. "I'd prefer that myself but alas, my bride has other plans for me. I'll doubtless spend years to come, following my darling Delaney all over Europe as her groom and competing myself when she decides I must."

"What do you mean?" Ainsley asked. "Oh, that sounds very grand and exciting," she said when he'd explained.

"It will be," he agreed, "and after I've returned home and slept for a month, I'll be up for it."

"You wouldn't miss it for the world," Chandler said with absolutely certainty, grinning at him.

"You're right, of course."

"I can fix you a mat so you can spend the night," Ainsley said, noting that he'd begun to yawn.

"Thank you. I'd appreciate that. Then tomorrow, I'll take the train to Southampton where I'll get a ship home."

"I'll look forward to seeing you when I get there," Chandler said. "I know everyone else feels the same."

Ainsley roused herself to make up the makeshift bed behind a screen at the opposite side of the cottage, and brew tea. Finn said goodnight and took his cup with him when he retired.

Chandler and Ainsley settled with a tea tray before the fire she poked into life. A light rain had begun falling beyond the open windows and door, lending the twilight the drowsy promise of rest, yet they were wide awake, sensing a new dimension of discovery between them.

"I envy Finn's going home so soon. I wish we were going with him." With his hand on the back of her neck, he tugged her closer so he could look at her closely.

She lowered her gaze, twisting her hands in her lap. "My darling, Chandler, you know I can't go with you."

"I know nothing of the kind. We both know we must be together . . . ."

She pressed one finger against his mouth. "I can't leave. Nothing sounds more lovely than to go with you to your beautiful ranch and live there with you for all the days of our lives. But it's not possible!"

He rested his head against hers. "Why not? What is so important that it can keep us apart, when we both know we must be together . . . ?"

"In case you've forgotten, I care for my mother and as a nurse, I have a very important job caring for the men who've been broken in the war and can't get well without months and years of patient care . . . ." She broke off, staring at him. "If I hadn't been here, who would've helped you fight morphine and begun regaining your strength?"

He met her worried eyes, trying to keep his equilibrium beneath the green magic that always sent his emotions into a muddle. "I will thank God every day for the rest of my life that you were with me when I needed you most. But, Ainsley, my beautiful, dear, dear Ainsley, I will always need you. When I set out for home and my family, I'll need your strength and good sense to help me find my way back to familiar ground. I love you so much and I can't imagine life without you . . . ."

"What about Yvette? What about the woman you promised to marry who longs to make a life with you at the *Mariposa*?"

Pain and confusion stabbed through him like a drawn knife. The thought of Yvette waiting for him and being forsaken filled him with self-revulsion. *How could he break her heart because he could no longer live without Ainsley?*

She left the seat and paced to the door to peer out at the rain that had thickened into a steady drizzle.

"I found a splendid stream and a battered old rowing boat this morning," he said at last, needing to steer them into less perilous territory.

She turned back, approaching him again. "You found my boat then!" She said, her delight returning in spite of herself as she perched on the arm of the bench and draped her arm around his shoulders.

"How can it be *your* boat. It must be at least a couple miles from here."

"Indeed, but when I first came here, I brought it with me I and rowed up and down the Codbeck most every day in summer. Will it still float do you think?"

"It was floating well enough today."

"Was it now?"

"Yes, tied to a tree."

"Well, then, the Kaley children have had it out. You and I will go rowing tomorrow and have a picnic beside the Codbeck. What do you say to that?"

"I say, what an excellent plan." He reached for her then and drew her across his lap, kissing her.

She wound her arms about his neck, opening her mouth beneath the exquisite attention of his tongue probing deeply. They remained there for a long interval, delighting in the first real intimacy they'd enjoyed, despite spending most all their time together for months.

Their attention to each other's body was eager and mutual. This was no virgin he was dealing with, he realized with growing gladness. Ainsley was a mature woman who was clearly familiar with ardent lovemaking. As they tugged at lacings and buttons in their burgeoning desire, he acknowledged glimpses of fiery images working in the back of his mind. What a plethora of joy and passion lay in store for them.

Scattering kisses over her throat and cleavage he'd laid bare in his growing arousal, he abruptly straightened, still hold her tenderly. "It's time, love. In another time, I'd carry you off to bed and ravish you. As it is, you'll have to get there under your own power but I still promise to ravish you." He arched a beseeching brow at her.

"My goodness, Mr. Whittaker." Laughter danced in the green pools of her eyes. "Shouldn't we have a care for your friend?"

"I daresay, he's out cold. And for my money, he doesn't give a rip what we're up to." His grin was roguish as he observed her a moment before heading toward the rear of the cabin where they heard Finn snoring in his makeshift bed on the floor. "I rest my case," Chandler said as they entered the bedroom he'd been using.

Ainsley suddenly dashed back to the kitchen for a bottle of sherry and two glasses. Once she'd returned, she lit a lamp and sat beside him on the bed. After she poured the wine, they contemplated each other in the yellow light before tapping glasses. "I've been saving this for a long time," she said with an eager smile and swallowed half of it.

They sat without speaking for a time. Presently, she traced a finger around his mouth before kissing him again. "We've done nothing you must lie to Yvette about," she said when she drew back. "Are you certain you want to change that now?"

"I've never been more sure of anything."

She moved nearer, burrowing her slenderness into the curve of his body as he laid back on the bed, embracing her to him. Surging longing filled them both, stirring their blood as she became weightless, boneless in his arms. The entire scope of their existence narrowed to this suspended time, their common need.

His fingers drifted down, undoing buttons in a fevered quest until he tugged her blouse from her slender shoulders. In turn, she pulled at his clothing and unbuckled his prosthesis to remove it. Once they were nude, he enfolded her, looking into her face, soft and golden in the lamplight. His hands played over her bare skin, fondling her small breasts, narrow belly and finally, lower still.

An overwhelming hunger bound them, a huge impatience bred of the many weeks they'd known they would sooner or later, come to this. Control was forgotten and they were soon one body, moving, worshiping.

Once it was finished and Chandler regained contact with himself apart from her, he considered her keen enjoyment of their lovemaking. He'd known she was no innocent, yet her giving her body with the same frank generosity she'd offered her mind and her help caught him off guard. On the rare occasions he'd had a woman in the past, they'd been of Clara Lou's ilk or wanton acquaintances during college. The enthusiasm had been great but smacked of theatrical performances, nothing like the wonder of this woman whose pleasure was a reflection of her love.

He glanced at her. She looked into some distant place he couldn't see. His purpose was now clearer than ever. He'd been torn in two directions since he'd awakened that long ago day to find her lovely face hanging over him in the hospital. For a long time, he'd pushed the truth away but inevitably, the quandary had grown painful, its sharp edges rubbing constantly inside his head.

Now, he longed to broach the subject again, to hear her say she would go to Wyoming with him. Yet, after their exchange earlier, he knew she wouldn't agree. There would be time enough to talk more tomorrow. He wanted nothing to push them apart tonight, nothing to break the spell of tenderness between them.

He pulled her close to the length of him and she nestled her head into the hollow of his shoulder, moaning softly as he stroked her hair. Soon enough, her breathing grew shallow in sleep.

As for Chandler, elation sang along every nerve as he lay with her. He didn't sleep until long after midnight.

Finn had already departed when Ainsley and Chandler awoke the next morning. When he opened his eyes, he saw her observing him from where she sat on the edge of the bed.

"Good morning, sweet man," she said with a smile, reaching out to stroke his cheek.

He sat up enough to grasp her bare arms as his mouth settled on hers. One hand cradled her face and he nudged her lips apart, his tongue, tasting, demanding, probing deeply until she eased away, trembling, meeting his gaze.

"Is this your usual way to say good morning?" She asked slyly.

"Only you rate such regard, my lovely Ainsley."

"I'm glad. And now I'm going to make breakfast and pack us some lunch before we go rowing."

"Ah, yes, we're going rowing."

"If we hurry, we'll have sunshine for a time," she predicted, ducking to look outside through a slit in the curtains.

"Then we must make haste," Chandler said with a chuckle, grabbing his prosthesis.

Within half an hour, they were underway along his usual path. "I've met interesting friends in the past week," he observed. "There's Perry shouting good morning." He indicated a rabbit standing on his hind legs, nose twitching as he watched them pass. "Hello, Benjamin!" He called gleefully to a madly chattering squirrel perched in an oak tree above the path.

Ainsley giggled. "I'm amazed by your talents for communication."

"You've no idea just how amazing I can be, my dear."

She stepped closer and put her hand over his on the cane. The drowsy quiet of the spring morning filtered through their thoughts as they continued toward the stream.

"Oh, it *is* all right!" She cried when they reached the stream. She ran ahead, inspecting the boat bobbing next to the unhurried current.

"You doubted my word, madam?"

"Of course not, silly man!" She swatted him as she passed and knelt to untie the rope. "But I always worry if it will make it through another winter. After all, this old tub's probably thirty years old. But now that the Kaley children enjoy using it, their father puts it in their barn every autumn and makes repairs on occasion. The kids gave it a new coat of paint last summer." She laughed. "It used to be green." She turned to survey Chandler waiting nearby. "Can you manage to get yourself aboard without tipping us over?"

"Have no fear, milady." He stepped as close the water as possible, then divided his weight between his artificial wooden leg and his cane while swinging his good leg over the side of the vessel. After tossing his cane in, he leaned down to grasp the sides as he made his way to the rear seat. He spread his arms, grinning at her in triumph.

"Good show, luv!" She clapped in delight, laughing while she rested her hands on her knees a moment before she untied the rope and hopped nimbly into the rowing boat, sitting to face Chandler. "You're becoming remarkably competent on your new leg."

Bending forward, he cradled her face in his hands and kissed her thoroughly for some minutes before easing back. "I'm going to take you dancing all in due time."

"Do tell? I shall be waiting with great anticipation for that occasion." Taking up the oars, she propelled them competently to the center of the Codbeck, then simply let the languid movement of the water carry them along.

They presently passed beneath an old stone bridge where three youngsters stood in a row, waving madly. "Ainsley! Who's your new beau?"

She slowed the boat and introduced Chandler to the Kaley children.

"Am I only the latest of many beaus?" He asked with a teasing grin.

She considered him peevishly. "After last night, you surely know the sincerity of my intentions."

"Actually, I'm a bit confused about your intentions where I'm concerned."

"I think I've made it clear I don't wish to think of anything beyond your time here. I'm loving every moment I have with you, but once you go home, I must continue with my life here."

"Will this life make you happy in thirty years?"

"Who knows what will make me happy when I'm an old woman. Perhaps I'll be mad, locked away in a nuthouse, or dead. There is no guarantee that a spouse hanging about will bring happiness."

"Personally, I think it gives one the advantage. In fact, I decided last night to ask you to marry me?"

"I believe you've already asked Yvette." Her face remained inscrutable and she didn't say more for some time. "Surely you aren't such a gentleman, you feel obligated to propose to every woman you take to bed."

"I wish you wouldn't make light of this, Ainsley. You've felt the same as I for a long time now."

"The problem is, I think, that we weren't in agreement about the end result of our feelings. This time with you here in the country was as far as I could see or wanted to look. I can't think of anything beyond my work and caring for my mother."

"Couldn't we find a place where your mother will receive the very best care?"

"I'd never do that even if I could afford to."

"I would insist on paying . . ."

"No, I'm determined my mother will stay in our home."

He had no means of counteracting the steel of her resolve.

She contemplated him glumly. "You expect me to leave everything here, my mother, my home, my work, my homeland. You flatter yourself that you're worthy of such a trade."

"I only know what I see in your eyes, my darling Ainsley. Love as deep as what I feel for you. When your mother is gone, you'll have no family here. I promise my family will love you as their own. Your life with me in Wyoming will be filled with such joy."

"What of Yvette?"

"She'll accept the truth in time and wish us the greatest happiness. I would do the same if it was she who broke our engagement."

"If I say no, will you marry her?"

"Yes."

She slowly digested this. "She should be terribly flattered to know how true you've been to her in your heart."

"I love her and she knows that will always be true whatever happens between us."

Dropping the oars, she reached for him, cradling his face, her gaze steady on his. He doubted he would ever find the right words to describe her eyes. The closest he'd come was pale green sea glass with a mesmerizing quality. So different from Yvette's Wedgwood blue. "You do make life on the *Mariposa* sound lovely."

His heart lurched at her change in tone. "Are you perchance still considering coming with me?"

Her pretty mouth pursed in thought. "I thought I'd decided beyond any doubt but now, I find myself still torn."

New hope surged through him. "Thank God for that!" He reached for her hands, holding them tightly in his as he studied her, barely able to breathe because it was so important he say the right thing, that he not lose her due to speaking carelessly. "Darling, I want you to be sure, absolutely sure because once I have you in my life, it's forever. I want a marriage as rock solid as my parents'. So let's not talk about this again until I get back from Herefordshire. That way, you'll have time to think very carefully about your decision. Just remember I'll give over my life to making you happy. I will cherish you always."

She smiled. "You are the most lovely man, my dear."

They consciously dismissed the matter during the short time before Chandler departed for Herefordshire. They played in the stream like children, made love in Ainsley's bed, and explored every corner of the farm, talking like very old friends. On Monday, they departed early in her derelict auto and she dropped him at the London depot before continuing to the hospital.

# CHAPTER TWENTY-EIGHT

**May 1919**

Chandler arrived in the village of Peterstow by afternoon. This being the nearest town to the estates where his parents grew up, he decided to find lodging for the night and go on to the country in the morning. Ancient gas lamps adorned every intersection as he walked from the depot along the narrow cobbled streets. He was once more reminded of all of the Dickens novels he had read as a child. Whenever he passed a particularly tiny slit of an alley that was surely black as pitch after dark, he half expected Fagin to leap out at him.

He presently came upon an inn that appeared quite comfortable and booked a room. The train ride had tired him more than all his walking about with Ainsley so after an early supper in a tavern, he retired.

The next morning he considered again the dilemma of reaching his destination in the country. He decided against a taxi because he had no idea when he might want to return to town. It was a bit far for him to walk so he presently settled on the solution of hiring a horse. It was high time he tried riding again so set out for a livery barn in search of a mount that wouldn't object to being ridden by a man with a wooden leg who wished to mount from the right side.

When he explained his need to the barn's owner, the man peered at him. "Why you want a horse like that?"

"I lost part of my left leg in the war."

The reason for the request slowly dawned in his ruddy face. "I got just the one for you, guvner." He turned into the barn and was soon back with an ancient beast reminiscent of one Ichabod Crane allegedly rode on his jaunt through Sleepy Hollow—spavined, skinny to the point of showing every rib, his spine sagging alarmingly. His owner stood back, appraising him with pride. "He'll not mind yer getting on the wrong side."

"You've nothing else?"

"Not jus' now. Mind you, Jeb won't mind you takin' him for a ride about."

Chandler gave the horse a final dubious inspection. "Let's give it a go, then. Put a saddle on him."

When this was done, the owner came to see just how he planned to get in the saddle. "Want me to heave you up, then?"

"If you could bring that crate over here, I think I can manage." He indicated a sturdy box nearby.

The man scrambled to drag it close to Jeb and Chandler gathered the reins and using the horse to lean on, stepped onto the box. The owner came to place both hands about his waist to steady him as he slowly lifted his good foot into the stirrup and with his helper pushing with all his might, managed to throw his artificial leg over the saddle and settle in. Sweat ran down his face and soaked his shirt and jacket as he sat there panting, every inch of him shaking.

"Well, there y' go," the man said with obvious admiration.

Chandler granted him a wan grin and shoved his boots more securely into the stirrups. He concluded that he'd managed the feat of getting aboard, not because Jeb had any preference but because he was too old and decrepit to give a damn. After mopping his face with his handkerchief, he secured his cane under his arm and prepared to depart. "Thank you, kindly, sir. I'll return . . . when I do," he finished hastily when he realized he had no idea when he'd be back.

The man nodded and he was underway, Jeb moving out with a remarkable show of energy but little speed which was ideal for Chandler's maiden trip on horseback. He soon discovered that his muscles still retained the memory of riding, and before long, he felt quite confident. The verdant countryside was serene and he was possessed by exhilaration as they bypassed several small herds of Herefords, the sight bringing home to him exactly where he was as nothing else could.

He'd heard his parents, Aunt Pris and Granville describe the two manor houses amid the towering willows and chestnuts so often they appeared as familiar to him when he came upon them as the *Mariposa.* He bypassed Laughlin, the smaller one, trying to put his mother as a child or Aunt Pris together with the elegant half-timbered mansion.

Once beyond the meandering expanse of the Layton River, he rode on toward Willow Rook and pulled up in the cobbled drive. His heart beat a rapid tattoo as he took in the grand structure. Forty-two years had passed since his parents had left this place and this knowledge left him momentarily bemused.

After a time, he slid off the crow-bait, holding fast to the saddle while he gained his balance and his injured leg grew accustomed to bearing his weight again. He acknowledged considerable satisfaction that he'd managed the ride with little difficulty.

He tethered Jeb to the fence enclosing a splendid old garden with ancient weeping willows holding court in the far corners. Taking a firm hold on his cane, he strode to Willow Rook's front entrance, being careful to step straight ahead so he didn't limp. Once he stood on a wide porch, he wielded the knocker.

No answer was immediately forthcoming. Bees hovered among the glorious peonies blooming nearby, their indolent sound soothing Chandler's nerves as he waited. He knocked twice more in the course of ten minutes and eventually, a frail old woman in a maid's uniform appeared and stood staring at him blankly.

"Good morning." He doffed his hat with a little bow. "Is Mr. Chancellor at home?"

"Who's wanting to know?"

"Chandler Whittaker."

"We don't know you."

He sighed and gave her a smile. "My father and uncle grew up in this house and I would like to speak to Mr. Chancellor. Is he home?"

She nodded doubtfully. "Kindly follow me."

"Thank you." He stepped into a grand hall that closely resembled the one at *Mariposa.*

Despite her age, the maid moved at an efficient pace and he limped more than usual trying to keep up.

Noticing this, she slowed abruptly, staring at his legs. "You're lame, then."

"I lost some of my leg in the war."

"Ah, there's the misery of that." She ducked her rumpled head and carried on at a more reasonable speed through a number of dim chambers, finally swinging open a door into what turned out to be a cavernous bedchamber.

Heavy drapes drawn over the windows made the room as dark as the rest of the house. Chandler was newly appreciative of the *Mariposa's* countless wide windows.

It took him a moment to see the enormous man propped up in the bed. Garbed in a filthy dressing gown, he was supported by a great pile of pillows, he watched Chandler's approach with bleary eyes, appearing every bit of the hundred plus years Pa-pa had estimated him to be.

"Mr. Chancellor?"

"Who's there!?" He shouted, still staring straight at him.

"Chandler Whittaker."

"He's lame," the housekeeper volunteered for no apparent reason before she retreated.

"Whittaker!" Garner Chancellor boomed. "Damien, is it?"

"No, I'm his son. Chandler."

"Brendon died . . . ."

"Yes, a very long time ago," he agreed, fast reaching the conclusion he'd come to a place where everyone was quite mad.

"You live at Laughlin then, Damien?" His voice was remarkably loud for someone so ancient.

"No, I live in Wyoming."

When there was no answer for several minutes, he was trying to decide if the old man would notice if he headed out. He'd turned toward the door when the brash voice startled him and he paused, slightly rattled.

"Those wild cows still making you and Brendon rich?"

"We raise only Herefords now."

He turned his gaze away and drifted into silence again. Chandler considered anew whether he might escape without notice when the man erupted again. "I always regretted pulling a fast one on your Pa-pa, old Moreton. I daresay he wouldn't have treated me so poorly but then . . . he never had my troubles . . ." he pondered what he'd said for a while before continuing. "Perhaps he had troubles but just kept them real quiet."

This was evidently a very humorous observation as he laughed heartily for a long interval, the sound gurgling up out of the rolls of fat smothering his huge neck. His tremendous bulk shook the bed so violently, Chandler half expected it to crash to the floor.

The old man finally wiped his streaming eyes and stared at his visitor, his gaze accusing now. "You didn't mind taking my Peggy like a harlot but you still wouldn't be happily married to anyone but the fine Harper Whittaker. Peggy was surely a . . . poor excuse for a granddaughter. I swept up her dirt from the time she was a small girl. Do you have any idea how tiresome that became." He paused, the sound of his labored breathing sawing into the still room. "M . . . my Meredith and Peggy living on a pension from . . . her husband." He thundered with mirth once again. "I . . . I was positively inspired when I spread that around. Everyone thought it true, never realizing Peggy was a bastard . . . I do wonder what your Pa-pa would've said to me had he known he forced you to marry a bastard . . . ." His crazy rambling ceased even as he continued holding Chandler in his hateful glare.

An alarm had begun clanging in Chandler's head while he tried sorting out what the miserable man had divulged in his muddled talk. "You say Peggy was a bastard?" He asked in genuine astonishment.

"Dammit, Damien!" Garner shouted, snatching his cane from where it lay on the counterpane and swinging it in a vicious arc that barely missed Chandler before he flung it at him.

"Good, lord! What the devil has gotten into you, you crazy old buzzard!"

Garner heaved himself up to lean on an elbow, shaking a crooked finger at him in a total rage. "Damien, are you deaf!? My bloody granddaughter, damn her, was a bastard! Hate to say it, even now," he added with a great heaving sigh. "But if I hadn't gone to Moreton, your first boy would've been the same. Bloody bad streak there . . . from Cleo, I daresay . . . ." Trailing off, he turned his attention out the window.

Who Cleo might be, Chandler hadn't the foggiest. Watching Garner with some dread, he presently concluded he had exhausted himself; now he stared straight up at the ceiling. Since there wasn't the slightest hope of having a coherent conversation with him, Chandler soon removed himself from the room as quietly as possible, still reeling from Chancellor's condition.

Fairly certain now the nutty housekeeper was the only other person in residence and she was unlikely to come out of hiding again, he poked around a bit, finding the condition of the once-grand house depressing indeed. The lavish furnishings were all covered by a greasy layer of dust and hair and everywhere he looked, a scrawny cat lay curled on a chair or sofa. When he escaped outside, he found a boy of ten or eleven feeding carrots to the cadaverous horse.

"Hello there. Who might you be?"

"Jimmy Carmody. I live there." He pointed across the river toward Laughlin.

"Do you now? Are your parents at home?"

"Only my mum. My Pa works in the village. What were you doing at the big house?"

"I'm Chandler Whittaker and I came especially to see Willow Rook. My father lived here when he was a boy and later."

"One of the Mr. Whittakers?"

"Indeed, you know of them?"

"But of course. They went off to be cowboys."

Chandler smiled, delighted to have found someone sane, with a fair grasp of the past.

Jimmy continued fondling Jeb's bony head. "You want to come to my house for lunch? My mum'll be ever so pleased to see one of you Whittakers."

"Thank you, Jimmy. I'd like that very much indeed. But now we have to figure out how I'm to get back on this handsome steed of mine."

Jimmy watched him quizzically. "We could walk if you like."

"Yes, we could but you see I'd really prefer to ride." He bent toward Jimmy with a wink. "Jeb might be offended if I didn't." He laughed when Jimmy stood gaping at him, then rolled his pant leg up past his knee so his prosthesis was exposed.

Jimmy stared at the straps and hinges, then lifted worried eyes.

"I lost part of my leg in the war."

"Crikey Moses!" Jimmy leaned down to inspect the contraption more closely.

"So the truth is, riding to your house will be only the second time I've been in the saddle since I was injured. I need all the practice I can manage. Will you help me?"

"What would I do?"

"Take my friend Jeb over by the mounting block and hold him steady."

He ran to fetch the horse from the fence while Chandler made his way to two large chunks of stone fitted together to form a wide step up from the ground with a wider slab on top from which mounting was executed. Having negotiated the span onto the block, Chandler stood struggling for his balance while Jimmy led Jeb into position. After collecting himself one last moment, he slid his prosthesis over the saddle and impelling himself with his good leg, he settled aboard.

"Well, now, we managed that rather well, my man," he said to Jimmy who'd jumped up on the block. He clapped him on the shoulder. "Good job! Now let's be off to lunch. I doubt Jeb will mind, if you care to ride."

The lad quickly slid on behind and they were on their way to Laughlin. "My pa was sent to France," he said after a bit. "But he was a clerk so didn't get hurt."

"That's good then."

They continued on in amiable silence, reaching the mansion within a matter of minutes. With Jimmy's help, Chandler dismounted without difficulty.

"I'll put 'im in the stable."

"Thank you." While he waited, he saw a striking woman of perhaps forty appear from house.

When the boy reappeared, his mother hurried forward with a smile. “I say there, Jimmy, who’ve you brought home with you?”

“It’s Mr. Whittaker, mum! I asked ’im to lunch.”

“How nice. I’m Sara Carmody. Do come in, please.” She extended her hand as Jimmy disappeared into the house. “Mr. Whittaker.”

“Hello, Mrs. Carmody. Your invitation is very kind. Thank you.”

She considered him closely. “Might I ask why you’re here?”

He granted her a smile. “I’m on a sentimental journey through my origins.”

“Are you related to the twins from the big house?” She asked as she led him into a modest hall, then into a sitting room where she gestured to a chair.

“Yes, Damien Whittaker is my father.”

“I must say your family’s fine reputation lingered on long after they left.”

“You’re very kind. I’ve enjoyed talking with Jimmy.”

“Jimmy’s a very wise lad. Speaking of whom . . . .” She turned, watching as the boy rushed into the room, bearing a tray holding glasses of lemonade and a bottle of Scotch.

He bowed before Chandler, then placed the tray on a table. “I thought perhaps you needed something after your ride on Jeb.”

“Thank you, Jimmy.” He accepted some Scotch.

When he’d drunk half the glass, he smiled. “Ah, this is excellent.”

Sara grasped her hands together, observing him with wonder. “I can’t tell you how lovely it is meet one of the renowned Whittakers. You’re as dashing as they say your father and uncle were.”

“My dear, lady,” he said with a smile. “You’ll make me blush.”

She laughed gaily.

“May I ask how your family came to live here?”

“My family has known Garner Chancellor since I was a small girl. Years later, after his daughter died during a trip to America, he wished to have people living in this house.

"My husband bought the Peterstow bank after we were married and we were in need of a country place. We would've preferred buying it but Mr. Chancellor merely added a clause to his will to the effect that we can purchase it from his estate after his death. The way he's going on, we may not be landowners for some years yet. He's a marvel. One hundred and three years old. I declare, I can't imagine living so long. Have you seen him?"

"Yes. How long has he been the way he is?"

"Oh, for at least five years. His mind went long before that, wandering back into the past. I must say, we were all shocked at what he babbled on about once he started."

"I assume you're talking about his granddaughter's illegitimacy," he ventured.

She nodded regretfully. "There wasn't a hint earlier and we were purely rocked to learn both his daughter and granddaughter were trollops. Once he let it slip, he seemed unable to stop talking of it and the time he married his granddaughter off to a Whittaker gentleman. He deceived Moreton Whittaker quite horribly you know and then Moreton forced your father's marriage."

Chandler waited for her to continue.

"He insisted Damien marry Peggy even when she was many months with child. It was matter of his marrying her or being disinherited . . ." she broke off, clapping her hands to her mouth in a startled gesture. "Oh dear, forgive me. Surely I haven't been saying such disparaging things about your mother."

Chandler laughed. "No. Actually, the infamous Peggy Whittaker died recently in an insane asylum. *My* mother was previously Harper Begbie who grew up in this house."

She considered him. "Ah, yes, Harper, whose heart was nearly broken when your father married Peggy. I believe Cleo was the name of his wife, Meredith's mother. I understand she was rather a hellion herself."

"He mentioned something to that effect."

She glanced toward the door. "Where *is* that Jimmy? You must be famished."

A moment later, her son burst in and flopped down on a hassock in front of Chandler. "I rubbed down your horse and gave him oats," he announced breathlessly. "Now he's resting in his stall."

"Thank you very much, my good man."

"Jimmy, you're a sight!" Sara admonished. "Run along and wash up so we can have lunch."

"I'd like to wash up myself," Chandler said.

"I'll show you." Jimmy hurried ahead to a small bath.

They soon joined Mrs. Carmody in the dining room for cold chicken, bread, cheese and tomatoes. "It's a shame your family's house is no longer as it was in the past. It must be dreadful to see it in shambles and buried in filth. It's so distressing to think of Mr. Chancellor's fine life reduced to living with that mad old woman pretending to be a housekeeper and all those horrible cats."

"This visit has shown me more than I expected," he said vaguely.

"Are you going to stay with us for a bit, Mr. Whittaker?" Jimmy inquired.

"Perhaps I'll poke about for a day or two before heading back. I've a comfortable room in Peterstow."

"Oh you mustn't go to Peterstow," he protested. "You can stay here. Can't he mum?"

"Oh, most certainly," she agreed happily. "What a splendid idea."

"Thank you, then. I'll enjoy that very much." Observing the two eager faces across the table, he wondered idly if Mr. Carmody was as hospitable as his little family.

After lunch Jimmy brought out a pony cart and drove Chandler to Peterstow to fetch his things from the inn. Later on they went on a lengthy tour of the two estates before dinner.

Aaron Carmody was a round, jovial man, as pleased to meet an unexpected guest as the rest. Still, Chandler was eager to get away the next day so took his leave after lunch and rode back to the village on his decrepit mount. His stay at Laughlin had exhausted him so upon reaching his room, he slept the remainder of the day and night, not even bothering to have dinner.

Once Chandler boarded the train the next morning, he had the opportunity to ponder his rather melancholy journey into the past. Above all else, he'd seen that nothing remains constant. The gracious life his father had enjoyed at Willow Rook had nothing in common with the present situation there.

Upon reaching London, he made a stop at the hospital where he'd been treated to make inquiries about passage to America. His doctors examined him and voiced their conclusion that he was quite fit and would not require passage home on a hospital ship.

So pleased was he with this news, he impulsively decided to phone Southampton to inquire how soon he could book a passage home. As luck would have it, he was told that a ship going to New York would sail within the week.

He left the telephone box with mixed feelings. He was pleased to have put in motion his return to Wyoming, yet filled with despair at the thought of leaving Ainsley behind.

With a new sense of purpose, he strode outside and hailed a taxi to travel to Ainsley's cottage. He had resolutely pushed her out of mind while he was away, unable to bear the agony of wondering what her decision would be.

When soon enough, he stood before the cottage, he glimpsed Ainsley in the window and his heart surged. But his elation died quickly when he'd gone inside and could see her clearly. Fear touched him like a cold hand and he knew she wouldn't be going to Wyoming with him.

She'd stepped to a window and now she wrenched around, her eyes desolate. "I . . . I didn't think it would be like this. I thought I could tell you without falling to pieces but as soon as I saw your taxi, I felt such sadness I thought I would break . . . ." In a mad rush, she launched herself at him and his arms went around her. After a space of minutes they still clung together in an attempt to bring some order to their scattered emotions.

He lifted her head from his chest, holding it steady. "Why Ainsley? Why are you doing this?" His throat ached with the knot of tears there.

"I can't go with you," was all she would say.

He suddenly wanted her body even though he couldn't have her. She wore only a dressing gown and opening it, he touched her with frantic desire.

Her need was as great as his, matching his urgency. She fumbled with the fastenings of his clothing as her mouth sought his, her tongue searching, seducing. Her body undulated in slow sinuous movement against his own. Half-mad with their hunger for each other, they groped their way toward the bedroom. Once they stood next to the bed, Ainsley helped him with the remaining straps and buckles.

Then they lay together, melded by the demanding heat. At the end, the dismal truth of his loss flooded back. He briefly despised Ainsley for denying them such a fierce, happiness.

Yet holding to her like a lifeline, he knew it was useless to talk of her reasons. Though they eluded him, they were apparently implacable in her mind. He knew they would never love again as they just had and her tears bred of this knowledge fell against the hand he'd lifted to her face.

"While I was away, I stopped at the hospital and the doctors told me I'm quite fit and needn't travel home by hospital ship after all," Chandler said presently. "I've booked First Class passage and will be leaving for Southampton the day after tomorrow."

It was a very long while before they fell into troubled sleep. Ainsley was already up when he woke the next morning and the day spun itself away in painful silence. Their sadness pushed them further apart just when they should have been taking care not to waste a moment of the precious time they had left. This reality gradually dawned on him toward evening and he approached Ainsley sitting at the window, staring out at rain that had been falling heavily all day.

"We have an entire night ahead of us."

She turned her head, then slowly stood and went to sit with him on the sofa. She allowed him to draw her onto his lap and she idly ran a finger around the curve of his chin. "This is madness. I've never felt this undone when a man was walking out of my life after a brief stay."

"That should tell you something," he murmured against her hair, struggling to keep his voice steady.

"Chandler, please don't."

The evening passed in quiet enjoyment of each other. Neither could stomach more interaction than simply sitting together, weaving a gentle, unhurried ending to their months together. They ate a light supper of bread, cheese and wine and slept in the same bed, holding each other close.

They breakfasted together soon after dawn, a subdued meal during which neither of them were able to get a firm grasp on the reality that within two hours they would part forever. Ainsley drove them to London and parked beside the depot before turning toward him.

"I won't wait with you or I shall embarrass us both with my hysterical weeping."

He reached for her and she slid into his arms, returning his savage kiss. "Goodbye, my dearest Ainsley."

"Goodbye, my love." With a final beseeching look, she turned back to grip the wheel, leaning her forehead against it.

Chandler stepped out, collected his bag from the backseat and watched Ainsley's car disappear. With a deep breath, he steadied himself and walked through the rain to the station.

# CHAPTER TWENTY-NINE

## May 1919 – June 1919

Dom pulled up Acer next to a clearing along the Lodgepole, his gaze settling on Yvette sitting on a cottonwood log, the aspen above making a wickerwork of the light and shadow around her. He dismounted still a short distance away and stood watching her for time.

Centaur, tethered behind the log extended his nose to snuffle against her shoulder. As she turned to push him away, she caught sight of Dom and lifted her hand in a little wave.

"Ah, my darling," he said as he strode toward her. "How lovely to find you here. It's such a nice day, I couldn't resist bringing Acer out . . . ." When he could see her more clearly, he stopped, looking at her closely. "What on earth! You've been crying. Whatever is the matter . . . ?" In one stride, he was beside her, lowering himself onto the log to take her hands. "Tell me, what's happened."

"Oh, Dom . . . ." Overcome by sobs, she collapsed next to him.

Wrapping her in his arms, he rocked her gently as she cried in great, gulping spasms. "Yvette, my beautiful Yvette."

After a long time, she pulled away from him a little and covered her face with her hands, her shoulders still shaking. "I've been such a fool. So unfair."

He peered into his face. "Please tell me what you mean. Darling . . . ?"

She had gone absolutely still, staring down at her handkerchief knotted in her fingers. After a long space of seconds, she moved a hand jerkily toward her jacket pocket and withdrew an envelope that she gazed at for a time before carefully withdrawing a letter. "I've heard from Chandler."

She lifted starry eyes to meet Dom's a moment before new tears spilled down her cheeks. With a gulping intake of breath, she scrubbed furiously at the wetness with the back of one hand. "Oh, Dom, I've been so foolish . . . ."

"Ah, my dear . . . ." He looked at her helplessly, then caught her hands again.

Abruptly, she wrenched free and leapt up. He didn't follow as she moved to the edge of the water and took Chandler's letter from the envelope, then merely stood, holding it by her side while she implored the sky, fighting back new weeping.

With sudden resolve, Dom stood, strode across the meadow and pulled her violently into his arms. "Yvette, have some pity! You're a wreck and I am more frightened than I've ever been in my life because I don't know what has happened to you. *Please* let me help you?"

She finally met his gaze a second before she hurled herself at him, weeping with no attempt at restraint now. He held her until the end of the dreadful storm of emotion.

When at last, she leaned limply against him, he led her back to the fallen log and drew her down with him, holding her. She slowly came back to herself, nestling her head in the familiar hollow of his throat as her breathing slowed back to its normal cadence.

"Chandler will be home next week."

He tightened his arms in reflex to the news. "So is a wedding in the offing?"

Her fists clenched and a renewed onslaught of tears dripped onto Dom's hand as he awaited her answer.

"I . . . I should think there will be a wedding soon." Laughter slowly curved her mouth. "But I won't be marrying Chandler." Looking down, she swiped at the wetness. "So, it appears I shall have to marry you . . . ."

Joy flared like a flame in the gray eyes that looked at her in astonishment. Settling her back in his embrace, he began stroking her hair falling over her shoulder. At last he craned his neck to peer at her. "Are you proposing to me then?"

"I am!" She steadied his face and let her lips travel along his jawline before settling on his mouth. The depth of love and compassion in her kiss extinguished all the doubt and confusion and pain of the past years.

"And what of Chandler?" He dared ask at last when she'd shifted back.

She looked at him forthrightly now. "As the time drew close for his return, I realized that I can't marry him."

"Because he's been injured?"

"Oh, heavens no!" She stared at him horror. "No! You think me that shallow and fickle that I'd break my engagement over something like that!?"

"My, darling, I definitely don't think any such thing. But I must say, you've caught me unawares here and I'm trying quite frantically to find out what has changed."

"*I* have changed, I daresay. Or perhaps I haven't. Perhaps I've just been dismissing the truth all this time."

He read something new and terribly vulnerable in her eyes and his heart began beating raggedly. "Are you telling me what I think you may be?"

She threw up her hands with a little laugh. "I have no idea why I'm muddling this so badly. The truth is, my dear, I haven't for a moment stopped being madly in love with you! I tried so hard not to but I can't help it."

"Oh, my lovely, sweet Yvette! I've waited so long for this day. I'd quite given up hope of it ever happening. Is it really true?" He consulted her again.

"I'm so awfully sorry I've been so unfair to you, the desires of my heart shifting back and forth along with my mind. But all that is finished now. I long to spend all the days remaining to us with you."

"Thank, God!" He wrapped her close, breathing in the floral fragrance of her hair. "I've prayed so long for this." Looking up, he studied her a moment. "But this is going to be very hard for you, I should think. Have you told Chandler what you've decided?"

"I've not." She sighed in spite of herself. "And I'm very nervous about what I'm to say to him when he arrives." She put up her hand when he started to speak. "Don't worry! I'll not change my mind. I just hate to hurt Chandler . . . Indeed I hate the way I've handled this entire matter. I couldn't blame you if you both ended up hating me."

"Whatever do you mean?"

"Oh, you know very well what I mean. I vacillated back and forth between the two of you, pledging my love to you and then Chandler. Never knowing for certain how I felt. I was truly awful to both of you."

Dom cocked a brow. "Let us not forget that my own behavior contributed greatly to the emotional chaos we suffered through. If I'd seen the light rather sooner, it would've made all the difference." He tapped the end of her nose. "If I hadn't been such a rogue for so long, we'd likely be long married by this time with half a dozen children."

Regardless of her lingering worry, she giggled. "I actually hope I'm not nearly as fertile as my mother. But two children would be nice," she added at his crestfallen look.

"Righto. Two exquisite little maids who look just as you did when you were a wee girl." Merry warmth filled his eyes. "How you enchanted me."

"Oh, I remember! And I thought you the most charming gentleman."

He tipped up her chin with one finger. "My darling, I feel as if I'm going to wake up any moment and discover this has all been an extraordinary dream since I found you here. Is what you've been telling me really true? Are you marrying me instead of Chandler?"

"I am!" Throwing her arms about him, she clung to him like a mooring in a storm. "I am so terribly happy and so relieved after all this time." Drawing back, she considered him anew. "But I'm afraid I don't know how to manage the next days after Chandler arrives. Any way I look at it, it seems I can't help hurting someone. This time it's Chandler that I promised to love forever. And now he's coming home to find it was all a lie."

"Darling, it was no lie. No one ever suffered and searched her heart more than you before making your choice. And I wasn't yet steady enough after my personal reformation to be of any help"

"The fault was entirely mine."

"I don't agree but in any case, we've reached an entirely new juncture where only blue skies abound."

"Ah, the way you say that makes it sound so very lovely."

"It will be nothing but lovely, my dear."

Abruptly, she straightened, regarding him with new resolve. "Well now that we both know how things stand, I must dash."

"Am I allowed to dash with you?"

"I'd love that."

When they'd walked to the horses and he'd given her a leg-up, she took up the reins. "Race you back," she challenged as soon as he was mounted.

"You're on!" He shouted and Acer jumped forward.

Clamping her heels to Centaur's sides, she propelled him into a run, promptly passing Acer. "Woo-hoo!"

Taller and in better condition than Acer, Centaur remained ahead until they pulled up near the *Mariposa.* Laughing, she leaned on the gelding's neck, inspecting Dom.

He dismounted, then came to help her down. "Let me acknowledge the superiority of your mount, my dear." He wagged an eyebrow at her.

"Thank you so much, darling," she said airily. "Yet, in most horse races, it's the jockey's performance that proves paramount." With a toss of her head, she fell in step with him as they led the horses toward the stable.

"You are such a delight!" Inclining toward her, he kissed her cheek before catching her hand that he tucked through his arm.

After stable boys came for their mounts, they headed along the driveway toward the *Mariposa.* Once they reached the piazza, Yvette stopped and stood looking out over the garden, where blooms were at their peak.

"What is it?" Dom asked as she stepped away from him.

"I must talk to my mother." Pressing her hands together, she glanced toward Trail's End beyond the garden. "I think I'll go now. Bye, love." With a hasty kiss for Dom, she was off, hurrying toward the house where she'd grown up.

Audra was in the front yard, cutting flowers. "Yvette, my dear, how nice. I was just headed down to the *Mariposa* garden to harvest some gorgeous roses I spotted yesterday."

"Oh, good, I'd love to walk with you." She reached for the shallow basket holding the cut blossoms. "I'll just run these inside."

Once she returned with the empty basket after delivering the flowers to Loretta, the maid, she and Audra set off along the driveway.

"What is troubling you, my sweet girl?"

Bailey, a new young beagle, capered out from the porch and danced around their legs. Yvette scooped her up and observed Audra over her bouncing head. "You've known all along how I feel about Dom."

"So now Chandler's coming home and you don't know how to handle this dilemma you're in?" She paused to fondle the puppy's ears. "Is that it, then?"

"Ma-ma, you know it is."

They continued walking in silence for a time before Audra veered toward a bench at the edge of the garden. Once they sat together, Bailey jumped down to hunt for bunnies among the peonies.

"Beneath the pain and worry I see in your eyes, I also see absolute joy and I can't begin to tell you how happy that makes me." She slipped an arm around her shoulders. "Ever since you decided to marry Chandler, I've worried about you because I knew you weren't happy, not really. Now I'm positively delighted by the certainty you will spend the rest of your life with the absolute treasure of your heart. And take it from your old mother who's known the deepest sort of love with your father, there is no greater blessing on this earth."

"Oh, Ma-ma, I love you so. But how am I ever going to tell Chandler? This will positively break his heart."

"Oh, darling, it's far better to tell him the truth now than years down the road when both of you might be desperately unhappy. Have you told his parents yet?"

"Only that Chandler's arriving home next week."

"Well, go now and talk with them. I have no doubt they will have nothing but good and loving advice for you."

She nodded, suddenly anxious to consult Damien and Harper who'd become like her own parents over the years she'd lived at *Mariposa.* "Thank you, Ma-ma. Now I'll walk back with you."

"No, you go in. Once I've cut some roses, I'll be fine getting myself home. It's such a nice evening, I believe I'll sit here awhile and ponder your good fortune."

"You're such a darling." Yvette kissed her lined cheek. "Thank you." With that, she hurried to the rear entrance.

The mansion was still as she passed through the kitchen into the hall. Voices led her to the parlor where Dom sat with his father and Harper.

"Ah, there you are." He came to embrace her. "How is your mother?"

"She's very pleased I've come to my senses at last."

"As are Harper and I," Damien said, rising to kiss her cheek.

"We're so very happy," Harper added, wrapping her arms around her.

"Since you didn't join us for dinner, Dom's been filling us in," Damien said, gesturing them to be seated.

Suddenly feeling vulnerable again, Yvette sought the solace of sitting next to Harper. Twisting her hands in her lap, she dared glance at her. "Are you very disappointed in me?"

She touched her arm. "My dear, we're not. We only want what will make both you and Dom happy."

"But what of Chandler?"

"You don't love him and that could only bring misery. I daresay there's another for him."

Yvette studied her intently, catching the curious light that'd crept into the knowing violet eyes. She'd only witnessed a time or two previously, the strange transformation of Harper when her *sight* manifested itself. Now she turned to her with keen curiosity. "What do you mean, there's another for him?"

"Oh, my dear, it's sometimes hard to pinpoint what I *see* at first but it always becomes clear soon enough." Wonder filled her eyes, banishing the rest. "This time I sense such joy over-riding all else . . . ."

"And that makes you think Chandler has found someone?"

Harper threw up her hands. "I truly can't explain whatever has fed this inexplicable knowledge into my mind all these years. Yet sometimes, I can interpret some of it. Because this rush of elation came to me today very soon after Dom told us of your change of heart, I can't help thinking your decision won't cause Chandler quite so much grief as one might think."

Yvette smiled. "How lovely."

"Yes, it is." She hugged her, then smiled at Damien who'd come to sit next to her, bearing the brandy decanter.

"Would either of you like some?" He asked. When neither accepted, he refilled his glass. "Now we must sort out how we proceed after Chandler is home. I'm speaking about the company now, of course. I've told Dom what I propose," he went on. After fortifying himself with a swallow of brandy, he glanced from Dom to Yvette. "As you know, I've recently purchased an additional tract of land some five miles from here. It's a thousand acres, adjacent to *Mariposa* land to the south. Harper and I wish to make you a gift of this parcel as a wedding present. You can use it as you see fit. Start your own Hereford operation perhaps. I've often thought it would be beneficial to cross some new strains with our bloodlines here in an effort to improve the breed as has always been our goal." He paused for reaction.

Dom, having already heard the proposal, smiled at Yvette. "I'm delighted at the idea. What about you?"

"I must say, I'm a little dazed but I can think of nothing nicer than having our own little ranch."

"It goes without saying, Dom will continue as a shareholder in the *Mariposa,*" Damien interjected.

"We'll still be close enough for you to continue teaching the children," Dom put in.

Yvette saw all the love and consideration in him as he strove to be certain her wishes were addressed. "Thank you so much for thinking of that."

"I know how much you adore teaching."

"Darling, I love you so much for that."

"Now we must decide about your wedding," Harper said. "Have you talked about that yet?"

"We've hardly had the time," Dom said with a rueful chuckle.

She granted him an indulgent smile. Before she could continue, Yvette spoke.

"I'd like a very small wedding before Chandler gets here. I daresay this entire matter will be very awkward for all of us, yet it may be tempered a bit for Chandler if it's already taken place. Do you agree?" She consulted them one by one.

"I think that's exactly the right tack," Damien said.

"I agree." Harper considered her and Dom. "We can make the arrangements quickly, just as soon as you decide when."

Yvette sat quietly a moment, then lifted her eyes to meet Dom's enraptured gaze. "Why not tomorrow?"

"That sounds splendid to me."

"Then we'll proceed toward that end," Harper said briskly, touching her hair in thought. "I'll talk with Mrs. Blanchard about the menu." She stood and headed out, only to turn back. "What about a dress?"

"Oh, I'm going to wear my mother's wedding dress. It's been my wish since I was five. She's already had it cleaned and altered."

"Oh, how lovely," Dom said, warm light in his eyes as he folded her hand between both of his.

"And as my attendant, Millie will surely wear one of Sawyer's latest creations. Which will likely make my mother's gown look a bit shabby but I hardly care about that."

"Quite right." Harper continued into the hall.

"I'm just so pleased you've accepted our gift," Damien observed. "I so look forward to you sharing full duties in the management of *Rancha Mariposa* once again."

"I, too, Pa-pa," Dom replied. "I can't recall ever being as happy as I am at this moment."

"My dear Dom, you have no idea how delighted I am that you've come to this place in your life. I've spent far too many years in torment because of the harm your mother and I caused you."

Dom leapt up and stood before him. "Pa-pa, I know how much you've always loved me. I was weak and petty for far too long. If I'd accepted that yours and Harper's love was strong enough to make up for what I never got from my mother, my life wouldn't have been such a debacle for so long."

Damien put a hand on his shoulder. "Let's not dwell another moment on the past." He drew him into a gleeful embrace. "You have always been one of the greatest blessings of my life."

At the conclusion of the wedding dinner at the *Mariposa* the following evening, Dom's best man Finn offered a toast and the diners faced the bride and groom, clicking glasses.

Millie turned to hug Yvette. "You look splendid."

"Not nearly as splendid as you in that sassy frock Sawyer whipped together for the occasion."

Sawyer laughed and tossed her flaming hair. Just as Yvette had predicted, she'd provided her most recent design, barely finished in time for the ceremony. An elegant two-piece number in pale blue silk and crepe, it was a style very much in vogue since the end of the war. It was a perfect compliment to Millie's eyes and her pale hair.

Sawyer had brought Yvette a lavender number with much the same panache for her to wear on her honeymoon. "I love it that you're wearing Audra's wedding dress but I can't wait to see you in my gift when you *go away* a bit later. With your build, you'll be quite stunning."

"It's such fun having a fashion designer as my good friend." Yvette kissed her cheek before turning to her new husband, positively dashing in his evening coat.

Even after so many years, looking at him still caused her heart to race and warmth to suffuse every part of her. He was more than ten years older than Chandler but the extra maturity had only made him more striking.

At the height of his drinking, he'd become bloated and generally unwell. Now his return to robust health had left him slender with the finely drawn features that had made him extraordinarily good looking. Indeed, he appeared much as he had when Yvette first became fascinated by him as a young man. Though a mere girl at the time, she'd thought him divinely handsome and eagerly gave him her heart from then on.

While in those early years, he'd been a formidable, often unnerving force in her life, time and his spiritual wakening had uncovered the honorable, gentler part of him. As she watched the gathering of family and friends drinking champagne and talking with one another, she was awed by her keen awareness of fate reordering itself to reach this moment.

Dom lifted his flute of Lemonade to her. "To my exquisite bride who has today made my dreams come true." He kissed her tenderly while the party offered cheers.

Settled beside him, Yvette found her parents at the opposite end of the table, still a handsome pair after so many years. Most of her sisters and some of their husbands filled one entire side; the opposite accommodated the rest of the adult guests while a separate festive table had been laid for the children, the girls quite in awe of attending their beloved teacher's wedding and celebratory dinner.

Yvette marveled at the scene. She reached for Dom's hand in an effort to steady herself. "It's so lovely sitting here with you, I can hardly bear it."

"You are the delight of my heart, my darling." He braced an elbow on the table, leaning so his lips were near her ear. "And our life spins before us in an idyll worthy of Robert and Elizabeth Browning."

"Will you write poetry just for me?"

He nuzzled her cheek. "Perhaps not but I shall read you poetry if you like."

"How gallant."

"You've no idea." He raised a roguish brow. "And now, Mrs. Whittaker, perhaps we should soon take our leave."

"Oh, yes, let's! I'd like nothing so much as to steal away into the night with my husband."

"Your wish is my own, my dear." He slid back his chair and stood, tapping a spoon on a crystal flute. "Our cherished family and friends, Yvette and I wish to thank all of you for sharing this, the happiest day of our lives. We treasure each of you and look forward to welcoming you to our new home at *Rancha Lirea* in the very near future."

"Now you must come with me," Sawyer said softly to Yvette. "Please excuse us." She grabbed her hand and the two of them headed upstairs so Yvette could don her going away dress.

"You've outdone yourself this time," Yvette said when she stood before a cheval mirror. The lavender silk floated over her slender body, ending just above the knee.

"I put every effort into your special frock," Sawyer said, nestling her head next to her friend's as they gazed into the mirror.

"And I love you for it." She reached up to pat her cheek. "We're off then."

"Oh yes, we mustn't keep your divine husband waiting."

As she started down the staircase, Yvette saw Dom waiting at the bottom, his eyes following her progress. "You look superb, my love."

With a little curtsey, she took the hand he held out to her and stepped into her future. One of the lads had brought Dom's automobile around to the front door. All the family and guests had spilled out into the piazza and threw handfuls of rice and rose petals as they emerged amid a clamor of shouted good wishes.

Harper, Delaney, Millie and Sawyer stood beside the car and caught Yvette in quick hugs before she joined Dom for the journey to Cheyenne where they would spend the night.

Lying with Dom after they'd made love, Yvette molding herself into his side while his hand stroked her hair. "I believe in you," she said softly.

He touched her chin to turn her face toward him. "Whatever do you mean?"

She considered him with such fervency he was a bit taken aback.

"I daresay I didn't fully understand what you've been through these past months while on your way to this day but now I do. I so believe in your promise to me and your new commitment to integrity and goodness. Although . . ." she smiled. "I believe these things have been within you all along."

His features eased into a smile. "I think you give me too much credit."

"Not true."

"Whatever goodness dwelled in me before was likely freed by your love."

"Perhaps that was part of it," she agreed since she was quite certain her love for him had kept him from straying further than he had.

"Indeed." One hand cupped the back of her head, bringing her still closer, into his kiss.

Much later, Yvette glanced about their stylish suite at The Plains as she hovered on the edge of sleep. How extraordinary that she was here on her wedding night. She thought of Chandler for the first time all day. Somehow the overwhelming worry of yesterday had faded beneath the certainty and joy.

Chandler's agony at leaving Ainsley had lessened a little during his journey to Wyoming. For a while now, he'd become quite numb and somewhat reconciled to his loss. Once he alighted from the train in Cheyenne in late June, he was taken aback by the congregation waiting on the platform.

He shouldn't have been surprised by the welcoming crowd since he'd seen similar assemblages at nearly every stop since he had left the East Coast—cheering, boisterous mobs that were seemingly unable to contain their delight at the arrival of whatever returning soldiers were due that day.

Yet, he was invariably made ill-at-ease by such displays and would've much preferred arriving unnoticed. Still, he was saved from a truly embarrassing spectacle by being the sole soldier returning to Cheyenne on this particular train. Thus, his reception committee was comprised of only his parents and a few townspeople hanging about around the edges of the platform.

Joy coursed through him as he rushed into Harper's arms. "Ma-ma, it's so lovely to be here! It seems forever."

"At least that," she said shakily, pressing him to her. "My darling, it's so good to see you. We've worried a great deal about you so it's going to be splendid having you back with us."

"Where's Yvette!?" He demanded, looking around with sudden agitation. "Why isn't she…?"

Damien put a hand on his shoulder. "We'll tell you everything on the drive out. We should be on our way."

Chandler looked helplessly from him to his mother, then got into the backseat of the automobile. *Something was very much askew.* He was abruptly swamped with dread.

After tipping the porter who'd loaded the baggage, Damien slid behind the wheel. Shortly, they were on their way out of town.

Harper had joined Chandler in the backseat so she could speak to him more directly. "Darling, what we have to say to you is very difficult but it's not fair to keep you in the dark so I'll simply say it. Yvette and Dom were married a few days back."

He could only stare at her, unable to speak. Shock went through him like a drastic change of temperature.

"This has got to be a hard spot you're in," Damien said from the front. "We're confident, your mother and I, that you'll deal with it as a gentleman."

Nausea assaulted him as he looked bleakly at Harper. "How can this be?"

"My dear, dear boy, you more than anyone should remember how it's been between Dom and Yvette. Since she was a little girl, she's adored him and he's felt the same. Her heart's belonged to him every moment since."

"I daresay," he agreed, an edge in his voice. "But I quite believed she was going to marry me as soon as I returned from the war."

Harper nodded. "I must say, we were all taken aback when they told us they were to be married. Yvette was positively devastated by the thought of hurting you."

"Did she remain devastated at her wedding?"

"No, actually they were both totally over the moon."

"Where is the gleeful couple now?"

"On a little jaunt to Cheyenne and Denver. They'll be home in a week." She reached for his hand. "Your father and I have quite a lovely gift waiting for them. As you know, we've been planning a trip to Europe for ages now. Ever since Granville arranged my entrance into the London and Paris art world actually. Now we're free to belatedly go and we're going to include Dom and Yvette."

Chandler absorbed the news without speaking. He might have been totally devastated to learn that just as he had come home from war, his family was leaving. Yet, curiously, he felt a sense of deliverance.

Since leaving England, he'd thought of nothing but Ainsley. The short span after their parting had blessedly soothed the jagged agony pounding in his brain. Still, he knew he had a long, desolate road ahead before he had any hope of being on good terms with his life again. And what he longed for most was solitude to lick his wounds and grow accustomed to the dismal direction his life had taken.

For the first time, he had a real sense of the heartache his parents had experienced when they weren't allowed to marry on schedule. Observing them now, and having grown up in the environment of love and joy that had attended them once they had ultimately married, he dared think perhaps fate still had some happiness in store for him as well.

"We're very excited about this trip, though I daresay we'll encounter many sad reminders of the destruction of war. One greatest regret is leaving just when you've arrived. The timing is quite wretched."

Calling up a smile, he shook his head. "Don't worry on my account, Ma-ma. I look forward to some time on my own. I can't wait to take long rides, reacquainting myself with the ranch. I've missed it a great deal."

Harper patted his hand. "I'm so glad you don't mind being left to your own devices. I promise when we return, we'll properly celebrate your homecoming. We are just so proud of you."

"Let me add to that sentiment," Damien offered from the front. "You've done a grand job in the war, Chandler, representing

Wyoming with the greatest honor. We're very gratified indeed. How are you getting on with your injury?"

"I've come to terms with it. It no longer causes much inconvenience."

"Well, that once again attests to your bravery and good sense."

"Pa-pa, I did nothing more than any man caught in that bloody insanity. It's going to take some time for all of us to come to terms with the things we've seen and done in the name of honor as you put it. I'm sure many never will."

His father didn't speak again for a long interval. "I spoke without fully thinking of what you've been through. Having never had experience with the military, I daresay I'm quite ignorant of the realities of that life, particularly in wartime."

"You meant no harm." He rested his hand on his arm a moment.

Harper smiled, impulsively embracing him before laying her head on his shoulder as they turned down the driveway beside the *Mariposa.* "Well, here we are, darling. It's just so nice to have you home. How does it feel?"

"Like a dream." He peered through the window at the front of the mansion. "It seems an eternity since I was here."

"Well, let's get you inside. Mrs. Blanchard has prepared luncheon."

"Jolly good. Mrs. Blanchard's wonderful meals are one of the things I've missed most."

As they entered the dining room a bit later, Granville came from the parlor. He drew Chandler into his embrace. "Ah, lad, it's a grand thing having you home."

"Thank you, sir."

Granville kissed Harper's cheek, then led them to the dining table where LuAnn set out the array of dishes she had brought from the kitchen on a tray.

Chandler was astonished to see Granville was as tall and striking as ever, looking very fit indeed, though he was likely nearing ninety. "Are you going along with the travelers to be their guide in Europe?"

"No, I can't imagine I could keep up with a touring party these days. I look forward to enjoying the serenity of *Mariposa* and catching up on my reading. I will be quite entertained imagining how your mother and Dom are enjoying all the magnificent art. How thrilling for Harper to find two of her recent paintings at the *Louvre.* I've longed for years to take her to Paris myself so she could see how well her work fits in among the Masters."

Harper hurried from the kitchen. "You've always been the loudest voice on my cheering squad," she said, draping her arms about Granville's shoulders as she leaned down to lay her cheek against his. "And I've always adored you for that."

He rose to hold her chair. "It has been one of the greatest pleasures of my life to have had a bit of influence in introducing your work to the world. And now I so regret I won't be with you in Paris so we can stand together at the *Louvre,* marveling at your latest. My heart would surely burst with pride."

"We shall miss you terribly." She slid into the seat next to Damien.

"Not to worry. I look forward to spending this time with Chandler." He smiled fondly at him across the table.

"I'll enjoy that also," Chandler said.

Yvette and Dom returned to the *Mariposa* the day before they were to leave for Europe. Despite the new circumstances between them, Dom looked forward to seeing his half-brother.

Now he and Yvette awaited Chandler who'd risen early to ride his gray Thoroughbred named Branson. Luke had been training the gelding especially to fit his needs since word of his injury had reached the *Mariposa.*

Having just arrived back in the stable yard, Chandler dismounted and handed the reins to a lad before heading along the drive to the rear entrance. A few minutes later, he stood in the door of the drawing room, observing the newlyweds.

He noted how self-possessed Dom appeared, one long leg crossed over the other, a glass of Ginger Beer balanced in slender fingers. It had never struck Chandler so clearly what a bloody attractive fellow he was. He was dressed all in black today, his white linen collar in stark contrast to his tanned face. Pa-pa once told him Dom had matured very early, appearing in adolescence much older than he was. Now the opposite was true. Though he was forty-three, only a silvery touch of gray at his temples betrayed the years. He could easily have passed for a man of twenty.

For the first time, Chandler looked directly at Yvette and his heart cramped with regret. In a delicate white lace dress, she was even more beautiful if such a thing was possible, her hair piled atop her head in a glorious, tumbled mass.

Bringing himself back to the moment, he stepped inside. "Hello, you two."

"Chandler!" Yvette leapt up and came to stand before him, smiling.

"You're looking fabulous!" He squeezed her hand.

"Oh, Chandler." Tears gathered. "I'm so sorry it had to be like this. I never meant to hurt you."

"My dear, Yvette. If I understand nothing else about what's transpired, I do know that you'd not willfully wound me. And I need only take a good look at you to see you're happy with my brother as you would never have been with me. Because of that, I'm very grateful the fates deemed we should take different paths for the remaining days of our lives."

"You've always been such a gentleman."

"Have a grand trip." He brought her hand to his lips, catching sight of Dom over her shoulder.

"I will, thanks." She turned quickly away.

Chandler reached toward his brother. "So good to see you."

With a ragged sigh, Dom pulled him into a hug.

"Likewise and I must offer my gratitude to you for managing so well in the war since you had to represent all of us on your own."

"I did my best to do my part. But so did Finn."

"Oh, I never meant to overlook his contribution."

"I know that," he said with a little nod.

"I've been frantic to know how you're dealing with all this." He indicated his cane.

"It was a huge calamity at first. I thought my life was over. But then after a very short time, I was in hospital and wasn't truly aware of anything for months. I was knocked out with morphine most all that time."

"No repercussions from that, I hope."

"Nothing lasting at any rate. And I've learned to manage this contraption so all is well, I daresay."

"I am truly sorry this happened to you."

He studied him, seeing the sincerity in his eyes and was reminded anew of his brother's transformation from the disreputable cad he'd been for so long. At least any lingering doubts he might have had about his suitability as Yvette's husband were now a moot point.

As he watched her approach Dom, Chandler was struck by the warmth drifting between them, so intense it was practically tangible. He wondered at the utter blindness that had caused him to miss the impact of it before. He appreciated for the first time the anguish Yvette had endured keeping her secret when their passion had clearly been so overwhelming.

The newlyweds soon excused themselves and climbed the staircase to Yvette's bedroom. For many days, he would hold close the fleeting image of her radiance as she looked at her husband.

The high level of emotion during the scant hours since he'd learned his life had been turned on end left him vulnerable to hope, however unfounded. Having been left alone, he found himself in the proper frame of mind to compose a letter to Ainsley, one last plea from the depth of his heart. Without further delay, he stepped to a writing desk by the window and found pen and paper.

***June 29, 1919***

***My Darling, Ainsley,***

***A few days back, Yvette married my brother Dom. I discovered upon my return here that I had not been unfaithful to Yvette***

*while you and I were together because I never belonged to her. It seems she has been madly in love with Dom for years, though she, like you, was afraid to give free rein to her feelings. Once she did, the transformation of both her and my brother was so remarkable that I am inspired to write to you one final time.*

*I know we agreed to look on our interlude as just that, likely the finest days either of us will ever know, but a time that could not be relived in another place. Yet if your initial weeks without me were half as wretched as mine on the ship and trains that brought me home but away from you, my beloved, then I pray that you will finally read this and listen to your heart instead of your very practical mind.*

*It is madness for us to throw away a love such as few are blessed, to live lives empty with regret. For this reason, I implore you, my darling, come to me.*

*Enclosed is a money order for your passage. If you should still refuse me, do not return it but think of it as a last gift from me. I shall not consider that distressing possibility but wait with the keenest impatience for your arrival.*

*With all my love,*

*Chandler*

Yvette came for a visit to the *Mariposa* in June, announcing that she was pregnant. For whatever reason, impending motherhood or wedded happiness, she positively beamed. Her report of life at the remote ranch painted a picture of life a good deal more basic than anything she was accustomed to, yet she had no complaints. When she was ready to return home, Garner stood with the group seeing her off.

As her smart little apple green convertible turned from the driveway to the road, he laughed, turning to Chandler. "Well, I do believe our lovely Yvette has found her heart's desire." He considered him a moment longer. "Has enough time passed now that you can be happy for her, my lad?"

Chandler looked at him with some surprise. "Yes, as a matter of fact, I've been feeling quite serene of late. Being back at the *Mariposa* makes me very happy."

As summer progressed, Chandler took up painting once again, finding his time in the war had unleashed a maturity that hadn't been part of his talent in the past. He seldom thought of Ainsley now and when he did, it was with a detached pleasure instead of the former wrenching hurt.

# EPILOGUE

Chandler was so reconciled to his quiet, celibate existence that it took him a moment to recognize the young woman dressed in a rather prim brown suit that a strange automobile deposited in the *Mariposa* driveway one evening in August.

He'd been sketching the rear garden, profuse with late summer blooms. He glanced up at the sound of the auto receding along the road, then watched the girl make her way hesitantly toward the rear entrance.

Connections slid into place inside his head and he threw down his pencil and sketchbook, grabbed his cane and started toward her. "Ainsley!"

She dropped her bags and ran toward him because he couldn't run to her. Then she was in his arms. "I came . . . ."

"My darling, Ainsley . . . ."

And they were adrift on the glorious river of love and need and the greatest hope that had spanned two continents and a great ordeal. At last, they were home.

THE END

# ABOUT THE AUTHOR

Jeannie Hudson grew up on a ranch in Wyoming where her rapport with animals was nourished in a country environment. She attended Casper College where she was the first and only student to serve as editor of the campus newspaper *The Chinook,* for two years which included a full scholarship

While at the University of Wyoming, she began writing full-time and began selling short stories to magazines. Over the next two decades she sold four suspense novels with the help of an agent, and raised Arabian show horses.

After a move to Minnesota, she continued writing and began raising show beagles. After marriage to her husband Adam, they returned west and now live in the Black Hills of South Dakota with two rambunctious beagles, Murphy and Bailey.

For more information about Jeannie Hudson, please visit her website: http://historicalauthor.wordpress.com

Coming soon from Jeannie Hudson

## THE YEARNING TREE

## BLOOD AND WINE ARE RED

If you enjoyed *MARIPOSA-BOOK III-SALVATION, please consider leaving a review and a rating on the site where you bought it: Amazon, Barnes & Noble, Kobo etc. Reviews and feedback are important to an author as well as potential readers, and would be very much appreciated. Thank you.*

Printed in the USA
CPSIA information can be obtained
at www.ICGtesting.com
LVHW092337020724
784553LV00030B/349